HAULING THROUGH

PETER BRIDGFORD
06-07-16

I HOPE YOU ENJOY READING MY BOOK.
DAMN THE TORPEDOES!

BRIDGE

Hauling Through

© Copyright 2016, Peter Bridgford

ISBN: 978-1-63381-074-7

Library of Congress Control Number: 2016903612

Designed and Produced by
Maine Authors Publishing
558 Main Street, Rockland, Maine 04841
www.maineauthorspublishing.com

Printed in the United States of America

To Mom and Dad: First of all, thank you for making me. Secondly, thank you for always encouraging me to follow my bliss.

To C.A.B., I.K.B., and W.R.B. (My girls): Thank you for never losing faith in me during this supremely ridiculous endeavor.

Prologue

Sergei Volentchko gasped in alarm as soon as he turned on the lights in his office and saw the faded green dossier sitting on his desk. Even though he'd received hundreds of these over the years, the mysterious arrival of each one completely startled him. Maybe it was because they always came during the night, like one of those unexpected snowfalls from his childhood in Stalingrad. But unlike those pleasant memories, there was nothing at all pleasurable about this surprise. And, as he walked over to hang up his coat and hat, his eyes remained focused on the dossier and his stomach felt heavy with dread.

It wasn't as if the dossier contained bad news—Volentchko knew it didn't. He'd seen enough of them to know that it contained no news whatsoever. Yet as he sank into his chair, he continued to treat the dossier like a cornered feral animal that he did not want to disturb. He hadn't even taken a full breath since seeing it, so he now looked up at the ceiling and inhaled and exhaled slowly. Then he looked back down at it and shook his head.

The dossier demanded Volentchko do the one thing he hated to do more than anything else—make a decision. Just by sitting there on his desk, it forced him to decide whether to read the useless document or just put it right into his overflowing file cabinets. This dilemma was an all too visible metaphor for the rest of his life. If he read it, he'd gain no new or relevant information, and those critics who said that he didn't do anything important in his office would demand that he retire. But if he filed it unread, there was the slightest chance that he'd miss some sort of valuable information and those same critics would call for his retirement due to incompetence. Volentchko knew that the means to this shared end dictated the real conundrum: whether to continue with this pointless debate or look through the new Turkish pornographic magazines he had just purchased at the black market next to the train yard. Ah, the fight between the good Russian and the horny old man was on again. Without making a decision, Volentchko lit a cigarette and stared off into space.

Oh, Kosmos2. It was easy to say that Kosmos2 was Mother Russia's crowning achievement and its most embarrassing moment wrapped in the same thin satellite shell. The American intelligence community, bloated with abundant funding and overconfidence, could never figure out why there was a Kosmos1 and a Kosmos3, but no Kosmos2. Volentchko remembered hearing arrogant Western double agents speak about this sloppiness as yet more evidence of a decaying Soviet Union. How embarrassed the West would be to learn the truth! But that was still a closely guarded secret, even in light of the new cooperation of the post-Cold War world. But Volentchko now had to wonder if Kosmos2 was such a secret because of national security or national shame.

In 1981, the leaders of the KGB had brought the Soviet intelligence community together. No one knew what they were going to say, so there was an uneasy excitement in the room. Their presentation started with a review of the history of the space race. Using colorful graphics, the KGB presenter outlined how the 1950s and '60s were nothing but a series of tit-for-tat, well-publicized achievements between the Soviet and US space programs. This elaborate game of leapfrog continued until the Americans grabbed the brass ring that was the lunar landing. Even the later impressive accomplishments of both space agencies, including the Soviet Salyut 1, the American Skylab, and the joint Apollo–Soyuz docking, were no longer able to generate the same glow of national pride for either country. The fact was, the space race was won as soon as Neil Armstrong took that damn first step on the moon!

But the KGB never let a defeat get it down. In that room filled with a rapt and eager audience, they now made the pitch that the time was perfect for a clandestine victory in space. Although the Soviet Space Agency's well-known accomplishments had had a powerful impact on the Americans, it would be something totally secretive that would give Mother Russia the real upper hand in the espionage battle. Their plan was simple: build a surveillance satellite with digital photographic capabilities and pirated American computer technology, and then secretly launch it in an Indian rocket. Everything would be done so quietly, not only would the Americans not know about it, but many of the communist leadership would be kept in the dark as well. Volentchko never knew whose idea it was, but he had to admit that it was fucking brilliant!

While the Americans wondered about the Indira Satellite Launch Vehicle with a larger-than-normal payload, the Indians stayed tight-lipped about their secret arrangement with the USSR. The Americans had no reason to worry. After all, weren't India and the United States both democracies allied against the spread of evil communism? Of course they were. But the Indians were also in the midst of a sustained and undeclared war with their Muslim neighbor, Pakistan. So when they were offered a secret shipment of weapons-grade plutonium in trade for adding a mystery payload to their scheduled satellite launch, they were all too happy to not ask any questions or make too many confessions. The launch went off without incident, and the Indian communication satellite deployed perfectly in Earth's orbit. Only the inner circle that the KGB chose to include knew that Kosmos2 had also been set free and that Russia now had a secret spy satellite focused right on the Americans!

Volentchko chuckled to himself. The successful launching of Kosmos2 still made him want to clap with excitement. But then he looked back down at the dossier and his smile vanished. There was no debate that Kosmos2 began as a Russian victory. As soon as it nestled into its geosynchronous orbit, it started sending back the most fantastic images. The KGB had been absolutely dead-on with their selection of the seemingly insignificant fuel depot hidden in a rural coastal American town. As predicted, Kosmos2 quickly revealed that the depot was actually serving as a secret base of operations for the entire American North Atlantic nuclear sub fleet. The satellite's images were so clear, it was easy to tell exactly which subs were being refueled and which were armed. Truth was, the photos were so crisp, Russian intelligence gatherers knew which American naval personnel needed haircuts and which ones needed to lose weight!

Ah, those first dossiers Volentchko received were as exciting and revealing as the pornographic magazines in his briefcase. And, as the recipient of this firsthand intelligence, his own status in the government had risen like a rocket. He found himself going from obscurity to being an important and respected man in an amazingly short amount of time. And he basked in that glory. Food. Vodka. Women. Gifts and privileges. During those early successful days of Kosmos2, he could not wait to go over the images with his magnifying glass—not that the photos needed much enhancement. Volentchko's reports were copious and thorough, and they were considered vital to national security. After all, because they contained the detailed movement and names of American attack submarines, entire military strategies could be planned from reading these reports. And who was at the epicenter of this crucial information? None other than Sergei Volentchko!

Then, without warning, the Americans shut down that facility. One moment, Volentchko and other Russian surveillance experts were getting their rocks off over secret information about sub activity that maybe even the American president didn't know, and the next, they were getting high-resolution photos of a deserted dock, a coniferous forest, and a sleepy little fishing village. It was as if the Americans had somehow learned about Kosmos2 and simply pulled the plug on the base. In an instant, Volentchko went from the golden goose upon whose words generals and admirals hung their decisions to a doddering old man in a nondescript office in the bowels of an unnamed government building. It just was not fair!

But that was not the worst part. If the Americans were going to relocate their secret base, the KGB just needed to find its new location. As any good intelligence officer knows, shifting targets is the name of the game in espionage. The KGB was confident that, once they knew where to re-aim Kosmos2, they could easily reprogram it for a new mission. But when they tried to get the satellite to reposition itself to take pictures of a newly identified American submarine base, a crippling design flaw in the software made it as disrespectful and disobedient as a teenager. Kosmos2 not only refused to be diverted, it insisted on continuing its original mission as programmed. So the dossiers with the photos of the empty dock, the pine trees, and the little fishing boats kept coming to Volentchko's desk. And coming. And coming.

When the Soviet Space Agency finally conceded defeat in re-aiming Kosmos2, the only solution they could offer was to wait for the Kobalt-class satellite's natural death. The experts all predicted that it would soon come crashing harmlessly back to Earth. And when it did, the Russian failure would flame out without the world being fully aware of either the momentary victory or the sour defeat that it represented. Ever optimistic, the KGB maintained that those early surveillance photos of the now-defunct sub base had been worth the gamble. And, since Kosmos2 had shown that the piggybacking of secret surveillance satellites onto the launchings of commercial satellites was possible, that method of delivery would be pursued for all future projects. Thus, whenever Kosmos2 ultimately died, it would be quietly revered as the pioneer for the modern Russian space espionage program.

But Kosmos2 didn't die and crash to Earth. No; over three decades later, the satellite continued to send useless photographs like love letters from an ugly mistress who stalks you long after your affair with her is over. And Volentchko felt stalked! No matter what demotion he received or where his office was moved, the dossiers somehow found him. And whenever he saw one on his desk, he had to decide whether he was going to look at it or jerk off to the beauties in his magazines. No longer was the weight of the world on his shoulders, just the weight of his conscience. As he thought about this now, he clenched his fists and roared with frustration.

The relationship between the man and the satellite had become cemented over the years, and even Volentchko had to admit that they were inescapably linked. Once the source of great national pride, they now were nothing more than embarrassments that everyone wished would disappear. And if the Russian leadership hoped that the satellite would accomplish this by burning up during its reentry into the atmosphere, what did they expect the man to do? Was he supposed to put his Makarov PM into his mouth, pull the trigger, and get a pauper's funeral?

Volentchko slammed his fists down and stood up to pace. All that had to happen was for the damn satellite to die and fall back to

Earth—how hard could that be? It was no secret that Soviet technology was dependable in its lack of dependability. Their cars fell apart when they hit the first pothole. Their electronics were so bad, the majority of crucial equipment was purchased secretly from Southeast Asia. And these days, their military technology did not stray from consistently underachieving: new attack subs sank when watertight doors gave way, fighter planes crashed when taking off, and battle tanks burst into flames when their gunners farted! But this antiquated piece of Soviet shit technology, hurtling through space and dodging meteors…no, this satellite continued to function like something made in Germany or even Korea! Why? Volentchko knew he'd been dealing with the damn thing for so long that he had ceased to have rational feelings toward it. But to him, there was no other way to look at it: the satellite's sole purpose was to torture him by chasing him around with its useless non-information!

He stopped his pacing and stood over the dossier. He slowly put his hand down to open it, muttering curses. "You illegitimate bastard son of a Bulgarian whore! You pus-filled wound on the cock of a Chechen! You know what you are? You're a useless bit of ancient technology taking pictures of a nonviable target! A big goddamn zero is what you are! So show me what you have, Kosmos2, which is nothing! Ruin my life yet one more time!"

It was a relief for Volentchko to finally flip open the cover and scan the material inside. He did this very quickly, for he knew the amount of time he would waste going over the dossier would be small and the breasts of the Turkish beauties in his new magazines would be big. The satellite's photos continued to have such stunning quality, he did not need to look too closely to see the vivid details of the landscape. Same rocky Atlantic coast. Same northern coniferous forest. Same decaying and abandoned fuel dock. Same fishing boats moored in their womb-like harbor. Same roads. Same this, same that. Useless information. He was about to close the dossier when he saw it. His eyes scanned the photos again, and something inside his brain registered just enough alarm that he looked closer. There! That was not the same. That hadn't been there in any of the previous photos. He frantically pulled his magnifying glass from the top drawer of his desk and peered through it. His skin tingled. His eyes struggled for a clearer view, but his brain was already telling him exactly what he was looking at. He just could not believe it. He sat straight up in his chair and said, "Now where the hell did that come from?"

1

Jamie Kurtz was sound asleep when his apartment door was viciously attacked, instantly jolting him awake. He glanced at the digital clock on the bedside table and saw that it was 11:00 a.m., but this only deepened his confusion. He was not late for an appointment. He was not expecting a delivery or a visitor. Truthfully, there was no reason for anyone to be pounding on his door at this hour. Yet the cacophony of the knocking not only continued, it grew in fervor. And, although his synapses were crippled with the hazy aftereffects of deep sleep, Jamie quickly surmised that the thunderous banging on his door indicated that there was some kind of catastrophic event occurring outside that required his immediate reaction. He threw on his clothes and ran toward the stairs to address the emergency. But, because he fully expected to be thrown into the midst of a dire circumstance that would require some kind of action, he took the extra time to put on his shoes. Only when they were securely tied did he continue on down the stairs.

The right hand doing the pounding belonged to none other than Ezra Jackson. Because of the man's short, stocky physique and his heavy brow, Jamie openly declared that his landlord was some kind of Neanderthal throwback.

Ezra Jackson was angry, and his anger was only building with each moment that his knocking wasn't answered. Why the man was dressed in a red union suit, big winter Sorel boots, and a knitted cap with earflaps on a warm June morning in Brementon, Maine, was anybody's guess, but it was clear that his mounting rage was making his ears and jowls the same color as his pajamas. The Neanderthal was like a volcano ready to erupt.

Ezra Jackson did not like Jamie Kurtz. Never had. He couldn't understand why a college graduate from the nearby fancy-pants

Bridgewater College would ever want to stay in a dead-end job just to be near his college girlfriend. And he certainly could not figure out why, when that same girlfriend ran off with another graduating senior, the Kurtz boy had acted like such a spineless wimp. Even a lowly landlord and part-time handyman could see how it was all going to play out, but somehow the boy was now still in a dazed and depressed state about it all. Not that Ezra felt an iota of pity for his situation or a sense of concern for his overall welfare; to Ezra Jackson, Jamie Kurtz was nothing but a worthless pussy who needed to move on.

The only reason he hadn't thrown the big baby out before today was that the boy's banker father paid the rent on time and in full. Ezra Jackson thought this man to be an even bigger fool to be supporting and enabling his overeducated and underachieving son, but his money was good. Of course, having a rich daddy paying all the bills didn't help build any respect for the boy; in fact, just the opposite. But even though he longed to evict the little puke, as long as his old man paid the bills, there wasn't any real reason to do so. Not until today.

The landlord continued to pound like a furious metronome meting out its vicious rhythm on the defenseless wooden door. However, as soon as he heard his tenant's footsteps coming down the last steps, he stopped. The last thing he wanted to do was fall flat on his face when the little prick opened the door. And although the silence was only momentary, it was vacuous, as if all the birds, all the trees, all the neighbors, and even the wind itself had suddenly stopped to see what would happen next.

Since Jamie was thoroughly convinced that he was being warned of an impending Armageddon, he opened the door with the adrenaline-enhanced strength of pure panic. His eyes were the size of saucers, and they frantically glanced back and forth looking for the source of the imminent disaster. He scanned for the fleet of emergency vehicles, the pack of rabid dogs, the approaching tsunami, the serial killer with bloodied knife upheld, the rogue cell of terrorists pulling off a suicide bombing, or the alien mothership hovering overhead to snatch unwary earthlings. But there was nothing there but his landlord in a red union suit, a winter cap, and winter boots, standing in front of him panting and obviously infuriated more than usual. When Jamie finally found enough of his voice to speak, it was nothing more than a croak. "What's going on, Mr. Jackson?"

The boy's eyes seemed pink around the edges, and Ezra Jackson felt that there was a real possibility that he'd been crying again, and this infuriated him even more. "What the fuck took you so long to answer this goddamn door?"

Jamie's was now overwhelmed with confusion, and he asked pathetically, "What?"

Ezra Jackson repeated himself, slowly enunciating each word. "I said, what the fuck took you so long to answer the goddamn door?"

"You woke me up. It took me…"

"Woke you up?" The landlord's face took on an expression of mock surprise. "Woke you up? Hell, boy, it's nearly noon! You're sleeping till noon now? Are you really that pathetic?"

Jamie sighed. "I work the late shift at the Hungry Rancher, Mr. Jackson. I have to clean the kitchen before I close down the restaurant every night. I get home late, so I sleep late. You know all of this."

Ezra Jackson shook his head. "Are you really gonna stand there and tell me that you stay at that horsemeat resty-rant to clean it? If you are, I'm gonna tell you that you're a goddamn liar! Cuz I know for a fact that that rat-trap ain't been cleaned since it opened."

"Well, I have to clean it every night. I mop the floors, empty the fry-o-lators, and then I…Um, what exactly do you want from me this morning, Mr. Jackson?"

The landlord looked Jamie Kurtz over from head to toe. "Have you been crying again?"

"What?"

"Your eyes, they're red. You've been crying over that lost piece of ass again, haven't you?"

Jamie spoke very calmly while rage welled up within him. "You woke me up, Mr. Jackson. Exactly what do you want? Why were you just pounding on my door so violently?"

The landlord's face sprang a crooked grin, and Jamie suddenly realized that, like a small boy using a magnifying glass to fry ants on the sidewalk, Ezra Jackson was getting ready to enjoy himself as he did something mean. The landlord put his hands on his hip. "Oh, it's *your* door now, huh?"

"It's my apartment, isn't it, Mr. Jackson?"

"No, you little asshole, it's mine! The door, the apartment, that house—they're all mine! They belong to me!"

"Yes, that's true, but I rent this apartment, and the door comes with it, I think. I'll have to look it up, but I'm pretty sure that when you rent an apartment, you also rent the front door."

"Not anymore."

"I can't keep the door?"

"You can't keep the door or the apartment, smart-ass!"

"Are you throwing me out, Mr. Jackson?"

"Yep."

"Just like that? Without any warning or reason?"

"Yep, just like that."

Jamie smiled smugly. "I'm no lawyer, but I think there are laws to prevent landlords from doing just these kinds of things."

The man now had such a shit-eating grin on his face that Jamie knew he had an ace up his sleeve, and he stiffened to face whatever the impact of the news was going to be.

Ezra Jackson said in a bad Irish accent, "It weren't me that's throwin' ya out, laddie!"

"What the hell are you talking about?"

"Oh, laddie," he continued in his mock Irish brogue, "yer old man is pullin' the plug on ya."

"My dad?"

"Aye!"

"You've got to be kidding me!"

Jackson cleared his throat, then said in his regular voice, "Him and me talked on the phone this morning. I hafta tell you, Kurtz, I didn't think much of the man before today. But after talking with him, I can say that we see things eye to eye. He's come to his senses and decided that he's wasted enough money on you. He's stopping his rent payments as of right now. No rent, no apartment. And technically, since your old man paid the rent, *he* was the tenant. So as tenant and landlord, we've already come to the agreement that you need to move your shit out of my apartment. Today. Got it? Good, now start packing."

Jamie's world started to twirl so fast that he gripped the door frame so that he didn't swing out of it. Ezra Jackson was smiling at him as if he had just hit a home run, and his cruelty seemed to bring Jamie back to his senses. "You're a fucking asshole!"

"Oooh, you gonna cry now? Boo-hoo, boo-hoo! I'll get you a tissue so you can wipe your eyes and blow your nose before you get the hell out of my apartment!"

"I'm going upstairs, Mr. Jackson, and I'm gonna call my dad right now. If you're lying to me, which I think is a fair chance with all that schnapps on your breath, I'm going to sue your ass off! When I'm done with you, all you'll have in this world is that silly union suit, that stupid hat, and those goofy boots."

"Well, ya better hurry, kid."

"Why? Cuz you're a sucky old man and you're gonna die soon?"

Jamie had always been terrible with verbal comebacks. In some ways, the inanity of his replies had saved him some major ass-whippings during his life. When the bullies were either laughing too hard or just trying to figure out what the hell he'd actually just said, they rarely had enough drive left to mete out the physical violence that might have come with better verbal parrying. His inability to defend himself with witty comebacks and voracious put-downs was yet another siphon of his self-confidence. In Jamie's mind, it was hard to be a winner or a real man if your only comeback was along the lines of "I know you are, but what am I?"

The landlord was currently enjoying the eviction of Jamie Kurtz too much to even think about what the boy had just said. He continued to smile and simply said, "No, kid, you better hurry cuz your daddy is also turning off the phone any minute now."

Ezra Jackson spun around and began walking away with a gait that made the earflaps on the hat bounce rhythmically over his ears. Jamie watched this departure with his mouth agape. When the landlord got to the door of his house, he turned around and yelled, "Anything not out of there by five o'clock today is mine. I don't want to see you again, Kurtz, unless it's to get the goddamn keys from you!"

Jamie slammed the door and ran up the stairs to call his father. When his father's secretary answered the phone and put him on hold, Jamie knew that Ezra Jackson's prophesy of his eviction was an undeniable fact. Margie never put him on hold. Usually she just chatted with him until his father was able to talk. As he listened to the awful Muzak, he thought about hanging up. This dream he was suffering through had so many psychological levels, it was able to shift and change and make him feel trapped no matter where he turned. But he continued to maintain that just hearing his father's voice would make everything all right again, and he was determined to stay on the line.

The Muzak stopped and Jamie's father spoke. "Hello?"

Jamie nearly dropped the phone. His father's voice was so emotionless, he could have been one of those automated operators. Jamie looked up at the ceiling and his world began to spin again.

"Dad?"

"Yes, Jamie."

"My landlord was just banging on my door. He threw me out of the apartment."

"He did, huh?"

"Yes, Dad, he did! He just told me that I've got a few hours to get all of my stuff out. That if I don't take it with me, it's his. He also told me that he's evicting me because you've decided to stop sending rent payments to him."

"Yes, that's all true."

"And?"

"I'm not sure I understand the nature of your question, Jamie."

"And...why would you do that to me, Dad?"

There was no momentary pause for contemplation or doubt. Jamie's father spoke clearly and succinctly. "Because it's time for you to walk on your own two feet."

"Uh, Dad?"

"Yes, Jamie?"

"What the hell's going on here?"

"Don't swear at me."

Jamie squeezed the receiver as if to break it. He looked up at the ceiling and mutely howled, before putting it back to his ear. "I'm sorry,

Dad. I just don't have any clue about what's going on, and I'm struggling to understand it all. I went to bed late last night after a grueling day of work thinking that everything in my world was just fine, and now I'm waking up to find out that I don't have an apartment anymore. I just thought you and I might have talked before it actually happened, that's all. Is that so unreasonable?"

"I'm cutting you off."

Jamie heard no conflict within his father. The statement was made with so much ease and coldness that it slipped from his father's lips, through the phone lines, into Jamie's ears, and down his spine like something lubricated with lithium grease.

"What, like a wart? Is that what I am to you now, Dad, a wart?"

"You have become something like a parasite, son."

"A parasite? I work! I work hard every damn day!" Jamie shrieked.

"Don't swear at me, Jamie. If you swear at me again, I'm hanging up."

"Sorry."

"You do work, son, but at that horrible restaurant. The Hungry Rancher? Come on, you're a college graduate, for goodness sake! You shouldn't be working at a place like that! It's beneath you."

"You know the history of all of this, Dad. When I came back to Brementon—"

"Jamie, you said it just now—it's history. And you, of all people, should understand how important it is to break the cycles of history. It didn't work out between you and Laura. You need to accept that, stop wallowing in self-pity, and get on with your future. I really thought I was helping you do that by paying the rent and your bills, but it's clear to me now that I've only enabled you to squander your talents."

"Who showed you the light? Good old Ezra Jackson?"

"Mr. Jackson has been most helpful in explaining what he's been seeing. I haven't thought much of the man until today. Talking with him, it is clear that he and I see eye to eye when it comes to you and your current state."

"Just to let you know, Dad, Ezra Jackson was wearing his bright red pajamas, winter boots, and his winter hat today! It's June! The man is definitely drunk, and I'm pretty sure he's certifiably insane.

So if he's the reason you're doing all of this, you might want to re-think a few of your choices."

"Hmm…Jamie, shall I do a short recap of what I know? You graduated from one of Cleveland's most prestigious prep schools and were accepted to every college you applied to. But you chose Bridge-water because Walter Whetstone, the world-renowned Civil War his-torian, taught there. And for four glorious years you were that man's personal project, protégé, and darling. When you graduated with the highest honors, you were the recipient of one of the most coveted American history internships in the entire country. And, even though the whole world was your oyster, you gave it all up to come crawling back to Laura in Brementon. Then she dumped you and left town, and you were too heartbroken to get yourself out of there. So now you find yourself in that dinky, dead-end little college town and continue to clean the fry-o-lator at that grubby restaurant while you cry yourself to sleep every night over a girl we all knew was going to leave you for a better ride at the first chance she got. So you see, son, I don't need Mr. Jackson's input to know the score."

Every word in his father's comment overwhelmed Jamie. The awkward pause in the conversation continued, and he knew that his father was looking down at his watch to see how much more time he was going to waste on this phone call. The image gave Jamie some focus. "Dad, what do you expect me to do without a place to live?"

"Get on with your future and apply to graduate school. Then you accomplish your destiny."

"Even if I wanted to do that, those applications take time to fill out and wait for acceptance, you know? How am I going to do any of that when I don't have a place to live anymore?"

"That's your problem now, Jamie. You've had everything handed to you, and you've failed miserably. Maybe you're like one of those bears in the national parks who get so much trash and food scraps from the tourists, they can't survive without help. That's not saying that I've lost complete faith in you, son. But now you'll have to work for everything you get. I'm hopeful that you can make it, but regardless, you'll succeed or fail on your own from here on out."

"I wish we could have talked about this first, Dad. A little more preparation time would have helped immensely."

"Mr. Jackson says that you've had more than enough time — sleeping half the day away and staying up half the night crying — to get your life in order."

"Dad, Ezra Jackson is a fucking asshole! He —"

The click was subtle, but when the dial tone came on, Jamie knew that his father had followed up on his threat. He hadn't slammed the phone down in anger, just merely hung up as soon as his ears registered the profanity. Jamie would have preferred there to be some emotion from his father, for that would have shown that the man still thought of him as a son, not a business transaction. But he smiled nonetheless because it felt good to call Ezra Jackson a fucking asshole. As a matter of fact, now that he knew that his father was conspiring with the pajama-wearing lunatic to make him homeless, his rising anger toward both men was pushing him to react to the situation. But how?

Jamie sat down on the couch to think. Because his shift at the Hungry Rancher began in a few hours, he didn't have a lot of time. So he decided to approach his problem the way Robert E. Lee would have prepared for a battle. The Virginian would use his cavalry to assess the situation, attack, react to his enemy's responses, and then choose the next target. Sure, it would be more fun to react impulsively and decisively like Stonewall, but Jamie respected the fact that the calculating Robert E. Lee was the man who died of old age and with both of his arms!

Jamie needed to assess his situation first. The fact of the matter was that his father's description had been right on the button: he was currently heartbroken, homeless, and stuck in Brementon, Maine. The impact of stating this took his breath away, but he thought about the veracity of this statement some more. Was he really heartbroken? Sure, when Laura first broke up with him, he was. But now that he'd had some time to heal, his heart showed signs that it was well on its way to being back to normal again. And he wasn't truly homeless either — not live-out-of-your-bags-while-you-push-a-grocery-cart-full-of-bottles-and-newspapers-and-urinate-in-your-pants kind of homeless. No, he really was apartment-less. There were plenty of other places to stay. With friends. Or at cheap hotels. Or in campgrounds. Even in his car, if he had to. Jamie smiled to himself as he realized that his situation wasn't really as bad as it looked.

Then he thought about how he was the fry-o-lator bitch at the Hungry Rancher, and this made him look up at the ceiling and groan, "Omigod, I work at the Hungry Rancher!"

Jamie got up and paced. The very name of the restaurant made him wince in pain. When he'd first gotten the job there, it had been reason for a victory dance. For it not only allowed him to come back to Brementon to be close to Laura again, but, in his mind, it was exactly what she wanted him to do to show his commitment to their relationship. By giving up the internship and then degrading himself further by working a menial job, he had assumed that she would see his sacrifices as proof that he was more than man enough to be her life partner. As Stonewall once said, "Sacrifices! Have I not made them? What is my life here but a daily sacrifice? Nor shall I ever withhold sacrifices for my country when they will avail to anything."

But Laura did not see Jamie's actions as a positive thing. Instead, she acted like she was *embarrassed* of him! When Alex Pettingill, a handsome Bridgewater senior from the lovely side of southern Connecticut, started wooing her, she saw her chance at a new life. After all, Alex was going somewhere in this world, and Jamie Kurtz clearly wasn't. And after he dealt with the initial devastation of getting dumped, he then had to watch as their new love affair grew and grew, until Laura drove out of town with Alex after graduation without even saying goodbye!

He could have moved on right then and there. He could have taken off in his car and gone far, far away. But his father was right—he had stayed and continued to live in a horrible garage apartment and work a terrible dead-end job. And why? To do penance? To acquire good Karma? Whatever the reason, it hadn't worked. It hadn't been anything but a senseless prison for Jamie. So while he was enslaved in his own Andersonville and peddled steaks that still showed the jockey marks, Laura was out there in the big world, screwing a rich frat boy from Connecticut and probably having multiple orgasms. It just wasn't fair! But that was the real scorecard of his life:

Alex and Laura, a million; Jamie Kurtz, a big fat zero!

"Wait a goddamn second!" Jamie yelled. He was slipping down the greasy path of self-pity again, and he would not allow himself to do that. Maybe he needed to just try looking at the problem from a different angle. Perhaps these recent events, as confusing as they seemed to be at the moment, were not kicks to the groin but hackings at the tethers that held him down. Could these seemingly insurmountable and incalculable betrayals by his loved ones, family members, and landlord actually be the agents that allowed him to be wholly and totally free? After all, if someone in a motorboat wants to go somewhere but can't get the anchor up, what happens? The boat is forced to circle around the anchor line in a giant and unending circle. And what happens as soon as that tether is cut? The boat can go anywhere it wants!

Jamie raised his fist and declared, "I can go anywhere I want and do whatever I want!"

He smiled because he wasn't in dire straits at all; he was facing a bold new future. No backstabbing girlfriend to sacrifice his life for. No emotionless father to seek an unattainable approval from. No mentally deranged landlord to tiptoe on eggshells for. No more fry-o-lators. No more expectations. Just an utterly free man making his own choices to live his own life!

With this clarity ringing in his head, he stormed off toward his bedroom to start packing. He grabbed the suitcase that had been stored under the bed and threw it down like it was an opponent in a wrestling match. Dust bunnies scattered in all directions. He pulled clothing from the bureau drawers and threw them into the suitcase. When he came across the rugby shirt that Laura had bought for him at L.L. Bean's outlet store, he lovingly fingered the frayed fabric of the blue shirt with the orange and yellow collar. She had only spent $4.99 on it, yet he had treated it with as much reverence as an Armani suit because Laura had given it to him. And after she left him, he would often wear the shirt, listen to his Sarah McLachlan CD, and walk around the apartment crying. Even now, he felt the urge to do this again.

"No! No more tethers!" Jamie bellowed as he threw the rugby shirt onto the bed. Then he heard Ezra Jackson talking to Julie Kersey outside, so he moved closer to the window to listen to their conversation. Julie worked as a secretary at a nearby shipyard. She'd been nice to Jamie, if not a little too nice. It was clear that Julie used her low-cut, tight-fitting white shirts, her ample breasts, and her warm smile to get what she wanted with most men. And as soon as Jamie had realized this, he'd steered well clear of her. Ezra Jackson, on the other hand, had fallen right under her cleavage spell. He was a few steps short of a drooling idiot, but he definitely was being led around by something other than his brain. As Jamie listened to them talking outside now, he heard the landlord brag about evicting the pain-in-the-ass tenant in the garage apartment. Julie not only cackled with laughter at his story, she promised to bring some brownies over to him later. She even flirtatiously said that, after acting like a big strong landlord and all, he would be hungry for some of her goodies.

Years later, Jamie would swear it was this very moment that gave him the sudden resolve to strike back. Instead of just slinking away with his tail between his legs, he knew that he had to counterattack like Lee against McClellan at Second Bull Run! And while God spoke to most of his prophets in the Bible in the form of burning bushes or other amazing happenings, Jamie swore that his holy call to action came from an awful secondhand rugby shirt and a conversation between a deranged landlord and a flirtatious secretary.

Jamie went to get a couple of boxes from the garage. While he was in there, the object under the gray tarp caught his attention. It was Ezra Jackson's pride and joy—a 1966 Porsche roadster in mint condition. The car only ever left the garage on the Fourth of July. On that one day, the car was uncovered and driven through the streets in the lavish patriotic parade to the Bridgewater football field, where it consistently won the infamous Brementon car show. As soon as Ezra Jackson had his trophy in hand, he drove back to the garage and put the car under the protective tarp for another year.

As Jamie now looked at the Porsche, the first idea for his counterattack came into his mind. He stopped and looked around at the inside of the garage and knew exactly what he was going to do. But he needed to pack all of his belongings first. So, once he saw that the coast was clear, he bolted out of the garage and bounded back up the stairs and into the apartment with the two boxes in hand.

It was time to purge all of Laura's things that were still lying around. Now that he was officially letting go of her, there was no reason to hold on to them anymore. For example, why the hell did he still have a partial box of tampons in the bathroom? Why was the stupid teddy bear that he'd won for her at the church fair still sitting on the couch? Why were some of her blouses neatly folded next to his shirts? Why did he hold onto that ridiculous rugby shirt? It was time to get rid of it all. He began to put her things into the boxes. At first, it was painful, but as more and more went in, he began to feel something akin to relief. And as he put the rugby shirt in, he felt like a free man.

After he finished packing his suitcase, he started to clear out the bathroom. He took Laura's toothbrush, a partial container of Midol, some leftover facial cleansers, and the half box of tampons, and put them all into a box. When he found an opened package of chocolate-flavored Ex-Lax in the medicine cabinet, the second idea for his counterattack popped into his head. He put the Ex-Lax down on the counter of the kitchen for later and smiled a devilish grin.

Since Jamie tended to eat lunches and dinners at work, there wasn't much food in the fridge. The freezer was full with the excess meat and fish from Ezra Jackson's previous hunting and fishing seasons—deer and moose chops and steaks, various fish fillets, and even some small waterfowl breasts—all wrapped tightly in white paper and labeled clearly with black wax pencil. As he looked at the contents now, the idea for his third and final counterattack came to him. He made a quick shopping list and ran to the convenience store around the corner to get what he needed.

Later, as he stirred the brownie batter in the bowl on the kitchen table, Jamie giggled and chortled like some kind of medieval witch. He had never made Ex-Lax brownies before, but it turned out to be pretty simple. The batter seemed so normal, he had to keep reminding himself not to lick the bowl or spoon like he usually did. He put the pan into the oven to bake, and then headed down the stairs and snuck back into the garage again. Thanks to a previous plumbing problem, Jamie knew that the access panel for the pipe from his apartment's toilet was up in the garage ceiling. The plumber had bitched and bellyached so much about that fact, Jamie was sure the guy had probably doubled his bill because of it. Of course, Jackson had refused to pay, and Jamie had paid for all the repairs out of his own pocket.

Jamie found a ladder tucked in the corner and set it up under the access panel. He climbed up and undid the screws that held the panel in place. There, just inside the drywall of the ceiling, was the large white plastic pipe that came down from the toilet. It elbowed near the opening and then ran parallel to the ceiling until it turned down behind the wall and went to the sewer. Using a hacksaw, Jamie carefully cut the junction of the elbow, and after wiggling it a little, he torqued it ninety degrees to face right at the Porsche. The trajectory was perfect. The next time the apartment's toilet was flushed, the foul contents were sure to hit the car. He left two screws on the access panel a little loose, creating the perfect nozzle to further aim the flow. He put away the tools and the ladder, then took his Swiss Army knife and gingerly slit the car cover from the front bumper to the rear of the cockpit. He wished he could see how it all went down, but he'd be long gone by then.

The brownies were done by the time he got back upstairs, so he set them out on the counter to cool. He was proud of his new vengefulness; it felt good to be on the giving end of the abuse, not the getting end, for a change. Whereas the first two counterattacks were aimed directly at Ezra Jackson, the third idea would sting Jamie's father the most. Explosive diarrhea and the damage to the Porsche roadster were two things his father could avoid any responsibility for. He could almost hear what the man would say to Ezra Jackson: "Well, sir, can you prove it was my son who did any of this? I mean, did you see him do it? He doesn't have any plumbing or baking skills that I'm aware of, so I don't think I'm liable for any of the damage. But if you want to contest this, I'll give you my lawyer's number and you can talk with him about it. He's the senior partner for the largest legal firm in Cleveland."

Although Jamie smiled at the thought of Ezra Jackson having to swallow his pride in the face of this legalistic power, it still meant that his father would get off scot-free, which was something he could not allow. That was why his third idea was so fantastic—it would leave his father with no chance to deny involvement. Jamie positioned a chair in the hallway under the entry panel that led to the attic, opened the panel, and put all the contents of the freezer up there in nice, neat piles. He put a cardboard sign in front of the piles that read, *You're a fucking asshole, Ezra Jackson. Signed, Jamie Kurtz.*

Now he was nearly ready to leave. He cut up the brownies, put them on a plate, and covered them with plastic wrap. Then, using handwriting that resembled a preteen girl's, he wrote a note on a card in Julie Kersey's script: *I hope you like my treats! We should get together later to share more!* :-)

He snuck the plate of brownies over to the front door of Ezra's house and put them down on the welcome mat and stole quietly back to his apartment. He took the two boxes of purged items and put them on the curb with a FREE sign on them. Then he loaded his Volvo wagon with the rest of his possessions. He did a final spot-check of the apartment to make sure that it was clean, and then, with measured humility, he walked over to Ezra Jackson's house and knocked.

The landlord threw open the door and scowled at him. "What the fuck do you want, Kurtz?"

"I'm ready to leave, Mr. Jackson. Here are the keys. Do you want me to lock it up?"

The landlord angrily snatched them out of Jamie's hands. "Don't bother. Just get the hell out of here."

"I emptied the fridge of all of my food, Mr. Jackson, but I didn't defrost the freezer because of all your stuff in there."

"I don't fucking care what you did or didn't do, Kurtz, as long as I never have to see your face again!"

"All right, then. Well, thanks for everything, Mr. Jackson. I talked with my dad and now I realize that you two are absolutely right—I have been wasting my time by being a bit of a fuck-up. I thank you for setting me and my dad straight about all of this."

"Whatever. What do you want, kid, a hug? Just keep moving."

"Oh, look, Mr. Jackson, you've got a plate of brownies here."

"Give them to me! Don't touch them! I don't want your mad-cow infested hands on my food! Julie Kersey made these for me. See what happens when you're a decent, hardworking guy, not a pitiful slacker like you, Kurtz? A beautiful woman brings you treats. And guess what? I'm going to eat each one of these, tell her how wonderful they were, and then I'll be poised to be enjoying her other treats, if you know what I mean. I've never had a girl screw around on me! You've got a lot to learn, dickwad!"

"You've said a mouthful there, Mr. Jackson. Well, thanks again for everything."

"Whatever."

As Jamie backed his car out of the driveway, he looked over at the apartment one last time. Ezra Jackson was still standing on his porch, wolfing down the brownies. When he looked up and saw Jamie about to drive away, he nonchalantly gave him the finger. Jamie shook his head and smiled a big grin as he put the car in gear, muttering, "No, Mr. Jackson; fuck *you!*"

2

At four o'clock on a Wednesday afternoon, the Hungry Rancher only had a few patrons. There were two senior citizens at one table eating an early dinner and a group of lost tourists at another. The elderly couple did not even react when Jamie walked in, but the tourists looked up with relief on their faces. The emptiness of the restaurant bespoke of something sinister with regard to the quality of the food, and the mere presence of another person choosing to walk in gave them all a shot of confidence that the place wasn't as bad as it looked or smelled. But, as Jamie continued on past them and toward the kitchen, their hopeful expressions fell into looks that betrayed the regret they now felt at having stopped at the Hungry Rancher in the first place.

Jamie had purposely entered through the front doors instead of the employee's entrance at the back so he could confront the manager, Adrian Goodsell, in public. This man had just the right mixture of anger, attitude, and cruelty to earmark him as a grownup bully, and those around him, both the restaurant's staff and its clients, quickly developed an appropriate fear of him. Goodsell's rages were legendary, and Jamie usually went out of his way to avoid pissing the man off at all costs. Now, as he came in the front door, he felt more like he was sneaking up on a black mamba than heading into work to quit.

As soon as Goodsell saw Jamie walking across the restaurant, he sped toward him like a middle linebacker cutting off a running lane. "Well, well, Kurtz, you're early for your shift—which never happens—and you've come in the front door, I see—which you're never supposed to do. So, what's up?"

Although his hair was thinning and his face showed that he was entering middle age, Goodsell was aggressive and strong enough to cause serious physical harm. Jamie just hoped that, by keeping the conversation in the public arena of the restaurant, Goodsell would refrain from snapping him like a twig. After all, the man didn't mind rubbing people the wrong way, but he had risen to the rank of manager with a full understanding of how not to permanently chase the customers away. Jamie looked at the way he was blocking his path now, and tried to keep the tone of his voice as calm as he could. "Well, Mr. Goodsell, I think it's time for me to move on."

Goodsell shrugged. "Uh-huh?"

"Well, I guess what I'm saying is that I'm quitting."

Goodsell scratched his chin, then turned suddenly and walked back toward the kitchen without another word. Jamie stood there not knowing what to do next. He couldn't tell if the man was walking away because he wanted to end the conversation privately in his office—something Jamie definitely did not want to do—or if he was walking away because the conversation was officially over. Jamie looked for signs of support from the patrons in the restaurant, but they were all too focused on dissecting their meals to take notice of his plight. He waited for Goodsell to turn around and make a gesture that either banished or beckoned, but he did neither as his wide shoulders hit the swinging door into the kitchen and he disappeared from sight.

"Coming through!" announced Vi, the bleached-blond waitress, as she entered the dining area with a pot of coffee. She was the one employee who'd been at the Hungry Rancher longer than Goodsell. No one was exactly sure when Vi had first started at the restaurant or why she kept working there, but she was reliable, polite, and seemingly un-fireable. As she got abreast of Jamie, she cooed, "Oh, hey, Jamie, what're you doing here so early, hon?"

Before he could answer, the senior citizens called her over. She went and poured their coffee, took their complaints with a smile, and then came back. She looked Jamie over from head to toe, then said matter-of-factly, "You're early, but you're not in uniform, and not ready for your shift. What's up, hon?"

"Did you see where Goodsell went?"

"His office, I guess."

"Shit! I wanted to talk to him out here in the restaurant. Did he look mad?"

"He always looks mad, hon! I'm sure that even when he's having an orgasm he looks mad!"

Jamie cleared his throat and said, "I'm quitting today, Vi."

"Good for you, hon. This place is like a roach motel, 'you check in, but you don't check out!' Get out of here before you're like me and you're too old to make it through a shift without pissing in your adult diapers."

The mention of both roaches and adult diapers caused the nearby table of tourists to look up with panicked expressions. Vi saw their reaction and said in a soothing voice, "Metaphors, just metaphors, guys; keep eating. Does anyone want refills on soft drinks?"

"I guess I have to go into his office to quit, huh?"

"Yep, looks like it. Well, it's been nice knowing ya, hon."

"Jesus, Vi, is it really going to be that bad, confronting Goodsell there?"

"What? Oh no, hon, I wasn't saying that. I'm just saying that I'm probably gonna be too busy to give you a proper sendoff when you're ready to leave."

Jamie's relationship with Vi had changed last Christmas. Up until then, she'd been like a kind and wise aunt to him. But at the Hungry Rancher's Christmas party—which was nothing more than the six employees standing in the parking lot and passing cheap liquor around—Jamie's outlook on Vi was forever altered. She'd been nipping from her private stash all night and was well on her way to being too drunk to drive home when she propositioned Jamie. It had been done quietly and no one else had heard her, but the invitation to go behind the dumpster for a hand job had been quickly issued and even more quickly refused. Vi seemed wholly unhurt and unfazed by his rejection, and had never mentioned it again. But the offer forever changed Jamie's perception. From that very moment, he could not help but notice that, despite her age, Vi was a woman who had an attractive face and a strong body. Even now, as he heard her comment about a proper sendoff, he had to admit that he was mildly excited. He shook his head vigorously and said, "Goodbye, Vi."

Jamie was surprised when the waitress hugged him, but he was utterly shocked when she grabbed his ass with her free hand. She winked at him as she walked back toward the customers saying, "Metaphors, just metaphors. Keep eating, darlings. But save room so you can grab some dessert—we've got pie!"

Jamie went through the swinging doors and found Goodsell at his desk doing paperwork. Jamie hoped that he was writing out a compensation check for him, but when he knocked on the door frame, Goodsell looked up and gave him a surprised look. "Oh, you're still here, Kurtz?"

"Um, yes, Mr. Goodsell. Like I said, I'm quitting."

"Yeah, I heard you in the restaurant. Thanks."

He went back to the paperwork. He signed something, restacked one of the piles, and then looked up again at Jamie. His expression was souring. "For God's sake, what is it, Kurtz? Why are you still standing there?"

"Well, you see, I got thrown out of my apartment—"

"Okay," Goodsell interrupted with some annoyance in his voice, "but why are you still standing at my office door? Do you want a medal? Do you want a handshake? Do you want a hug?"

"Well, Mr. Goodsell, I need to…collect my…um, last paycheck."

"Oh, it's about the money, huh? Don't worry, we'll mail your last check to you. You're quitting about five days before payday, so you'll just have to wait until it arrives in the mail. Okay, Kurtz? Thanks for everything."

Goodsell once again looked down at his desk and started to organize the papers on it like that would make the annoying Kurtz boy disappear. Jamie cleared his throat and said, "Well, that's just it, Mr. Goodsell, since I got thrown out of my apartment today, I don't have an address for you to send the check to anymore. So, I was wondering if you could just write the check now and give it to me."

"No, it's not payday, Kurtz, and I don't write checks unless it's payday. You'll have to wait until I mail you your check."

"But I don't know where I'll be on payday!"

"Do you have any fucking idea how many times I've had this same goddamn conversation with outgoing employees? With the continual flow of ex-cons, college students, lowlifes, and overall degenerates that have come in and out of this place to work here over the last eight years, I'd give a conservative estimate that I've had this conversation over fifty times since I've been manager. So don't expect any special treatment from me, okay?"

He stopped talking and went back to his paperwork. Jamie waited for him to say something more, but he didn't. So he meekly added, "But, Mr. Goodsell—"

"I think what I'm trying to say here, Kurtz, is that I don't give two shakes of a rat's rectum that you're quitting right now. That freak Blanton will cover for you tonight and then I'll hire someone new tomorrow to replace you. And you know what? They'll quit in about three months. And on and on. Everyone always thinks they're indispensable, but they're not—no one is in this world. You walk out, someone else is begging to come in. And you know why? Cuz people always need the money. Some for legitimate reasons, some for not-so-legitimate reasons. And truthfully, I don't give a shit which. I just need them to do their work or get out of the way so someone else can do it. So don't act all high and mighty and expect me to cry cuz you're quitting today, okay? Truth be told, I'll forget your name in about a week. The only constant here at the Hungry Rancher is me and Vi, and I honestly don't know who's gonna outlast who.

"So, Kurtz, goodbye, farewell, *auf Wiedersehen*, so long. Don't let the door hit you in the ass on the way out. Thanks a million for all your hard work. You're a trooper, and we love you. You were, without a doubt, the best fry-o-lator bitch we've ever had. Now get the fuck out and stop blocking my goddamn office door."

"I just want my check, Mr. Goodsell. Can you hold it for me here?"

"Yes, you can get it...on payday!"

Goodsell looked down at his desk one more time. He spoke suddenly, as if conversing with the piles of paper there. "If you are still standing there when I look up again, Kurtz, I swear to God and all His saints, I'm gonna ring your goddamn neck, rip out your fucking heart, and then eat your liver. Get the fuck out, *now!*"

Jamie edged backward quickly, certain that Goodsell was not bluffing. He walked into the kitchen and went straight over to where Elmer Blanton was scouring pots and pans in the sink. When he saw Jamie edging over, he said, "Yo, J-man, what's up?"

"I just quit, Elmer."

"Ah, dude, good going. I mean, I'll miss ya, but you're better than this fucking place! Me, I'm right behind you. As soon as I get enough money saved up to buy me a car, I'm quitting and heading to California."

Elmer had told this dream to Jamie many times before. But whenever he started to ask about the specifics of the dream, he seemed to hurt Elmer's feelings. He did not want to do that now, so Jamie just smiled and nodded. Elmer clapped Jamie on the back and said, "So, dude, what're you gonna do now?"

"I don't know, Elmer. I was also evicted today, too."

"No way! Wow, you must have done some bad shit to get evicted."

"My dad told the landlord to evict me."

"No way, dude!"

"Yeah."

"Why's your old man so pissed at you?"

Jamie took in a deep breath, nodded, and said quietly, "I guess I haven't lived up to his expectations, Elmer. In his eyes, I'm nothing but a failure!"

"Sounds like me and my old man. I sure hope I don't ever make my own son feel like such a loser. Hey, you know what? You should drive to Cali with me. You've got the perfect road-trip car, and we could head off together, just you and me, and then we could be roommates in San Fran."

Jamie smiled at Elmer. If nothing else, the boy was persistent. "Aw, Elmer, I like it here. I think I'm going to stay around a while longer."

"So no San Fran, huh?"

"Not quite yet."

"Maybe when you're ready to go, bro, I'll have saved up enough money and be ready, too."

"Yeah, maybe."

"Hey, you know what? You should head over to the Job Service office to get a new job."

"Where's that?"

"It's at the Corners. They've got all kinds of jobs listed there. If I was you, I'd head over there right now and check it out. I'm sure there's some work you could do until I've saved up enough money. Then we'll head west together, right, dude?"

Jamie clapped the boy on the back. "You'll be the first one I call when I'm ready to head to California, Elmer."

3

No one knows exactly when the Corners got its name, but most agree that it came about because it was the intersection between the main overland route and the primary access road that headed south to the many small towns on the coastal peninsulas. For generations, the people who lived in these remote and isolated fishing villages made their way through a network of smaller roads to get to this main thoroughfare into the Corners to sell their catches and buy their supplies. The advent of the automobile and the designation of the coastal route as US Route 1 completely transformed the area in the early twentieth century. Although it continued to be a center of local business, the Corners was now awash with waves of eager tourists in search of shopping, entertainment, and food. As a result, countless attractions were hastily constructed to entice these travelers to stop, as companies of commerce and entertainment vied for the best position and exposure.

After World War II, developers, drunk on the postwar economic boom and with the burgeoning population of the nearby naval station in mind, proposed building a modern shopping mall at the Corners. When it was finally constructed, the sprawling complex of stores and restaurants included the biggest Sears store in the state of Maine and a giant movie theater with an unprecedented eight screens. The Corners became a destination for people from near and far, and residents thought that the area was going to enjoy unending prosperity.

But it didn't. After several decades of steady economic decline, nearly all the stores of the Corners were closed down and the buildings had fallen into such a state of disrepair that some people wanted to raze the whole place. Just before that happened, however, a spark of revival came in the form of several national chain stores, who, for reasons no one could fathom, forecasted that the area was going to rebound. Outdated buildings were renovated to look fresh, and new modern structures were built, and the Corners' validity as an eating and shopping destination was restored.

But even as the big box stores sprang up like giant portobello mushrooms and the roads became clogged with traffic, some businesses in the Corners resisted the change. The pawn shop not only continued to defiantly advertise used guns and guitars, but seemed to revel in the fact that it was still a good spot to make shady transactions. The greasy mechanics at the tire warehouse between the luxurious motel and the shining new movie complex seemed to relish the way that the blasts of their air wrenches disturbed the patrons of both establishments. The roofing business with the inflatable Santa out in front seemed more proud of the yearly patches on that Santa than the mismatched coats of paint on their building. And, nestled anonymously in a grove of small pine trees, the windowless white cinderblock Job Service building looked like a bunker in which to hide from the ravaging effects of an explosion, especially one that involved redevelopment.

Although he was stunned to be following Elmer's advice, Jamie knew that looking for a new job made sense. With his life an empty slate now, he was completely free to pick any job he wanted. However, when he saw the Job Service's sign in front of that featureless building, he thought some high school students had switched the signs around as a prank. Even as he got out of his car and started toward the door, he wondered if Elmer would be so cruel as to send him to a biker gang's headquarters as an elaborate punishment for questioning him too much about his dreams of going to California.

The steel door looked so imposing, Jamie expected it to be locked. But when he turned the handle, it opened easily, and he walked inside. Once his eyes adjusted to the dimness of the interior, he saw a small waiting room with several chairs and coffee tables positioned around it. There were two offices in the back. The walls were paneled with fake wood the color of butterscotch, and two battered ceiling fans twirled overhead like drunken men.

A large blond woman in one of the offices stood up, straightened her skirt, and started to walk toward him. Her smile was beaming, but the dark red lipstick accentuated the fact that the woman's hair was nearly white from peroxide. She was wearing a tight black skirt and a white shirt that hugged her substantial chest. As she approached, she thrust her hand out like the prow of an icebreaker. "Hello, my name is Beth."

"Oh, hi," Jamie said, shaking her hand a bit awkwardly.

"I'm sorry, what is your name?"

"Oh, it's Jamie. Jamie Kurtz."

"Okay, Jamie Kurtz, first things first. If you're here, you're looking for a job. And if you're looking for a job, you have to make sure that you do everything you can to get that job. And the way to do that is to present yourself in the best manner possible. Rule Number One: A person who introduces himself and smiles at a potential employer is a person that is immediately seen as self-confident, polite, and dependable. What that old shampoo commercial said is true: you cannot make a second first impression. Always remember that this process of finding a job is more about presentation than anything else."

Jamie said nothing. From Elmer's brief description of the place, he thought all he had to do was walk in, survey the job listings, and pick a job—not receive a spiel about his mannerisms by this bleached-blond woman. He was unsure how to proceed without inviting another critique.

"Jamie Kurtz?"

"Yes, Beth?"

"*Do* you want to find a job?"

Jamie straightened his shoulders and put some attitude into his reply. "That was the main reason I came to the Job Service today, Beth."

"Well, you need to fill out our questionnaire first."

"Questionnaire? I was told that I could just look over your listings and find a job."

"Well, to serve you best, we need you to fill out a questionnaire first. We pride ourselves on serving our clients' specific needs."

"I just want a job."

"Of course you do," Beth laughed. "That's why you're here, right? But look over at that table. See all those three-ring notebooks piled on top of each other? Each one is full of jobs. Now, you could spend the next few hours wasting your time by searching willy-nilly through them, or you could spend just a few minutes and fill out the questionnaire so I can narrow down that search. Okay?"

"I just want a job," Jamie repeated weakly. It was too late, for the woman had already spun around and headed over to a table just outside her office. She grabbed a paper from a stack there, put it on a clipboard, and took a pencil out of a cup on the table. When she came back, she handed him all of this and told him to take a seat and answer all the questions. Jamie started to say something, but the woman just pointed down at the chairs. Reluctantly, he sat down in the closest one.

The questionnaire was not short. It asked for educational and employment background. It asked for interests and hobbies. It asked about allergies. It asked for references. There was much more to fill out than Jamie wanted to be bothered with—he just wanted to find a job, not fill out ridiculous forms. He was quickly becoming irritated at the whole damn process. Why was this woman wasting his time with senseless paperwork when she had already said that the jobs were listed in those notebooks?

An idea popped into his head. He sat up in his seat and tried to inconspicuously looked over the top of his clipboard at the woman in her office. She was focused on something on her desk and wasn't paying attention to Jamie anymore, so slipped over to a chair that was right next to the table with all the notebooks. Each of them had a label declaring their category on the front cover. He saw one that said CONSTRUCTION and one that said SALES. He reached for CONSTRUCTION. When his hand touched the cool vinyl cover of the notebook, he glanced up to make sure that Beth was still in her office. But she wasn't. Somehow she'd not only gotten up, but had walked stealthily over to where he was. She was now towering over him so closely that her ample bosom obstructed his view of the bottom half of her chin. With her hands on her hips in full confrontation mode, she asked, "Are you done with the questionnaire already, Jamie Kurtz?"

Jamie's face flushed and he laughed nervously. "Um, just about."

"Well, let's see what you've got so far."

Beth scooped the clipboard out of Jamie's hands. She glanced at it, then eyed Jamie with renewed suspicion. "Well, well, well, Jamie

Kurtz. A Bridgewater College graduate, huh? Oh, how the mighty have fallen. And here you are, at the Job Service, cheating on a job placement questionnaire."

"I'm not sure you could say 'cheating.' I was merely looking through the notebook before my questionnaire was entirely finished."

Beth put up her hand to silence him. Her fingers were short and stubby and covered with golden rings. "Did you think that because you're a college graduate, you deserve to get special treatment?"

"No."

"Good. Let me tell you something, Jamie Kurtz. I am also a college graduate. A lot of the people I help are college graduates. You're not special because you went to Bridgewater College. Rule Number Two to finding a job is that everyone's crap smells like crap—no one is special! An employer is going to pick you for who you are, not which college you attended, okay?"

"Okay," Jamie said with a shrug.

This seemed to annoy the woman. "Rule Number Three, Jamie Kurtz, is never shrug while in a job interview. It shows an apathetic and almost contemptuous reaction to a question."

Jamie rolled his eyes. "Okay, I won't shrug anymore."

The woman shook her head with disapproval. "I grew up in Brementon, in the very shadow of Bridgewater College. I wanted nothing more than to go to school there, so I worked hard in high school. Very hard. I was an excellent student. I got myself elected to the Student Council and I did all the extracurricular activities that the guidance counselor recommended to enhance my value as an applicant. So when I applied to Bridgewater, I was confident that I would get in. But I didn't. Even though my grades and SAT's were all above average and I was a well-rounded person, I guess I just wasn't good enough. Maybe I wasn't pretty enough or my parents weren't rich enough to make a whopping donation to the college. Whatever the reason, Bridgewater College rejected me. Guess how that made me feel, Jamie Kurtz."

He was too stunned by her diatribe to do anything more than shrug, which annoyed her even further. She inhaled sharply. "Like dirt, Jamie Kurtz, that's how it made me feel. Even worse than dirt—more like dog poopy! And although most people would have quit with their dreams right then and there, I didn't give up. I applied and got in at the University of Maine at Orono, and I went there to prove to Bridgewater College that I was better than they thought I was. I studied hard, put my heart and soul into all of my classes, and graduated with high honors. I could have had any job I wanted, but I chose to work here at the Job Service because I want to help people turn their lives around. And that's just what I do, Jamie Kurtz."

"Hmm…that's interesting, Beth."

"No, probably not. But do you know what I do find interesting? Even though you were deemed good enough to get into Bridgewater College, you're here now at the Job Services asking for *my* help in finding you a job. Isn't the world a funny place?"

Jamie was now thoroughly uncomfortable with the way the whole experience seemed to be tumbling out of control. He had thought that Beth was odd the moment she walked up to him, but now that she was apparently getting revenge on him for her rejection from Bridgewater College, he was becoming scared of her. He cleared his throat and, as he'd been taught in crisis management training during his sophomore year in college, he spoke very calmly and slowly. "Well now, Beth, I don't think that the college you attend makes you the person you are. Actually, I think it's essential to separate the two. After all, Bridgewater College and I are not synonymous in any way. While it's true that I graduated from that institution, I certainly didn't have anything to do with who was being accepted or refused admission to the school, now did I? Of course not. And it certainly seems that you've proven, without a doubt, that Bridgewater made a tremendous error in not accepting you. As for me, I only came here today to see the listings of available jobs. You see, Beth, I was evicted from my apartment this morning and I just quit my job at the Hungry Rancher, so I'm looking for some work that will help me get back on my feet."

Beth's expression instantly softened. "Did you just say that you worked at the Hungry Rancher?"

"Yes, I did."

"Oh my!"

Jamie waited for the barrage of insults that were sure to follow. If this woman found humor in a Bridgewater College alum looking for a job, he knew that she would be beside herself with one working at the Hungry Rancher. But Beth's face now reflected nothing by pity. She even spoke to him with a purr. "Do you know how many lambs I've sent to slaughter over at that place?"

Knowing the Hungry Rancher like he did, Jamie wasn't sure if the question was metaphorical or factual, so he shook his head. She continued, "That manager! That awful manager…what's his name?"

"Adrian Goodsell."

"Aw, that's right, Goodsell!" she hissed. "He has chased away or broken more good workers than I can shake a stick at! What did you do there?"

"I cleaned the fry-o-lator," Jamie admitted.

Beth gasped. "You were the fry-o-lator bitch?" She looked at him with complete seriousness as she said, "You poor, poor little lamb!"

"It doesn't matter; I just quit today. I want to start a new life."

"Good for you, Jamie! But I'm getting the vibe that you started working at the Hungry Rancher for a woman. Am I right?"

Jamie did a double-take. "Uh, yeah, you are."

"I'm like that. I can figure things out quickly from body language. I'm nearly psychic. I just knew that you were working at the Hungry Rancher for a woman's love. Did she work there?"

"Good God, no! Laura wouldn't even step foot inside the place! No, she was a student at Bridgewater. After she graduated, we parted ways."

"She dumped you?"

The woman was filleting his past with such precision and from such minimal clues, Jamie had the unshakeable feeling that he was being filmed for some kind of reality TV show, and he now looked around for the hidden cameras. Beth continued, "Oh my gosh, that's so sad! Here you were, working in that horrible meat dump for that bastard manager just to be close to the woman you loved, and she left you for some other guy! You must have been crushed. Of course you were crushed, Jamie Kurtz. After all, you're in here now, looking for a new job, aren't you? Oh, my poor, poor little lamb!"

It was now completely clear to Jamie that Beth was psychologically and emotionally unstable. He stood up abruptly and said, "Wow, would you look at the time? I've got to go! Hey, Beth, thanks for all your help."

"No, wait, Jamie, don't go. I need to help you find a job."

"But I haven't filled out my questionnaire yet," Jamie croaked.

"Let's dispense with the silly questionnaire. Just tell me what you're looking for in terms of a job."

The whole experience had been like some kind of disturbing psychological experiment. Jamie felt as if this woman Beth was trying to alternate shame, pity, anger, and compassion to break him. And although he wanted nothing more than to leave before she succeeded in doing so, the fact remained that he needed a job. He inhaled and said, "Well, Beth, I want to work outside. I've been cooped up inside for too long. And I want to work a job that will make my body tired at the end of the day. I need a job that is hard enough to beat some sense into me."

"Hmm," Beth muttered, biting her lower lip. She gazed down at the notebooks, but then shook her head. Jamie thought she was going to refuse to help him. She seemed to look past him, then she spoke haltingly. "You know, I do have something. It came in just the other day. I wonder…"

She walked away from Jamie and back to her office, where she picked up a paper from her desk and looked at it. Slowly, she came back toward him. "I've got this listing from an employer that I've helped before, but it's for a seasonal temp. But you know what? This just might be the perfect job for you, Jamie. It's going to be a hard job. I mean, a *really* hard job! But maybe that's just what you need right now. Maybe a really hard job will make you forget that little hussy and move on. That's what you need, right?"

Jamie was intrigued enough to ignore her jab at Laura. "What kind of job is it?"

"You'd be a sternman on a lobster boat out of Kestrel Cove."

Jamie liked to *eat* lobster, and what he knew about lobstering came from the placemats at the restaurants. There were traps and different-colored buoys, but beyond that, he knew nothing. He nodded thoughtfully. "Huh, that doesn't sound too hard."

"Well, it is, Jamie. Lobstering is a very physically demanding job. You bust your ass from sunup to sundown, lifting traps all day and being up to your elbows in stinky bait. Most of the people I send out to do this kind of work come back the next day and want to try something a little easier. Do you think you're up to something this challenging?"

Jamie's pride was affronted. "If I can last as the fry-o-lator bitch for six months, I think I'm tough enough to do this job!"

"Okay. Like I said, this captain's a regular. He usually lists a third man position through us every spring. He has his regular ace man, but he hires someone for the summer months to make the work go faster on the boat. He's the type of person who never goes easy on anything or anyone, especially his crew. He works them hard—sometimes too hard. He's chewed up and spit out a lot of the guys I've sent him—on the very first day! And now, with this…" She glanced down at the paper and absentmindedly scratched her chin. She paused with her mouth open, and her eyes darted around the room.

Frustrated with her elusiveness, Jamie asked, "With what, Beth?"

"Well, Joe Quinn—that's the captain's name—he injured himself last year in an accident. So there's an additional aspect to this job listing. He's hiring someone because he *has* to. His injury was severe enough that a lot of people said he wouldn't be able to go back to fishing at all. Now that he's going to try, he needs the extra man to haul through his gear."

"What kind of injury?"

"He crushed his hand while fishing last winter."

"Oh, God."

"Are you still interested, Jamie?

"Well…"

"It's outdoors, close by, and a helluva lot better than working at the Hungry Rancher."

The job sounded almost too hard. Sure, he wanted a challenge, but not to be chewed up and spit out by an injured captain who was also probably self-medicating! But there was something in it that seemed to fit, too. So Jamie nodded and said, "Okay, Beth, I'll take it. When do I start?"

"Oh, no, Jamie, it doesn't work like that. I'll give you Joe's phone number to call tonight. He'll probably ask you a few questions, and either he'll like what he hears and tell you to show up the next morning, or he'll pass. If the latter happens, which I really don't think it will, you should come back here and we'll work on getting you a different job."

Beth gave him Joe Quinn's phone number, and they exchanged another awkward handshake. Before she let him go, she said, "Just promise me one thing, Jamie—and this is serious."

"What?"

"You must wait to call Joe. Don't go out to the nearest phone and call now, because he won't be home. He's a fisherman, so he gets up before the sun and then works all day long. The *last* thing you want to do is call too early and talk with his wife. That would be a kiss of death for your getting this job with Joe! I cannot caution you enough—wait until after dinnertime to make the call."

As Jamie walked to his car, he looked back at the Job Service building. It seemed so innocuous from the outside, but what had transpired inside was anything but ordinary. He shook his head in disbelief. And, although he had to admit that it had been one of the most uncomfortable experiences of his life, he felt a glimmer of hope that he was now on the right track. And if he was, he'd owe everything to that crazy blonde woman.

The rest of the day seemed to pass at a snail's pace. Jamie didn't want to go into any of the stores at the Corners, so he took to driving around aimlessly to kill time until it was late enough to call Joe Quinn. When he saw a hand-painted sign for the Sinking Buoy Campground on the road to Kestrel Cove, he decided to follow the signs all the way to the campground to ask about availability and pricing. After the owner informed him that there were plenty of empty tent sites that were only $20 a night, Jamie drove the campground's horseshoe-shaped road to find the spot he wanted. All of the prime campsites near the water were already taken by parked RVs, but just past these, he found a vacant site that had enough trees around it to ensure privacy, even if neighbors showed up later. He memorized the number and drove back to the office to pay.

By the time Jamie finished setting up his tent, the sun was low in the sky, and he knew it was late enough to call the captain. He'd noticed the public phone right outside the bathroom building when he'd driven the campground road, and he set off now to make his call. When he got there, the phone was occupied by a teenage boy with bad skin and ripped jean shorts who was just finishing up an extended conversation. And even though he knew it was irrational to worry that this conversation would continue so long that it would be too late to call about the lobstering job, Jamie suddenly felt his armpits dampen with anxiety.

After the boy finally hung up and walked away, Jamie put the money in the slot, dialed the number, and waited. On the fourth ring, Joe Quinn answered. "Hullo?"

"Hello, my name is Jamie Kurtz, and Beth over at the Job Service gave me your name for a temporary job on your boat."

There was a momentary silence on the other end. "Yeah, she called earlier to tell me about you. Have you ever been lobstering before?"

"No."

"You ever work on a boat before?"

"No."

"You ever *been* on a boat before?"

"Yes."

"Hmm…okay, that's a start. Why don't you come down to the wharf at five a.m. tomorrow morning and we'll see how things go? Don't worry about gear; I've got extra skins and boots. Just bring your own food for the day, and be ready to work."

"How do I get to the wharf?"

"Where you coming from?"

"The Sinking Buoy Campground."

"You're camping?"

"Yes."

"Huh, that's a first. Well, take a left out of the campground and go straight till you come to a T intersection. Take another left. Go about three miles till you come to a white church. Take a right there. That road'll take you to the wharf. Don't be late."

"I won't. Thank you for this chance. I'm a hard worker."

"You better be."

Jamie started to respond, but the fisherman had already hung up. He'd sounded young, but his tone was so abrupt, it made Jamie exhale sharply. There wasn't any way to find out if he could handle this job without stepping right into it, and then it would be too late. What if he couldn't hack it? What if these fishermen laughed him right off the boat? Jamie tried to remember some Civil War quote that would inspire him, but the fear of failure completely blocked his attempts at recall.

He started walking toward his campsite. If Jamie had been less absorbed in his thoughts, he might have noticed that the car he was walking around to go to the tent was not his. But he was so distracted, he was nearly atop the two people having sex on the picnic table when he realized he'd walked into the wrong campsite.

He should have turned around the second his befuddled brain registered that the people in front of him were copulating, but he was too shocked to do that and he froze in place. The couple was having doggy-style sex. The woman had her shirt on, but her pants and underwear were on the picnic table that she was leaning on. The man's pants were down around his ankles, and the gas camp lantern on the table highlighted the whiteness of his thrusting ass. The woman was moaning and adding sensuous words of encouragement, and the man was grunting as he thrust like an animal. Jamie stared for a moment, then realized what was happening and gasped loudly.

The couple stopped, but neither person moved away or covered themselves up. Their heads turned toward Jamie, but the man remained inside the woman, and she continued to lean against the table. The man growled, "Can we help you with something, dickwad?"

Jamie was too stunned to speak or avert his eyes. He just stood there, staring.

"What the hell do you want?" the man asked with growing impatience.

"Maybe he wants to watch, Norm. Ooh, we haven't done that before!"

Jamie tried to say something, but he could not make his neurons work properly enough to speak. He stood there, sputtering and making odd sounds.

"What are you, some kind of retard?" the man grumbled.

"Oh, honey, do you just want to watch me and Norman have sex? Is that what you want? Come on, Norm, it'll be fun. We'll just put on a show for this young man. It's kinda exciting, isn't it?"

She reached down and stroked the man's thigh, and his glare at Jamie wavered. He began to slowly thrust again. Eventually, his pace and intensity built back up to what they had been.

For Jamie, the crazy events of this epic day suddenly crashed down on him like a wave and incapacitated him. His muscles didn't work, his thoughts didn't flow, and his mouth was useless. He stood there, helpless to escape. Finally, he came out of his stupor and was able to get enough control to start backing away.

"Oh, honey, don't go! Not yet! I'm so close!" the woman said in a strained voice. "Stay. Here, let me make the pot sweeter!"

With that, she stood more erect and quickly lifted her shirt and sports bra up and off. Her large breasts fell out and thumped onto the picnic table. Jamie recoiled, and he turned and ran.

"Oh, don't go, honey, I'm so close! Come on, Norm, make me come, make me come before he leaves!" the woman urged.

"Goddamn it, you little puke, stay here until she comes! Just one more second, goddamn it!" the man snarled in desperation.

But Jamie didn't stop. He kept running until he reached the safety of his own campsite. He quickly unzipped his tent and crawled into his sleeping bag. He closed the tent against a world that felt as if it had gone completely mad. In one day, he'd dealt with his father, Ezra Jackson, Adrian Goodsell, weird Beth at the Job Service, a horrible pimply-faced teenager, a bizarre couple having public sex, and a probably addicted fisherman he was now sure was hell-bent on breaking him. The world seemed out of control and totally against him. It was all too much, and although it pained him to do so, he curled up in a fetal position and began to cry quietly.

5

When his mini alarm clock beeped, Jamie fumbled to put on his clothes in the predawn darkness. As he drove around the campground, he could tell that all the other campers were sound asleep, and he let out a contented sigh in this moment of solitude. He didn't know if it was the calm before the storm or not, but he was determined not to waste the serenity nonetheless. He paused for just a moment before turning onto the main road and driving toward Kestrel Cove.

Joe's directions were good, and Jamie had no difficulty finding his way. When he got to the white church, he turned onto the wharf road. There was a white house across the road that sat low and menacingly like a sentry. Although the house itself didn't attract much attention, the numerous items on its lawn did. Boats of varying length and condition, engines, farm tools, cars, a tractor missing a wheel, and a rusted metal statue of Jesus were among the assortment of junk. Although it was clearly more than just a cluttered yard, there wasn't quite enough detritus to be considered a junkyard. Jamie mused that it was more like a postindustrial midden pile, and he was captivated by it as he drove past.

As the road wound its way down toward the water, it went past several battered mobile homes, two or three tiny cottages, and the open expanse of a wide treeless lane. Just beyond this there was a huge Quonset hut with three garage doors that was surrounded by an odd assortment of cars in various stages of disrepair. A big sign on the side of the building read *Jerry Shute Garage*. Jamie drove down a steep hill and pulled into the gravel parking lot next to the ancient wooden wharf. Directly across the road was a renovated grand old home with a widow's walk and a hand-carved sign identifying the house as the Ocean's Swell Bed & Breakfast.

Jamie parked and got out of his car to take a look around. The wharf consisted of a series of weathered piers that ran parallel to the shoreline. There was a ramshackle wooden building with a hand-painted OFFICE sign on its door. Another building, which looked like a small battered barn, sat perpendicular to the office, and the small alleyway that ran between the two buildings gave access to the docks. Out beyond all of this, Jamie could see the small cove where a dozen lobster boats were tethered to their white mooring balls. Behind him, there were so many lobster traps, outboard motors, fish traps, and steel fishing drags stacked around the perimeter of the parking lot, the whole space felt enclosed.

The morning's purple, blue, and orange sky was the color of a fresh bruise, and Jamie felt some uneasiness as he watched the colors mingle and change. Suddenly, a man came running from inside the wharf complex. In the predawn light, it was impossible to see clearly, but he appeared to have long hair that fluttered behind him as he ran, and, for a moment, he looked like the crazed Hidetora in Kurosawa's movie *Ran*. But as soon as the old man spied Jamie there, leaning against the back of his car, he stopped short and stood in place as if in a game of freeze tag. After an awkward moment of silence, the old man put his finger over his pursed lips and shushed him before sprinting up the hill and into the woods.

Jamie was still staring after the strange old man when a pickup truck came barreling down the hill and into the lot. It parked well away from Jamie's car, the doors flew open, and two men got out and walked silently toward Jamie. One man was short, but he walked as if he were a much bigger man. His right arm dangled awkwardly at his side. The other man was well over six feet tall and had very broad shoulders, and he lumbered along like a bear.

"You Jamie?" the smaller man asked with a voice so devoid of emotion that Jamie felt that he would not have cared whether the answer was yes or no.

"Yes, I'm Jamie Kurtz. You must be Joe."

The man nodded. Jamie put his right hand out to shake hands, but Joe stared at the outstretched hand with disdain. The taller man rolled his eyes, and Jamie immediately understood his blunder. But he continued to stand there with his hand extended, unable to retract it gracefully, and he felt his face flush with shame and anger at himself.

"That hand don't work so good no more. This is my ace man, Jimmy. Get your food, and let's get going. We've got a long, long day ahead of us."

Jamie nodded toward Jimmy, who reached out and shook Jamie's still extended hand with a very strong grip. Even though he continued to smile, he hissed quietly at Jamie, "Smooth move, Ex-Lax! What're you gonna do for your next trick, call him short?"

"Uh, I…I'm not…I dunno."

Jimmy leaned down closer. "Before we get going, I've got one question for ya."

"What?"

"You're not a retard, are ya?"

"What?"

"I always like to ask the fresh meat from the Job Service if they're retarded. It makes me feel better about getting on the boat with them, I guess. One time, a guy answered that he *was* a retard, and it was clear that he actually was. So me and Joe treated him like a retard, and he nearly made it to lunch. So tell me, you're not retarded, are ya?"

"No."

"Slow? Socially inept?"

Jamie looked at Joe for help, but he was staring out at the water. "No, I'm not slow nor inept. Actually, I'm a college graduate."

As soon as the words left his lips, Jamie knew he'd made another mistake.

"Ah, ya hear that, Joe? We got a college boy here. A real genu-ine college boy. So, if that's true, then your answer most definitely should have been, 'Yep, Mr. Jimmy, I sho' am a retard!'"

"Jimmy, let him be!" Joe barked impatiently. "At least let him get on the boat before you make too much fun of him. We need him to get some traps hauled today, which we sure as shit ain't gonna do flapping our gums out here in the parking lot. You ladies ready to do some work today?"

Jimmy looked away sheepishly from the scolding and then nodded. The two men silently turned and started walking toward the wharf, leaving Jamie behind. He'd obviously made a horrible first impression, and things would only get worse once he was trapped on the boat with them. He was half tempted to hop back into his car and quit. If he just did that and drove away, he imagined that the two men would keep on walking without acknowledging that anything had just happened.

"Don't quit yet, college boy. There's money to be made today! Just get your food and come on," Joe said without looking back.

Jamie grabbed his snacks out the car and ran to catch up with the two men, who were already halfway down the wooden alleyway.

"Watch where you step. There could be piles of shit on the wharf. Don't step in 'em," Joe said.

"So, Ed's still at it, huh?" Jimmy asked.

"Crazy bastard can't stop now even if he wanted to."

The wooden beams of the wharf shifted and murmured under their weight as they walked between the buildings. They continued past two covered gray plastic bins that reeked of fish, some battered old gas pumps, and onto a metal ramp that ran down to a floating dock. A small fleet of dinghies and skiffs were tied up there, and they shifted with the waves like a school of fish.

The brooding waters broiled as if something was alive just beneath the surface, and Jamie looked farther out to the lobster boats on the moorings in the cove. The vessels were a collection of newer boats and older tubs that seemed barely seaworthy. Jamie suddenly realized that he'd never thought to ask what Joe's boat looked like. And although he hoped that it was one of the newer ones, knowing his luck, it'd be one of those barely floating death traps.

`"Do you know how to operate an outboard?" Joe asked, breaking into Jamie's dark thoughts.

"I guess," Jamie replied.

"What the hell does that mean, college boy? Yes or no?" Jimmy chirped.

"It means that I could do so if asked to, I guess."

The two men stared at Jamie as if he'd spoken in an ancient language. Joe shrugged. "What I'm trying to ask you is, have you ever used an outboard motor before?"

"Uh, no."

"Jesus, you're as useless as tits on a boar, aren't ya, college boy?" Jimmy stated evenly.

Joe shook his head at Jimmy. He then pushed the skiffs around with his foot while he pulled on the bowline of a black skiff with a small battered outboard motor. The boat's sides were chipped and scratched, and several empty beer cans were awash in the standing water on the bottom.

"Here, hold this bowline," Joe said to Jamie as he hopped in.

Jimmy jumped into the stern, next to the engine. He put his cooler lunchbox on one of the seats and began working on the engine. The boat, with just the two men aboard, was already low in the water, and Jamie wondered if it would still float with the three of them in it. Jimmy pulled the draw cord, but the motor did not start. He pulled it again with no response. He squeezed the rubber ball on the fuel line and muttered, "Come on, you fucking cunt!"

On the next pull, the motor burped and then started. An oil-rich blue cloud of exhaust spewed out the back, skimmed across the surface of the water, and floated downwind like a ghost. Jamie watched it as it went out to sea. Jimmy said roughly, "Well, what do ya think we're gonna do, college boy, waterski your ass to the boat? Hop the fuck in and let's get going!"

Jamie jumped into the bow. He landed awkwardly, stumbled, and rocked the small boat. Water sloshed around inside and the gunwales smacked against the other small boats. Jimmy throttled away from the floating dock, but over the loudness of the motor he asked again, "Are you sure you're not retarded, college boy?"

Joe tapped his ace man's knee and motioned with his head. Jimmy nodded and headed the skiff toward an ancient white lobster boat at a nearby mooring. The boat was in such bad shape, the only discernible reason for it to be floating was because it was made of wood. The paint was peeling in giant strips that looked like birch bark, revealing the gray primer below. The boat was listing hard to the starboard side, and Jamie gulped audibly. If this was Joe's boat, he was no longer worried about not being able to last through the day—he might just die when the boat sank!

The lobster boat was listing so badly, Jimmy had to steer the skiff to the lower side to get Joe aboard. Jamie tried to catch hold of the gunwale, but pulled off a handful of paint chips instead. On his second grab, he succeeded, but got a painful splinter in his left hand. Joe effortlessly hopped aboard and disappeared into the wheelhouse.

Even though he knew that he should keep quiet, Jamie couldn't stop himself from asking a question. "So how old is this boat?"

"How the hell should I know?" Jimmy replied with obvious annoyance.

"Is she a good boat?"

"Doesn't look like it, does it, brainiac?"

Jamie shut his mouth as the sour taste of bile began to work up his throat.

Just then, a stream of water shot out of a hole in the hull just in front of the skiff, and Joe appeared back at the gunwale. He motioned for Jimmy to shut off the motor. When he did, it got quiet enough for Joe to report, "Geez, the pump's wires are disconnected again. There's a shit-ton of water down there in the bilge. We're gonna be here awhile while it drains out."

Joe looked down at Jamie and noticed the ashen color of his face. "Jesus Christ, kid, what's the matter with you? You're as white as a fucking clean sheet! You're not seasick already, are ya?"

"No, I'm fine. It's nothing."

"Naw, you look like shit," Joe continued.

"Yeah, you do," Jimmy chimed in, "and you keep asking the stupidest questions about this boat!"

"Well, how long before we can board her?" Jamie asked with a gravelly voice.

"Board her? What are you, team leader on a commando mission or something? And why in God's creation would we be going on board this piece of barely floating shit anyway?" Jimmy sneered.

Jamie looked over at Joe, but the man's facial expression hadn't changed. He shrugged his shoulders. "But you hired me to—"

Jimmy started cackling, and his laughter was sharp and mean. When he finally regained his ability to speak he sputtered, "Oh, I get it! Joe, you're gonna fucking love this! The kid thinks that *this* is your boat!"

Joe looked at Jamie with an inquisitive face. Then his expression softened as the laughter began to seep out. Whereas Jimmy's reaction was one of ridicule, Joe's was of pure humor. He laughed a little longer, and then his face tried to resume its steely expression. The corners of his mouth remained upturned in an impish grin as he explained to Jamie, "Naw, kid, this isn't my boat! It's Sanford Hughes's boat. He's an old fisherman who's just done with it all. At this stage, he doesn't really care what happens to her. So he keeps doing crazy things like disconnecting the bilge pump in hopes that the old tub will fill up with water and flip over and sink. We pump her out whenever we can. I know that I'm—what's that fancy term I'm always hearing on Oprah?"

"Enabling," Jimmy said, nodding.

"Yeah, I'm enabling him by saving his damn boat and I *should* let her settle to the bottom, but I want Sanford to leave with some dignity, so we bail her out whenever we can. My boat is that one over there. The *Bobbie C.*"

Jamie followed Joe's pointed finger and saw a black lobster boat a couple of moorings over. It looked like a well-kept workboat that was in much better condition.

"Goddamn, you shoulda seen your face, kid! You were scared shit-less!" Jimmy hooted again. "But you've got a right to be scared of this boat; it's an accident waiting to happen. I've told Joe a thousand times that he's only being an accessory to its ultimate sinking."

"I'm just trying to help an old man who's helped me out more times than I can count, Jimmy. That's the way we do it—help someone out and then *get* help someday. Fishermen have to look out for one another 'cause no one else is going to, right?"

Jimmy nodded. "Sure, but it seems like you're just delaying the inevitable, Joe. This boat's gonna be underwater any day!"

"Hey, we all know that it's going to pop the one flake of paint that's holding the whole shitty thing together, and she's gonna sink right down to the bottom, leaving a slick that won't be just from the fuel."

Jimmy chuckled. "Yeah, right, it's in such bad shape that even the seagulls won't land on it anymore!"

The two men enjoyed a short laugh together, but when they looked back over at Jamie, he wasn't laughing. Joe clucked his tongue at him. "I can't believe you thought this was my boat!"

"If you knew my luck, you'd understand. I've got some bad Karma," Jamie said softly.

"What did you just say?" Jimmy asked.

"Oh, nothing. You wouldn't understand."

Jimmy pointed his finger at Jamie. "You think 'cause I'm just a big ol' dummy I don't understand the philosophies of them rice-eating, slanty-eyed Chinks and Japs, huh? Well, I sure as shit understand Karma! That whole spiritual checkbook of deposits and withdrawals makes good sense to me. But if it were your fate to show up for a temp job as a master baiter on this piece of shit boat because of some bad Karma, you would've had to fuck up wildly in a previous life, wouldn't you?"

There was a momentary silence as both Joe and Jamie digested what Jimmy had just said.

"Discovery Channel?" Joe deadpanned.

"Yep, I was watching this cool show about karate the other day, and then it got all goddamn serious and boring about this shit called Buddhism. The only thing I can remember about any of it was how, with Karma, if you screw up once, you'll be paying for the rest of eternity!"

"You'd better hope that isn't the way things happen, huh, Jimmy? With the amount of screwups you've had in your life, you'll be paying in spades!" Joe said with a straight face.

"Hullo, Pot! This is Kettle—you're *black*!" Jimmy bellowed, and both men laughed loudly.

When the stream of water had slowed to a mere trickle and the boat wasn't listing as badly as it had been, Joe disappeared down forward again. He came back up and hopped into the skiff. "Well, we did our good deed for today, huh? Now, let's go catch some lobsters."

Jimmy started the outboard and they motored over to the *Bobbie C.* Once alongside, Joe jumped aboard, clipped the bowline's carabiner to a ring on the gunwale, and went into the wheelhouse. Like before, Jamie waited for some instructions, but Jimmy just stared hard at him, then finally barked, "So, are you gonna just sit in the skiff all goddamn day and daydream about catching lobsters, or are you gonna go aboard and actually do it?"

Jamie shook himself. "What?"

"This is our boat, retard! We don't go around the harbor pumping out *all* the boats—just Sanford's." Jimmy slowed his speech in a patronizing way. "This is the boat you are going to be working on today."

Jamie lifted his left leg over the gunwale, but as he pushed up from the skiff with his right leg, the small boat drifted away from the lobster boat, and he almost lost his balance and fell into the water.

"Okay, Grace, now that you're on the boat, grab these lunches as I hand them to you. And be careful. I swear you'll be swimming after mine if you drop it in the drink!"

Jimmy handed up two lunch coolers and Jamie's bag of food, and Jamie put them safely on the deck. While Jimmy came aboard, Jamie looked around. There wasn't much to see. The deck was a small space that had dark tiles on it, and the open stern of the boat led directly to the water. Behind him, against the wheelhouse, there was a silver lobster tank and the bait box. Suddenly a buzzer went off from down below, and then the engine rumbled to life.

"What do you think you're doing now, college boy?" Jimmy said.

Jamie shrugged. "Standing?"

"You're good at that!"

"I'm just trying to stay out of the way, Jimmy!"

"Now that's the first good idea you've had all day!" Jimmy sneered.

Joe came out of the wheelhouse holding a pair of orange overalls and some black rubber boots, "These were left by another sternman. They should fit you or be close enough for the day."

Jamie put on the boots, which were a couple of sizes too big. As soon as he tried to put his boots through the pant legs of the overalls, he realized that he should have put them on first. The damp rubber of the boots stuck to the vinyl overalls, and he teetered as he struggled to push them through. When he finally succeeded, he looked up and saw that Jimmy had been watching him the entire time. "I'm telling ya, that was like watching a chimpanzee try to build a computer."

As Jamie now fumbled to tighten the straps on the overalls, Jimmy came over to him. He'd quickly gotten dressed in his oilskins and boots and had a cigarette hanging out of his mouth. "Okay, kid, Joe says that you've never been on a lobster boat before?"

"Right."

"Do you know how we catch lobsters?"

"Yeah, in lobster traps."

"Yep, that's true."

Jamie was unsure of Jimmy's intentions. He'd been insulting and ridiculing him up to this point, but now his tone was much kinder and informative. "Okay, this'll all become clearer when we get out there and get started. Joe has eight hundred and eighty traps in all, but we'll haul only half of them today. The way it works is pretty simple. When we come up to one of our buoys, I'll gaff it and then run the line through the hauler to reel it in. Once I break the traps onto the side of the boat, Joe and me will take the lobsters and crabs out while you take out the old bait bag and put a new one in. Then I'll stack the rebaited traps on the back of the boat until we put them back in the water. Your job is to band all the keepers and keep the bait bags full. That's pretty much our day—buoy, haul, lobsters, bait, reset. Got it?"

"Yeah, I think so."

"Are you ladies done talking? Do you want to continue your knitting circle, or do you want to head out and catch some lobsters to make some money?" Joe called.

"Aye, aye, captain," Jimmy retorted. He undid the carabiner and walked up to the front of the boat with the skiff in tow. At the bow, he attached the skiff's bowline to the mooring pendant and Joe backed the lobster boat off the mooring. Jamie expected them to head right out of the cove to start fishing, but the lobster boat headed back toward the wharf.

"You look confused again, college boy," Jimmy chuckled.

"I'm just taking it all in. Why are we headed back to the pier?"

"Wharf. We call it a wharf, not a pier. And we need to load up with enough bait and diesel fuel for the day."

When they got up to the pilings of the wharf, Joe cranked the wheel hard, put the diesel engine into reverse, and the boat swung into place. Jimmy motioned Jamie to follow him. The tide was high enough that they were able to get out of the boat right onto the wharf, and the two men stood looking back at Joe in the boat.

"Jimmy, I left five fish totes yesterday by the fire extinguisher. Grab 'em. I want three herring and two redfish today."

"You got it, boss."

Jimmy led Jamie back to an old-fashioned rolling fire extinguisher. It had once been silver and red, but now the whole rig was brown with rust. Next to it was a stack of five empty rectangular plastic fish totes.

"There they are. Bring 'em back over to those big bins over there. I'll get the pitchforks so we can start pitching bait."

While Jamie struggled to drag the five totes, Jimmy reappeared with two pitchforks and took off the lids of the bins. An overwhelming odor of decaying fish filled the area immediately, and it was strong enough to make Jamie gag. The left bin was filled with salted herring, and many of the fish had rotted to the point where their stomachs had exploded. In the other bin the severed heads of redfish sat in a similar briny and bloody soup.

"All right, you heard the captain. You fill them two totes with redfish heads while I fill these other three with herring."

The pitchfork's wooden handle felt gritty with salt and blood, and Jamie noticed that, although Jimmy was wearing rubber gloves, he hadn't been offered any yet.

"Well, let's go! This bait ain't gonna jump in by itself, college boy. Break down that stack of totes and spread them out so we can fill them."

Jamie tried to pull apart the stack of totes, but they were held firmly together by the vacuum created by the wet plastic. Jimmy let him struggle for a moment or two then pushed him out of the way. "I'd love to watch you waltz with these goddamn totes all day, but I know I've got to make enough money to pay some of my fucking bills today!"

With one mighty thrust, Jimmy pulled the first tote away from the stack. Once the seal was broken, the others came apart rather easily. Immediately, Jimmy went straight to spearing herring with his pitchfork. He worked so fast, he was finished with his three totes before Jamie could get one of his filled. The tines of the pitchfork kept catching on the eye sockets of the redfish heads, and Jamie kept having to stop to scrape them off on the side of the tote. He tried to work fast, but Jimmy sighed impatiently as he waited for him to finish.

"Now we gotta drag them back over to the boat with these tote hooks." Jimmy handed Jamie a ferocious-looking metal hook, and they dragged the totes over to the edge of the wharf. Then Jimmy and Jamie hopped back down onto the gunwale to swing them down onto the boat's deck. Each tote weighed well over a hundred pounds, and Jamie struggled to hold up his end. Once they had the totes secured against the port gunwale, Jimmy showed Jamie how to put three big herring and one redfish head into the bait bags. And after he put the deck hose into the lobster tank to fill with saltwater, Jimmy snarled, "Joe and I can empty traps in our fucking sleep, college boy, so you're gonna hold us up. You need to keep up with the bait. Try not to screw us up too much today!"

Jamie began to fill the bait bags. He still didn't have any rubber gloves, and his hands were gross and slimy. Grabbing the herring was like grabbing yogurt, and the fish squished and spread between his fingers. The oily feel of his hands and the smell that alternated between fecal matter and salty copper coated his nose until he felt nauseated. The redfish heads were the opposite. They were rough and full of spines, and he already had several small bloody wounds on his hands from handling them. But by the time Jimmy and Joe had the fuel tank topped off, Jamie had most of the bait bags filled. Joe looked back at Jamie and said, "Okay, college boy, this is your last chance to jump ship. So what're ya gonna do?"

Jamie looked up at Jimmy and Joe and said confidently, "Let's get going. We won't catch any lobsters standing around here and flapping our gums, huh?"

◇◇◇◇

As they motored away from the wharf Joe arched his eyebrow just a fraction as Jimmy came back into the wheelhouse, and, in that subtlest of gestures, the two men exchanged a wordless dialogue about the kid's response. There had been the usual awkwardness at the beginning with this newbie, but they had the first inkling of hope that this one would survive the entire day.

The diesel engine rumbled loudly as the *Bobbie C.* steamed toward the first string of traps. The exhaust pipe came up right behind where Jamie stood, and the heat coming off the metal tube forced him to edge away toward the cooler air. But the intense warmth seemed to follow him and saturate his clothes and skin. All of the available bait bags were full now, so Jamie relaxed as the landscape streamed by. None of the landmarks were familiar, and he had no idea where they were, so the endless rocky shoreline was hypnotizing in its anonymity.

Joe throttled the boat down and said in a booming voice, "And here we go!"

Jimmy used a long wooden-handled gaff to grab a lobster buoy that was painted like a bumble bee. He pulled it toward him and heaved the attached line over the block that hung from a metal davit on the side of the wheelhouse. Joe took the loose end and wrapped it quickly between the two steel plates of the hydraulic hauler, and, with his elbow, he pushed a bronze lever that was on the dashboard of the lobster boat. The hauler turned with a drone until it took a bite of the line, and then the weight of the traps made it grumble with a throaty snarl. It wasn't long before the first trap came up out of the water and dangled from the block. Jimmy expertly wrestled the trap onto the gunwale, slid it back a little bit, and undid the bungee straps holding the trap's lid down. He and Joe quickly rifled through the trap, throwing all the small lobsters and crabs back into the water and tossing the keeper-sized lobsters onto the bait table. Then Jimmy yelled, "Okay, college boy, empty the old bait bag and put a new one in!"

Jamie was unsure how to do this, so he came up behind them hesitantly. Jimmy grabbed the old bag out of the trap and thumped it against the side of the boat. Rotten pieces of old bait and loose fish bones fell out of the bag and into the water, and several circling gulls dove down to get at the morsels. Jimmy impatiently snatched the full bait bag out of Jamie's right hand. He picked up the skewer-like bait iron from the side of the table, put the full bag onto the bait iron, threaded the string in the trap through the eyelet of the iron, and flicked the bag into the trap. It was all done in seconds.

Throwing the empty bag at Jamie, he snarled, "Got it? You gotta be faster than *that*, college boy! We've got 440 traps to do today! If we spend this much time on each goddamn trap, it'll take us five fucking days to haul through!"

When the next trap of the string came up, Jamie didn't have to be told what to do. As soon as the hauler stopped and it was on the gunwale and opened, he came around Jimmy, took the old bag out of the trap, beat it against the boat, and put a new bag in with the bait iron. Jimmy shut the trap and brought it back next to the other one on the deck at the stern of the boat. By the time Jimmy walked back up to Joe, the hauler was stopped and there was another trap at the block. The lobsters from the first two traps were starting to flop around on the bait table, so Jamie quickly measured them with the gauge and banded the claws before darting in again to bait the next trap.

Jamie began to get the rhythm of the process. He saw that his job was not so difficult, just crammed into a short time period and a small space. Like an officer in Jeb Stuart's cavalry unit during the 1863 Confederate invasion of the North—who had to scout, skirmish, and retreat in the same moment—his job involved juggling three different responsibilities simultaneously. Jamie understood that there had to be a certain timing to his movements: he had to be ready to bait the trap, band the keepers and get them into the tank, and bait the empty bags so he would be ready for the next trap. And it was also clear to him that Joe and Jimmy were not going to help him in any way. In fact, they seemed to be going faster to make it harder on him. He figured if he could stay calm and do what he needed to do, he'd be just fine.

Once the ten traps in this first trawl had been hauled, emptied, and re-baited, it was time for Joe and Jimmy to work together to set the traps back out. Joe positioned the boat where he wanted and Jimmy began to let the traps slide off the deck into the water. Jamie saw this momentary respite from hauling as a chance to drop the keepers into the tank and refill bait bags. Although he was interested in seeing what Joe and Jimmy were doing, he only watched out of the corner of his eye as he worked. He knew that if he missed this opportunity to stay ahead, he'd get overwhelmed, and Joe and Jimmy would never let him catch up.

Professor Whetstone had always said that what made Jamie an excellent student of history was that he simultaneously saw the big picture, the little picture, and all the pictures in between. As a freshman in one of the professor's upper-level Civil War courses, Jamie's essays and class discussions clearly demonstrated that he fully grasped the importance of Chamberlain's actions at the Battle of Gettysburg, as well as the impact of Stonewall Jackson's death on Robert E. Lee and the Southern army. It had taken less than a semester for the venerable college professor to become most impressed with Jamie. Now his ability to see the complete picture might allow him to thrive on the deck of this lobster boat.

◇◇◇◇

For Joe and Jimmy, the first string had been grossly disappointing because they usually had the new guy bawling by the end of it. Once they had him crying, they'd go even faster until the guy demanded to quit. Joe liked to say that the wheat and chaff were best separated by a hard beginning. Yet this scrawny bookworm had not only managed to get all the lobsters banded and into the tank by the time they were approaching the next string, he had also baited all the empty bags. He hadn't even taken a break in between strings like most of the newbies did, and was all caught up before they were ready to grab the second string's buoy. And while they were disappointed to be missing the fun of making the college boy cry, they were, at the same time, mildly impressed. However, it was going to be a long day, and they were both confident that they would ultimately break him.

◇◇◇◇

The second string went smoother than the first. There were plenty of lobsters in the traps, which made Joe almost smile, and Jamie kept up on all his duties. But he noticed that Jimmy and Joe were setting the trawl back into the water and searching for the next buoy much quicker. Instead of becoming frustrated by this, Jamie was determined not to fall behind. As he worked, he had to wonder why he was so good at menial jobs. After all, even that asshole Goodsell had praised him for being the best fry-o-lator bitch the Hungry Rancher had ever had. Why was it that he could do these kinds of things so well, but failed at more meaningful aspects of life? Like relationships. If he'd been as brilliant seeing everything in his relationship with Laura, he'd have known that she was going to leave him. If he had been so great at managing to stay ahead of the pace of life, he should have seen his father's ultimate cut-off. But he'd let everything blindside him. The truth was, when it came to life, Jamie was noticeably challenged.

◊◊◊◊

By the end of the fourth trawl, Jimmy and Joe were completely bored. The new kid kept staying ahead of them and thwarted their every attempt to have some fun tormenting him. If they couldn't rattle Jamie's chains by working too fast and giving him the silent treatment, they'd have to try other things. Having worked together for so long, the two men had a lot of tricks in their torture bag. A lot of tricks.

Joe turned on the boat radio to a country-western station. Since a speaker hung right over Jamie's head at the bait station, he could hear the twang of the steel guitars in the pit of his stomach. At first the volume was manageable—loud enough to be heard throughout the boat, but drowned out by the sound of the hauler. But with each string, Joe subtly turned up the volume of the radio. Jamie was working so hard to keep up, he seemed oblivious to the rising volume. But, by the end of the trawl, the music was loud enough that it could be heard back at the wharf. When the college boy seemed not to be fazed by the ridiculously loud country music blaring directly over his head, Jimmy and Joe grimaced at one another. They hated having the radio so loud, but it usually worked to rattle the new guy. Yet this kid seemed happy as a goddamn clam to be working furiously while the music boomed right over his head. Jimmy nodded at Joe, and he turned the tuning knob on the radio just a hair. The blaring music disappeared, and screeching static filled the air in its place. Joe and Jimmy continued working as if nothing had happened.

They hauled through another two strings with the radio static blasting. But, although Jamie was somewhat curious as to why two grown men would spend forty minutes listening to loud radio static, it was far from getting under his skin. After the last trap from this trawl went back into the water, Joe idled the boat and turned off the radio. Jimmy looked at Jamie and said harshly, "Break time!"

"What?" Jamie asked warily.

Joe came out onto the deck and headed toward the stern. He turned to Jamie and said, "We've been working straight out for a couple of hours, and we need to take coffee and piss breaks every so often. Got to keep OSHA happy, right?"

He continued to the very back of the boat, lowered his orange bib overalls, and peed off the stern.

Jimmy cut in, "Did you bring some kind of snack or drink, college boy?"

"Yeah."

"Well, dig in. You ain't gonna get another break until lunch."

Jamie waited until Joe came back to the wheelhouse, then he headed over to the port gunwale to wash his hands in the ocean water. It was cold, and it stung the small cuts on his hands. He pulled an apple from his paper bag and bit into it. Joe had poured a cup of coffee from his thermos and Jimmy was drinking from a Mountain Dew and eating a Twinkie.

"So, you from Maine?" Joe asked.

"Cleveland, actually."

"You know, I drove through Cleveland once," Jimmy said, "and it didn't seem all that nice. A fucking dirty and old rat trap."

"The city certainly has had a hard past," Jamie said with a smile.

"You know, it was so dirty there that a river actually caught fire," Jimmy chuckled.

Jamie nodded. "Yep, the Cuyahoga River in the seventies. Some people mark that event as the real beginning of the greening movement in America."

"Oh yeah, I remember that!" Joe declared. "That was kind of embarrassing for Cleveland, huh?"

"It was an embarrassment for the entire country. Most lakes, ponds, and rivers were nothing but industrial cesspools back then. That fire forced everyone to see how dirty the world was and that we all needed to help clean things up. Nowadays, the river's clean and there's ritzy condos along the shore."

"So you're a tree-hugger, huh?" said Jimmy.

"What brought you to Maine?" Joe interrupted.

"School."

"Oh yeah, I forgot you're a college boy."

"Where'd you go?"

"Bridgewater College."

Jimmy smiled sardonically. "Bridgewater College? Holy shit, that place ain't cheap! Does it ever bother you to think that you paid a hundred thou on your education, and Joe and me spent absolutely nothing on ours, and yet here you are, working for us?"

"Working for me," Joe added firmly.

"Yeah, yeah." Jimmy flicked his hand at Joe, but then turned back to Jamie. "So does it bother you at all that you wasted all that money?"

"I don't think you can put a price on education."

"But a hundred grand?" Jimmy shrieked. "For the same amount, you could own a decent house, a good lobster boat, a whole farm, a chunk of land somewhere, or even a fucking Ferrari. And what are you doing with your high-priced education now? Baiting traps! Doesn't seem like a good return on your money."

"Maybe it wasn't his money," Joe said, arching his eyebrows.

"Sure, but at this rate, he'll never pay back those loans!" Jimmy said.

"Maybe he doesn't have loans," Joe deadpanned.

"What do ya mean, Joe? If it wasn't his money and he doesn't have any loans, what else could it be? Were you on a scholarship?" Jimmy asked with a tilt of his head.

"Bridgewater doesn't give out too many scholarships, Jimmy," Joe declared.

"Well, where else could the money come from? It just doesn't fall from the sky, right?"

"Maybe his daddy paid all his bills."

"Whoa, whoa, whoa! Is that true, college boy? Did your daddy pay for all your college tuition?"

Jamie answered reluctantly, "Uh, yes, he did."

"Well, no wonder you're fine with working on a boat after plunking all that money down—it weren't your goddamn money!" Jimmy said with a vicious laugh.

"My father and mother wanted me to get a good education," Jamie said defensively.

"Still," Joe said with a nod, "after your daddy invested that much money to send you to Bridgewater, he can't be totally fine with you baiting traps on a Maine lobster boat, can he? Didn't he think you'd be joining him in his practice or something?"

"He's a banker, not a lawyer."

"See that?" Jimmy sneered. "See why I don't trust banks, Joe? There's his old man sitting on millions and millions of other people's money and his little boy goes to good ol' Bridgewater College! Makes you wonder where the money came from, huh? Maybe Daddy took it from the coffers!"

"Unless," Joe calmly stayed on his course of interrogation, "your father doesn't know exactly what you're doing right now. Does he know that you're baiting traps on a lobster boat today?"

"Or maybe you think he loaned you the money," Jimmy said, "and you're gonna save up your fucking nickels and dimes and pay the old man back before he croaks, huh?"

For the first time, Joe and Jimmy had Jamie on the ropes. Faced with their simultaneous lines of questions, he couldn't mount a good defense, and they were hitting nerve after nerve. And they were clearly loving it. Like sharks in a feeding frenzy, they had gotten a taste of blood and were circling in for the kill. Jamie knew they'd been impressed by his work ethic and his ability to keep up with their pace and mental abuse, but now they were finally getting a chance to enjoy putting the irons to him.

Jamie felt like a boxer trapped in the corner. Joe and Jimmy were mercilessly pounding on him with their rapid-fire questions, and some were landing and hurting him. In just a matter of minutes, they'd managed to find his weaknesses, and they seemed content to keep hitting him. He knew that the only way for a boxer to get out of a corner was to fight his way out. So he lifted his chin, looked right at them, and said,

"Actually, my father does think I'm a failure. When I graduated from Bridgewater, which he did pay for out of his own pocket, I got one of the top American history internships in New York City. It would have taken me far in the history world, but I couldn't leave my girlfriend. So I gave it up to come back here to Maine to be near her, and I got a job at the Hungry Rancher to pay my bills. None of this endeared me to my father, for obvious reasons. But when she dumped me for another guy and I stayed around, my dad finally had enough of me. He cut me off and had me evicted from my apartment yesterday. Then I quit my job at the Hungry Rancher and went looking for a new job at the Job Service, and that's how I came to be working with you two."

Joe and Jimmy exchanged glances, but remained silent. Jamie's answer was the perfect way to get himself out of the corner. By exposing all his skeletons voluntarily, he'd derailed their efforts to batter him into revealing them, and they were confused and confounded by his startling honesty.

Finally, Jimmy recovered and chuckled meanly, "Sounds like a lot of rich-boy *wah-wah* to me!"

Ignoring Jimmy, Joe said, "What was her name?"

Jamie thought about lying, but he answered softly, "Laura."

"Did she have a hairy twat?" Jimmy asked with a lewd grin.

"What?"

"Ignore him; he's got this thing about hairy bushes," Joe said, waving his left hand dismissively.

"I found this website the other night, Joe. Fucking A! It was full of these women who didn't shave nothing. Not their legs, not their pits, not their bushes! The videos were like watching gorillas mate! Grossest fucking thing I've ever seen in my life!"

Joe stared at Jimmy for a few seconds longer than was necessary, and they all seemed to be waiting for his rebuke. Joe's face didn't change expression, so it was impossible to tell whether he was annoyed, perplexed, or amused at the moment. Finally, he opened his mouth, exhaled, and said slowly, "Let's haul some more traps. At lunch, I wanna hear more about this Laura, college boy."

Jimmy looked relieved that Joe had not reamed him out, and he said to Jamie, "So, we've hauled about fifty traps. That means that we're an eighth of the way through the day. You've only got three hundred and ninety more traps to bait today, college boy! Isn't that exciting?"

Joe didn't wait for Jamie or Jimmy to get to their stations before he hit the throttle. Jamie struggled to walk on the pitching deck, but he made his way back and kept baiting empty bags. They hauled through several more strings without incident. The sound of the line in the hauler, the traps coming up, the scurrying of the three men as they emptied and loaded the traps, the mountains of lobsters needing banding, and the continual stink of the bait all began to take on a normal feel to Jamie. And, although neither exciting nor exotic, the work appealed to him, and he actually found himself enjoying it.

When one of the traps came up with a small cusk in it, Jimmy and Joe smiled cruelly at one another. The fish had blown out its stomach on the rapid rise from the bottom, and it flopped in the bottom of the trap. When Jamie came around with the bait iron and a full bag, Jimmy nodded at the cusk. "Hey, college boy, put that fish on as bait, too."

Jamie stared down at the cusk. Its eyes were bulging and its belly looked like pink bubble gum coming out of a mouth. He looked at both Joe and Jimmy, but they had their poker faces on. He wasn't sure what they wanted him to do, so he asked, "And how should I do that?"

Jimmy barked, "Jesus Christ, kid! Put the goddamn fish on the bait iron—through the eyes—and let's get going! We can all gather 'round the traps and sing campfire songs later, okay? Not all of our daddies pay our bills, you know! Some of us actually have to work for a living! Let's get going, college boy!"

Jamie reached into the trap and grasped the slimy fish, pulled it out, and thrust the metal skewer of the bait iron through its eyes. The fish thrashed wildly as Jamie flicked the bait kabob into the trap, and eye juice dripped down his hands as he returned to the bait station. The cusk continued to writhe pathetically in the trap as Jimmy lugged it astern with the other traps. Joe ordered, "Let's keep adding that kind of interesting bait whenever we can, okay?"

Jimmy guffawed, "Yeah, it's more fun to do that!"

The next trap had a large rock crab in it. Joe nodded to Jimmy, who then said to Jamie, "Put that crab on the bait line!"

Jamie looked at the two men again, and understood their game. He reached in and grabbed the crab, pulled it out of the trap, and stabbed it through the midsection with the bait iron. When he flicked the bait bag down on top of it into the trap, the crab struggled, its legs frantically straining at the bait line. As Jamie watched Jimmy take that trap back, he wondered how far these two would take this. Would they kill one of the seagulls circling the boat and ask him to put *it* into the trap? And although it seemed overly cruel to be impaling fish and crabs just to torture a new crew member, Jamie was not too disturbed by any of it—and he wouldn't let it get the better of him. So, as they continued to tell him to skewer any fish or crabs that came up with the trap, he did so mechanically and robotically, without losing time or feeling anything at all.

By lunchtime, Jimmy and Joe had grown bored of this game as well, and they suddenly stopped asking him to put anything but the bait bags into the traps. They gave each other silent looks that indicated how startled they were by Jamie's resolve. Just like the static on the radio and the quickened pace, they could not seem to find the way to take this scrawny college kid off his game, and they continued to be impressed with his solid performance.

Joe said to Jimmy, loudly enough for Jamie to hear, "Let's head out to the deep gangs, and we'll eat lunch out there."

The boat sped up and headed toward the open ocean. Jamie kept on filling bait bags until they were all full. Then he looked around at what they were going past. He could see several other lobster boats working the waters of this area, and each had a cloud of seagulls following it like a swarm of flies. They cruised for a while, then suddenly Joe slowed the boat until it wallowed in its own wake and the diesel engine idled warmly.

Joe and Jimmy grabbed their lunch boxes and headed toward the starboard gunwale at the stern. There was no announcement that it was lunchtime, but Jamie went over and washed his hands, which seemed permanently stained with the stink of bait, and joined them on the gunwale. He'd just taken the first bite of his sandwich when Joe smoothly asked, "So why *did* Laura leave you?"

Jamie was so surprised that Joe had held onto the earlier topic that he almost choked on his food. He swallowed and said, "Well, she was my college girlfriend. I didn't know that everyone has a college girl-friend they break up with right after graduation. I honestly thought Laura was the girl I was going to marry."

"How many girlfriends have you had?" Jimmy asked.

"What—in my life?"

"Yeah."

"I dunno."

"Make an educated guess, college boy. Is it twenty, thirty, forty?"

Jamie seemed to think on this for a moment. His eyes looked up and his face took on an expression of concentration. Finally, he stated, "Um, three."

Now it was Jimmy and Joe's turn to almost choke on their food. Joe bellowed, "Jesus Christ, kid! You only had three girlfriends before this Laura?"

Jamie shook his head. "No, Laura was the third."

"Holy shit," Jimmy brayed, "I've had more girlfriends than that in one goddamn week! You can't be telling the truth!"

"I am. I guess I've been lucky. I've met some wonderful women and formed long and meaningful relationships with them," Jamie said proudly.

"*Long and meaningful relationships*," Jimmy mocked. "And you thought the third one was the charm, huh? After only two other wom-en, you really thought Laura was your true love?"

"Yes, I did."

"Which one of those three did you lose your virginity with?' Joe asked with a smirk.

"What?" Jamie gasped.

Jimmy grinned. "Which one of the three women from those long and meaningful relationships popped your cherry, college boy?"

Jamie looked at Jimmy and then at Joe, but their faces were cold and impersonal, so he looked down at his sandwich.

"You ain't still a virgin, are you?" Jimmy asked incredulously.

"No, I'm not."

"So, which one of those three women popped your cherry?" Joe repeated.

"Laura."

"Oh…my…God! He gets his first piece of ass and he thinks she's the one!" Jimmy exclaimed, his mouth open and the chewed-up sandwich clearly visible in his mouth. "You say you're not retarded, but maybe you're Skinner's child?"

"Who?" Joe stared straight at Jimmy.

"B. F. Skinner. He was this American psychologist who kept one of his kids in a box to see if he'd come out normal. He didn't."

There was silence on the deck of the boat for a moment. A lone gull flew low to survey the bait on board, but another one came in and chased off his rival.

"Discovery Channel?" Joe said with a straight face.

"Naw, National Geographic. It was on after *Cops*."

"Which episode?"

"The one with the big fat nigger who steals some Twinkies from the convenience store and then tries to run away from the cops until his pants come off. Remember that one? His big fat black belly was flopping all over the goddamn place before they tackled him. It took three of them to take that fat nigger down!"

"Oh yeah, that's one of my favorite episodes. I love it when the nigger says, 'Come on, man, this is poleece bru-tal-ity,'" Joe said, mocking the black man's accent.

Jamie stared at Jimmy and Joe in disbelief. They had just been grilling him effectively about his relationship history, then they'd slid too easily into a tangential dialogue about TV that was full of the n-word. He was sure he'd never been part of a conversation of this sort in his whole life.

Joe turned his head to look at Jamie again. "I take it you were not Laura's first."

Shocked again at the swift change in topic, Jamie gulped, "What do you mean?"

"She'd had other cocks inside her before yours," Jimmy added with a grin and a nod.

Jamie hesitated to answer, but he knew that he had to maintain his composure. "No, I wasn't her first."

"And not her last, that's for sure!" Jimmy chuckled.

"Hey, I loved her, and she loved me. Okay?" Jamie said defensively.

"Obviously not enough," Jimmy snorted.

"So what happened?" Joe asked.

"Colleges, especially small liberal arts ones like Bridgewater, are very insular. Inside their quads, they're their own little world living with their own rules for solving their own problems. And just like the wardrobe in the book *The Lion, the Witch, and the Wardrobe*, once you enter the magical kingdom, everything changes. You feel that the rules of the outside world don't apply to you. You begin to believe the delusion that what you're going through on the college campus is reality, but it's not. And you find that out as soon as you graduate."

"Joe?"

"Uh-huh, Jimmy?"

"Do you have any fucking idea what he just said? I mean, I heard something about 'insulation' and 'quadriplegic' and something about a fucking lion or something, but then he completely lost me. Did you understand one goddamn thing he just said?"

"He thought that Bridgewater was the real world, but it isn't. As soon as he hit the outside world, he learned that."

"Oh," Jimmy said, taking another bite of his sandwich.

"So, you came back from New York after quitting your internship, and then Laura dumped you?" Joe continued coolly.

Jamie shook his head. "Well, not right away. I came back to Maine, and it took me a while to get a job—"

"You know you were being goddamn pathetic, right?" Jimmy said. "You have the whole world at your feet, and you go and waste it on some pussy! I mean, that's truly pathetic!"

Jamie looked at Jimmy coldly. "But I thought Laura was the one. I didn't know that I was making an ass of myself until it was too late."

"Was the new guy younger?" Joe asked.

"Yep, he was in Laura's class—a year behind me. When I came back to Brementon, I couldn't find a job at first because all the college students had already taken everything. I know it sounds insane, but I was really proud of myself when I finally got the job at the Hungry Rancher and found an apartment near the campus. I thought I was doing the right thing by sacrificing for the relationship and showing my commitment, but the only thing I was doing was making myself less of a man in her eyes. She hooked up with this rich beefcake, Alex Pettingill, and she dumped me. She left town with him right after graduation. And I stayed."

Joe shrugged his shoulders and kept chewing his sandwich. Jimmy's mouth opened, but nothing came out, so he closed it. He opened it again, and a scratchy voice came out. "Did you really work at the Hungry Rancher?"

"Yes, I did," Jamie said with a sigh.

"Holy shit! When you said that before, I thought my ears were playing tricks on me. I mean, no one in their right mind works at a shit-hole like that."

"I did."

"What the hell did you do there?"

"I helped fry the food."

"You were the fry-o-lator bitch!"

"Yes, I was."

"Whoa, you've come up in the world, haven't ya, college boy? Few people ascend so quickly from fry-o-lator bitch to master baiter! No wonder you've been a tough nut to crack today—any survivor of the Hungry Rancher has the emotional and physical scars to endure the worst tortures, huh?" Jimmy said with a wink.

"If Laura showed up tomorrow, what would you do?" Joe asked seriously.

His question was so out of context from Jimmy's line of questioning that Jamie looked at him with suspicion. But Joe looked genuinely interested in the answer, so Jamie exhaled before answering, "Depends."

"On what?"

"If I could find it in my heart to forgive her. After someone breaks your heart like she did, it's hard to trust them again, right?"

Jimmy started laughing. The tone of the laughter was almost identical to the sounds that hyenas make on the African plain. He laughed alone for several moments, then said, "Lemme get this straight! This chick's boning a rich beefcake right now, but *if* she came back to you, you being a loser and homeless and all, you'd take some time to look into your heart to forgive her before you took her back? Did I get that right? Did you actually just say that?"

"Yes, that's what I said."

"And you're sure that you ain't a retard?"

"Yes, I'm sure."

Jimmy poked Jamie in the breast with his finger. "I hate to be the bearer of bad news, college boy, but she's upgraded. She ain't never coming back to you 'cause it's always upward and onward with chicks. Why would she ever come back down to you unless she was slumming it?"

Jamie looked at Joe for some help, but he was now staring coldly at him. He stammered to answer Jimmy. "I don't know, maybe she'll realize that we had something good together."

"Here's a question, kid. Would you *ever* go back and work at the Hungry Rancher?" Jimmy inquired.

"I doubt it."

"You *doubt* it?"

Jamie shook his head. "No, I *know* I would never go back and work at the Hungry Rancher."

"Good answer. Maybe you ain't a *total* retard! But you know *why* you wouldn't? 'Cause once you've escaped something like that, you never go back to it. Same with this chick Laura. She's never coming back down to the minors to be with you, college boy."

Jamie turned up his hands. "Haven't you guys ever been dumped?"

"Sure, everyone has at some time in their life," Joe answered unemotionally.

"Well, are you telling me that if, afterwards, one of those women came back to make nice with you, you wouldn't think about getting back together with them, even if they had been with another guy?"

Joe calmly put the sandwich bags into his lunch box and closed it. "Kid, if any of those fucking bitches ever came back to me after boning another guy, I'd part their skulls with an axe and dump their lifeless bodies in the water out here."

For the rest of the afternoon, Jamie continued to find the repetition of the job somehow comforting. As the traps came up, were unloaded, re-baited, and then put back in, he became proficient enough in baiting and banding that he was never too far behind in the process. He was even able to spot their bumblebee-colored buoys out in the bay.

When the deep-water trawls were all hauled through and the boat headed back toward shallower waters, Jamie was tired to the bone. His legs and shoulders hurt from standing all day and rocking with the boat. His hands were cut and sore. And the day's direct sun had burned the skin on his arms, nose, and forehead. Joe hadn't said another word to him after lunch, but Jimmy kept riding him hard with stinging criticisms or outright put-downs. He chastised Jamie for knocking into him when he put the bait bags into the traps; he erupted into a huff about how many redfish heads were in the bags; he snatched the bander away from him and showed him the proper way to do it. Jamie felt he had made mistake after mistake, all afternoon.

As they steamed to the last gang of traps that needed hauling, Joe came out of the wheelhouse and looked at Jimmy, who was sitting on the gunwale smoking a cigarette, and then over at Jamie at the bait table. He shook his head. "Okay, boys, only four more trawls to go till our day is done. 'Course, we don't get paid for these last forty traps!" He stopped for the dramatic pause, then, just as Jamie was about to ask why, he continued, "These last traps, boys, will be going straight to the government for welfare for all those fat, lazy niggers to sit on their porches and drink their malt liquors and smoke their designer ciga-rettes! So enjoy these last forty traps—'cause some lazy good-for-nothing is loving life because of all of our hard labor!"

Joe spun and went back into the wheelhouse, and Jimmy shook his head angrily. Jamie was tempted to say something to rectify Joe's inflammatory remark, but he knew better than to try. The worldview of these two men was so startlingly different from his!

As the hauler noisily labored to raise the next trap, Jamie took a good look around. The whole bay felt full and fecund in the gorgeous afternoon sunlight. The lobsters in the tank splashed, and the boat felt strong and stable under his feet. The afternoon wind was blowing the waters into a minor chop, but it also brought the fresh smells of pine trees and salt water. Jamie saw several now-familiar lobster boats working nearby, and he breathed in deeply and closed his eyes for a brief moment of enjoyment.

It was around this time that Jamie started to feel the sadness soak into him. From the way that Joe hadn't talked to him and Jimmy had been correcting him all afternoon, Jamie knew that they didn't want him to come back. And even though the job had been repetitive and a tad boring, he was sad that he had not been up to the task. He didn't like to fail at anything. Plus, he'd have to head back to the Job Service again and deal with that awful blond woman to get another job. He shuddered to think about that. But first things first. He would finish these last trawls, head to the wharf to collect his money, and drive right back to the campground and shower to get the stink of bait off. Then he'd go straight to bed and rest up for the next day.

After they hauled through the last four trawls, Jimmy barked that Jamie needed to take the deck hose out of the lobster tank and spray the entire back of the boat. The pump for the hose ran directly off the engine, so as soon as it revved up to take the boat back to the wharf, the water sprayed out of the hose with greater force. Jamie carefully washed out the empty bait totes and all around his baiting area. He squeezed the mouth of the rubber hose to focus the spray, and aimed at the back deck of the boat. He took the short-handled white brush and began scraping the mud and seaweed off the gunwales. When he turned around to see what Joe and Jimmy were doing, they were up in the wheelhouse, smoking cigarettes and talking. He felt a twinge of anger about being the only one working, but it disappeared quickly when he thought about having to search for another job. Bad work was always better than no work.

As the boat entered the cove, Joe slowed it down as they approached the moorings. Many of the lobster boats they'd seen earlier in the morning were gone now, replaced by the other fishermen's skiffs. Jamie looked back out at the bay and could see several boats heading in toward the cove and others working hard to finish the day's hauling. Jimmy came out of the wheelhouse and began to inspect the cleaning effort like some kind of naval officer, and Jamie scoffed to himself since the boat looked better now than it had at the beginning of the day.

"All right, not bad, not bad. You could have cleaned up under the gunwales a little better, but not bad. Now, take the deck hose and put it over the side. I'm gonna start draining the lobster tank. Once we're tied up to the wharf, you go ahead and start putting the lobsters in those bait totes. Always put them right side up, got it? And count the lobsters as you put them in there. Whatever you do, don't lose count, okay?"

"Okay."

The wharf was alive with activity. Men of all shapes and sizes in orange oilskin bibs were walking around and doing specific tasks. Somewhere, a radio was playing '70s rock music. The drone of a lawnmower could be heard nearby, and an ascending commercial jet skeined out a wispy white contrail as it labored its way through the sky. After spending the day on the back of a boat doing a very isolated and routine job, the world seemed like a suddenly very loud and busy place.

Jamie looked down at the mound of lobsters in the emptying lobster tank. There were so many! As instructed, he began to count as he took them from the drained tank and put them into the totes. The lobsters were cold to the touch, and although they were banded and couldn't pinch, they still managed to cut his hands with their sharp tail shells and pierce his fingers with the spines on their knuckles. Jamie had seen plenty of lobsters before, but he was caught off guard by the variations of their coloring in the tank. Some were a deep forest green, while others were coppery brown or pumpkin orange. The flecks of orange, blue, and even white on some of their shells caught his eye as the tank of lobsters took on the image of an Impressionist painting.

Joe disappeared from view up onto the wharf, but Jimmy came back with several more empty totes and set them up next to the tank.

He started working with Jamie and asked, "So what number are you on now?"

"Forty-seven."

"Oh, good. You know, one time we had one thousand forty-four lobsters at the end of one day! Think of that! That's about two or three lobsters per trap! That doesn't happen much anymore. Now, we're lucky if we have five or six hundred lobsters a day."

"Uh-huh," Jamie responded halfheartedly, trying not to lose his count.

Jimmy started taking two or three lobsters in each hand to put them in the totes, and Jamie began to work faster to keep up with him. Because there was only space at the top of the lobster tank for one man at a time, the two of them quickly worked out a synchronized movement, and they bobbed and dipped into the tank like two orthodox Jews at the Wailing Wall.

"Oh, how many you got now?" Jimmy asked quickly.

"Um...sixty-five." Jamie was less than sure. He hadn't lost count, exactly, but he wasn't totally sure what number he was on.

"You sure? I thought you were on sixty-five last time I asked."

"Naw, I'm sure."

"Speaking of sixty-five, did you know that in 1965 there were celebrations for the twentieth anniversary of World War Two? That war seems so very far away now, but back in those days, it was almost current. When I was nineteen, the Vietnam War seemed current. Now that we're more than forty years from it, it seems like ancient history. But ya know what? I was watching a show about it on Channel Fifty-seven yesterday, and I learned some new things about that war. Imagine how you're going to remember things that happened when you were thirteen or fourteen years old. It'll be a lot different, right?"

"Uh-huh."

"I wonder how much they got for lobsters back in 1965. I mean, if we get three forty-five a pound now, it must have been a lot less back in '65. I mean, gas was so much cheaper back then, it probably took less than a hundred bucks to fill the tanks in those days. If gas was eighty-five cents or even seventy-five cents a gallon, it would have been downright cheap, don't you think?"

"I dunno," Jamie replied, completely panicked that he'd now really lost count.

"I mean, if we have about five hundred pounds of lobsters here, and the price is three fifty, then this load is worth what? Let's see, three times five hundred is…three times five is fifteen, so that would be fifteen hundred dollars, and then you would add the fifty cents times five hundred, and that's two hundred and fifty. So, if you add them together, that makes seventeen hundred and fifty bucks….Gee, I wonder what the price *was* back then."

Jimmy was being chatty for the first time all day, and Jamie struggled to keep counting the damn lobsters as he listened to him go on and on. He tried not to get hung up on the numbers and math Jimmy was talking about, but it was impossible.

When they'd topped off the first tote with lobsters, Jimmy told Jamie to grab the other end, and together they lifted it up to the gunwale. Then they both hopped up and lifted the tote up to the wharf, which was about waist high. An older man in orange bib overalls came over to the edge of the wharf with an elongated ice hook. His face was etched with wrinkles like a walking woodcut. His lanky arms were dark mahogany brown, and he put the ice hook onto the handle of the tote and started to drag the tote toward the scale.

"Hey, Alfred?"

"Yeah, Jimmy?"

"How much were lobsters back in '65?"

"How the fuck would I know?"

"Well," Jimmy said with a smirk, "you were still working on this goddamn wharf back in those days, weren't you?"

"Hardy, har-har! Actually, I was too busy screwing your mother back then to work as much as I do these days. Why are you bothering me with such dumbass questions today?"

"Just curious, Alfred. How much ya figure lobsters were back then?"

"If I had to guess, I'd say about a dollar a pound."

"Huh, so five hundred lobsters would be about five hundred pounds, right?"

"That's right, Jimmy," Alfred said with impatience in his voice. Jimmy thumbed toward Jamie, who was clearly concentrating too much on the count by now. Alfred's face suddenly lightened and he chuckled and wagged a finger. "Oh my, it does seem to be hazing up out there."

Jimmy smiled an alligator grin at him. "Hey, it happens."

"Well," Alfred began slowly, "your fucking count better be right on the goddamn button today or I'm going to have to tell Drake, and you know how pissed he'll be!"

Jamie and Jimmy filled another tote and put it on the wharf. "What are you on now?" Jimmy asked.

"One thirty-five."

"I'm on two oh five. Together that's…three thirty-five…no, wait, three forty!"

"Uh-huh."

Jimmy chattered on about birthdays, TV channels, and his favorite baseball player's statistics, and when the last partially filled tote was put up on the wharf, Jamie had absolutely no idea how many lobsters he had counted. Sometime, either with the blabbering about the price of lobsters throughout the '70s, or the diatribe about the porno channel numbers on cable, or the passionate oration about the batting averages against left-handed pitchers of Red Sox hitters during the early '80s, he'd completely lost track. He was in a panic and his mind raced to figure out what to do—guess high or guess low. He was in a real sweat when Jimmy asked, "Well, how many did you count?"

"Three hundred and thirty-five," he said, trying to sound confident.

"Wow, three thirty-five? I was only on three thirteen, and I thought I was taking a lot of lobsters out at a time."

"I did start earlier than you," Jamie declared.

"Yeah, yeah, you did. That's six hundred and forty-eight lobsters together, right?"

"Uh-huh."

"You're sure it was three thirty-five?"

"Yes!"

"Just don't want to be off. One time we were wrong in our count and Drake almost had a fucking cow over it. He threatened to not buy our lobster anymore. Okay, Alfred, it's definitely six hundred and forty-eight lobsters in total!"

"Ya better be right!" Alfred bellowed menacingly.

Joe came down from the wharf and went into the wheelhouse. He threw off the side line and Jimmy threw off the stern line, and the boat backed away from the wharf, heading toward its mooring.

"Aren't we going to wait until they count?" Jamie asked, pointing to Alfred and another man who were transferring the lobsters from the plastic totes into a wooden box that was sitting on the platform scale.

"Naw, they'll tell us when we come in," Jimmy said with a grin as he went into the wheelhouse and laughed with Joe.

As Joe brought the boat up to the skiff, he backed the boat down, and Jimmy used the gaff to snag the bowline and pulled it to him. He took the carabiner off the mooring pendant and fastened it to the ring again. Then he walked the mooring pendant up to the bow cleat and secured the boat to its mooring.

"Is she on?" Joe thundered.

"Yeah, she's on!" he yelled back.

"You sure?"

"Yeah."

Joe shut the engine down. In the sudden silence they all peeled off their oilskins and boots, and Joe and Jimmy lit fresh cigarettes. Then they climbed into the skiff and chugged back to the floating dock. They walked the gangplank up to the wharf and stood there for a moment. Finally, Jamie clucked his tongue. "Well, thanks a lot for giving me a job for the day, Joe. I really appreciated earning some money. Do you want me to come back on payday to get my check?"

"What?" Joe sounded genuinely perplexed. He looked over at Jimmy, who simply shrugged his shoulders.

"Well, I was just wondering how I'll get my money for the day, that's all."

"Jesus, kid, what's the rush? We were hoping you'd drink a few beers with us," Joe said with a nod toward Jimmy.

"Oh. I just figured that, since I didn't do so well today, you two would just like to be rid of me."

"Do you know what the hell he's talking about, Jimmy?"

"Nope. But I have to admit that I haven't understood a third of what he's said today."

"Hey, come on, I know I did everything wrong. I wasn't fast enough. I couldn't do anything right this afternoon. It's clear that Jimmy hates my guts. Plus, I lost count on the lobsters. Our number, six forty-eight, is way off, and now Drake probably won't even buy your lobsters. I guess I'm not cut out to work on a lobster boat after all."

Joe laughed briefly with Jimmy and said, "Tell ya what, kid. Follow us to the store, we'll buy some beer, and then we'll head to my place. We can discuss all that other shit there, okay?"

Jamie was confused by the invitation. "Um, sure, okay."

As they walked on the wharf, Jimmy and Joe stopped to talk to a few of the other lobstermen, but no one introduced themselves to Jamie or spoke to him. In the parking lot, Jimmy and Joe got into the pickup truck and Jamie followed them as they drove to the main road. They turned left and went a short distance to a small convenience store. Jimmy hopped out of the truck and ran in. Joe rolled his window down and hollered over to Jamie, "Jimmy'll get us some beer and smokes."

Jimmy came out a few minutes later with a fresh pack of cigarettes in his shirt pocket and a twelve-pack of Budweiser under each arm. He hopped into the truck, and Joe nodded at Jamie before driving away. Less than a mile down the main road, they turned suddenly onto a dirt driveway. As the two vehicles bounced through the potholes, they looked like fighters bobbing and feinting. At the end of the driveway was an attractive new house.

The pickup truck stopped in front of the garage door, and Joe and Jimmy climbed out. Jamie parked right behind the truck, and as he got out, he pointed at the two twelve-packs. "A few beers, huh? Some would say that two twelve-packs is more than just a few."

Joe said with a straight face, "One twelve-pack is for us, the other one is for Jimmy. Hey, I'll go tell the old lady we're here. You guys head over to the picnic table and get started."

Jimmy lumbered off toward a picnic table at the edge of the yard, and Jamie hurried after him. Before he even sat down, Jimmy opened a beer and started to drink. When he had taken a couple of hearty chugs and sat down, he looked up at Jamie. "Oh, you probably want one too, huh?"

"Sure."

Jimmy took a beer out of the other twelve-pack and handed it to Jamie.

"This place is nice," Jamie said, pointing at the house.

"Fucking A-grade stuff, man. Joe paid for this whole house with lobster. His old lady's family owned the land and they gave it to Joe and Sally when they got married. She never lets him forget that. He works his tail off to make enough to build this friggin' mansion, and the bitch lords it over him that he wouldn't have none of it if her family hadn't given them the land."

Through an open window, Jamie and Jimmy heard an argument escalating in the house. They caught snippets of words as the woman's voice rose to a screech. They heard Joe's voice turn into a deep yell, and then a child began to cry.

Jimmy lit a cigarette and continued as if nothing was going on, "Yeah, I look at this house and I know I'm in the right business. One day, I'm gonna be my own captain and I'm gonna build me and my wife a house just as nice as this one."

Jamie was uncomfortable. Inside the house, the argument was still building, yet Jimmy kept talking as if there were no sounds of yelling, cursing, or crying spilling out. Jamie wasn't sure what to do, so he kept the conversation going with Jimmy. "When do you think that'll all happen?"

"How the hell would I know that? One day."

"Well, how long have you been a sternman?"

"Fifteen years."

"Fifteen years!" Jamie said with surprise. "How old are you?"

Jimmy crushed his empty beer can and threw it onto the table. He got another beer out, opened it, and took a big slug. "I'm twenty-nine, and I've been sterning since I was fourteen. Been working with Joe here for eight years now. I've already got my lobstering license and some traps out there, but I need to save up for the boat."

A door slammed, and they turned to see Joe walking toward them with a shotgun clutched in his good hand and a revolver tucked into his belt. He put both down on the picnic table, then grabbed a beer, opened it, and took a heavy swig. He shrugged and said, "Thought we could do some shooting later."

"Guess Sally didn't like us sitting out here, huh?" Jimmy asked.

"Fucking bitch! God, if it weren't so warm and soft on the inside of her vagina, I'd take this shotgun and blow the top of her fucking head off!"

"Least she didn't throw anything this time!"

Joe chuckled at Jimmy's comment and said, "Remember that *Cops* episode when that big beaner bitch threw a cast-iron frying pan at her husband and brained him? He was a scrawny spic and was all woozy from being hit by it. He sounded just like a dazed Speedy Gonzalez!"

"Ha-ha, that was a classic! *'No, señor, I have had nothing to dreenk!'*"

"Ha-ha! Goddamn stinking wetbacks!" Joe stopped laughing and looked directly at Jamie, who sat in stunned silence. "Are you always this quiet? Has he talked at all before I got out here?"

"Yeah, he asked a dumbass question or two," Jimmy said with a smile.

"Good. I don't trust nobody who's too quiet. So you thought you did terrible out there today, huh?"

Jamie took a swig from his beer. "I fell behind a couple of times and Jimmy found something wrong with everything I did this whole afternoon."

"Naw, you did goddamn great today! Didn't he?"

Jimmy pushed his empty can away and opened another. "Hell yeah, kid, you did great! You weren't perfect, but you did pretty damn good for your first day."

"But you two seemed pissed with me all day!"

"Aw, that's just what we do to newbies," Jimmy said indifferently.

"You mean, you're purposefully mean to them?"

Joe answered, "Sure. We need to see if they have what it takes to work on the boat with us. Most don't, but you do. You didn't crack once today. Did you see ever him crack, Jimmy?"

"Hell, no!" Jimmy grinned.

"I don't see how belittling and being purposefully abusive to someone makes any sense," Jamie stated.

"Hardship usually results in bonds that are stronger than those formed under happy circumstances. Veterans, survivors, and convicts usually have bonds of friendship that are much stronger than ordinary ones. This is a direct result of the hardships they've endured together," Jimmy said knowingly.

Joe turned to Jimmy. "National Geographic Channel?"

"Health Channel. The show was called *Psychological Connections of Adversity*. It was actually a pretty kick-ass show!"

"Health Channel?" Joe asked incredulously.

"Hey, I was flipping through the channels and saw some lady's bush. Turned out they were showing babies being born on the Health Channel. They kept showing these women's bushes as they popped out their babies. One chick on the show had old Hitler's mustache down there. Got so interested in seeing all that pussy, I kept watching. The show that came on next was this one about relationships. It was interesting while they talked about concentration camps, disasters, and soldiers, but then they got into some psychobabble, and I flipped to something more interesting."

Joe shook his head at Jimmy, then turned to Jamie again. "We had to test you today, kid. And you passed with flying colors! We're actually pretty impressed with you."

"Testing me? So the radio static, the baiting living creatures, the silent treatment all afternoon, and not giving me any gloves—those were all tests?"

"Yep, yep, and yep. And even more than that."

"What else?"

Jimmy and Joe smirked at one another, and Jimmy said, laughing, "We don't have to count the lobsters. Drake and Alfred weigh 'em. I was just messing with you. You got all wigged out about that one!"

"Hey, that's not funny! I really thought that old man Alfred was gonna be pissed when I lost count!...I can't believe I spent the whole afternoon thinking I was doing everything wrong. "

"But you weren't. You did great, college boy. And now you've got a job for as long as you want," Joe said with a nod.

"What?"

"Me and Jimmy think you'll work out great as the third man on the boat for the whole summer, if you want to. I'll pay you by the hour. Jimmy gets a quarter share of the whole take, but you'll make more consistent money if I pay you by the hour. We have to catch something for Jimmy to make money, but you just need to be on the boat working to do that. And from what I saw today, I'm willing to offer seven bucks an hour. We don't usually work less than twelve hours a day, so you figure that's about eighty-four dollars a day. We work six days a week and take Sundays off. You could make over five hundred a week. That's two grand a month. That ain't bad. 'Course, most of that will go away in taxes to keep those welfare mothers pumping out illegitimate bastard babies and buying fancy clothes, but you'll have enough left over to buy yourself some beer."

"Don't forget," Jimmy added, "that we get the culls and dead ones. And when the stripers and mackerel start running, we'll find time to catch some of them for dinner, too."

"Yeah, that's right. So, what do you say, kid?"

Jamie was stunned by the turn of events. He swallowed and asked, "Will every day be like today?"

Joe took a sip of his beer and nodded. "If you mean the long hours and hard work, then yes. But if you mean the radio static and other shit, then no. I mean, we'll definitely still fuck with you from time to time. You're a monumental challenge—we still got to find your Achilles heel. But most of the time we'll stick to just working hard and catching lobsters. And that's one thing you should know: we're the hardest working boat in Kestrel Cove!"

"That's the truth, kid. And it's a good thing for you working hourly, too," Jimmy chimed in. "I worked on a boat hourly once, but the captain was a lazy son-of-a-bitch and we never went out fishing, and I made nothing. With Joe and me, you'll be working hard and making money hand over fist."

"So what do you say?"

"So you really don't hate my guts, Jimmy?"

"Naw, you're kinda likable for a rich and spoiled college boy, I gotta say. I ain't sure if you're retarded or not, but you're definitely entertaining to have around."

"And I wasn't screwing everything up today?"

"Nope, you did pretty good out there," Joe declared, "for never having been on a lobster boat before. You'll get even better with practice."

Jamie thought about it for a moment. He liked the work and he found Jimmy and Joe to be interesting, albeit somewhat cruel—and crude—people. He could think of worse ways to spend a summer. For one thing, it was definitely a step or two up from the Hungry Rancher. "Yeah, sure, I'd like to work with you guys."

"Excellent!" said Joe.

Jimmy pushed his empty away before opening a new can. "Cheers! Here's to a new team!"

The three clunked their beer cans together. The early summer dusk was still warm, and a few mosquitoes buzzed around them. Jamie noticed how quiet it was now, and he felt good.

Joe asked, "You're staying at the Stinking Buoy Campground?"

"Sinking Buoy."

"Whatever," Joe said with a shake of his head. "Why are you staying there?"

"It's cheap."

"Yeah, but it's where all the freaks go to get outside!" Jimmy commented.

"And it's like, what, twenty bucks a night?" Joe said.

"Yeah, about that."

"That's ridiculous. Tomorrow morning, take down your tent and bring everything with you when you come to work. After we're done hauling, we'll show you where you can camp for free, and I mean on a sweet little chunk of land where nobody'll bother you. Plus, you won't have to hang around with a bunch of freaks. Not only will you be earning decent money, you can live for free on this spot. If you do that for the rest of June, July, August, and part of September, you'll have saved up plenty to rent a cheap place for the fall and winter."

"Why? What happens then?" Jamie asked.

"We'll take up all the traps and sit back and enjoy ourselves. You can either collect unemployment and watch TV, or you can find some fishing jobs or odd jobs around here to do. Then we'll start up again in April."

"That all sounds pretty good to me," Jamie concluded.

"Good!" Joe declared.

"Let's shoot!" Jimmy suddenly bellowed.

"Yeah, let's shoot," Joe said nodding. "Jamie, put our empties on that log down there."

"What?"

"Take these empty beer cans and place them on the log over there," Joe said slowly.

"The one off the path right there?"

"Yes, the one off the path right there."

"Um, okay."

He gathered up the empty cans in his arms and walked down to the log. It was a white pine that had been cut down some time ago. The bark was pocked and jagged from previous target practices. He put the cans out on the log, and when he turned around, Jimmy was standing with the shotgun aimed right at him. Jamie dropped down to the ground and covered his head with his arms. There was a silence, then Jimmy and Joe started laughing hysterically.

"Hey there, soldier! I want to see a belly crawl and then drop and give me twenty!" Jimmy yelled between fits of laughter.

The two men were gasping and sputtering with laughter. Jamie stood up and swiped the dirt off his pants and shirt. He shook his head and wondered what he'd gotten himself into by signing on with these two maniacs.

"Did you really think we'd shoot at you?" Joe finally asked.

"Jimmy looked ready, and I just figured you two might do stuff like that."

"You think we're capable of that?" Jimmy asked, slightly offended.

"You two have just spent the last ten hours mentally and physically torturing me to see if I had the stuff to work on a lobster boat with you. Is it really such a stretch that, as part of that twisted regimen, you might see how I react to being shot at?"

"Hey, wait a minute, that's not a bad fucking idea!" Jimmy boomed.

"Yeah, next time we get a temp guy from Job Services," Joe exclaimed with a huge smile, "we could shoot at him and see how he reacts! That's a great idea, Jamie!"

"No, I didn't mean that!" Jamie spit out. "Someone could get really hurt!"

The sudden blast of the shotgun made Jamie jump. One of the cans on the log had vanished. Jimmy was smiling broadly, and he gave a thumbs up. Joe grabbed the revolver with his left hand and slowly cocked and aimed it. He squeezed the trigger and the gun bucked with the explosion. The bark underneath the next can in line on the log split open, but the can stood firmly where it was.

"Shit!" Joe cursed.

He raised the gun and pulled the trigger again. He missed a second time. "Goddamn it to hell!" Joe yelled, and spittle flew from his mouth. When Jimmy took a heavy drink from his beer, he caught Jamie's eye with a troubled look.

Joe took a step forward and fired again, but no cans moved. He cursed again and his body, which had been fluid and relaxed before, stiffened into a statue of frustration. He took another step forward and fired. No can moved.

"Goddamn it!"

He leaped forward and took two quick shots. One can fell off the log just from being jarred by the errant shots. A torrent of swear words came out of Joe's mouth, as if he were speaking in tongues, and his finger continued to pump the trigger, causing the revolver to click like a stuck record. Joe slumped down into a sitting position with the gun lying on his thigh. Jimmy whistled and rolled his eyes. Joe's head spun around and he yelled, "What was that you just said, asshole?"

"Nothing, Joe."

Joe stood up and slowly stepped back toward Jimmy and Jamie. His eyes were red with rage. When Jamie looked over at Jimmy to make sure everything was okay, Jimmy was looking straight at Joe.

"Well, you two are suddenly quiet as goddamn nuns! What's the matter? You feeling sorry for the cripple? Is that it?"

"Come on, Joe, calm down. We didn't do nothing," Jimmy said soothingly.

"That's it! Get the fuck out of here! I don't want to see you two fucking assholes anymore today!"

"What about Linda? She's supposed to pick me up here."

"I don't give a shit about any of that! Just get the hell out of my goddamn sight!"

Jimmy downed the last of his beer and crunched the can in his hand. "Okay, Joe, we're going. Jamie, do you mind giving me a ride toward town? We'll bump into my wife, Linda, along the way, I'm sure."

"Naw, that's fine." Jamie was completely confounded by what had just happened and wondered again what he'd gotten himself into.

Joe grabbed the shotgun off the picnic table and stomped off toward the house. He didn't turn around as he barreled through the garage doorway and slammed it shut behind him. Jimmy grabbed a couple of beers out of Jamie and Joe's twelve-pack and added them to the remainder of his. He picked this up and tucked it under his arm. "Let's get going before he turns around and comes after us."

Jamie asked nervously, "Is he going to be okay?"

"I ain't worried about *him*, kid. It's us who's in more danger right now. If he's pissed off enough, he'll reload and come back out here. I think we want to be gone by then. If you want your rear window intact, we might want to make a hasty retreat!"

"Are you serious?"

"As serious as the clap, man. Let's get going."

"What about his family?" Jamie asked.

Jimmy gave him a meaningful look. "Believe me, they know how to take care of themselves when he gets like this. Come on, let's go!"

They hustled to the Volvo, sped off, and drove for a while without speaking. Jimmy was sipping his beer, and Jamie was focusing on the road. Finally, Jimmy said, "This Volvo is a smooth-riding vehicle, but it must be pretty expensive to fix."

The two sat in silence again. Jimmy finished off his beer and tossed the can out the window. He opened another can.

Jamie couldn't hold it in any longer. "Jimmy, what the hell just happened with Joe?"

Jimmy lit a cigarette and blew the smoke out the window. "That temper tantrum back there? Oh, I've seen Joe explode like that lots of times. Once, a few years back, he couldn't get his lawnmower started. He tried and tried and tried. Finally, he just went inside, got his shotgun, and shot the shit out of it! But that wasn't enough. He was so mad at it, he set it on fire. The gas in the tank caused a small explosion, and the Kestrel Cove Volunteer Fire Department had to be called in to put out the fire. Joe's dad is the mayor of Kestrel Cove, so the firefighters didn't ask too many questions. Afterwards, Joe just went to Wal-Mart and bought a new one. Hasn't had any problems with that one yet."

"He got really mad at us just now. And so quickly, too!"

"Joe's still dealing with the injury to his hand. He doesn't like being crippled. He's pretty cocky about being a good fisherman, and yet he let his hand get crushed in the hauler last winter. That's something an amateur would do. And it left him unable to do things like he used to, like shoot. Joe could hit butterflies with a .22 rifle, but now he can't even hold one with that bad hand of his. He thought shooting with the revolver would be easier because he can hold it in his good hand, but Joe ain't left-handed, so he's having to learn how to shoot all over again. I shouldn't have whistled when I did, but I knew we were in for it. He was just angry about not being able to hit the cans and we were standing there watching. He didn't mean anything by it. He'll be all better tomorrow morning, you'll see. Don't worry."

A car came toward them with the left headlight out. Jimmy yelled, "Whoa! Flash your high beams and pull over. That's my old lady there!"

Jamie did as he was told, and they waited as the other car went past them, turned around, and came up behind them. Jamie and Jimmy got out and walked back to the other car. When a woman got out, she asked, "Hey, Jimmy, what's going on?"

"Oh, we were at Joe's, but he flipped out and sent us both away. Jamie here was giving me a ride until we came across you."

"That's why I didn't recognize the car. Hi, Jamie, I'm Jimmy's wife, Linda."

Jamie reached over and shook her hand. The woman was tall and pretty, with long brown hair pulled back in a ponytail.

Jimmy patted Jamie on the back. "He's gonna be our new third man! Today was his first day, and he did great."

Linda looked Jamie over and then at the Volvo behind him. "You don't seem the type to get involved with these two beasts. I already feel sorry for the torture you're gonna endure from them."

"Yeah, today was pretty interesting," Jamie chuckled.

"Hmm, it'll get worse. You still have time to run away from it all," she said sweetly. A child started crying in the car and Linda turned to Jimmy. "Let's go, honey, Jimmy Junior is getting fussy."

"Okay, okay. Let me get my stuff. He went back to the Volvo and got his twelve-pack and his lunch cooler. When he started walking back, Linda stood with her hands on her hips. "Jimmy, what the hell is that?"

"Beer."

"Have you been drinking and driving, too, Jamie?"

"No, I haven't. I swear, I just had one beer before leaving Joe's. I never drink and drive. Never!" Jamie stated emphatically.

"You hear that, Jimmy? He never drinks and drives! Maybe he'll be a good influence on you. Do you remember what the sheriff said the last time he busted you for a DUI? He told you that, if he ever caught you near a vehicle with a beer again, you'd never get your license back! NEVER! Forget suspensions, he'd take your license forever. Then I'd be stuck schlepping your ass all over God's creation for the rest of my life. Do you really want that?"

"No."

"Me neither. After working my fingers to the bone in that stupid store, I have to come down here to pick your drunken ass up. Does that seem fair?"

"Cut me some slack, woman, I was just having a couple…Whoa! Christ on a crutch, Linda, you ain't wearing any underwear! I can see your tits and crotch through your dress with that headlight behind ya like that! You've been giving Jamie quite a show here! He's gonna have to go back to his tent and jerk off into his sleeping bag!"

"Jimmy Coleman, you're a piece of work!" She reached out to shake Jamie's hand again, then said, "Welcome aboard, Jamie, and may God have mercy on your soul. You'll have to come over for dinner sometime soon. Come on, James Earl Coleman, get your drunken ass in the car so we can do the Driving Mr. Daisy thing all the way home!"

As she turned and walked back to the driver's side door, Jamie watched her moving in the light of the car. He hadn't noticed the translucence of the dress before Jimmy's comment, but now he was startled by how clearly he could see her body. Jimmy slugged him hard on the shoulder. "I see you watching my old lady's ass! She's got a fine one and I'll be riding it later tonight, college boy. But you sure as shit shouldn't be looking at it like that. You'll go to hell!"

Jimmy grinned and punched Jamie again. "I'll see you in the morning, college boy. You did a goddamn great job today. See ya tomorrow! Don't be late!"

When Jamie finally drove into the campground, it was eerily quiet. He could hear the sounds of people around their campfires as he went straight to the shower and got cleaned up. When he came back, he opened up one of the two beers Jimmy had left him and drank from it while sitting at the picnic table. The day had been, without a doubt, a strange one. But there was something in the craziness of Joe and Jimmy that made him look forward to working with them. He was a bit offended by their crude language and racial biases, but there would never be many boring moments with them, that was for sure! And now he had a job for the entire summer and fall—he didn't have to go to the Job Service and see that crazy woman ever again!

The beer was warm, but it tasted good. He would snack on something quick before he went to bed. He was tired, and it was completely dark now. A loon warbled mournfully from somewhere out on the water, and he smiled at the familiar sound. This job was either going to be an incredible adventure or a colossal train wreck, and, truth be told, Jamie wasn't sure which one he preferred right now.

When Jamie woke up the next morning, his entire body ached. He moved sluggishly as he took down the tent and put everything in his car, but he hurried to drive out of the campground and get to the wharf early. He parked in the exact same spot as the day before, and, since no one else was around, he grabbed his lunch and walked down the alleyway. Just outside the office, the long-haired old man he'd seen the day before came running toward him again. This time, when he saw Jamie, there was a glimmer of recognition in his eye. The man pointed his bony finger at Jamie and hissed, "You're Joe's new third man, ain't ya?"

"Yes, sir."

"You ain't told nobody that you saw me yesterday, did ya?"

"Nope, I didn't tell anyone."

The old man cackled, "Good lad, good lad!" And then he ran off into the shadows and disappeared.

When Jamie heard Joe's pickup come down the hill, he tensed up to face Joe after the unpleasant scene of the previous night. But it was immediately clear that those events had been either forgotten or swept under the carpet. As the two men walked up to him, both were grinning and in a good mood, and Joe even gave Jamie a jovial pat on the shoulder as he asked, "Did you bring your camping gear, college boy?"

"Yep."

"Good. We'll get you all set up on your new spot after work."

Jimmy blurted out, "Hey, do you think he should park his car somewhere else today?"

Joe looked over and swiped the air with his hand. "Naw, it's okay where it is."

"It was fine there yesterday," Jamie said with a shrug.

"Yeah, that's true," Jimmy started to say with a heavy sigh, but then shook his head. "But Drake can be a bit of a prick sometimes. Parking in the wrong place could get you on his bad side, and *nobody* wants to be there! He has certain things that push his buttons, and when he loses it, it's all over. There ain't no redemption with ol' Drake!"

Joe said, "You know that white house with all the shit in the yard there when you turn off the main road?" Joe asked.

"Sure," said Jamie.

"Well, that's Drake's. All the land from there to here is his. Hell, most of the land around these parts is his or his family's. His ancestors were some of the first ones to set up shop on this peninsula."

As they continued down onto the wharf, Jimmy and Joe took pains to tour Jamie around, and he was grateful to have the answers to some of his questions. By the time they walked down the ramp to the skiff dock, he felt he was beginning to learn his way around.

"Hey Jimmy, while I go out and get the boat off the hook, why don't you give Jamie the lowdown about each boat?"

Jimmy looked at Joe uncertainly. "Really?"

"Sure."

"Okay, I guess I can do that," Jimmy said with a shrug.

"All right then, Jamie, listen to Jimmy and try to remember as much as you can. I like for my crew to know all the captains, the boats, and the buoy colors of the cove."

"Okay."

Jimmy anxiously watched Joe head down the gangplank to the floating dock. And, as he puttered away and the skiff's wake formed a lacy tessellation of waves behind it, Jimmy said quietly, "Huh, that's interesting."

"What is?"

"Well, this is the first time he's gone out alone to get the boat since the accident. That bum hand makes it hard to do all the things you have to do to get the boat off the mooring and in to the dock."

"Well, is he going to be okay?"

"Joe's a big boy, he'll do fine."

"Should we tell him to come back?"

Jimmy gave Jamie a withering look. "Yeah, let's pick up our skirts and run to the edge of the wharf shrieking! Maybe Joe'll come back and save us!" He shook his head in disgust. "He'll be fine. Just interesting that he's choosing to do it today. Hmm… Okay, look at the boats out there, college boy. Do you recognize some?"

"Sure," Jamie declared confidently, "I know ours and I know Sanford's."

"Good. See the big gray one right here?"

Jamie looked at the fishing boat at one of the closest moorings. The boat was large and ancient. It was painted gray, but the paint was chipped and flaking off as if it had a tropical disease. It had an empty net spool and some rusted booms on its stern, and a sign on the bow that announced its name as the *Norma Jane*.

"Well, that's Drake's boat. Hard to miss her, especially when she's all started up and smoking. He's got her set up so he can fish for anything. He uses her to catch lobsters, scallops, shrimp, and ground fish. We'll see this boat steaming around the bay all the time, but we won't ever come alongside when she's just idling."

"Why not?"

"Well, Drake takes Ed Simmons's old lady, Wilma, out as his sternman, and they've been each other's fuck buddy for years. If the *Norma Jane* is ever just sitting out there, there's a good chance that those two are down below decks getting it on. And believe me, no one wants to see that!"

"What about the woman's husband?"

"Well, hell, Jamie, he sure as shit doesn't want to see his wife banging someone else!" Jimmy retorted.

"No, no, Jimmy! I mean, does the woman's husband know about the affair?"

"Sure. Everyone here knows about it."

"What does he do about it?"

"Nothing. You see that crappy little fiberglass rowboat with the black outboard motor at the mooring next to Drake's?"

"Yep."

"Well, that's Ed's boat. His hauler shit the bed a couple of years ago and he's too poor to fix it, so he hauls his traps by hand. He's as strong as an ox…and crazy as a Betsy Bug!"

"Jesus, does he ever see his wife and Drake together?"

Jimmy looked at Jamie with mild irritation. "Their boats are on moorings next to each other, college boy, so what do you think? Ed watches Wilma and Drake head out together every damn day."

"And he knows that they go out and have sex?"

"They go out to catch lobsters; the sex happens afterward."

"And the husband *knows* this?"

"Like I said, everyone knows."

"Jeez, that's harsh."

"Well, Ed's taken to shitting on the wharf for revenge, but that isn't gonna stop Drake and Wilma from screwing around."

The *Bobbie C.* started up and its initial burst of exhaust puffed into the wind. Jimmy said, "Anyway, we better keep going. Joe'll be here soon. So, you see the smaller red boat just beyond Drake's? That's Hai's boat. He's a gook straight from Vietnam. He's a really good fisherman, and he stays mostly to himself. He brought his whole family over here, so you'll see countless other little monkey people working on that boat from time to time. The boat ain't much, but she's clean and painted better than my goddamn house! Hai and his family fish the hell outta her."

Before Jamie could say anything, Jimmy continued, "And you see that white boat right next to Hai's red boat? That's Nigger Bob's rig. He doesn't take as good care of his boat, but he fishes pretty hard from her.

"And the ugly monster near Nigger Bob's, with the really tall gunwales, is Matt Jay's boat. He built that fucking scow himself, and it looks like it. Matt's a fag, but doesn't tell anyone. He's pretty cool for being a homo, plus he's a damn fine fisherman. He's never tried any funny business with any of us, so it's okay if he's a cocksucker."

Joe was steering the boat toward them, and his approach seemed to ease some of Jimmy's concern and unleashed the urgency of finishing the tour before Joe reached the wharf. "And that white boat that was right next to our mooring is Bobbie Schmidt's. He's a good shit. You'll meet him and his sternman, Wiley. That Wiley is one crazy motherfucker! The two of them fish almost as hard as me and Joe do. On days when the weather sucks and the surf is raging, we'll see those guys right next to us, fishing through it.

"Let's see…next to Sanford's boat are the boats of other old-timers that don't fish too much. They still talk tough in the fish house, but nobody listens anymore.

"Oh, that green boat over there is Vernon Quigley's. He's a damn slimy one, that one. He keeps getting accused for keeping shorts and for bleaching eggers, but nothing ever sticks to him. He's a complete asshole, but for some reason, he's one of Bobbie Schmidt's best friends."

Jamie had no idea what a short or an egger was, but he figured he wouldn't make an ass of himself by asking for clarification. Jimmy seemed finished with his presentation, but Jamie wanted to know about some pleasure boats moored farther out in the cove, so he asked, "Who owns those nice-looking boats out there?"

"Who the hell cares? They're summer people, and they don't matter since they ain't one of us. Just focus on the fishing boats; they're the only ones you need to know."

Out at the farthest point of the cove, almost hidden by a hare-lipped section of the shoreline, was a jet-black lobster boat. Jamie pointed at it and said, "Whose black boat is way out there?"

"That's Bill Hand's."

"Who's Bill Hand?"

"Come on, you've heard of Bill Hand."

Jamie shook his head. "Nope, never have."

"Sure you have—he's in the news all the time."

"Nope, I don't think I have, Jimmy."

"Everyone's heard of Bill Hand."

"Okay, if you say so. Just remind me, 'cause I can't remember who he is."

Jimmy rolled his eyes and exhaled loudly. "He's a billionaire who's always in the news. He invented something huge, but nobody knows what. Some say Velcro, some say the artificial heart. Nowadays, he runs a gigantic computer company called Veritech Industries. He's got more money than God, and lives in a huge mansion on top of Mt. Buxtor. But he ain't just a regular old sit-on-his-ass-and-drink-scotch rich guy. He wears the plainest black clothes and he's as quiet as a statue, but he's definitely good people. Good, but a little odd."

"It seems like a really nice boat."

"It is, but there's something about it that ain't quite right. It's brand new, and as soon as you hear the engine running, you know it's got some real power. I mean, Joe and I once saw it out in the bay and watched Bill open up the throttle on her, and I swear that boat was doing over sixty knots! Now, why anyone would need a completely black lobster boat that can go that fast is anyone's guess, but there it is. And the weirdest part about it is that no one from the cove—and I mean *no* one—has ever stepped foot on that boat! Joe and I've talked about sneaking over and checking her out, but we haven't yet. There's something definitely mysterious about the man and that boat."

As soon as Joe brought the *Bobbie C.* up against the wharf and tied it off, he started barking orders for Jimmy and Jamie to start pitching bait. When Joe handed Jamie a brand-new pair of heavy orange rubber gloves, he grinned because he knew that yesterday's hazing was officially over. He slid his hands into the gloves and felt their warmth, and then held his hands up like a minstrel to show off his good fortune.

Once they were out on the bay fishing, the feel of the day continued to be different from the day before. Whereas yesterday Joe and Jimmy had worked at a breakneck pace to bury Jamie, now they almost leisurely hauled through the gear as they took the time to explain the workings of it all in more detail. Joe even took great pains to tell Jamie the names of the fishing holes and the nearby islands, and they motored into several bays and inlets to show him the best places to catch striped bass and mackerel. And they sought out other lobster boats and pulled alongside to proudly introduce Jamie as their new third man.

Right after lunch, they came across Ed Simmons. He was standing in the stern of his rickety runabout working on the outboard motor. The ancient Mercury had its cover off, and the blackened inner workings of the motor were exposed. Ed smiled and waved when the *Bobbie C.* pulled up, and Jamie instantly recognized him as the long-haired old man he had seen running from the wharf the past two mornings.

"Motor quit on you again, Ed?" Joe inquired.

"Yep."

"Wanna tow?"

"Nope, I've got oars. I think she's just flooded. She'll start working pretty soon. Thanks for the offer though, Joe."

"Ya know why they call Mercury engines the niggers of the sea, don't you, Ed?" Jimmy asked loudly.

"I can only guess," the old man replied with a chuckle.

"They're both black and they both never want to work!"

They all laughed, then Joe cleared his throat and said, "Hey, Ed, this is my new third man, Jamie."

The old man looked at him with the same twinkle Jamie had seen that first morning on the wharf. "Yeah, we've met."

"Huh. So you're sure you don't want a tow, Ed?"

"Naw, she'll start up soon as she breathes a little. Thanks, though."

"You know, you should really get a new motor."

"Yeah, but I'd need to have some money for that," the old man replied.

Joe nodded. "I think we're due for a good summer of fishing, Ed. If so, we could all be rolling in it this year."

"Ah, I sure hope so. But you know, Joe, if I didn't have bad luck, I'd have no luck at all!"

Joe chuckled. "I'll keep my eye out for you later this afternoon on our way back in. If you're still having problems then, wave me down and we'll tow you in."

"Right kind of you, Joe. Bye, Jimmy. See ya later, Jamie."

They were barely out of earshot when Jimmy announced, "Shoot me if I ever get like that, okay, Joe?"

Joe smirked. "Oh, don't worry, buddy. I might just shoot you today in a preemptive effort to curtail the whole damn process!"

The rest of the day seemed to fly by. Now that the guys weren't hazing him as much, Jamie was surprised when Joe announced that they were going to head in early to get him a new campsite. As the boat lumbered toward the cove, Jimmy even helped wash the gunwales this time. And after everything was cleaned, Jimmy motioned for Jamie to follow him into the wheelhouse for the rest of the ride. He stood next to Jimmy and listened as the two men joked and joshed loudly over the engine's rumble.

At the wharf, Alfred winked when he told Jamie to do a better job with the count on the lobsters this time, and it seemed to take no time at all to empty the tank and head back to the mooring. As they rode back in the skiff, Joe outlined the afternoon plans. "We'll head over to the store and buy a case of beer, and then we'll get you all set up at your new campsite, Jamie."

At the top of the ramp, Joe smiled and grabbed Jamie's shoulder. "Hey, I want to introduce you to Drake now. If you're gonna work for me and be around the wharf, you should know who he is, and he should know who you are."

They found Drake in the doorway to the office. He was a short man, and his face was so tanned and leathery that the crow's feet around his eyes seemed highlighted with salt. His hair was orangey-red, and the main tuft in the middle of his head swirled like flame. He wore stained khaki pants, a faded blue work shirt, and dock shoes that were molded to the shape of his small feet.

"Hey, Drake, I want to introduce you to someone," Joe said proudly.

Drake's expression was a perpetual scowl. "So who's the kid, Joe?"

"He's my new third—"

"Oh no, Drake, Ed's done it again!"

The wharf rat who had interrupted Joe was so skinny, Jamie could not help staring at him. He looked like a walking skeleton in his orange bib overalls.

"Oh, Christ on a Crutch, Vincent, where now?"

"Over by the gas pumps, Drake."

"Argh, that bastard! He's a sneaky old bugger, that's for sure."

"Ed Simmons again?" Joe asked with a snicker.

"Yup, the old coot is still shitting on my wharf almost every damn morning. It feels like I spend half my day just trying to find where he shat before I step in it or sit in it. Naw, it ain't funny, Joe! It's goddamn gross! And what's worse, if the health inspector were to drop in and step in a pile of human shit, we'd be shut down just like that!"

"Maybe if you just talked to him, he'd stop doing it, Drake."

"No, he wouldn't. He's crazy enough that he'll keep doing it forever! I'm telling ya, Joe," Drake said slowly, coming closer to Joe's face, "the next time I see him out on the water, I have a mind to try and run him over!"

Joe laughed. "Do you think the *Norma Jane* could catch his scow?"

"Watch yourself, Joe! No one makes fun of my *Norma Jane*! She can get moving right quick when duly inspired," Drake crooned, and his scowl softened into a grin.

"I'm trying to imagine that scene," Joe said between laughs, "you in the *Norma Jane* chasing Ed Simmons around the bay. It'd be like destroyers laying down a smoke screen, that's for sure!"

The two men chuckled over that for a minute, but then Jamie spoke up. "Why don't you just ask him to leave the cove?"

"What did you just say?" Drake growled, giving Jamie a dark look.

Joe turned sharply toward him, but Jamie continued. "Ed Simmons. Isn't he paying you for his mooring in the cove?"

"'Course he is! Everyone pays for their mooring," Drake grumbled, shaking his head.

"Well, if he's shitting on your wharf, just tell him he's got to put his boat somewhere else. You know, sort of evict him."

Joe rolled his eyes and blew out air like a muted whistle. Drake puffed up and thrust his chest out. "What do you think I am, a heartless bastard? You can't fuck around with a man's livelihood like that! If old Ed Simmons wants to shit on my wharf, let him crap away. I ain't gonna make it personal."

Jamie thought that screwing someone's wife seemed like a very personal thing to do, and even though he knew he shouldn't ask, he couldn't help himself. "But weren't you just saying that you'd like to run him down in your boat for crapping on your wharf?"

"All I'm saying is that I don't like Ed Simmons messing up my wharf."

Jamie melodramatically looked around at the rusted fire extinguisher, the battered fuel pumps, the various sections of fishing nets hanging akimbo, the rusting bait irons lying in plastic buckets, and the other pieces of fishing detritus that clung to the old wooden wharf like fungus. "Yeah, but look at this place. I mean, how could you really tell if someone was messing it up?"

Joe stared at Jamie with disbelieving eyes and shook his head like he regretted introducing him to Drake in the first place, and then he turned toward the older man and braced for impact. Drake's face reddened and his eyebrows lifted. "What the fuck did you say this little puke's name is?"

"Jamie. Jamie Kurtz. He's my new third man."

"Well, I don't like him, Joe! I don't like him at all! He's an uppity little prick. Don't let him come onto my wharf without ya, got it, Joe?"

"Yeah, Drake, I hear you."

Then Drake turned to Jamie and jabbed him in the chest with his finger, which felt as strong as re-bar and made him wince. "I don't like you. From now on, whenever you see me, walk on the other side of the wharf. You don't want to come face to face with me. Got it, you little shit?"

Yes, Drake. I get it and I—"

"And don't call me Drake. Only my friends and family call me that. To you, I'm Mr. Muldoon. Got it?"

"Sure, I got it."

"I don't like him, Joe. I don't like him at all."

"I know, Drake, I know."

Heavy silence followed as they walked to their vehicles and drove to the store for the beer. This time, instead of heading to Joe's house, they went in the opposite direction, past the turn-off for the wharf, and down a ways on the main road. When Joe braked hard and turned into a random dirt drive off to the right, Jamie followed, wondering what would happen when the three of them were face to face again. They dipped down from the main road and parked in a clearing near the water. As soon as Jamie got out of the car, the smell of spruce and pine trees hit him like a wave, and he grinned tentatively over at Joe and Jimmy, who grinned back. Apparently, the fracas with Drake was already on a back burner.

Each of them took a beer from the case, popped the top, and sat down on the tailgate of the truck.

"Well, here's your new digs, Jamie," Joe announced. "Pretty impressive, huh?"

"Is this public land?"

Jimmy snorted. "Well, not exactly public. The owners just don't come around!"

Joe elbowed Jimmy. "The owners live in Charlotte, North Carolina. They wanna build a retirement house here someday, but for now, they only come to town once a year."

Jamie looked around. The woods seemed to be endless. "Gosh, there's no neighbors anywhere nearby, huh?"

Joe grinned. "Just Bill Hand. He owns the land all around this property and on the other side of the main road, and he's pretty protective about it."

Jamie rolled his eyes. "It sounds like this Bill Hand has quite a lot of power."

Jimmy jerked his thumb toward Jamie. "College boy says that he's never heard of Bill Hand before!"

Joe shook his head. "Everybody's heard of him!"

Jamie shrugged. "Sorry, but his name still isn't ringing any bells. Maybe if I ever meet him, his face will look familiar."

Joe said, "Oh, you'll meet ol' Bill Hand soon enough. His house is on the other side of the road, so he'll be over to visit as soon as he discovers you're here. He's pretty cool, and I'm sure he won't care that you're here. But, you're right, Bill Hand is pretty powerful—he goes fishing with the governor and has dinner with the president."

Jimmy nodded. "Like I told you this morning, he may be an odd-ball, but he's good people. You'll definitely meet him when he comes to the fish house meetings."

"Uh-uh, Jimmy, I'm not sure Jamie here will be invited to any fish house meetings anytime soon. Remember, he pissed off Drake this afternoon."

"Oh yeah, smooth move, Ex-Lax. Is it your habit to piss off the biggest and baddest dog in the pack? I mean, of all the people in this area to make your enemy, you had to choose Drake!"

"I didn't mean to," mumbled Jamie.

"Whatever. Just keep away from him," Jimmy replied as he took a big slug from his beer, crumpled the empty can, and threw it on the ground. He opened another can and took a drink. "I mean, he's a mean bastard when he *likes* someone. I can't even imagine what he'd do to someone he hates! I'm telling ya, college boy, avoid him at all costs and try to stay on his good side. You never know, he just might forgive you someday."

"No, he won't," Joe interjected. "Drake does a lot of things, but forgiving ain't one of them."

"Well, anyway," Jimmy continued, "try not to piss Bill Hand off when you meet him, okay? He's got more money than God and he has connections. I mean, you see the weirdest people coming to visit him—rock stars, government officials, foreigners—you name it."

Joe took a sip from his beer. "I remember when Bill Hand first came to Kestrel Cove. When he bought Mt. Buxtor, everyone was devastated. My old man still talks about hiking up there when he was a kid and being able to see the ocean all around. A group was right in the middle of the process to get that property designated as a state park when Bill swooped down and bought it. There were a lot of people pissed off at him back then.

"'Course, there were others who saw him as a savior. Because he's an internationally known gazillionaire, some people thought he'd be handing out new and crisp hundred dollar bills to the citizens of Kestrel Cove every Christmas. Oh, there was even talk of him setting up Veritech's world headquarters here. There was speculation that we'd be seeing limos and private yachts all headed to Kestrel Cove, and preparations were made for a flood of all of the Veritech employees coming to live here. Committees were set up—one to propose a high-speed ferry to and from Portland, and another one was to develop the old Naval Air Station into an international airport for executives and clients. The supporters all said that it was going to become the Silicon Valley of the midcoast region of Maine!

"But of course, none of that happened. Bill Hand bought more and more property, but he only built his mansion on top of Mt. Buxtor and stopped with that."

"Why do you think he didn't build the company headquarters here?" Jamie asked.

"Well, some people say the governor of the state where Veritech headquarters is currently located really sweetened the deal to keep everything there. Others say he got scared away from developing this area because of the...the problems with this town. Whatever the reason, he didn't build any headquarters here. But, over the years, he's become a big part of the community, even if he acts like a recluse!"

Jimmy broke in. "Yeah, well, Bill Hand ain't a recluse. A recluse is a person who has willingly chosen to live a solitary life away from the rest of society. Bill doesn't fit that definition, since he's quite social when he gets to the fish house meetings and other business dealings."

"Discovery Channel?"

"Yep, I watched a show about Howard Hughes. It was fascinating how he went from a rich playboy to a lonely old man who let his fingernails and hair grow creepy long. Now, *that* poor bastard was a recluse!"

"Yeah, you're right; Bill Hand isn't like that. Private is more like it. He comes to town and goes to the store. He comes to the fish house meetings and listens to us talk about things. But you never really know what's going on in his head. He's pretty damn secretive," Joe said with a nod.

Jamie looked around again. There was a pile of empty beer cans behind them in the bed of Joe's truck, and the sun was beginning its final descent into the western sky. The shadows in the clearing were lengthening and stretching around trees and the truck like snakes, and Jamie had to admit that he was enjoying himself. But he had a question. "Have either of you ever been to his house?"

Joe cleared his throat. "Well, you're gonna learn that me and Jimmy are curious by nature. And when someone says we can't do something, we try to see how far we *can* do it, till we know we're gonna get in serious trouble. But when it comes to Bill's land and house, we both know to leave it alone. No one I know from Kestrel Cove has ever been on his property."

He took a sip of beer and continued, "What we do know is that Bill Hand designed all the buildings on his property and did most of the construction work himself. When he needed help, he only hired companies from out of state. Me and Jimmy talked to a bunch of the workers afterwards, so we know that his house is wired up with technology and security shit that would make a spy jealous. To open the screen door, for example, you have to do a retinal scan. And then there's a computer that won't open the inside door unless it recognizes your voice. And they told us, after a few beers, that there are machine-gun nests around the property that can fire automatically when the thermal imaging units pick up the body heat of any intruders. We also know that he's got a tunnel running under that whole property. This ain't speculation—them construction guys told us."

Jamie felt a little tipsy. He leaned forward with his beer held high. "Jeez, Kestrel Cove definitely is an interesting place! You got a bunch of fishermen who are all unique, old guys crapping on wharves, that asshole Drake, and even a secretive millionaire. Ha! I thought I was in for a boring time here, but that isn't the case! Is there anything else I need to know about this place?"

Jamie had asked this question innocently, but as he swallowed another sip of beer he could see that Joe and Jimmy were reacting strangely. Their eyes began to dance as they pantomimed a secret message to each other. Jamie put the beer down, tilted his head, and asked, "What?"

Joe cleared his throat again and mumbled, "There *is* one more thing you should know."

Jimmy leaned forward as if to tell a secret. "Yeah, there's something you should definitely know."

"Huh, that sounds serious!" Jamie chuckled. But as he put his can up to his lips, he could tell that Joe and Jimmy were not in the mood to joke around, and he let the beer can down slowly like it was on hydraulics. "What?"

Joe exhaled. "Well, if you're gonna live here, you should know about the big secret. Now, I ain't saying that I totally, absolutely believe all of it, but there's a lot of people around here who do. "

"*I* sure don't believe all of it!" Jimmy chimed in, nodding furiously.

"All of what?" Jamie asked, now suddenly interested.

Joe inhaled sharply. "During the Cold War, this area was pretty important. Back then, Russian subs with enough nukes to blow up an entire continent were sailing all over the world to look for the best place to launch an attack on the U.S. So it was mighty important for the American military to know where those subs all were. That naval station near the Corners was sending out a nearly constant stream of P-3 Orions to look for them. They'd fly over to Greenland and drop so many sonar buoys along the way that people used to say you could walk right to Europe by stepping on them."

"And all those planes needed lots and lots of fuel!" Jimmy added.

Joe took a swig of beer. "Yeah, right; they were drinking down more fuel than could be delivered by just trucks or trains. So the Navy built a tanker dock down at the end of this peninsula to unload all that fuel, and built an underground pipeline to get it from the dock to the base. The old-timers will tell you that they spent a good portion of their fishing days either avoiding those tankers or salvaging their gear after them big ships barreled through it. It's hard to imagine it now, but this whole area was a real hub of activity."

"Yeah, which is why the Russians would totally put it over this area," Jimmy said knowingly.

"It?"

Joe nodded as he said, "Yeah, *it*—the satellite."

"The Russians put a spy satellite over Kestrel Cove?" Jamie yelped incredulously.

"I know, I know, it sounds fucking ridiculous. But you gotta think about the way this place was back then. If the Russians knew the tanker schedule, they'd not only know when the American sub hunting planes had enough fuel to fly to look for their subs, they'd know when to attack the tankers if a war ever started."

Jamie was skeptical. "So they put a satellite over Kestrel Cove to watch this?"

"That's what people say. It flies overhead every night at eight o'clock to take pictures of this whole area."

"Eight o'clock specifically?"

"That's the time the Navy scheduled the tankers to be at the fuel depot, I guess," Jimmy said.

"So do the tankers still offload their fuel at eight o'clock?" Jamie inquired.

Joe said, "No, as soon as the Cold War ended, there wasn't the need for as many flights of those P-3's, so the Navy didn't need the tankers to bring the fuel anymore. That fuel dock's been abandoned for years."

"But people still think the satellite keeps flying overhead at eight o'clock every night?" Jamie asked dubiously.

"Yeah, yeah, I know. That's why Jimmy and me don't personally believe all of this."

"Naw, definitely not!" Jimmy chirped.

"But you gotta understand that most people of Kestrel Cove do. They'll even stop whatever they're doing at eight o'clock because they don't want those Russians to know what they're doing."

"Your making this up!" Jamie howled.

Joe shook his head firmly. "No, I'm not. Once people get to know you, Jamie, they're gonna warn you to be particularly careful whenever you're out and about at eight o'clock. They might even herd you inside if the barbecue or baseball game goes too late."

"Oh, I can't *wait* to see this! It'll be so funny—"

"No, that's what I'm trying to say to you—you *cannot* laugh at them. I mean it, Jamie. People are really sensitive about this one. They totally believe that it's real, and I'm not sure what people would do to you if you made fun of it. Okay?"

"Okay, but it does seems really far-fetched, doesn't it? I mean, why the hell would the Russians want to know anything about Kestrel Cove? I mean, is seeing Drake and Wilma having sex out on the *Norma Jane* how they plan to win the war these days?"

Jamie was chuckling, but Jimmy and Joe sat as still as stones. Finally Joe spoke, but his voice was tight with emotion. "That's exactly what I'm talking about here, Jamie. I don't believe it all totally, but I'm ready to pop you in the face for making fun of it just now. I'm not telling you that you've got to believe any of it, but you better realize that for most of the people of Kestrel Cove, the satellite is as real and powerful as God. I can tell you for a fact that Ed Simmons ain't crapping on Drake's wharf anywhere near eight o'clock at night! The people of Kestrel Cove really believe that a satellite is watching them, Jamie, so whatever you do, don't make fun of them about it."

Jamie heard the seriousness in Joe's voice. He nodded solemnly and said, "I'm sorry. I know that I screwed up by making Drake angry at me today, but I won't make that same mistake about the satellite."

Jimmy said lightly, "Yeah, well, what this all really means for you, college boy, is that if you're gonna pull your pud, you better do it before or after eight o'clock! 'Cause you don't want those Russians to know how many times a day you choke the chicken, right?"

At that, the three of them broke up with laughter. Then Joe said, "Well, since we've got to get up early tomorrow, we should call it a night. Let Jimmy and me help you get your tent set up."

They jumped off the tailgate, and Joe went around to the cab, started the engine, and turned on the headlights to illuminate the ground in front of the truck. He yelled over, "Jamie, go get your tent out of the car. Right there is a great place to set it up."

The site in front of the truck was level and overlooked the bay, and Jamie was impressed that Joe had chosen such a perfect camping spot. He started to set up the tent, and Joe and Jimmy came over to help. Once it was up, Jamie turned to Joe and asked, "Hey, what do I say if anyone bothers me about being here?"

Joe looked at Jimmy, then said coolly, "Just tell them you're my third man—everyone will know to leave you alone. But don't worry too much; nobody comes here. You'll be fine. See you tomorrow morning!"

"Hey, Joe?"

"Yeah, Jamie?"

"What time is it right now?"

Joe looked down at the dashboard clock in the truck. "About seven forty-five."

"Is that why we're calling it a night right now? So the satellite won't see us?"

Joe chuckled. "Naw, we just have a full day ahead of us tomorrow. Plus, I don't care if the Russians know that I'm having a beer with you."

"So you *do* believe they're watching us, huh?"

"See you tomorrow, college boy!"

As the truck headed back up toward the main road, the darkness engulfed it and turned it into a disjointed pair of far-reaching headlights and a pair of floating red taillights. These lights flew through the woods like sprites until they disappeared from view. Jamie listened as the distant drone of the truck's tires on the pavement faded until he could no longer hear it. He felt a sharp pang of loneliness, and he stood like a statue as he contemplated the significance of this on his newly forming future. The relaxing sound of the waves on the rocks nearby let him lose himself deep in his own thoughts, but when the mosquitoes found him and began to buzz in his ear, he was compelled to move.

He unloaded his sleeping gear from the Volvo, brushed his teeth, and went into the tent. He was exhausted from another physical day on the boat and more than a little drunk from drinking beers on an empty stomach, and he let out a mighty yawn. He opened the flap of the tent so that he could lie on his back and look up at the stars that were peeking through the holes in the forest canopy. He tried very hard to see the infamous satellite streaking across the sky, but sleep came too quickly and if it was really there, he completely missed it.

Jamie had hoped he wouldn't see Ed Simmons again, but the next morning at the wharf, he caught a glimpse of him running through the woods and heard his giggling just as Joe's truck came flying into the lot. Joe and Jimmy were clearly still groggy from waking up, but they smiled as they approached. Both men seemed more at ease and ready to treat Jamie as part of the team, and he really enjoyed the growing feeling of camaraderie.

The day of fishing went well. The lobsters were plentiful, but Jamie could tell that the honeymoon was over. Now that he knew what he was doing, Joe and Jimmy were less vocal in giving him advice or praise. As they hauled through the gear without much fanfare, each man was expected to effectively do his own job. Their silent synchronicity was not only a vote of confidence, it made Jamie's job easier. By the end of the day, however, he had the feeling that this summer of working on a lobster boat was going to be more about the mundane and routine, and less about adventure and excitement. But he was all right with that.

As the three of them walked up the ramp from the skiff, Joe nodded toward the other boats now approaching the cove. "See, my lads, we're done first again. There's still light to enjoy, for God's sake!"

When Joe announced that he needed to talk with Drake for a minute and that Jimmy would have to wait for his ride, Jamie decided to head right to his new campsite. But as he walked the wharf, he noticed how everyone was giving him a wide berth. He even saw a few guys with cruel grins on their faces. Although he thought it odd, he paid no attention and stayed on course toward the parking lot.

When he saw that the Volvo was in a much different position than he'd left it in the morning, he stopped cold. At first, he thought he was the victim of a prank. But when he noticed the shattered driver's-side window, he knew that something terrible had happened, and he strode quickly toward the vehicle. As he got closer, he gasped at the destruction. The front end of his car was grotesquely crumpled and twisted, and the front wheel lay akimbo and was only attached to the axle by what appeared to be a mere thread of metal. Jamie looked around for someone to share his shock with, but the parking lot was empty.

He turned to walk back to the wharf, but stopped when he saw Drake, Joe, Jimmy, and a posse of orange-bib-wearing wharf rats coming toward him. He opened his mouth to say something, but when no words came out, he pointed frantically at the damage with exaggerated gestures. Some of the men in the group chortled at his pantomiming.

Joe came forward. "Hey, Jamie, Drake just told us what happened."

Drake cleared his throat and grumbled, "Yeah, I kinda backed the bait truck into your car today. But it shouldn't have been where it was, right in front of a No Parking sign. See the sign?"

Jamie turned and looked. Right where the front of his car had been parked, there was now a No Parking sign. The fresh dirt at the base of its post clearly indicated that it had been put there just a few hours before. He clamped his hands to the sides of his head and stared at the ground in silent fury.

Joe said, "Come on, Jamie, it's gonna be okay. Let's all just stay cool and calm."

Jamie jerked his head up and pointed back at the damage to his car, and Joe nodded. "I know, I know. It got smashed up. But let's call Jerry Shute, the mechanic, and he'll come down here and pick it up. He'll be able fix it." Joe stopped and turned toward Drake. "He can fix that, right?"

Drake shrugged his shoulders nonchalantly, which caused several of the men to snort with laughter. Jamie looked angrily at Drake. The little man stood as impassively as a rock, and there was no sense of remorse in his demeanor. This made Jamie mad enough to say, "I'm just wondering how in the *hell* my car got this much damage."

Drake spoke with an even tone. "Well, I was backing up the bait truck and *WHAM!* I slammed right into your car. Never thought to look, since there's not supposed to be anything parked there."

"Well, then, Mr. Muldoon," Jamie's voice was terse with anger, "I gotta ask you a question."

"Yeah, what?"

"Were you going forty or *fifty* miles an hour when you collided with my car?"

Some of the wharf rats found this funny, and Drake's face flushed. "Hey, the bait truck's a heavy old gal. When she gets up momentum, she hits like a hammer! I never thought to look behind me, since it's a no parking zone."

Jamie hissed, "You know, Mr. Muldoon, from the way my car is completely turned around, I can certainly see that you were operating a dangerous piece of equipment. I think your insurance is sure to increase because of this accident."

The effort to remain unemotional was taking its toll on Drake, and he inhaled sharply and then spit through clenched teeth, "My insurance ain't gonna go up one fucking penny, you shithead. Your car was not where it was supposed to be, so you're at fault here, not me."

"Huh, I wonder what the sheriff would say about that."

"Well, let's call him and find out, shall we? But I already know what he'd say."

"Oh really? How do you know that?" Jamie asked impatiently.

"Sheriff Gus is my brother, you shithead, so I know exactly how he thinks. He'll not only see it my way, he might even give you a citation for wasting his time."

"I don't think we need to call Sheriff Gus on this one," Joe interjected calmly.

Jamie stared hard at Joe, then raised his voice for the first time. "No sheriff? Well, how in the hell are the insurance companies gonna hear about this accident unless we report it?"

"No sheriff. No insurance companies, Jamie," Joe said, shaking his head.

"Joe, look at my goddamn car! He smashed the shit out of it! And why? 'Cause I insulted his precious wharf yesterday. I pissed him off, and now look at my car! And, for the love of God, Mr. Muldoon, couldn't you make that new sign look like it had been there longer than a few minutes? I mean, which one of your guys still has the shovel in his hands?"

Some of the men standing around chuckled with laughter, but it was full of tension and evaporated quickly. Several of the men shuffled their feet, and Jamie felt they were all acting like skittish horses afraid of their master.

"No sheriff. No insurance companies," Joe said again.

"And who's gonna pay for the repair, Joe? I can't afford to pay for a new front end!"

"You can work that out with Jerry. He'll give you a good deal. Besides, Drake will help you pay the bills."

Drake was standing there with a subtle grin on his face until Joe's words sank in. Then he started sputtering, and his eyes started to blink and twitch. "What? I'm gonna help him pay for the repairs?"

"See, Jamie? That was a nice offer right there."

Drake's jowls swung with the bobbling of his head. "Aw no, Joe! Over my dead body! I ain't helping this little puke do nothing of the sort."

"Well, I just thought you might want to do something to help the kid out, Drake. I mean, news about this little incident will travel far and fast. In no time at all, it might go all the way up the chain of bigwigs to the state representatives. And you know how those politicians gossip like old women. And if it reached the ears of someone who had a beef to pick with you over the zoning of this wharf or certain tax loopholes that you're quite comfortably lodged in, it could start a landslide of negative attention toward you. I just figured you might want to help the kid out and avoid any of that."

Drake scratched his chin and stared straight at Joe. Then he looked down at the ground and shook his head. The other men in the group seemed to hang on every word of this confrontation. Drake finally shifted position and spit on the ground. "All right, I'll help a little—but no more than I think is fair! Alfred, go to the office and call Jerry to get his ass down here so he can take a look and give us an estimate."

Because the garage was so close to the wharf and Jerry Shute's phone was turned up loud, the men standing in the parking lot could all hear it ring. Suddenly, Drake looked around the silent group and his face grew red. "What the hell is everyone just standing around for? Get back to work! We've still got lobsters to get out in orders. Get going!"

The men looked at Drake with disappointment, but he stomped his foot and yelled, "Get back to work or I'll fire all of your goddamn good-for-nothing asses!"

As the men slowly sifted back into their jobs on the wharf, the tow truck started up, headed down the hill, and parked right behind the Volvo. Jerry Shute got out and, without acknowledging anyone, gave his full attention to the wrecked car. He was a skinny man with black hair that was slicked straight back. He wore navy-blue work pants that were ripped in places and darkened by oil. His light-blue work shirt had his name on a patch on the breast pocket. His leather work boots were scuffed and faded, and the steel toes showed through tattered holes like the skull of the Terminator in the movie. He moved closer to the battered car and whistled loudly.

"So, Jerry, can you fix it?" Drake growled.

The mechanic nodded slightly and said, "S'pose so."

"Well, how much will it cost?"

Jerry looked at Drake, then back at the car. He crouched down on his haunches and felt the crumpled metal. Then he stood up, sucked in a breath of air, and let out another whistle. "Can't say. Never worked on a Volvo before."

"Jesus, Jerry, give us a goddamn ballpark figure. Is it gonna be hundreds? Thousands? How much?"

Jerry seemed to think about his next comment carefully. "Depends on the parts. Can't say till I start calling around for those."

The mechanic wiped his hands on a grimy rag that only spread the dirt around, and he looked over at Jamie. "This yours?"

Jamie nodded.

When Jerry spoke again, he was looking down at the car and it was unclear exactly who he was talking to. "It'll be expensive. The frame's definitely bent. And I'll have to cut things off, which means that I'll have to weld things back together. I've got a buddy who gives me good deals at a junkyard outside of Freeport, so maybe he's got an old Volvo or two in there that I can get the right parts from. Maybe. Maybe not. If I had to guess, though, I'd say thousands probably."

"Well, I sure as shit ain't paying thousands!" Drake said to Joe, crossing his arms.

Joe said, "Jerry, you've always given me a clearer estimate once you've got some work into a car. Why don't you take it up to the shop and start tinkering with it. If you find it ain't worth the expense, let us all know, and we'll go from there. How does that sound?"

Jerry looked over at Joe and smiled slightly. "Yeah, that works for me."

"I ain't paying thousands to fix this little puke's car! It shouldn't have been there. It ain't my fault!" Drake exclaimed.

Joe tilted his head. "Let's just let Jerry get it up to the garage and start working on it. He'll give us an idea of what it's gonna cost to fix it, and, once we know that, we'll go from there. Okay?"

"I guess," Drake grumbled.

"Okay, Jamie?" Joe asked.

"Don't have much choice, do I?"

"All right. So Jerry, take it up to the garage and start working on it. We'll figure out the details after you tell us some more."

"Okay, Joe."

Jerry headed back to the tow truck and backed it up to the front of the Volvo. Drake signaled Alfred that it was time to get back to work, and they started walking away. But Drake turned around and barked, "You know I ain't paying thousands, Joe. No threat you make will make me pay that much."

"Fine, Drake. I'm sure you'll help out as much as you can."

Drake pointed a stubby finger at Jamie. "Next time, kid, don't leave your car in the no parking zone. Shit like this wouldn't happen if you parked where you're supposed to!"

Without waiting for a response, Drake and Alfred lumbered off. Joe shook his head and looked at Jamie, who was watching Jerry attach the tow truck's cables to the Volvo. He came up quietly behind him and put his left hand on his shoulder. "Come on, kid, we'll give you a ride to your campsite."

Jamie was on the verge of crying, but he choked it down and nodded. As the tow truck began to winch the car up, it seemed to shiver and the loosened tire snapped its thin steel tether and started rolling toward the wharf. Jamie groaned as Jerry caught it and wrestled it back to the tow truck.

"Don't worry, Jamie, Jerry knows what he's doing," Joe said.

"Jerry Shute, but he won't," Jimmy said with a German accent.

"What?"

"It's what people around here say about Jerry."

"Why do they say that?"

"'Cause he's a good mechanic, but sometimes he needs to be guided as to what to do. He ain't lazy, but he tends to do the minimum unless you tell him otherwise," Jimmy said with a smile.

"That's not going to be a problem with your Volvo though, Jamie!" Joe said quickly, throwing Jimmy a disapproving look.

The three of them sat in complete silence as the pickup rumbled up the hill past Jerry's garage, up the winding road to the main road, and then toward Jamie's campsite.

"Well, are you gonna tell him about the coffee can, or am I?" Jimmy suddenly asked with a goofy grin.

Joe's face darkened. "You're about as sensitive as a goddamn rock sometimes, ya know that?"

Jimmy nodded and said in his best Elvis voice, "Well, thank you very much!"

"What about the coffee can?" Jamie inquired.

"Well," Joe stated slowly, "Jerry has a certain reputation. He really *is* a good mechanic, Jamie, he is. But after he fixes a car, he usually hands the owner a coffee can with some leftover nuts and bolts in it and says, 'These are extra. I can't figure out where they go.'"

"Are you kidding me?" Jamie shrieked.

"Well, it's not like our cars and trucks have their axles falling off or their trannies letting go. I mean, his repairs always work," Jimmy added reassuringly. "It's just that Jerry always has 'extra' parts left over after a job."

"Good God!"

"Now don't let dumbass over there get you riled up," Joe said sternly, looking straight at Jimmy. "Jerry's an ace mechanic. He'll fix your car or he'll help you replace it. Either way, Drake's gonna pay his share."

"Stupid Drake—what an asshole!"

"Hey, mess with the bull and you're gonna get the horns!" Jimmy stated with a shrug.

Jamie inhaled sharply. "Wait a minute! You don't think this was my fault, do you? You know that sign wasn't there before, right?"

Jimmy remained silent, and Joe gave him a glare for bringing it all up. He sighed, then addressed Jamie in a gentle voice. "Hey, you just pissed the wrong person off. When you criticized the wharf right to Drake's face, you put a target on your back. Guys like him don't mind stepping right on anyone who makes them mad. But he'll pay his share for the repairs, don't worry."

"And that's *it*?" Jamie exclaimed. "That psychopath purposely drives his bait truck into my car, and it's *my* fault for making him angry? You two not only think that's normal, but now you're taking Drake's side on this one? I thought you guys were my friends."

Suddenly Jimmy jabbed Jamie with his finger. "You little shit! You have no fucking idea what Joe just did for you, do you? You pissed off maybe the most powerful person on this whole peninsula, other than Bill Hand, when you insulted Drake. You gotta learn, college boy, that you can think things in your head, but you can't say them out loud—not in a small town like this. I mean, sure, you can say them to us on the back of the boat, but not right to the man's fucking face! You can't walk in front of a bad-ass bull like Drake and not expect him to charge you!

"And don't pull that whiny pussy bullshit, 'I thought you guys were my friends' crap! Do you know how many people would have risked going head-to-head with Drake to get him to pay his share? Not fucking many, I can tell you that! As a matter of fact, any other captain in this cove would have just shrugged and said, 'Tough shit! You mess with the bull and you get the horns.' But not Joe. He *threatened* Drake, for God's sake! Nobody talks back to that man, let alone threaten him! But Joe just did! And how do you repay him? You keep on whining and crying like a little fucking baby. You can be mad at Drake all you want, but you better show some goddamn gratitude for what Joe just did for you! You gotta show that you ain't the little puke Drake says you are!"

Jamie looked over at Joe, who was wholly concentrating on driving now, and his silence told him that Jimmy had just nailed it. Jamie was suddenly ashamed of himself. The whine of the truck's tires on the road was the overwhelming sound in the cab as the three of them stared straight at the road ahead of them and didn't speak.

Finally, Jamie said quietly, "Jimmy's completely right, isn't he, Joe? I didn't realize that standing up to Drake was such a risky proposition, and I thank you for doing that for me. I'm really sorry for being such a whiny prick."

"Hey, Jamie, don't worry about it. I'm sure it was a shock to see what had happened to your car. Just get some rest tonight, and we'll talk to Jerry tomorrow. I'm sure he'll have a better idea of what he needs to do to fix it."

"Yeah, okay," Jamie nearly whispered.

"Tomorrow morning, just wait for us on the side of the road near your campsite, and we'll pick you up there. It can be our new morning routine, okay?" Joe said.

"Okay, thanks."

After the truck pulled down the dirt road and came to a stop in front of his tent, Jamie slid out and jumped to the ground. Jimmy pulled the door shut, and he and Joe yelled, "See you tomorrow."

Jamie watched them drive away, and then he turned toward his tent. His movements were so leaden and sluggish, it was as if gravity had intensified during the day. Even the beauty and solitude of his campsite could not permeate the sense of darkness he was feeling. He peeled off his smelly clothing, crawled into a clean pair of shorts and a T-shirt, and wandered down to the shoreline to sit on a piece of granite the size and shape of his smashed car to catch the sunset.

An osprey flew overhead with a fish clutched in its talons. Jamie watched the black-and-white raptor disappear into the treetops behind him, and although the scene should have inspired him, all he could feel was the sourness of regret flooding into him. He fought to push it down and away, but it overwhelmed him. Had he made a huge mistake in coming to Kestrel Cove? Sure, it hadn't been all roses up in Brementon—what with his insane landlord and that asshole manager—but at least his car had been in one piece there! All he felt now was embarrassment, anger, and a sense of worthlessness. And what was worse, with his car smashed into a twisted wreck at the moment, he was now completely trapped. No matter how much he might want to flee from this place and these people, he couldn't.

His stomach grumbled, and he realized he was incredibly hungry. He got up from his rock and walked back to the campsite to cook something for dinner. When it dawned on him that all of his cooking supplies were still in the back of the Volvo, he glared at the ground and clenched his fists in anger. This was the final straw. He was about to vent his frustration with a primal scream when he remembered that he had a box of Pop-Tarts in his tent. He opened a few of the foil envelopes and devoured the breakfast pastries. Then he got ready for bed—even though it was early, he wanted nothing more than to curl up in his sleeping bag, close his eyes, and make the whole world disappear.

◦◦◦◦

When Jamie went up to the main road to wait for Joe and Jimmy the next morning, he felt a little better. The good night of sleep had helped him come to terms with the events of the previous day, and he was eager to put his energies into lobstering. But while he stood there gazing into the awakening woods, a soft voice with a subtle lisp said from behind him, "So are you comfy camping on the Petersons' land, Jamie?"

Jamie whirled around. Standing next to him was a gray-haired man wearing a black sweatsuit and black Kung Fu shoes, and looking earnestly back at him. Jamie was too startled to speak, and the man said, "Oh, I'm sorry for surprising you. I was just out on my morning stroll when I saw you standing here. I figured that you must be Joe Quinn's new sternman who's squatting on the land across from mine, so I came over to introduce myself. I'm Bill Hand."

"Oh, yes, I've heard about you."

"Oh, I'm sure you have." The man seemed to have more to say, but he tapped his teeth with his index finger before continuing. "Are you comfortable down there on the Petersons' land?"

Jamie looked down at the ground and kicked some dirt. "Are you going to have me rousted?"

"Rousted? Good Lord, who uses that term anymore? No, Jamie, I'm not going to do anything like that. And I must say that I don't think the Petersons would care about you being on their land, as long as you take care of your trash and your sewage in the proper ways and don't burn down the trees. I mean, you're going to have to move when they drive up in their RV for their annual one-week visit in August, but other than that, I think you can stay and respectfully enjoy their land."

Jamie nodded. "I promise that I'll care for the place like it's my own."

"Good. Well, Jamie, I'm trying to get a photo of this pileated woodpecker that's making quick work of a dead pine on the eastern side of my land, and he gets skittish and camera shy after sunrise, so I better get going. It was nice to meet you, and I'm sure that I'll be seeing you again soon, maybe at one of Drake's next fish house meetings."

"I doubt that," Jamie scoffed. "Drake hates me!"

"Oh, yes, it's a pity that he had to act out so childishly on your car."

"What? You know about that? It only happened yesterday afternoon!"

Bill Hand chuckled. "News travels on the wind in this little community, Jamie. You better learn that if you're going to spend any time here with us. Anyway, Drake will let you in because he has to—all fishermen and their sternmen are required to attend. It's not his place to pick and choose who can go. Plus, I'm betting that he'll kinda forgive you at some point."

"Joe says he'll never forgive me."

"Fishermen are a funny breed, Jamie. They have such a different set of rules to play by, and their worldview is a little skewed, but they respect hard work, fairness, loyalty, and toughness. I'd even be willing to wager money that, if you continue to show any or all of those qualities, Drake just might stick up for you or go to bat for you someday. Now, that doesn't mean he'll ever *like* you, but he might end up respecting you."

Jamie saw headlights coming down the road and heard the familiar rumblings of Joe's truck approaching. "Well, here come Joe and Jimmy!"

Bill Hand nodded. "Yep, and if you don't mind, I'm going to slip into the woods to see if I can find that woodpecker. I'm not antisocial, but there are times when I don't feel like talking with too many people.

But it was good chatting with you, Jamie. I'm sure we'll get some more chances to do that in the future."

Bill Hand stealthily slipped into the trees and disappeared from sight. Jamie was so focused on trying to see where he went, he wasn't paying attention when Jimmy hopped out of the cab to let him into the middle seat. He whacked Jamie hard on the back and said, "Hey, college boy, are you getting ready to wax poetic about the fucking spruce trees, or do you want to go make some money today?"

10

It didn't take Jamie long to figure out that the passage of time in Kestrel Cove was measured by the week. The entire community was so aligned with the daily routines of the lobstermen that the only relief from each day being a mechanical clone of the one before was on Sunday, when the fleet took a day off. While the lobster boats slumbered peacefully at their moorings on that day, the town seemed to catch its collective breath and do all those things that were impossible to do during the busy workweek. After going to church, some people went to the Corners to shop and eat, others did work around their houses, and a few sat and watched television.

On his first Sunday off, Jamie woke up before dawn, as usual. But when he realized that he didn't have to go to work, he went back to sleep. When he woke up the second time, it was a beautiful day outside. Coming out of the tent, he stretched his arms over his head and the rank odor of his armpits and the rest of his body wafted up and socked him in the nose. He hadn't noticed before just how bad he smelled, but now that he was aware of it, he had to do something about it. But with no car, the task of getting to a shower or a laundromat seemed impossible.

He'd retrieved all his camping gear from the Volvo, so he was now able to cook for himself. As he began to make instant coffee and a breakfast of pancakes from a box, he glimpsed an approaching figure in his peripheral vision. Since he wasn't yet comfortable with being a squatter, he immediately assumed that whoever was coming planned to throw him off the land. But as the person neared, he recognized the unexpected visitor as none other than Bill Hand.

"Well, good morning, Jamie!" Bill Hand said with a smile. "Sorry if I frightened you yet again."

"Oh, you didn't frighten me," Jamie countered a bit too quickly.

"Well, it looked like you were bracing for a fight or something when I first came up. I was just looking for a nearby osprey nest when the most repulsive smell drew me here. I can see now that it was the unmistakable stink of boxed pancakes and instant coffee."

Jamie looked down at his camp stove. "Yeah, I was just cooking myself some breakfast."

Bill Hand shook his head. "That's not breakfast, Jamie, that's a travesty. No one should be forced to eat that stuff!"

"It's all that I have, Bill."

"Hmm, you know what? You should come to my place for a decent meal this morning."

"Your place?" Jamie said doubtfully.

"Oh, that's right—you've already gotten Joe Quinn's and Jimmy Coleman's version of me. Hmm…let's see…what would they have told you? Oh, right: first, I swooped in and stole Mt. Buxtor from the naive and unsuspecting natives, some of whom have ancestors buried atop that tallest peak on the peninsula. Then there's the construction of my super top-secret manse by out-of-state workers, who, even though they were sworn to secrecy, told people about the tunnels, the retina scanners, and the thermally aimed machine-gun nests! And what else? Oh, right, nobody has ever been on my mysterious black boat and lived to tell about it! So, how'd I do?"

Jamie laughed because Bill Hand had nailed each and every rumor that the guys had told him. He rolled his eyes. "That's *exactly* what they told me."

"Well, they're definitely predictable. I guess I should clear up some of that stuff, but I kinda like it that people give me space and let me be. If there's safety in numbers, my sanity lies in prime numbers less than ten. So, since there's only one of you, I feel totally comfortable inviting you over for some real food."

Jamie nodded. "I would love to, Bill. But I also just discovered that I…uh…kinda stink."

"Well, I didn't want to say anything, Jamie, but your aroma is definitely competing with the abominable odor of the coffee and pancakes right now!"

"That bad?"

"Oh, I think the smell of fish and body odor trumps instant pancakes and coffee every time!"

"Well, with no car, I can't go anywhere to clean up."

"You can shower at my house."

"You wouldn't mind, Bill?"

"No, and actually I insist. I'm not sure I would want your current aroma to linger in my house too long."

Jamie chuckled nervously. "Oh, thank a lot, Bill. I really appreciate it."

"Sure. Go get rid of that noxious breakfast and then get what you need to clean up. While you're doing that, I'll try to find this osprey nest. Yell out when you're ready, okay?"

Jamie poured out the coffee and dumped the pancake batter into the ocean then rinsed his dishes with the cold salt water. He hurried back to gather up his clean clothes and his toiletries, worried that Bill Hand would get annoyed with him for having to wait, but the man seemed far more interested in looking around the forest than anything else. When he was finally ready, Jamie called out, "Okay, Bill, I've got all my stuff!"

Bill Hand appeared from behind a large tree and looked down at Jamie's feet. "Uh, Jamie? Do you have any other footwear than those rubber boots? They're not really the best for walking around these woods."

Jamie said sheepishly, "Of course, I'll put on my sneakers. I've just gotten so used to slipping on these boots for work, I don't even realize when I'm wearing them."

Jamie changed his shoes, and then announced, "Now, I'm really ready."

"All right, let's get going. With that breakfast properly disposed of, your body odor is starting to take over this whole woods."

They walked the driveway up to the main road and waited for oncoming traffic before crossing. Jamie said, "Thank you so much for letting me shower, Bill. I really need to figure out how I'm gonna clean up during the few weeks that my car is out of commission."

Bill Hand did a double-take, then said slowly, "Oh, Jamie, your car isn't going to be ready any time soon. I'd say maybe in a few *months*."

Jamie was shocked. "A few *months*?" he said in disbelief.

"Or many months. Hopefully, less than a year."

"But Joe assured me that Jerry is a good mechanic!"

"Jerry Shute *is* a good mechanic, Jamie, but he'll put off working on your car unless you stay on top of him."

"Wait, are you really telling me that I need to *supervise* him?"

Bill Hand nodded. "If you don't show up from time to time, he'll forget all about your car. All those other cars in front of the garage belong to owners who haven't pushed hard enough for their repairs. If I were you, I'd start going up there every day after work to remind him. You might feel like a pain in the ass doing that, but it'll motivate him. You're in a war of attrition with Jerry Shute now, Jamie, and you must do everything in your power to win."

They crossed the main road to the head of a narrow hidden trail. Jamie fell in behind Bill Hand, still thinking about this latest road-block in his life. "Holy cow!" he finally said. "I don't know if I can survive being trapped without a car for that long!"

Bill Hand started to respond, but the call of a Canada warbler made him stop and tilt his head to hear the bird better. Then he said, "You don't need a car to get around and do things here in Kestrel Cove."

Jamie spread his arms. "I dunno, Bill, things are pretty spread out around here."

"Huh; you don't know Kestrel Cove very well yet, do you?"

"Well, I think I've seen most of it..."

"But you've always been with Joe and Jimmy."

"Yeah..."

"Well, those two drive to get to their mailboxes at the end of their own driveways! They may not be the best guides on how to navigate this area without a car. You know, Jamie, it's just hitting me how dif-ficult this whole move to Kestrel Cove has been on you. You're new to the area, stranded without transportation, and nobody's bothered to tell you how to get around on foot. No wonder you feel so trapped! I bet no one's even talked to you about the pipeline yet, have they?"

"The pipeline?"

"Okay, it's time to set you free, young man! After we get you cleaned up and fed a decent breakfast, we're going to take a walk. I'll show you how to get around without a car. That way, even if Jerry takes his time fixing your car, you won't feel so trapped."

"That would be great. Thanks."

There was another bird call and Bill Hand turned to listen. He shook his head as if he were vigorously disagreeing with someone, then turned back and kept walking. After they had stopped a few times for other bird calls, Jamie cleared his throat and said, "I didn't know you were interested in ornithology."

Bill Hand spun around. His usually serious face gave way to a grin. "A polysyllabic word? I've been conversing with the guys from Kestrel Cove for so long, I half expected you to say, 'Gee, you sure like birds.'"

"Or maybe, 'So you're a tree-hugger, huh?'" Jamie offered, smiling back.

Bill Hand chuckled and continued walking. He spoke over his shoulder. "Yes, Jamie, I'm interested in the natural world. These woods and waters have treasures that most people are too busy to take any notice of these days. I find the ways of nature to be very inspiring. I watch the chickadees flitter and flutter, and I wonder if they truly understand the dangers and perils out there. Sparrow hawks, pesticides, and global warming—do these ever dominate their whole beings the way we humans let our petty fears run rampant over us?"

Jamie added, "Well, don't forget that those fears can be very useful to people in power to control the masses who have the numeric advantage over them."

Bill Hand stopped walking again, turned and pushed his hand against Jamie's chest to stop him. "What, exactly, do you mean by that comment?"

Jamie was startled by the physical contact and the serious tone of the question. "Well, as you've probably heard, I'm interested in the study of history. I like it for many reasons, but one of the greatest inspirations has been that famous old quote, 'Those who don't learn the lessons of history…'"

"'Are doomed to repeat it,'" Bill Hand said.

"I think that most history can be boiled down to a few main

themes that get repeated again and again. For example, the murderous events of the pogroms, the Holocaust, the Khmer Rouge, and the Balkan War all strike me as being similar, yet one has to wonder why we humans haven't learned to eradicate that kind of behavior after the first time it happens. I think it's because we put our trust in the leadership to keep us safe. But they're not really the solution; they're the problem. They manipulate our greatest fears to make us an obedient and easy-to-manage flock. After all, by keeping the boogeymen of our own pantheon alive and well, they know exactly how we're going to respond. They can enslave us with our own fears."

Bill Hand whistled under his breath. "Jamie, this entire peninsula is wrapped in so much fear, we truly *are* slaves. But I think we can be freed from those fears. It'll just take one person to step forward and do something."

They resumed walking. After a little while, Jamie asked, "Were you just talking about the satellite?"

Bill Hand stopped and faced Jamie squarely. "Ah, so they told you about that, huh?"

"Yep."

"Hmm, they usually wait much longer to tell the new people about our little secret. It seems as if you've won their confidence faster than usual. That's very interesting."

"You don't think the satellite's real, do you?"

Bill Hand's eyes squinted with emotion. "Oh, it's definitely real, Jamie. I know for a fact that there's a Russian surveillance satellite in the skies above us. But the people of this town have made it into an omnipresent and omnipotent entity, and have given it so much power, they've turned that satellite into something much bigger than it really is. It's become the source of all of our problems, the excuse we use to shove our real issues under the rug, and the thing that we blame when we're not strong enough to stand up and be judged. It's my personal dream to set us all free from it, and I'm going to try everything I can to break its hold on us."

Jamie was astounded at what he had just said. Bill Hand believed the satellite was real and wanted to do something about its weird hold on the town! That was certainly food for thought!

They came to a clearing, and Bill Hand announced, "Well, we're here. This is my home."

Jamie knew that the house was new, but it looked like a big old Adirondack cottage. The foundation and porch were made of rough boulders mortared together, and it had a large, low-slung roof that covered the house like a shawl. The gray paint was the shade of charcoal, and even the wood trim seemed weathered and old.

"Wow, this isn't what I pictured at all."

"Really? What did you think it was going to be?" Bill Hand asked with a grin.

"Like something from Woody Allen's movie, *Sleeper*."

"Not futuristic. I wanted something that reminded me of my past. The most perfect house I've ever seen in my life was my grandmother's summer cottage outside of Saranac Lake. I found the architectural plans and had an exact copy built here. I updated some things, but the overall design and outward appearance is the same."

"It's beautiful."

When they walked through the front door, Jamie noticed that there was neither a retina scanner nor a voice-recognition computer there. Bill Hand guided him right to the bathroom. Everything inside was polished to a shine, and the faucet, toilet, shower, and the washing machine and dryer were the best brands on the market. After Bill Hand left to cook breakfast, Jamie put his dirty clothes in the washer. Then he let the hot shower and the fancy French buttermilk soap wash away the salt, the bait, and the unpleasant events of his time so far in Kestrel Cove.

When he came out, Bill Hand was chopping cilantro on a cutting board in the kitchen. He looked up and asked, "So, how was that?"

Jamie just shook his head and said, "Ahhhh."

Bill Hand nodded knowingly and went back to his chopping. A Miles Davis song was playing, and the notes of the music seemed to ride the rays of the sunshine that was streaming through the big windows of the house.

"Coffee's ready, Jamie. Grab a cup over there in the cupboard and help yourself."

"Can I help you do something? I'm pretty good in the kitchen."

"No, thanks. I think I got this. Plus, there's no fry-o-lator."

Jamie stopped with his hand on the cupboard doorknob. "What did you say?"

Bill Hand was chuckling. "There's no fry-o-lator. I figure you probably got pretty good using the one at the Hungry Rancher."

"And how would you know that?"

Bill Hand kept his eyes on his chopping. "Adrian Goodsell and I are best buds."

Jamie froze. After a moment, he croaked weakly, "Goodsell? You know Adrian Goodsell?"

"Sure, we go bowling every week."

Jamie's expression of disbelief made Bill Hand laugh. "No, I went to the restaurant to check up on you."

"You did?"

Bill Hand stopped chuckling and looked up at Jamie. "Yep, as soon as I learned that you were going to be a neighbor of mine, I needed to see if you're on the level or not. So I did some quick investigating. Your landlord had some interesting comments about you and wanted to know where you are, especially now that he's got everything cleaned up. Your old friend, Professor Walter Whetstone, was like a grandfather bragging about his own grandchild. And Adrian Goodsell called you the best fry-o-lator bitch he's ever had."

"Boy, Bill, you were pretty thorough!"

"Sorry, Jamie, but I can't help myself. Call it a professional hang-up of mine. I always do thorough background checks on the people who are around me. Kestrel Cove is such a small and insular community, I just find it prudent to know something about anyone who's coming to this place to call it home, even for just a summer."

Although surprised, Jamie was basically unfazed by this news because his father had a similar penchant of researching the backgrounds of all his employees and family friends. He resumed getting his coffee and shrugged, "So I guess I passed?"

"Yep, the crazy landlord, the glowing history professor, and the sadistic boss all sort of cancel each other out. The little dirt that I found on you actually made me like you more."

"So, do you have the dirt on all the residents of Kestrel Cove?"

"Yes, I do, Jamie. But the people of this community have enough dirt to form their own sod farm. It's not too hard to find out some pretty incriminating things about them. However, if you're looking for me to say that Drake wears dresses, you won't get that from me!"

"Ooh, now there's an image," Jamie said, shaking his head.

They laughed for a moment, but then Jamie said seriously, "It seems that you have a distinct advantage—you've got a lot of information on me, but I don't really know anything about you."

"Yes, that's definitely true."

Jamie waited for him to say something else, but he didn't. He just went back to making breakfast. Maybe some of those rumors that Joe and Jimmy had told him about Bill Hand's love of privacy were more than a little accurate.

After a filling breakfast of huevos rancheros with chorizo and handmade hash browns, they headed outside for their walk. Standing in the dirt courtyard in front of the house, Bill Hand pointed up the hill. "Maybe we should start this trek with a visit to the top of the mighty pinnacle of Mt. Buxtor."

They came to a junction where the road split—half went up the hill and the other half went down. Jamie pointed down and asked, "Does that go all the way to the main road?"

"Yep, it's the driveway from the main road to the house. At the bottom, there's a small gatehouse that functions as my guest house."

Jamie turned to the road going uphill. "So, this one goes to the top of Mt. Buxtor?"

"To the very tippy-top."

Jamie noticed that the soft dirt of the road was crisscrossed by some deep ruts, so he said, "It sure looks like there's been some recent traffic on this road."

Bill Hand stopped walking, turned, and put his hands on his hips. "Are we now in the middle of a Hardy Boys mystery?"

There was just enough annoyance in Bill Hand's reaction that Jamie felt the need to clarify his remark. "What I meant is that every time I've seen you, you've been walking around the woods. I just assumed that you didn't drive."

Bill Hand dropped his hands and visibly relaxed. "Actually, I've got quite of motor pool of vehicles. One of my life's passions is antique cars, and I own several that I keep in a garage that's tucked away down the hill from the house. I'll show you my collection another time. We've got enough on our docket today."

Jamie thought about how hard it was to gauge Bill Hand. Even though he made a lot of comments that seemed humorous, it was tough to tell exactly when he was joking and when he wasn't. And, although much of their conversation seemed comfortable and friendly, there had been several moments when it was clear that Jamie was being kept at arm's length. He had to wonder if he and Bill would ever be real friends, but the way the guys had talked about the man seemed to indicate that he was too protective to let anyone get close to him, and this made Jamie shake his head with some sadness.

As they walked up the hill, the trees were thick around them and shielded the road from direct sunlight, and the mosquitoes murmured in the shadows. They came to another junction where the road split at a giant Y. One arm of the Y was blocked by an imposing metal gate with numerous NO TRESPASSING signs on it. When Bill Hand motioned for Jamie to follow him onto the ungated road, Jamie whistled. "All those signs seem like a little overkill, don't they?"

Bill Hand turned around so quickly that Jamie nearly ran right into him. When he spoke, his voice was tight. "Jamie, this land is my home. Because I have a certain status in the world from my successes in business, there are real threats against me out there. So security is something I take very seriously."

Duly chastened, Jamie apologized and they resumed their walk in silence.

The road narrowed gradually until it became a small path that made its way through the forest and came out onto a huge exposed rock face that overlooked the end of the peninsula and the open water of Casco Bay. The view was unbroken for miles, and Jamie gasped at the profound beauty of the scene in front of him. Pleasure boats skittered here and there among the islands that dotted the bay, and, farther out, a handful of sailboats flowed on the breezes, their white sails full and contrasting starkly with the dark-blue waters. Down at the end of the peninsula, Jamie could see the concrete and steel of the abandoned naval fuel dock. He tried to spot his campsite. When Bill Hand noticed this, he pointed and said, "See the crown of the tallest white pine tree down there?"

"Sure."

"Well, that tree's right over from your tent. You've probably never noticed it before, but you're camped right next to one of the tallest trees on this entire peninsula. It's so old that it has, quite literally, pieces of Kestrel Cove history hanging off its branches. I've tried to tell the Petersons how important it is, but I'm sure they'll just cut it down for wood to build their retirement house. They're nice people, but they don't quite value nature the same way that I do."

Now Jamie looked for the wharf, and, when he found it, he smiled when he realized that he was looking straight at Joe's boat. Seeing it gave him a feeling of pride.

Bill Hand gently clapped his hands together. "Well, let's get going. I want to show you how to get to the wharf from your campsite, how to use the pipeline, and how to get to the store on foot. You ready?"

"Sure. Although it's pretty nice up here."

Bill Hand smiled. "Yes, it is, Jamie. There's usually a red-tailed hawk who plays in these updrafts until the crows chase him away, but he's not here today. You have my permission to come up here anytime you want."

"Really?"

"Sure. Whenever you want to catch a sunrise or a sunset, or just want to see this vista again, you can come on up. Just make sure you take the same road we took today."

"Okay…and thanks, Bill."

When they got down to Jamie's campsite, they took another trail that followed the shoreline like a shadow all the way to the wharf. It had been in front of him all this time, but Jamie had never seen it. Now he knew how he could easily walk to work every morning, and he instantly felt more independent. As they walked around the fish house, past the dormant bait truck, and toward the wharf itself, Jamie was surprised to see so much activity. The lobstermen weren't hauling, but the wharf was far from closed down. Alfred and some other of the wharf rats were helping to fill lobster orders while Drake barked his orders.

"Want to stop and say hi to Drake?" Bill Hand asked with an impish grin.

"Oh, he looks kinda busy right now."

"Yep, he sure does."

Jamie tilted his head. "Bill, do these guys work seven days a week on the wharf?"

"Well, just because there are no lobsters coming in doesn't mean that there's none heading out. They fill orders and sell fuel to recreational boaters. Sundays are probably less stressful than the regular days, but the work is pretty constant."

They went through the parking lot and past the infamous No Parking sign. It now leaned so far to one side that it threatened to fall down. Right behind it a trail headed up the hill toward Jerry Shute's garage, and when Bill and Jamie got there, they found that nothing more had been done to the Volvo. Jamie clucked his tongue and shook his head at the state of his car.

The trail meandered on through the trees, sticking close to the property lines of the trailers and cottages that were just off the wharf road. When they crossed a gap in a stone wall, they entered a wide clearing that ran in both directions like a giant swath of ribbon cutting through the forests of the peninsula.

"I present to you, the pipeline," Bill Hand said with a note of excitement in his voice.

Jamie looked both ways. "How far does this thing go?"

"It was the buried fuel lines that pumped the aviation fuel, back in the day, so it goes all the way from the fuel dock to the Naval Air Station near the Corners."

"Where does the pipeline go when it gets near my campsite? I mean, I've never seen this kind of opening anywhere near me."

"Ah, good observation. Yes, you're absolutely correct; the pipeline had to be diverted around the base of Mt. Buxtor. From here, it takes a big jog across the main road and heads up the other side of my property. Once past the mountain, it crosses back over the road and resumes its course."

"Huh, I see. But why is it so important?"

"Have you ever heard of a paper road?"

"Nope."

"A paper road is a planned road that was never built, but everyone treats it as if it exists. In terms of legality and right of way, the issues can get blurry. But in small towns, paper roads can be a common way of getting around. The pipeline is sort of like a paper road. It's a sustained cleared path that runs the length of the peninsula, so it's become like a paper highway."

"So a lot of people use it?"

"Oh, yeah! So many that there are times when there should be a traffic cop out here. I personally tend to wait until after rush hour to do any traveling on it."

Jamie thought he was joking again, but he seemed to be absolutely serious. Just then, the noise of two small revving engines drifted around the bend in the pipeline. Bill glanced toward it. "Ah, sounds like we might want to seek some protection."

As they walked back to the stone wall, a dirt bike came flying over a rise, its engine howling. As it shrieked by them, Bill Hand nonchalantly reported, "That's Wiley."

A rugged-looking pickup truck, missing its windshield and headlights, was right behind. Its tires spewed mud as it roared past, and Bill Hand deadpanned, "And that's Michael Lewis."

"Are they *racing* out here?" Jamie asked incredulously.

"Nope, playing tag. When Michael's pickup touches Wiley's back wheel, they'll turn around and Wiley'll have to bump the pickup's bumper."

"Isn't that dangerous?"

Bill Hand gave Jamie a that's-a-really-stupid-question look, and started walking in the direction the motorbike and truck had just gone.

"Shouldn't we head the other direction? Away from those guys?"

"No. I want to show you how to get to the store and to Joe's house, and those are both in this direction." He shrugged. "Plus, we'll be able to hear them coming from a mile away!"

The sun-heated air was quite warm in the open clearing, and the insects shrilled loudly in the foliage. Jamie found himself deep in his own thoughts as he walked. "So does the sheriff know about the pipeline?"

Bill Hand grimaced. "Of course. Everyone knows about it."

"Does he ever bust people for using it?"

"The main roads are his jurisdiction, not the pipeline. Whenever there's a crash on the pipeline, those involved in the incident take care of themselves. Unless there's a blatant abuse of the law that he can't ignore, the sheriff doesn't intervene. But you should ask Jimmy about *his* arrest on the pipeline sometime."

"What?"

"Oh, yeah, one time he drove his SUV onto it to go mudding after drinking with Joe and he drove his car into a tree."

"Oh my gosh! Was he okay?

"Not a scratch."

"Did he total the car?"

Bill Hand chuckled. "Nope, the car was in perfect shape. He still has it, I think."

"Wait a minute! How can you drive a car into a tree and not damage it?"

"Well, it seems he hit a rise and went airborne near an infamous oak tree that has massive, low-lying branches that kids have been climbing and swinging on for generations. The SUV landed perfectly in the crook of one of those branches like it was a cradle! Jimmy was so drunk he thought he was stuck in the mud, and he almost burned up his engine gunning it to get free. People still laugh about finding a slobberingly drunk Jimmy Coleman revving his engine like a NASCAR driver, while his car was stuck three feet up in a tree! But the sheriff had to be called in on that one, and Jimmy had to pay the piper, as they say."

He stopped and gestured for Jamie to look through the trees at a large building with a dumpster and piles of cardboard boxes out back. "That's the store."

They followed a short trail from the pipeline into the store's parking lot, which held a handful of pickup trucks. Bill Hand said, "The store will be your best bet to stay supplied while you don't have the use of a car. You can buy everything you need here. Plus, it's a destination for this entire community. The fishermen stop here in the morning for their coffee and cigarettes, and the local kids come here at night to buy beer and do doughnuts in the parking lot. But most of the time, it's quiet like it is right now."

A young woman came out of the store's back door to throw a cardboard box onto the pile, and when she saw Bill Hand and Jamie standing there, she froze in place. She appeared to Jamie to be in her twenties, and she was very attractive. She gave a slight nod toward Bill Hand and a crooked smirk at Jamie before she turned and headed back inside.

"That was Shelley Vanes. You were just identified as my friend, so people might begin to treat you differently. Some will treat you like you're rich. Some will treat you like you're a fag. And some will treat you like you're a spy. Whatever their personal perspective about me is now transferred to you—sorry about that."

"You mean that girl will tell other people she saw us together?"

Bill Hand laughed ruefully. "Right now, your exact whereabouts and your involvement with me are being disseminated throughout the network."

"Gossip, huh?"

Bill Hand gave Jamie a serious look. "No, not gossip. Gossip is the spreading of lies and speculation by a few individuals who like to talk about other people in an attempt to gain power over them through their words. What Shelley and the rest of the inhabitants of Kestrel Cove do is spread information about the community in an oral tradition. We don't need a TV station to broadcast our news; we've got eyes everywhere to see and report everything that happens. There's a huge difference between gossip and this system, Jamie. One is something that's reprehensible. The other is a fact of life here in Kestrel Cove. Like I said before, if you're gonna live here for any length of time, you better understand that quickly."

Jamie nodded. Then he asked, a little shyly, "So, who is Shelley Vanes? She's kinda cute."

"She *is* wicked cute. I'm glad you noticed that. She's cute, smart, and full of spunk. And if I were a young buck getting over a broken heart, I'd think about coming to the store to talk with her sometime soon."

Bill Hand suddenly turned and started up the trail back to the pipeline. The tortured sounds of the truck and dirt bike could be heard coming back their way, and they watched as the truck came careening around the muddy corner, the driver barely in control of the vehicle. Right behind the truck, the bike sped dangerously close to its rear bumper. The two vehicles flew past and continued down the pipeline.

"Huh, Wiley's about to tag him out again," Bill Hand said matter-of-factly.

They were about to continue onto the pipeline when Bill Hand pointed out a small clearing near the store. "See that?"

Jamie looked, nodded.

"If for any reason your present campsite doesn't work out, that would be a great place to camp. There have been several squatters there already, so the area is set up for a long-term camping experience, including a homemade outhouse. If you camped here, you could get all your groceries and hot food at the store, and you'd be in the center of the town's activity, which would provide outstanding accessibility and safety."

"That makes some sense."

"Yeah, so whenever you have to move, just remember this place."

"Whoa, Bill! First you said *if,* and then you said *when* I have to move. Do you know something I don't?"

"No, I said *whenever.*"

The blue sky overhead was spotted with puffy white clouds, and the sun was summertime bright. Every once in a while, a cool ocean breeze brushed through the treetops and down over them, and Jamie and Bill Hand would feel the air turn colder and smell like salt, as if a cold fish was suddenly pressed up against them.

They had not gone too far from the store when they came upon an armless plastic baby doll that was skewered through its bottom onto a tall pole that was stuck into the ground. The doll's eyes, nose, and mouth were smudged black with makeup, and its wiry hair had been plastered to its plastic skull by rain and wind. One of its blue eyes was half shut in a wink that seemed cruel and foreboding. The doll's skin, which once had been overly pink with health, was now faded to a deathly shade of paper.

Jamie whispered, "Bill, what the hell is that?"

"It's the marker for the trail to your captain's house, Jamie. Joe and Jimmy found one of his daughter's dolls and they made it into a totem. Isn't it cute?" Bill Hand snorted.

"No, Bill, it's not. It's kind of screwed up!"

Jamie could not take his eyes off it, and its one-eyed grin seemed to follow him. He shuddered as Bill Hand said in a low voice, "Jamie, you need to understand that the Joe Quinn you know is very different from the young man we knew before the accident. Because his father's a powerful man of the peninsula who gave his son certain privileges, Joe grew up like any kid who understands that they're above the law. And when consequences are not something to you worry about, you don't give them much thought.

"So Joe not only did whatever he wanted, he cultivated a bad-boy image that verged on truly insane. When I first came to Kestrel Cove, I have to admit I was rather fearful of Joe. He seemed to have no concern over safety or the repercussions of his actions. I thought he was dangerous. But once I got to know him, I realized that he's deceptively intelligent and sensitive. I've wondered often what he would have become if he hadn't set out to be a fisherman. I think he was smart enough to get into any college and do well. But the ocean called him and he was powerless to resist.

"As a young fisherman, Joe figured out that if he acted tough and crazy to the point of being psychopathic, the other fishermen would give him a much wider berth. They did. As he got more established, he learned that he didn't have to act like that anymore, and he was able to show his other good qualities, too.

"Then the accident happened, and it changed him, quickly and dramatically. And now I find myself fearing him again."

Jamie added, "But he seems to get along just fine, Bill. Most of the time, I don't even think about his right hand anymore."

Bill Hand shook his head. "It's not what he can do or can't do that's really changed. It's more the overall tone of the man. Before the accident, he'd do some pure crazy and somewhat mean things, but everyone saw a spark of light in his countenance that told you it was all in fun. But that spark was lost after the accident. There's a darkness in him now that makes people nervous. This wretched doll is a visual reminder of Joe's awful dark potential."

As they got closer to Joe's house, they heard yelling. The voice was that of Joe's wife, Sally, who was screaming, "Goddamn it, Joe! Don't get so upset! For the love of God, I'm sorry that she knocked over your beer! But accidents happen! Don't yell at her!"

Then Joe's voice boomed out, "Come here and say that to me again, you goddamn bitch!"

"Jesus, Joe! It was only a little beer..." Sally pleaded.

"Just a little beer? Look at my goddamn pants. I'm so sick and tired of you two ruining my life and then bonding together against me like I'm the fucking bad guy! I've sat around and let it happen for too long!"

"No, Joe! Don't get up. I'll clean it up and wash your pants! *No!*"

Jamie found himself being pushed back toward the pipeline by Bill Hand, and like a panicked sheep, he submitted until the two men were back at the doll on the pole.

Jamie gasped, "Shouldn't we do something?"

Bill Hand threw his hands up in the air and said quietly, "Like what?"

"I don't know, maybe knock on the door and intervene?"

"We'd just get ourselves shot."

"But it sounded like Joe was going to hurt his wife and his daughter."

"Yes, it did."

"Should we call the sheriff?"

Bill Hand grabbed Jamie roughly by the arm. "Do you know what people would do if they found out that we called the law on Joe Quinn because we heard him yelling at his wife in his own house? They'd string us up, Jamie!"

"We could call anonymously. No one would ever need to know it was us."

"Jeez, Jamie, you just don't get it, do you? The sheriff would need to know, because the last thing he wants is his community wondering who's the snitch who called the sheriff to intervene in the business of another man in his own house!"

"So we just walk away? Even though we know that Joe's going to hurt his wife and daughter, we just walk away?"

"Yes, we walk away. We don't really know what's going to happen. Joe could spout all of that and then go watch TV and pass out. We don't know, and truthfully, I don't want to know. Let's keep going."

"This is wrong, Bill, really wrong!"

"Hey, I didn't say that living in Kestrel Cove was always going to be warm and fuzzy! There are times—many times, actually—that living here is gut-wrenching. And this is one of them. You need to get used to it if you're going to stay here."

"No, I won't get used to it, Bill. I've got to do something!"

Jamie started back toward the house, and Bill Hand nearly tackled him. "Jamie, I can't let you do that. I know we should do something to help, but we can't. If they were fighting out in the parking lot of the store or on the wharf, then we could. But not inside his own house."

"This is bullshit! We need to do something now!"

Bill Hand got right in Jamie's face. "There are rules here in Kestrel Cove that cannot be broken, just like there are laws in nature that can't be broken. And this is one that sucks, but it is taken very, very seriously by the people of this community. What happens in a man's house cannot be stopped. We must walk away now. Let's go."

Jamie felt defeated. "Why would anyone talk to their family like that?"

Bill Hand seemed to think for a moment before speaking. "Jamie, everyone has skeletons in the closets of their life. Unfortunately, we just heard Joe's. Some people drink, some do drugs, some have affairs, some lie, some steal, and some cheat. If you go around picking the scabs off everyone's life, all you're gonna do is cause a lot of bleeding."

"Do you think he'll hurt them?"

Bill Hand shook his head. "Probably not. Joe knows the rules, too. Bruises and marks and hospital visits are there for the whole community to see and judge. Harsh words aren't. I think, once his verbal tirade is over, they'll be fine. Come on, let's go. We'll take the pipeline back to your campsite."

"Hey, Bill?"

"Yeah?"

"What if he does hurt them?"

Bill Hand pursed his lips and said simply, "He probably won't."

"But what if he does? How will we be able to live with ourselves knowing that we could've stopped it?"

Bill Hand looked at Jamie with emotionless eyes. "You know, Jamie, this world can be a very, very tough place sometimes, and all you can do is make your way through it. No one ever said it was always going to be palatable."

11

The next day, Jamie woke up to find a bag with his clean clothes in it outside the door of his tent. He hadn't heard Bill Hand drop them off, but he figured he'd done so during his predawn stroll. After their hasty goodbye the day before, Jamie had completely forgotten that his clothes were still in the washing machine at Bill's house. Now he opened the bag and took them out to smell their pleasant fragrance before getting dressed. Compared to Bill Hand's French pressed java, Jamie's cup of instant coffee tasted so horrible, he fought to drink it down. He ate a packaged donut, prepared his snacks for the day, and went up to the main road just in time to hear the approach of Joe's truck.

Joe and Jimmy both seemed hung over, but no worse for the wear. Jamie kept his voice even when he asked them about their weekends, but both men merely shrugged and talked about the TV shows they'd watched. When he told them that Bill Hand had showed him around the area, they acted as if he was giving them old news. He tried to emphasize that he'd been right outside Joe's house in the afternoon, but Joe didn't react. Jamie then pointed out that he'd still not officially met Joe's wife or daughter, and there was a cold, stony silence that lasted until they pulled into the wharf parking lot. As they got out of the truck, Joe said harshly, "Consider yourself lucky that you haven't met my old lady yet—she's a real fucking bitch."

The day was hot and cloudless. The relentless sun made working on the boat absolutely miserable. There was nowhere to hide from the solar intensity, and it bore down on them with unerring purity and sapped their strength. The work seemed harder in the heat, and the bait began to reek more than usual. When they'd hauled through all the gear, the three men were eager to get back to shore and find some relief in the shade. But as they shuffled past the office doorway, Drake came flying out and grabbed Joe's arm. "I need to talk to you."

Drake moved closer and spoke directly into Joe's ear. "I'm calling a meeting in the fish house tonight."

"Okay…"

"I think we need to talk some things out."

"Sounds good, Drake."

"We'll start it at seven o'clock sharp."

"We'll be there."

Drake hesitated and threw a glance at Jamie, who was gazing down at something on one of the pilings. "Don't bring the little puke. I don't want him there."

"He's my third man, Drake, he's got the right to come."

"I don't like him."

"You've made that quite clear, but he's my third man. If you're letting other sternmen come to the meeting, you've got to let him come, too."

Drake stepped back and put his hands on his hips. "Oh, maybe that's what I'll do then. Maybe I'll just make it a captains' meeting. Maybe I'll exclude *all* the sternmen, including your third man!"

"It's your fish house, Drake, and your meeting. Make it for whoever you want."

"I will."

"Okay, then."

The two men faced each other down, and finally Drake growled, "All right, the meeting'll be for everybody. You just keep that little fucker away from me. If he gets anywheres near me, I'm gonna punch him right in the fucking nose."

"Okay."

"Tell him to mind his manners at the meeting. He can come, but I don't wanna hear him speak. I don't want him drinking my booze, neither. And if there's any snacks, I don't want him mooching the food. Got it?"

"I'll talk to him, Drake. We'll see you at seven."

Joe went back to Jimmy and Jamie. "There's a meeting in the fish house at seven tonight."

"What's it about?" Jimmy asked as he exhaled a cloud of cigarette smoke.

"Dunno. Drake's got a hair across his ass about something."

"It ain't about us, is it?"

"Don't think so."

"Good. I hate walking into that kind of meeting."

Jamie seemed confused, so Joe turned to him and explained, "Whenever there's something important to talk about with the other captains, Drake calls for a meeting in the fish house. He's calling one for tonight. All the captains and their sternmen will be there. You should come, Jamie."

"But Drake won't let me in his fish house."

"He said you can come, but you can't talk, eat, or drink."

"Wait—he said that?"

"Yes, he did."

"I can't talk or eat or drink?"

"Right."

"What can I do?"

"Show up."

"And what else?"

"Listen."

"Listen?"

"This isn't a social event, Jamie. Drake's obviously got something important to say, and we've all got to listen to him. Most sternmen don't talk at these meetings, anyway."

"Okay. Anything else?"

"Yeah, don't get close to him. He says he'll kick your ass if you do."

"So that's it, huh? Can't talk, eat, or drink, and I've got to stay away from Drake in a shed that is smaller than my tent?"

"Yep."

"Maybe I shouldn't come."

"Suit yourself, college boy, but I think you should. You're part of this community now, and that means you go to these kind of things."

"What time did you say it starts?"

"You should definitely be there by seven. I'm sure guys will be there earlier, to eat and drink, but you can't do any of that, right?"

"Right. I'll bring my own snacks and drinks in my ol' pic-a-nic basket!"

Joe laughed at Jamie's comment and slapped him on the back. They walked toward the truck, but Jamie stopped halfway. "Hey, remember how I told you guys that Bill Hand showed me around yesterday?"

"Yeah…"

"Well, he showed me how to get from the wharf to my campsite. I think I'll start walking to and from work from now on, okay?"

"Sure, kid."

"I need to go up and talk to Jerry about my car anyway, then I'll head back to camp in time to eat and drink enough to get through this meeting tonight."

"Okay, see you later."

Later, after a dinner of Spaghetti-O's, Jamie was still unsure whether he should go to the meeting. He was definitely curious about what was going to go on, but he didn't want to give Drake any ammunition for further humiliation. As he sat on his rock and watched the sun sag in the western sky, the familiar lispy voice of Bill Hand came from behind him. "Hey, Jamie, are you ready for the meeting?"

Jamie shook his head. "I'm thinking about skipping it, Bill."

"Oh, I wouldn't do that if I were you. It's a big deal around here when Drake calls a meeting like this. We all know that someone's going to get the what-for tonight, and people are really buzzing about who it's gonna be."

"What if it's me?"

"Ah, don't worry, it isn't you. You're small fish compared to what he's going to tackle at tonight's meeting."

"I don't want to be stuck in such a small space with Drake breathing down my neck, waiting for me to screw up again."

"Hey, lots of guys'll be there. It's not like you're going to be standing around alone with Drake. I'll be there."

"You will?"

"Technically, I'm a fisherman of this cove. I have my lobstering license, but I don't fish, so Drake always invites me to these meetings. They're usually pretty entertaining!"

Jamie looked forlorn. "But Drake hates me."

"So what?"

"He told Joe I could come to the meeting, but I can't talk, eat, drink, or come too close to him or he'll beat the shit out of me!"

"Oh, come on, Jamie, don't be so dramatic! What did you do at those fraternity parties at Bridgewater College? Did you go over to the biggest and drunkest football player and get up in his grill and piss him off?"

"Of course not," scoffed Jamie. "I stayed far away from them and tried to make it through a night off their radar.

"So do the same thing with Drake."

"But the fish house is a lot smaller than a frat house, Bill. I don't see how I can avoid him there all night."

"Well, truth be told, his silly little list of do's and don'ts for you isn't any different from the other sternmen, except for the part about kicking your ass. Most sternmen are expected to be there to be seen, not heard. Just stay close to them, keep your mouth closed, and if Drake moves to the left, you move to the right."

Jamie stood up and tried to sound chipper when he said, "Well, I guess if we're gonna go to this meeting, we better get going, huh? I know the *worst* thing I could do would be to show up late."

As they neared the fish house, they could hear the sounds of a small party. All the lights inside were on and spilling out into the surrounding woods. Bill Hand stopped and turned to face Jamie. His eyes shimmered like embers. "Just remember, when we go inside, you head over toward the other sternmen."

"Okay."

"And don't expect Joe to talk to you. There are no real rules about all of this, but sternmen and captains don't usually mix or socialize at these things. It's not segregation, but an unspoken tradition of separa-tion. If you don't get more than a cursory nod from Joe, don't be hurt by that, okay?"

"Yeah, sure." Jamie was having strong second thoughts about staying at the meeting, but he kept following Bill Hand. They were greeted by several loud hellos and a few curt nods of acknowledgment at the door of the fish house. Jamie was about to go inside when some-one hollered, "Hey, college boy!"

It was Wiley. He was outside the fish house smoking a cigarette, and he motioned Jamie to come closer. "I was starting to wonder if

Drake was going to scare you out of coming tonight, but I'm glad to see he didn't."

"I wanted to see a fish house meeting."

"Harrumph! They ain't nothing too special. Although tonight could be pretty entertaining. Usually Drake just wants to tell us to double-check our measurements or make sure our skiffs don't sink, but there are rumors that he's got something heavier he wants to talk about tonight. Come on, let's go inside."

Wiley got so close to Jamie's face that he could smell the aroma of smoke and whiskey on his breath as he whispered, "When we get in there, keep an eye on Ed Simmons, Drake, and Wilma. They're playing out a scene that should be a hoot to watch. Ed's been drinking straight since he heard about this meeting, and he's higher than a fucking kite. Watch how he keeps forgetting his place and touches Wilma. I know it sounds twisted, but you don't try to flirt with your wife in the fish house of her lover. It's gonna get heated before too long. I'm telling ya, this shit's better than TV!"

Inside, Jamie saw Joe talking with Bobbie Schmidt, and Nigger Bob was talking with Matt Jays. The Vietnamese fisherman, Hai Hien Ngo, was standing alone, but he nodded almost warmly when he saw Jamie. There were several older men he didn't recognize, seated in a booth with large drinks in front of them. They were talking to each other, but when they spotted Jamie, their yellowed and watery eyes seemed to be searching for something.

A hearty and wheezing laugh caught Jamie's attention. Ed Simmons was standing in the corner talking with Vernon Quigley. Wilma was standing next to Ed, but her eyes were darting around the room. The expression on her face was so sour, Jamie wondered where the noxious aroma was. Ed swayed like a reed in the wind as he talked, and Jamie saw that Wiley's description was true—the man was quite drunk. For his part, Vernon Quigley seemed amused to be in the middle of it all, and he continued to feed Ed with chances to joke and talk, but kept his discerning eyes on Wilma's discomfort.

"Well, I'll tell ya, I wouldn't be half the man I am today if it weren't for this little lady right here!" Ed boomed out, slurring some of the words and attracting too much attention.

Then the man not only put his arm around his wife's shoulders, he deliberately brushed her breast with his right hand. Wilma instantly shoved him into the wall of the fish house hard enough to make him fall to the floor. All conversation in the fish house ceased, and everyone waited for the scene to unfold.

Wilma barked, "Ed, what the fuck are you trying to do?"

"Can't a husband touch his wife?"

"You're drunk and gross. I'd rather be touched by rotting bait than by you!"

Ed Simmons stared up at Wilma and shook his head. He started to struggle to get up, but his wife stood over him, feet apart and fists clenched, as if she was posturing for a fistfight. Meanwhile, across the room, Drake looked like a dog with its hackles up. He took a few steps forward to intervene, but halted when he saw that Wilma had things in hand.

"Wilma, you're my goddamn wife!" the man bellowed pathetically.

"In title only, Ed, in title only."

Ed Simmons clawed at the floor to get enough traction to stand up. When he was finally on his feet, he spoke in a harsh and despondent rasp. "Actually, Wilma, the title of *wife* ain't the way you're known around these parts. Usually I just hear people refer to you as *that whore*."

"I'd rather be called a whore any day than be touched by you, Ed Simmons."

He glanced around the room with an embarrassed look, then nearly whispered, "Isn't it a wonderful thing when we reach our goals, Wilma?"

She turned and stormed out of the fish house. The men near the door nearly tripped over themselves to get out of her way. The assembled fishermen watched her leave, then all heads turned back toward Ed Simmons, who was still standing against the wall. He swayed a little and looked down at the floor. He reached over to the bench nearest him, grabbed his plastic cup, and took a healthy drink from it. After he wiped his mouth with his sleeve, he muttered, "Ah, women—you can't live with 'em, you can't live without 'em." His cackle was like listening to sandpaper on wood, and the men in the fish house remained silent.

It was Vernon Quigley who suddenly broke the silence with, "Come on, Drake, now that the goddamn soap opera's over, let's get this meeting going and done with. I've got a lot of shit to do tonight!"

Drake's eyes tightened into slits of anger. He took a sip of his drink and licked his lips. Vernon Quigley shrugged, then slowly made his way toward the workbench that had the bottles of alcohol on it. He poured himself a big slug of rum as he kept a wary eye on Drake.

"Huh," Drake mumbled, glancing quickly over his audience. "All right, let's get this meeting going, then. There's not too much on the agenda—just two things that need to be talked over."

The men nodded respectfully. Drake continued, "As Vernon so aptly said, we all have a lot of shit to do, so I'll make this a quick one. Speaking of shit, Ed, how about you quit shitting on my goddamn wharf!"

The room erupted into laughter, but it was as brittle and fragile as a dried leaf. Ed Simmons looked up from his drink with a grin that could have etched glass. "Huh, Drake, that's an interesting accusation to make at such a public forum without a shred of proof. It's not like that rat-trap of a wharf's got any cameras to catch the person who's doing that. And you ain't got no witnesses, neither."

Ed Simmons's eyes scanned the group of men in the fish house as though trying to increase the drama of the situation. But when the old man's eyes locked onto his, Jamie knew he was sending a message straight to him, and the hair on his arms stood up from the apparent threat. Then a speckle of humor flew across Ed's eyes, and Jamie understood that it had been more like the line from the wedding ceremony—"Speak now or forever hold thy peace." When Jamie answered by smiling back, the old man grinned broadly and looked back at Drake.

"I don't care whether I've got a witness or not, Ed, I know it's you. Stop shitting on my wharf, it's private property!"

"Seems to me, Drake, that everyone in this room knows 'private property' means something that belongs to another man and shouldn't get fucked around with, right?"

Ed Simmons's retort was as bold as Drake's initial accusation, and the men in the fish house braced for a real fight. Several of them cleared their throats, but most remained silent and stared at the combatants.

Drake drew himself up to his full height. "I don't give a flying fuck about the definitions, Ed, I just want you to stop shitting on my wharf."

"Our friend *up there* sees everything, doesn't He?" Ed Simmons said, looking up toward the ceiling. "Do you ever worry about Him watching you two, Drake? Do you ever worry about being judged by Him?"

"Aw, Ed, you're completely drunk. You're sputtering and rambling like a crazy man tonight! What I'm worried about is what the Health Department might think if they found out that the lobsters we ship around the globe are coming from a place that's covered in human shit!" The men in the fish house giggled at this. "And truth be told, I'm sick and tired of stepping in your poop piles on my goddamn wharf! It's gross, and you need to stop!"

"We've all got our problems, right, Drake?" Ed Simmons said to the floor.

"Harrumph!" Drake snarled.

"Actually, I think rubber may be the solution to all your problems," Ed Simmons said with an indifferent shrug.

"Oh, really?" Drake said sarcastically.

"Yep, if I was you, I'd start wearing rubber boots to protect yourself from the shit on the wharf. And I'd also put rubbers on other parts of your body to protect yourself down there, too. Ya sure don't want it to burn when you gotta pee, right?"

The two men glared at each other, and even Jamie understood the seriousness of the showdown. Everyone was transfixed with a mixture of curiosity and disgust; this exchange between Drake and Ed Simmons was likely to have earth-shaking impacts.

Drake looked around at all the faces staring back at him, and, as he waved the other man off, he said brusquely, "You're just drunk, Ed. Stop doing what you're doing on my wharf!"

"I'm just drunk," echoed Ed Simmons as his knees buckled and his body sagged onto the bench. "I'm always just drunk, right?"

"Come on, Ed, just stop shitting on my wharf," Drake said, nearly pleading.

"Then just stop doing what you're doing with my wife," Ed Simmons mumbled into his drink.

"Can we finally get onto some goddamn fishing business tonight?" Vernon Quigley shouted.

Drake's head snapped up to stare fiercely at Vernon, but he didn't speak right away. When he did, there was a hint of a snake's hiss in his voice. "Oh, ye*sss*, let's get on with some fishing busine*ssss*, *ss*hall we?"

Someone in the fish house whistled softly but audibly. The fight between Ed Simmons and Drake had only been the first card in a prize fight, and it was clear that Drake was now primed and ready for the next battle. He took a long, deliberate drink from his cup. "It's come to my attention—*again*—that we've got a fisherman in this cove who continues to break the rules. I've been made aware that one of us is bleaching eggers!"

Drake stopped to let the news sink in. Someone in the group sucked in air and others shook their heads and avoided making eye contact. Vernon Quigley froze with his drink halfway to his mouth and stared angrily around.

Jamie elbowed Wiley gently and whispered, "What's happening, Wiley?"

Wiley whispered back, "Someone's been catching female lobsters that still got their eggs on 'em, and they've been using bleach to make 'em drop those eggs. It's not only really illegal, it's totally a fucking lowlife thing to do!"

Jamie nodded his understanding, and Drake picked up where he'd left off.

"I was hoping this individual would stop without being brought into the public light, but I've heard that it keeps happening. I've called this meeting tonight because I need to make it clear to that person that this illegal and unethical activity will stop. And it will stop *right now*!"

Jamie watched as most of the fishermen fidgeted and stared down at their feet. Vernon Quigley, on the other hand, was looking around with smoldering eyes. Jamie craned his neck to see what Joe was doing, so he didn't see the beer bottle flying through the air toward the sternmen. The next thing he knew, a bottle smashed against the wall right near where he was standing, showering his hair and shoulders with broken glass and beer.

"You goddamn snitch!" Vernon Quigley bellowed. He pointed his finger at the group of sternmen. "I'm gonna come over there and kick your scrawny ass!"

Jamie, who was swiping his hair to get the shards of glass out of it, looked up and saw Vernon Quigley pointing in his direction, and he shook his head a little and flinched.

"It weren't me, Vern! I swear I didn't tell nobody!" a voice shot out behind Jamie. It belonged to Quigley's sternman, Jay Reynolds. Jamie hadn't noticed him at all before, but now he realized that he'd been standing right behind him the entire time.

"No, Vernon, it wasn't him who told me," Drake sputtered. He seemed shocked that Vernon Quigley had reacted the way he had, almost giving himself away. "Another person came to talk to me."

Vernon Quigley ignored Drake and continued to glare at Jay. He shook his head violently. "I've had nothing but trouble since hiring you, you cocksucker! Now, I'm gonna do what I should've done a long time ago!"

The big fisherman moved with surprising agility toward his cringing sternman. In an instinctive and mildly protective move, Jamie stepped into his path. When Vernon Quigley bowled over him and sent him sprawling to the floor, everyone started yelling at once. Instructions, warnings, and epithets flew as pandemonium filled the fish house.

Jamie would try to remember the next events with more clarity later, but he'd be unable to do so. In the movies, fight scenes were always slowed down and choreographed carefully to catch each and every move. But now, as Vernon Quigley swept in, Jamie was surprised by the rawness, the speed, and the lack of grace of the attack. All he knew was that, as he struggled to get back to his feet, he heard two punches hit someone's midsection like a rug being beaten, followed by the sharper sound of a snapping branch. Then there was the unmistakable sound of a breaking bottle. The mayhem was a blur that was suddenly pierced by a booming voice shouting, "Wiley, don't!"

Regaining his feet, Jamie saw Jay Reynolds out cold on the floor and Vernon Quigley down on one knee with Wiley holding a broken bottle against his neck. Blood dripped from a cut on Vernon's cheek, and his eyes swam in their sockets.

Bobbie Schmidt's calm voice carried over the chaos as he took a step closer. "Okay, Wiley, it's over now. Just put the bottle down, okay? Nobody else needs to get hurt tonight."

Wiley's eyes still blazed with anger. "Hey, Bobbie, is it fair that this fucking scumbag thinks he can do whatever the hell he wants and get away with it? Bleach eggers without getting in trouble, throw bottles at us sternmen, and then come over and attack us without facing the consequences? Well, I say he can't do any of that shit without paying for it. And I say that payment should happen right here and right now!"

"But Wiley, you've made him pay already. You tattooed him right on the cheek there, and I can see he felt that punch, buddy, so why don't you just put down the bottle."

Bobbie Schmidt's voice was calm and friendly, but there was enough of a hint of fear in it that Jamie understood that Vernon Quigley's life was in jeopardy.

"Not so high and mighty now, huh, Mr. Bigshot?" Wiley sneered down at Vernon.

Bobbie Schmidt continued in the same calm voice, "That's right, Wiley, you showed Vern that he can't do this kind of shit at a fish house meeting. I'm sure that, once he gets his bearings back, he'll apologize to you and all the sternmen for what he's done tonight. Now come on, Wiley, back down and let him go!"

Jamie shuddered when he saw that the jagged edge of the broken bottle had nicked the skin on Vernon Quigley's neck and opened an incidental incision that was now trickling blood. When he looked at Wiley's cold obsidian eyes, he saw no fear and no indecision. The boy was completely calm as he held another person's life in the balance, and Jamie involuntarily shook his head in sadness over yet another example of humanity's seemingly unlimited cruelty.

Wiley noticed and said, "What was that, college boy?"

"Nothing!"

"Naw, I saw you! You just shook your head at me. Why'd you do that?"

Jamie quickly surveyed the room for support, but all he saw were the other fishermen clearly using body English to indicate that he should proceed with caution. He cleared his throat. "Well, Wiley, I shook my head because I was just realizing how many times this very scenario has happened throughout human history, that's all."

Wiley smirked and his eyes lit up. "Human history? Ah, that's right, college boy, I've heard that you like history. I know, let's play a history game to decide how this—what did you just call it?—oh, yeah, *scenario* ends. Let's pretend that we're gladiators in that big stadium in ancient Rome, what was it called?"

"The Colosseum."

"Yeah, right, the Colosseum. I'm going to play the famous gladiator, Wilius Maximus, and I've just beaten the shit out of my opponent. And you're going to play the emperor who gets to decide whether this worthless scumbag lives or dies."

The men in the fish house collectively stiffened. Almost everyone present agreed that Vernon Quigley needed a royal ass-kicking, but few men wanted to see his throat slashed. And they all knew it would only take a wrong comment for Wiley to do that right now. And, in their own ways, they pitied the college boy for being in such an unwinnable situation.

"Constantine."

"What did you just say, college boy?" Wiley snarled.

"I want to be Emperor Constantine."

"I don't give a flying fuck if you want to be Dick Clark, I'm the fucking gladiator and you're the goddamn emperor. You've got to decide this man's fate."

"I want to be Emperor Constantine," Jamie repeated.

There was a collective groan from the men in the fish house, and Wiley actually pulled the jagged edge of the bottle away from Vernon Quigley's neck. "What the hell, college boy? I already said I don't give two shits about which emperor you are, as long as you're the motherfucking emperor and you give me a thumbs-up or thumbs-down to decide this man's fate."

Jamie watched Wiley put the bottle back on Vernon Quigley's neck and continued, "But it's important to *me*, Wiley. I will only play this game if I'm Emperor Constantine."

Suddenly Drake cursed loudly, "Jesus H. Christ, you little prick! You're screwing this all up! You're gonna get someone killed here tonight!" He paused for breath, then said, "Wiley, for the sake of everybody here, cut this shit out!"

"Shut up, Drake! You mind your own business, you dried up old goat! Just shut the hell up! This is between me and Vernon…and the college boy!"

Drake opened his mouth to speak again, but closed it and took a step back when he realized Wiley was beyond reason. He shook his head and stared at Jamie with contempt.

Wiley said, "Okay, college boy, you can be Emperor Constant—"

"Emperor Constantine."

"Right, Constantine," Wiley said with a malicious grin. "Okay, college boy, you're him. Now give me the thumbs-up or thumbs-down on Vern, here."

In his best royal voice, Jamie said, "I cannot do that, Wilius Maximus."

There was a collective gasp, then dead silence settled on the fish house.

Wiley snorted, "What the hell did you just say?"

"I said, I cannot do that, Wilius Maximus. You see, Emperor Constantine was the Roman emperor who converted to Christianity and outlawed the barbaric death matches somewhere around 325 AD. So, if I am Emperor Constantine, and you just said that I am, then I have to remind you that you're better than this, Wilius Maximus. You have felled your opponent, so now it is time to go out and get a drink or get laid. There will be no killing here tonight. You must do the right thing here."

"But this fucking scumbag attacked us!"

"Yes, he sure did. He threw a bottle, knocked me on my ass, and then beat the snot out of his sternman. But then you clocked him and he's done now. You've won and he's lost. We're all looking at him, beaten, and he's pathetic. It's over—Drake got to get his message across about the eggers, and now the man's been verbally and physically humiliated in front of everybody. That's enough, right?"

"I'm not so sure about that," Wiley retorted, poking Vernon Quigley's neck with the broken bottle.

"It is. And I say that it is."

"Oh, really?"

"If I'm Emperor Constantine and you're the gladiator, Wilius Maximus, then you *have to* do what I say, and my decree is for you to let him go and have a drink with me outside."

Wiley's face relaxed and he chuckled. "Hey, kid, you just might be as fucking crazy as I've heard."

"Yeah? Well, Wiley, you're definitely as crazy a motherfucker as *I've* heard. So how about us two crazies having a drink outside?"

Wiley waggled his finger at Jamie. "That was pretty fucking clever, choosing Emperor Constantine, college boy. Very, very clever! But don't think you'll fool me the next time we're in this kinda situation, okay?"

Jamie spoke dramatically with his arms widespread. "Wiley, do you really honestly think that you and I will ever be in this kind of situation again?"

Wiley snorted with amusement. "Eh, you never know, college boy. But I do know for certain that ol' Vern ain't gonna ever attack me again, right Vern?"

"Right," Vernon Quigley mumbled.

"Well, if my emperor says to let you go, I guess I've got to let you go."

Wiley smiled at Jamie, and the tension in the room began to dissipate. A few of the men even started to turn their grimaces into tentative grins and drink from their cups again. But then Wiley, in a move that looked like he was releasing Vernon, suddenly had a small bloody chunk of flesh between his fingers. Jamie's head spun around with the resulting outcry, and he saw that Wiley had sliced Vernon's earlobe off. The boy had a cruel smile on his face as he bent over to say, "But I never want you to forget, Vern, that you should never, *ever* fuck with me or any of us sternmen again! Got it?"

Some of the men pushed past Jamie to get to the wounded fisherman. Jamie was frozen with shock at what Wiley had done. He could see the bloody piece of flesh, the drops of blood on the floor, and Vernon Quigley being rushed out of the fish house and into the dark night. Outside, a truck started up and raced out of the parking lot. The unconscious Jay Reynolds was then peeled off the floor and helped out of the fish house. By then, some of the men had gathered around Wiley, who flashed Jamie a defiant grin. Finally Drake boomed out, "Get that crazy sonofabitch out of my goddamn fish house!"

Nobody dared to touch Wiley at this point, so the men surrounding him just gestured toward the exit. He waved and headed for the door. When he got there, he turned toward Jamie and chortled, "See ya later, Emperor Constantine. I guess we'll have to have that drink together some other time."

Drake had gone over to the area where Vernon had been sliced, and as the remaining fishermen talked excitedly about what had just happened, he shook his head silently. Jamie looked over and felt momentarily sorry for him. The whole meeting had been nothing but one big fiasco, from the marital drama of Ed and Wilma Simmons to the embarrassing debate with Ed about him pooping on the wharf to the bloody ending with Vernon and Wiley. Even Jamie's having some success in talking Wiley down must have caused Drake some chagrin. In the end, however, Drake knew that not only had his warning to Vernon Quigley about bleaching eggers been diffused to the point of being ineffective, his attempt to exert his authority over his cove had been completely eclipsed by the silly fight and the bloody conclusion. Drake pointed at the disaster on the floor and rumbled, "Who in the hell is going to clean up this damn mess?"

Jamie skirted the bunched-up men and left the fish house unnoticed. When he got to the shoreline, the reflection of the alabaster full moon shimmering on the waves created the illusion that they were covered in bejeweled scales from a magical fish. He stopped and gazed out at the scene. There were no longer any sounds other than the soft and sensual winds brushing through the tops of the trees and the murmur of the ocean caressing the rocks. The peacefulness here was a stark contrast to the chaos of the fish house fight, and Jamie closed his eyes and enjoyed the feeling of being alone.

"Pretty damn beautiful, huh?"

The lisping voice came out of the darkness and startled Jamie so badly that he spun and fell down on his rump.

Bill Hand said softly, "Jesus, Jamie, I didn't mean to startle you." He reached down and helped him stand up.

Jamie laughed, "Oh, don't worry, Bill, this is just the perfect ending to a totally crazy day."

"You do know that not all fish house meetings are quite as dramatic as tonight's, right? Usually, it's like going to a cheap bar. Not much serious business ever takes place, only serious drinking. Tonight…well, you were there."

"Unfortunately," Jamie warbled as he brushed the forest duff off his pants.

"Hey, you won some major points at that meeting tonight. Showing up, stepping in front of the charging Vernon, and the way you handled that situation with Wiley—it was a real trifecta for getting respect from that group. Hell, before he cut off part of Vernon's ear, you had actually bested Wiley. That little historical role-playing trick was brilliant. He not only seemed impressed, I'd even say that you've got a friend in him now, and that'll come in handy sometime. And although I know that it's not your main goal in life, I think you may have even impressed Drake a little tonight."

"Sure, Bill, we're best friends now. He's coming over later to have a toenail-painting party with me in my tent!"

"No, seriously, Jamie, you'll notice a difference in the way that people'll treat you in the future."

"Yeah, right. I'm sure I'll be the headlines tomorrow morning."

"Actually," Bill Hand chuckled, "by tomorrow, it'll be old news."

"What?"

"The phone lines are probably filled with the details of tonight's meeting as we speak. The fight at the fish house and the way you handled yourself negotiating with crazy Wiley and outfoxing him—that's all the buzz of the community right now. Tomorrow morning, I'm sure Mrs. Viceroy's third drunk-driving charge or the length of Joshua Chamber's dick will be the headlines again. But for now, it's all about you, Wiley, and Vernon, I guarantee you."

"My fifteen minutes of fame?"

"Hey, Jamie, don't discount what happened tonight. In a small town like this one, it's important to make connections with the people. You've seen what happens when you make enemies, even if unwittingly. Tonight, you definitely earned a spot of respect in this community, and that's a very important thing, believe me."

"I just want to go to bed, Bill."

"Yep, I think we're all ready for a good sleep after that one," Bill Hand said with another wry chuckle. "Come on, I'll walk you back to your Great Palace, Emperor Constantine."

12

The dream was grainy like an old black-and-white newsreel. It came in a series of amorphous and befuddling scenes, but Jamie could see himself in a packed courthouse. He was sitting at the defendant's table wearing padded headphones. It did not take his subconscious long to figure out that the scene was straight from the Nuremberg war trials of 1946. But then, as dreams are wont to do, fuzzy objects in the periphery came into sharper focus, and Jamie could see that he was the only human in the courtroom. The defense lawyer, the prosecutor, the judge, members of the jury, and the audience were all giant lobsters. Their onyx eyes were glaring at him as they burbled from armored mouths. Jamie could hear what they were saying translated in his headphones.

A sad female lobster was on the stand. When the prosecutor asked her who had killed her father and mother, she pointed her crusher claw directly at Jamie. The gasps of the audience were deafening in the headphones. Another witness came forward and implicated Jamie as "the Butcher," a notorious member of a death squad that was killing innocent lobsters. The flow of witnesses was nonstop, and Jamie squirmed in his chair as the tension in the courtroom rose with each testimony. One of the witnesses was an egg-laden female who slumped in the witness stand with her caviar-like eggs mounded out in front of her like a pillow. She described how Jamie was the one who was getting ready to put her into the chamber with the other condemned lobsters, but another human with a wounded claw had intervened and freed her and her unborn babies. Before she left the stand, she defiantly pointed her claw at Jamie and shrieked, "Baby-killer!"

The stream of witness was so unceasing, the dream actually sped up to fit them all in like time-lapse photography. Each witness decried

Jamie's murderous guilt before vacating the stand. On and on it went, and the crowd glared at him with their beady little black eyes, the hate coming off of their carapaces with microwave-like intensity. Jamie turned away from the repeated chant of "Murderer!" from the witness stand.

Suddenly the judge stood and announced that he'd heard enough. With his huge crusher claw poised, he glowered at Jamie. "You, human, and your death squad have condemned nearly five hundred lobsters a day to death for more than thirty days. These actions have resulted in the deaths of over fifteen thousand lobsters!"

The courtroom shrieked with disbelief, and the judge banged the gavel several times to silence the angry outbursts. Jamie frantically yelled, "Your honor, I'm innocent! I was only doing my job!"

The judge angrily silenced him by announcing that he was ready to pass sentence. He slowly lifted both claws into the air and addressed everyone in the courtroom. "Lobstercide is a reprehensible crime against nature, and that crime will continue endlessly and unchecked as long as we allow the perpetrators of this crime to live. The entrapment, torture, and death of innocent lobsters can no longer be tolerated, and the only way to implement this change is to punish each and every one involved in this activity. Hopefully, when they see that our responses are severe but just, the humans will choose not to perpetuate these acts of murder upon our species."

The judge paused. There was a silence that ached in the courtroom. Jamie leaned forward as the judge pointed at him. "Jamie Kurtz, I find you guilty of lobstercide. I deem your sentence to reflect the seriousness of the heinous acts you have perpetrated upon our innocent species. Therefore, it is my decree that you should be put to death by boiling at six o'clock tomorrow night."

With this, the judge stood up, as did everyone in the courtroom, and he left through a side door. The bailiffs grabbed Jamie's wrists with their claws and began leading him out through cheers from most of the courtroom. In the midst of the cheering, Jamie could also hear the grumblings of those lobsters who were against capital punishment. It was their belief that the perpetrators of these crimes should be stuffed into a lobster trap for the remainder of their lives. The courtroom became a whirl of claws and steely feelers as Jamie was escorted out of it.

The dream fast-forwarded to him standing on a platform in front of an audience of lobsters in a large space that resembled an empty airplane hangar. A pair of metallic lobster claws came down from the ceiling and grabbed Jamie by the ropes that bound him. He was lifted into the air and swung out over the side of the platform. Below him, on the floor of the hangar, was a huge glass vat full of vigorously boiling water. Jamie screamed. The judge came out of the group of the lobsters and pointed up at him. "Jamie Kurtz, do you have any last words before you are boiled to death?"

Jamie started pleading. He mentioned his parents and his ability to make the world a better place, and he gave historical examples of murderous mobs that had exhibited great moments of mercy to the condemned throughout history. The judge waved him off like he was trying to smash a piñata with his claws, but Jamie continued talking a blue streak. The judge signaled to the lobsters in the control booth overhead, and the metal claws opened. Jamie screamed as he began to fall and the warmth of the steam from the water started to scald his skin. As his body hit the water, the dream went dark.

Jamie awoke in a sweat. His soaked sleeping bag was wrapped around him like a burrito. He shed it and frantically unzipped the tent to get outside. He looked up at the sky to catch his breath, and up above in the cloudless and moonless heavens, countless stars twinkled brightly. He was tired enough to need more sleep, and the nightmare, albeit a terrible and shocking one, was just a dream. He got back into his sleeping bag and tried not to think about it anymore. After a moment or two of restlessness, he drifted back to sleep.

The next morning started as regularly and innocently as any other day. He walked down to the wharf to meet the guys. Joe seemed especially motivated to get through their gear as quickly as possible, and, during the morning hauling, Jamie struggled to keep up. The hauler droned on endlessly as the traps came up, and he felt overwhelmed by the number of keepers that needed to be banded and the unending bait bags that needed to be filled.

Then it happened. He looked at the lobsters on the bait table and suddenly saw them as bedraggled concentration-camp victims staring back at him. He shook his head to chase away the visions, and for a while, this worked. But when he gazed into the lobster tank, he saw nothing but a railroad car full of victims of the Holocaust. He held tight to the table, but the dream and all of its emotions and fears came crashing over him like a warm wave, and Jamie felt himself lose his grip and begin to fall. Everything went black.

"Hey, kid, come on!" Jimmy's voice boomed through the darkness.

"Jamie, sniff this!" Joe barked.

He heard a snapping sound, then the ammonia seeped into his sinuses and cracked open the darkness like an eggshell. Joe and Jimmy were bent over him, their faces tight with concern.

"Whoa, what happened?" Jamie asked in a befuddled voice. He was lying on the deck of the boat looking up at the blue sky.

"You passed out," Joe said matter-of-factly.

"You ain't pregnant are ya, college boy?" Jimmy teased.

"Aw, shut up, Jimmy," Joe said with annoyance.

"Or did you tie one on last night?" Jimmy asked, ignoring Joe. "I sometimes get a little woozy after I overdo it."

"You? Overdo it with the booze?" Joe asked with mock surprise.

"Oh, fuck you!"

"Whoa, that was weird," Jamie said as he started to stand up.

"Hey, why don't you stay sitting for a while," Joe cautioned. "I don't want you puking on the deck of my boat!"

"Naw, I'm fine, really. Huh, that was pretty weird," Jamie said as he rubbed his head.

Jimmy shrugged. "You know, women and girls used to faint all the time back in the early nineteenth century. People used to call it 'the vapors,' and men used it as evidence that women were the weaker sex. It wasn't until recent times that it was understood that the real reason behind all those women passing out back then was the incredibly tight corsets they were forced to wear. It turns out that it had nothing to do with weakness, but rather a forced suffocation from their clothing. Some feminists mark that as the birthplace of modern-day chauvinism."

Joe and Jamie looked at Jimmy with their mouths open. Finally Joe asked hopefully, "*The View?*"

"History Channel. Why the fuck would you ever think I was watching a woman's show?"

"Well, you did watch the Health Channel about relationships!" Jamie reminded him.

Joe laughed, but Jimmy said, "Hey, smartass, if you're ready to start giving me shit, you're ready to get back to work again."

Jamie stood up and went back to the baiting table. Joe and Jimmy kept their eyes on him, but he seemed to be fine. He completed his tasks all afternoon without any problems, but he was greatly unnerved by all that had happened to him. First the dream, then the visions, and finally, the passing out on the deck—clearly, something was deeply troubling him. He decided to ask Joe and Jimmy about it during the lunch break, but he regretted doing so as soon as he heard himself ask, "Do you guys ever think that what we're doing out here is evil?"

Joe and Jimmy shot confused looks at him. Jimmy was smoking a cigarette, and he took several long drags from it before talking. "What? Smoking?"

"No," Jamie said, shaking his head, "what we do on the boat."

"You mean talking about niggers on television and stuff?" Jimmy questioned again.

"Aw, never mind."

"Naw, college boy, what the hell are you talking about?" Jimmy asked, blowing smoke into the air.

"Jamie, you don't mean…lobstering, do you?" Joe asked, stiffening as he said it.

"Yeah."

Joe said, "No, I don't think lobstering is evil."

"But we kill so many of them. Think about it—each boat in the cove probably kills five hundred lobsters every single day! Think about how many that is in a week or a month. We kill tens of thousands of them!"

"Whoa, I don't kill nothing," Jimmy replied defiantly. "I catch 'em, but that's because other people want to eat them. The real killers are all those people who are ordering lobster dinners!"

"Yeah, but we're the ones who go out and catch them. Ultimately, we send them to their deaths!"

"Hey, wait a goddamn minute!" Joe roared. "I cannot fucking believe you're equating us to killers! We're lobstermen, so we catch lobsters. There ain't nothing evil or bad about that. Lobsters are nothing more than bugs, Jamie. It's not like we're slaughtering whales or elephants out here—though I've always wanted to do that! The idea of throwing a harpoon into the back of a whale and doing the Nantucket Sleighride, or taking a really big elephant gun and shooting a bull elephant between the eyes on the savannas of Africa—now that would be fucking cool! But lobstering—it's only a few steps up the rungs from bug exterminator. You don't shed tears for the cockroaches of the world that are being exterminated, do you?"

Jamie shook his head. "Never mind. I'm sorry I brought it up. I've just been having some weird dreams lately, that's all."

Jimmy held up his index finger and said, "Maybe you're like Rasputin. He had dreams and visions. He was the powerful confidant of the royal family of Russia, then the Tsar couldn't kill—"

"Please shut up, Jimmy!" Joe commanded. "I don't feel like one of your meandering regurgitations of information from a TV show right now."

"Jeez, sorry, Joe!

"And Jamie, just what the hell are you talking about?"

"I wish I knew, Joe. Last night I had a dream that I was on trial for murdering all these lobsters. They dropped me in boiling water! It was so real! Then today I was thinking about that dream and I started seeing the Jews from concentration camps every time I looked at the lobsters we've caught. I think that's what made me pass out."

Joe's confused expression began to twist with anger. He opened his mouth, but then shut it when nothing came out. Jimmy closely watched his reaction, but did not say anything. Finally, Joe took off his baseball cap and rubbed his face and head with it. He put his hat back into place, opened his mouth, and said tightly, "Are you really equating lobsters with the Jews from the concentration camps?"

"Yes."

"So, you're trying to tell me that you see a connection between the Ultimate Solution of Hitler and lobstering? Do you really think that the SS troops, the trains, the concentration camps, the gassings, and the ovens that the Nazis used have anything to do with what we do on this boat?" Joe's voice was even and low, but Jamie sensed there was some powerful and explosive force being held back. The words had come out of his mouth like the steam from old radiators.

"Well, we do catch hundreds of lobsters each day, transport them to holding tanks, where they are concentrated until it is their time to die. The judge lobster in my dream actually called it 'lobstercide.'"

"*Lobstercide?*" Joe exploded. "For the love of Pete! Jamie, you gotta be kidding me!"

"Oh, kinda like genocide. I see," said Jimmy. "That kinda makes sense."

"Don't you encourage him!" Joe barked. Then he leaned in toward Jamie and hissed, "We catch lobsters so people can eat them. We're no different than farmers or ranchers—we provide food for people to eat, for God's sake! We're not performing ethnic cleansing or murdering innocent people out here! We're not doing anything wrong!"

"I know, I know! But these dreams and visions have been so disturbing! I'll get over it, I swear."

"Yeah, you better," muttered Joe.

"Maybe you need to talk to somebody about it," Jimmy offered tentatively.

"Who does he need to talk to, Jimmy? A goddamn shrink?"

"I dunno, Joe. Sometimes when I'm having problems, it helps to talk to somebody. Usually it's with Linda. But sometimes I need a person with more knowledge or experience on the subject at hand than her. Sometimes just hearing that somebody else went through what I've been going through is enough. Most of the time, they have something to say that clears it all up for me."

Joe crossed his arms defensively and said, "So who the hell would Jamie talk to to help him get over this? Should he confess to a goddamn priest?"

"I was thinking more of a rabbi," Jimmy said quietly.

"*What?*"

"Well, Jamie said he's been seeing a connection between the victims of the Holocaust and lobsters. Maybe he needs to talk to a Jew. You and I aren't Jews, so how can we reassure him that there's no connection between lobstering and what happened to the Jews with the Nazis?"

"There is *no* goddamn connection between lobstering and the Nazis!" Joe howled.

Jimmy continued with a shrug, "Maybe a rabbi could say something to help him get over his concerns."

Jamie broke into the argument excitedly. "Hey, Jimmy, that's not a bad idea. I hadn't thought about that. Yeah, maybe talking with a rabbi could help me get over this!"

Joe looked at Jamie first, then shifted his shocked expression to Jimmy. Finally, he erupted. "Am I the only sane motherfucker on this entire goddamn boat? Have the two of you finally gone batshit crazy? This is the stupidest conversation I've ever had in my life! Lobsters are bugs and we catch them so other people can eat them. If you can't deal with what we do, then you two should just go get new jobs."

"No, Joe, I think Jimmy's onto something here. If I could talk to a rabbi, maybe I could absolve myself. Just talking with someone invested in the Jewish situation, like a rabbi, will clear everything up for me."

Joe's eyes opened wide. "And where are you going to find a goddamn rabbi in Maine? I bet I could count the Jews in this whole state on the fingers of my working hand. Kestrel Cove sure as shit doesn't have a synagogue. I doubt that Brementon even has one. Even if you go through with this asinine plan of talking to a rabbi, where are you going to find a goddamn rabbi to talk to?"

"Portland," Jimmy replied evenly. "It's the biggest city in Maine. Every time I go down there, I see all them Africans and Arabs walking around the streets like they own them. I bet they've got a Jew or two down there. I mean, in a big city like that, you can find almost any type of people."

"Hey, I bet you're right, Jimmy. I'm sure there's gotta be a synagogue in Portland!" Jamie said.

"Sure," Jimmy nodded, "you could go down there and talk to a rabbi about all this stuff and feel better about being out here murdering all these lobsters!"

"Hello-o-o-o," Joe howled, "we're right in the middle of our summer fishing season here. When do you propose to go on this ridiculous trip? We're fishing every day except Sunday, and I'd bet that a rabbi won't be in then."

"Actually, I'll go tomorrow."

"Tomorrow? Tomorrow's Thursday, Jamie. You ain't going to Portland tomorrow 'cause we're fishing tomorrow. We've got some more lobsters to murder!" Joe sneered.

"But, Joe, you've been telling me all this week that we're not fishing tomorrow because you're gonna beach the boat and replace the zincs, clean the bottom, and inspect the propeller. Remember?"

"That's right, Joe, you did say we're doing that tomorrow! The boat's gonna be out of the water almost all damn day. We don't need him—me and you can do all that by ourselves. He *could* go to Portland and talk to a rabbi tomorrow."

"Oh, yeah, that's true, I did say that," Joe admitted, "but how the hell are you gonna get down to Portland, Jamie? Your car's still in the shop, right?"

"Jimmy, can I borrow one of your cars?"

"Sorry, dude, but Linda'll need the car to get to work after she drops me off at Joe's in the morning."

Jamie turned to Joe, who waved his left arm around like he was spreading incense. "No fucking way! I don't lend my cars out to nobody. Especially to go down to Portland on a ridiculous mission like this one!"

"Well, you could take the Green Meanie," Jimmy offered.

"The Green Meanie?" said Jamie.

"Yeah, that's right, he could do that! Why don't you tell him to try swimming there, instead," Joe said with a cackle.

"Hey, it's cheap transportation, Joe, and he could get all the way to Portland and back again in one day. He could find a rabbi, talk to him, then be home for dinner!"

"What's the Green Meanie?" Jamie asked again.

"It's a bus run by a nonprofit agency called the Coastal Cultural Center. They started the bus service so people around here would have a way to commute to and from Portland for their jobs," Jimmy explained.

Joe said, "Oh, yeah, the Coastal Cultural Center are a bunch of heroes! All they want to do is save our kind. You know—us mentally slow coastal and island residents."

Jimmy shook his head. "Hey, come on, Joe, they just try to help out people living on the coast!"

"They stick their nose into things that don't concern them. Did you know they approached me after the accident? They came right to my house to offer me some kind of grant to retrain me to work a job I could do with one hand. Can you believe that shit? I have no goddamn idea how they heard about my accident or found out where I live, but they had the gall to come to my home and say that, with my new disability, there were actually more openings and opportunities for me. I told them I had something in the basement I wanted to show them. Went down and got my shotgun and came back to finish the conversation—you never seen white people run so fast! Couldn't get a clean shot at the rear window of their car—I still have to clean up the lines of fire at my house."

"Anyway, the Green Meanie," Jimmy continued, "is an old Greyhound bus that's painted green and takes riders from Kestrel Cove to Portland."

"Where do you catch it?" Jamie asked.

"It leaves from the store parking lot at 7:30 in the morning," Jimmy said, "early enough so they can get people to work."

"I wouldn't get on that bus, even if somebody paid me!" Joe declared. "That Frenchie driver is drunk half the time. I'm telling ya, he's gonna kill somebody someday."

"I think I'll risk it, Joe. I mean, don't you think it's worth a shot if it makes me a better worker on your boat?" Jamie said.

Joe smirked at him. "Do what you gotta do, kid. Just know, if you die in a bus accident, Drake'll pay Jerry Shute and put your car out on his lawn as a goddamn trophy!"

13

When he got to the store the next morning, Jamie found that the coffee was all gone and no one had made any more. As he tried to tilt the urn to get the last drops into his cup, the two cashiers openly laughed at him from their registers. Undaunted, he headed back to one of the coolers in the rear of the store to get a bottle of green tea. But when he found that all the drinks had been pushed into a jumbled pile in the back, he got down on his knees to scrounge through them all. After a few moments of searching, he finally pulled out the one he wanted.

"Hey! Close that damn door! What are you trying to do, air condition the whole store?"

Jamie stood up to see where the snarling voice had come from, and the dark-haired cashier was staring back at him with her hands on her hips. When he held up his drink to signify that he'd succeeded in his search, she sputtered a few more obscenities at him. He made his way back to the front of the store, giving the dark-haired cashier a wide berth, and went to the other register. Shelley Vanes, the attractive young woman he'd seen with Bill Hand, was standing there, looking intently at him. Jamie felt a twinge of excitement as he put the bottle of tea next to her register. He coughed and said, "'Morning."

"Uh-huh, it is," she replied with a slight smile. She rang up his purchase and said, "You're Joe Quinn's third man, right?"

"Uh-huh," Jamie responded, taken a bit by surprise.

"Well, I heard he had a new third man who's a stuck-up college boy, and you seem to fit the profile. I also hear that you're now not only Wiley's friend, but Bill Hand's too."

Jamie rolled his eyes. "Wow, you sure hear a lot of things."

"Uh-huh, I certainly do." She looked down at her watch. "Um, it looks like you're a little late for work today, especially since Joe and Jimmy already came in for their morning coffee a few hours ago."

"They're beaching the boat today to work on the bottom, so I'm taking the Green Meanie to go to Portland."

"Buckle your seat belt and pray to your god!"

While Jamie chuckled at her comment, the other cashier said sourly, "Yeah, I really hope you don't die today!"

"Well, thanks, I guess," Jamie said with a hopeful grin.

"I was being sarcastic, asshole. If you do survive your little field trip and you come in here again, make your choice before you open the cooler door."

"I knew exactly what I wanted. But all the bottles in that cooler are so mixed up, I couldn't make my selection without getting down on the grubby floor to move them all around."

The cashier's face began to darken. "Are you trying to say that me and Shelley don't do a good job stocking and cleaning this store, dickwad?"

"No, I wasn't trying to be overly critical—I'm just saying that I don't think that customers should have to play a giant game of Husker Du with mismatched drink bottles while rolling around on a floor that has obviously not been mopped since the Great Depression..."

"All-righty, then. Well, have a nice trip to Portland!" Shelley interjected.

"So you think you can come in here and start talking smack about us and our store like that, huh, you little puke?"

Shelley leaned in. "Psst, you better run before she goes completely postal!"

"Okay, thanks, Shelley!"

The unauthorized use of her name caused her to stop smiling. But as the other cashier started another tirade of curses, she nodded quickly at the door. Jamie took the hint, grabbed his bottle of tea, and hurried away. When he turned at the door and looked back again, he had to admit that Shelley Vanes wasn't just pretty, she was drop-dead gorgeous. And, for a moment, he was too mesmerized by her beauty to move. But he caught the sight of something flying toward him, and he ducked just before a cellophane-wrapped square of fudge hit the wall next to him. When he saw the angry cashier picking up another round from a basket by her register, he whipped open the door and scurried out.

Jamie felt ridiculous waiting alone in the empty parking lot, but then he heard the throaty diesel and the grating gears of the approaching bus. It swung wide into the gravel lot and came so close to him, he had to step back to avoid having his feet run over. After the air brakes made their flatulent sound, the bus door flew open. A lanky man with a greasy pompadour and bushy sideburns bounded out of the bus, bowed slightly as he neared Jamie, and said in a heavy French accent, "*Bon jour, monsieur.* I need *mon café de matin, no?* After, we go, *oui?*"

"Uh, sure," Jamie replied uncertainly.

The man walked directly into the store without another word, and Jamie looked at the bus as it sat there idling. It was just as Jimmy had described—an old Greyhound Scenicruiser that had been painted forest green some time ago. The paint was flaking off in places, revealing the original silver color underneath. It looked as if the bus was some kind of treasure that had been covered to hide its true value, but clearly, there was nothing of any value beneath *this* new paint job.

The door of the store opened suddenly. "*Ah, mes petits amours, merci* for my *café.* You two are *belles femmes. Ah*, if I were a younger man, I would give my left *noix* for a *ménage à trois* with you *deux belles femmes, no? Har-har-har!*"

A cellophane-wrapped square of fudge burst into a cloud of crumbs next to his head, and the lanky man let the door close, which stifled the string of accompanying obscenities. He shrugged and grinned at Jamie as he walked back onto the bus. "Ah, they want me!"

When the driver announced that it was time to board, Jamie turned around to see who the man was talking to. He was stunned to find that he was now the head of a line of over a dozen other people, and he had to wonder where they'd all come from. He was so preoccupied with this that he didn't move. When the driver revved the engine and harshly asked him if he really wanted to go to Portland, Jamie sheepishly stepped aboard and stood there to buy a ticket. After a moment, the driver said, "We do that later, *cher.*"

Jamie sat down in a window seat a few rows back and watched as the rest of the passengers filed aboard like livestock. There were so few riders, each person had an entire row to themselves. The driver closed the door, pulled the bus onto the main road, and ground the gears a couple of times as he got the Green Meanie up to speed. Then he started talking nonstop to no one in particular. "You *Americains* drive your cars *si lentement*. You live *si rapidement*, but you drive *si lentement*. It is so, how do you say, *ironique, no? Le Quebecois* and *le Francais* do it the right way—they drive *rapidement, vivant lentement, et amour profondement!*"

As Jamie watched the driver's reflection in the round overhead mirror, he saw him start to move his lower jaw in an exaggerated sweeping motion. When a pink plastic edge protruded from his lips like a miniature tongue, it was clear that the man was manipulating his dentures within his mouth. He did this until both the upper and lower plates were free, and he continued to move them about with his tongue. Jamie couldn't imagine what the purpose of all this was, but he was so transfixed, he was helpless to stop staring.

It was at this moment that a young girl plopped down next to him. She was so little that she had snuck into the seat without him fully noticing her at first. But her jasmine and vanilla perfume betrayed her invasion of his space, and he dropped his eyes to stare at her. She seemed to be a young teenager, and although she was a pretty girl, she wore too much makeup. Her brown hair hung down past her shoulders, and she had bangs that looked like they were designed to keep rainwater off her face. The multiple earrings in her left ear jingled like the bells cats wear to warn away songbirds, and Jamie could not help feeling that he might be this girl's prey. He was about to say something to her, but she cooed softly, "You're Joe Quinn's third man. Your name is Jamie, right?"

"How does everyone know that?"

"Kestrel Cove's a small town. Believe me, we all know way too much about each other. I've heard all about you."

Jamie shook his head and chuckled, "Yes, I'm Jamie Kurtz and I work for Joe."

The girl extended her hand, and its fragility made Jamie grasp it gently so he wouldn't break it. "My name is Angie Williams."

"Nice to meet you, Angie."

"So where are you headed today, Jamie?"

"Portland."

"Yuh…no, *duh*. That's the only place this bus goes, right? We're all going to Portland. If you weren't going there, you'd be shit out of luck."

"Oh, right."

"So I guess what I meant is, what are you going to *do* in Portland today, Jamie?" She tucked her slim legs up under her. She was wearing a very short skirt, and this movement exposed her thighs.

"I need to talk to someone."

"Why?"

Jamie was thrown off by her questioning, but he was flattered enough by her attention that he forgave the intrusion. "I'm going to Portland to ask a friend for advice."

"Oh, I see," Angie said as she readjusted her legs underneath her. Her skirt rode up a little more, and Jamie found it difficult to keep his eyes from roaming. He blinked a couple of times. "And why are *you* going to Portland today, Angie?"

She smiled. "I'm going to my class."

Since Jamie assumed that she was a high school student, he figured she was being forced to do summer school in Portland. "Oh, really? What class?"

"A college course, actually."

He sat up with more interest because he realized that he'd completely misjudged the situation. Instead of a high school student needing remedial help, it was clear to him now that this girl was actually some kind of gifted and talented student who was taking enrichment courses at a college in Portland. The chance to talk with someone academic, albeit young, was exciting. "Oh, a college course. Which college?"

She smiled with pride as she said, "The Atlantic College of Cosmetology."

Jamie thought she had said something about the cosmos. And, since he was so excited to have an intellectual conversation, he began to rattle off his knowledge of the universe and astrophysics.

After a while, the girl giggled, "I don't know nothing about any of that stuff you just said, Jamie. I'm taking classes to become a beautician."

He suddenly understood his error, and he felt like a pompous moron. He looked down at his feet, cleared his throat, and tried to recover. "So, is that what you're going to do after you graduate, Angie?"

The girl seemed confused by Jamie's question. She pursed her lips into a seductive pucker and tilted her head as she pondered an appropriate answer. Then she opened her mouth and a warm, sensuous laugh came out. "Oh, you think I'm a high school student! Don't worry, I get that all the time. Everyone assumes that I'm sixteen, but I'm actually twenty-one years old! I'm just little for my age."

"Oh, Jeez, I'm so sorry!" Jamie blurted apologetically.

"Hey, I take it as a compliment—I hope I never look as old as I really am. But to answer your question, yes, I do want to open my own beauty shop in Kestrel Cove. Actually Drake—you know Drake, right? Oh, right, I've heard about how he *loves* you! Anyway, he's told me that I can rent the building that he owns across from his house. Right now, it's abandoned and full of his pogy nets. But with a little cleaning and remodeling, it could be a cute little shop in a perfect location."

"Sounds like it needs some work," Jamie replied.

"Oh, I know a lot of guys who owe me some favors and will work on the building for free. So I'm totally sure that I can get it fixed up pretty quick. Having my own business is a dream of mine."

Their conversation went on from there and continued easily all the way to Portland. Jamie found Angie to be an interesting contradiction—she appeared youthful and innocent at times, but she also came across as experienced beyond her years and more than a little flirtatious. And while she seemed so small and fragile, he caught so many subtle undertones of a strength and rugged determination in her stories that it was clear she could take care of herself.

The bus exited the highway and pulled into the parking lot of a large supermarket. Without any announcement, the driver opened the door to let the passengers off. Angie stood up and hurriedly gathered her belongings. "Jesus, today's trip seemed longer than normal, but then I usually sleep the whole way. Today, I had a good reason to stay awake."

Jamie grinned. "I enjoyed talking with you, Angie. Maybe we could—"

"Well, I've gotta run to make it to my class on time. I'll see you on this afternoon's ride back to Kestrel Cove. We can talk some more then, right?"

Jamie smiled. "Oh, sure."

"But let's sit farther back on the way home, okay?"

"Okay."

She bent over and kissed him lightly on the cheek. This took him by surprise, and the combination of the kiss and the aroma of her perfume made him feel a twinge of movement in his groin. She went to the door, turned, and waved to him before leaving the bus.

When Jamie tried to walk past the driver, he stuck out his arm like a fleshy turnstile. "*Monsieur, cinq* dollars, *s'il vous plait.*"

"How much?"

"*Cinq.*"

"Five dollars, you moron!" an angry voice shouted behind Jamie.

"Oh, sorry. I didn't know," he said nervously, as he started going through his pockets.

"Well, now you do, *Monsieur.*"

The people behind Jamie chuckled, but then they all seemed to sigh with annoyance that their path was blocked. He tried to move out of the way, but there was nowhere to go. "I wish I'd known before how much I had to pay; then I'd have been ready."

The driver, who had clicked his dentures and chattered to himself nearly nonstop throughout the trip, now sat as silent as a statue with his hand outstretched. Finally, Jamie found a five-dollar bill and handed it to him.

"*Merci, monsieur!*"

Jamie hurried off the bus and walked toward the supermarket. He didn't know where the synagogue was, but he figured there had to be a public phone with a phone book outside the store that he could use to find the address. He found this fairly quickly, but he was surprised to discover that there were five synagogues listed in the yellow pages. Three of them were clearly in different towns, so he eliminated them from his search. Another one had a large ad that described it as being close to the Jetport, which was too far away. That left one in downtown Portland, and, using the street map in the telephone book, Jamie was able to plot the most direct course to it.

But when he was finally standing outside the three-story brick building that was set back from the street and almost completely hidden behind a clump of spruce trees, he was skeptical about its current status. A stone placard with carved Hebrew letters and a small circular stained-glass window with the Star of David were the only clues that the building was more than a derelict warehouse. When he tried to open the front door, it was locked. There was no knocker and he didn't see a doorbell, so he tried banging on the heavy wooden door with his fist until he felt as futile as an Avon lady making a house call to a castle.

Then the door creaked open and an old woman dressed completely in black came out. She seemed neither surprised nor concerned by Jamie's presence and allowed him to hold the heavy door open for her as she shuffled past. She looked down and mumbled, "You must be here to see the rabbi."

"Yes, ma'am."

"Well, he's in his office."

"Thank you. Can you tell me where his office...?"

But the woman kept walking and didn't respond. Jamie shrugged his shoulders and let himself in. It was very dark inside, so he called out, "Hello-o-o?"

When no one answered, he set off to find the rabbi's office. Like a rat in a maze, Jamie made his way through the labyrinth of darkened hallways until he came around a corner and abruptly found himself right in front of the desk of a very startled rabbi. The ensuing yelling match would have been almost comical if the older man hadn't fallen backwards off his chair and onto the floor. As Jamie rushed forward to help him, the rabbi screamed, "There's no more money in my desk! I've got some change in my pocket that you can have, but please don't beat me up again, you dirty goy thug!"

"Oh, no, I'm not here to do anything bad like that, sir! I just need to talk to you!"

As the rabbi slowly got up off the floor, he examined Jamie with distrustful eyes. He bent down to pick up his yarmulke and put it back in place. Then he asked, "How did you get inside?"

"An old woman let me in. She told me you were in your office."

"Mrs. Abrahms, that old coot," he said with a growl. "And my congregation wonders how I've managed to get mugged three times in the safety of my office during these last six months!"

"I'm so sorry! I didn't mean to startle you!"

The rabbi sat back into his chair and sighed deeply. "Well, what can I do for you today?

"My name is Jamie Kurtz. And I need a rabbi's perspective on a couple of questions that I have."

"Hello, Jamie Kurtz. I'm Sal Reubens. Have a seat and ask your questions."

"Okay, Rabbi Reubens. I'm not sure you can help, but some disturbing things have been happening to me recently and I'm confused. I'm hoping that you *can* help me."

"I'll certainly try, Jamie. And just call me Sal."

"Okay. Well, you see, I live in Kestrel Cove, which is near Brementon."

"Brementon? My wife loves to shop at the Corners. Hmm, you came a pretty good distance today just to ask a rabbi a couple of questions. I guess you didn't know there's a synagogue right there in Brementon, huh?"

"Uh, no, I didn't."

"It's okay, not many people know how many Jews live in this state. There's far more of us than anyone wants to admit."

"Well, actually, I also thought that a temple in a bigger metropolitan area would have a more ecumenical outlook on things."

"Ah, my young man, I may be too much of an old codger to be either ecumenical or metropolitan, but I'll do my best nonetheless."

"Okay, but this is going to sound a little absurd…"

"No, there's no such thing as a stupid question," the rabbi said glancing at his desk, "but I do need to get some other things done today, so maybe we can move this along?"

"Uh, sure. You see, I work on a lobster boat. I'm the third man, which means that I bait the traps and band the lobsters."

"Hmm, that sounds interesting."

"It is, but it's hard work. And it's the reason that I'm here today. I had a really horrible nightmare the other night about the lobsters we catch."

"Well, the subconscious can certainly percolate up into our conscious world from time to time, but that's really something for a psychoanalyst to help you with."

"There's more, Sal. Yesterday, I had such horrific visions that I passed out while working on the boat."

"My goodness! It sounds like you may also need someone in the medical profession to look at you."

Jamie shook his head. "No, Sal, I think I just need to hear your opinion. You see, I'm being haunted by the similarities between what we do to lobsters and what the Nazis did to the Jews during the Holocaust."

The rabbi stared at Jamie, and there was an uncomfortable silence between them that was only broken by a clock chiming somewhere in the synagogue and a city bus rumbling by outside. Finally, the rabbi cleared his throat. "I'm sorry, Jamie, you said that you had some questions, but I didn't hear any in that last statement."

"Oh, right. So do *you* think there's any connection between 'lobstercide' and the genocide the Nazis perpetrated upon the Jews?"

The rabbi sat rigidly and stared at him wordlessly for too long. When he finally did speak, his voice had a sharp metallic edge to it. "Let me get this straight. You traveled from your little lobstering community to the streets of Portland to find this well-concealed and out-of-the-way temple just to get my perspective about some kind of connection between the systematic slaughter of over six million innocent Jewish men, women, and children by a diabolical regime of mentally deranged and murderous thugs and the local fishery of a crustacean that, due to the strict Kashrut dietary rules of my religion, I cannot even eat?"

Jamie rolled his eyes. "Well, when you say it that way, Sal, it does sound a bit perverse and more than a tad insensitive."

"That's because it is."

The rabbi's comment stung, but Jamie plunged on. "But I've never experienced anything like this before in my life! These dreams and visions have been so clear and have felt so real! I'm desperate. I just don't know what to do! I thought that if I talked with you about it all, maybe I could understand the connection that my brain is making, and I could get some relief."

"You seem like a good young man, Jamie, but you've wasted your time on this quest today. There is absolutely *no* connection between lobstering and the Holocaust! And that's not only my Jewish perspective, but the perspective of any normal and sane person."

"But do you have any advice for me to get rid of these horrible feelings?"

"Quit your job and become an animal rights activist."

"But I can't do that, Sal. It's a good job and I'm making money doing it."

"Then I really don't know what to tell you, Jamie. If the job is adversely affecting you, quit. If you don't want to do that, then you have to try to find some other solution to your problem."

"But what, Sal? I'm telling you, I think I'm being driven insane by this!"

The rabbi looked up from his desk and his eyes were softer. "When I was a much younger man in New York City, members of another synagogue asked me if I would go talk with their rabbi. They were all terribly worried by the way that he'd been acting. For some unknown reason, he'd been staying in his home and staring out the window, day and night. So I went right over to talk to him. His apartment overlooked a park, and we sat in his sunny living room and exchanged pleasantries while we drank some tea. Before too long, however, I told him exactly why I was there.

"He then launched into the telling of the most amazing story. According to him, a young man in his congregation had recently come back from the war in the Middle East, and he'd come to the rabbi wanting to talk about some strange feelings he'd been having. In a nutshell, because of the horrors he'd seen over there, the young man had become so discouraged with life that he wanted to do something radical. He was going to turn himself into a tree! Well, you can imagine the old rabbi's reaction—he pulled no punches as he tried to reason with the young man. He pointed out the silliness of this solution and even suggested a few psychologists who could help with what were obviously symptoms of PTSD. But the young man said that he would not be swayed and that he was going to try to do it. Well, the elderly rabbi had had enough, and he sent him on his way with a good dose of ridicule. Not too long afterwards, the young man disappeared. There was no note, no body, no eyewitness. *Poof!* he was just gone!

"When the old rabbi stopped talking, we sat in silence for a moment or two. Then I had the chutzpah to ask him if it was the guilt he felt from sending the young man away that was making him too sad to leave his house. The old rabbi looked at me with a genuine expression of surprise and said that he didn't feel any guilt or sadness. I then foolishly went into a long diatribe about the fact that, as rabbis, we do the best job that we can, but we should never let our failures eat us up. The old man waved me off as he nodded for me to look out the window. Then he nearly whispered, 'I can't leave my home because I need to watch over him!'

"When I looked out the window, I saw that an oak tree sapling had recently been planted in the park across the street. I looked back at the old rabbi and he just smiled as if to say, 'There he is.' He explained that the tree's arrival had been on the very day that the young man had disappeared, and the only conclusion that he could draw was that the young man had, in fact, succeeded in turning himself into a tree. Even though I spent the next half hour trying to reason with the man, nothing I said could change his mind—he was bound and determined that the troubled young man was now the young tree, and it was his job to watch over him! I left his apartment unable to convince him otherwise."

The rabbi went silent and Jamie found that, somewhere in the midst of the tale, he'd crept forward in his chair and was leaning in with anticipation. When the man continued, his voice was low and dark. "That old rabbi never left his apartment again. When his congregation went over to look in on him the next time, he was dead. He was still sitting in his chair, facing the window that looked out over the park and its new tree."

The rabbi's story was like a Zen koan for Jamie, but it jarred him into a most unpleasant enlightenment. With painful clarity, he suddenly understood just how asinine his whole 'lobstercide' quest had been. It was as if a distorting lens had been removed from his eyes and he could see just how ridiculous it was to look for a connection between lobstering and the Holocaust. And though he felt an almost unbearable embarrassment at his behavior, he also noticed that a weight had now been lifted from his shoulders. He thrust his hand out toward the rabbi. "Thank you so much, Sal! I get it now. Thank you—thank you for your story."

The rabbi managed a weak smile and then asked, "Is there anything else that you need from me today, Jamie?"

"Yes, Sal. Could you please help me find my way out of here?"

14

Jamie was now free—both mentally and physically—to enjoy the remainder of his day. As he ambled up the cobblestone streets and brick sidewalks of Portland, he let the history of the city sweep him up. He imagined the clopping of the horses' hooves, the shouts of merchants hawking their wares on the corners, and the smells of a nineteenth-century port city. He wound his way up to the history museum to take a tour of the home of the great poet, Henry Wadsworth Longfellow. And when he came out of the museum's gift store, he had a few new books to read. He checked the time and discovered that he would have to run to get back to the supermarket parking lot if he was going to make the bus.

The Green Meanie was idling there, already loading passengers, when Jamie got there. He took his place in line, nodded at the driver as he passed, and walked down the aisle. He decided to follow Angie's advice and sit in the rear of the bus, and he found a window seat in the last row. When the door closed and the bus began to pull out of the parking lot, Jamie felt a pang of disappointment that Angie hadn't made it. He had spent the afternoon eagerly waiting to talk with her on the way back to Kestrel Cove, and he'd even practiced how he was going to ask her out on a date.

"Hey, stud! How was your day?"

He was startled to see Angie now snuggling next to him, and he smiled. "Oh, good. How was class today?"

The girl grinned. "You know—nothing but bad haircuts and dirty hair. Actually, the best part of my day is just getting started!"

Jamie blushed, and Angie tickled him as she said seductively, "You're blushing! Oh, my God, you're too cute, Jamie Kurtz!"

She leaned over and kissed him on the neck. He was stunned by her forwardness, but the tingling as she continued made him powerless to protest. She worked her way up to his earlobe and nibbled playfully on it. As she nibbled, she put her right hand on his rapidly engorging member and started stroking it sensuously. And even though Jamie knew that he should push her away, the haze of pleasure was beginning to engulf him. In a feeble attempt to stay afloat, he blurted out, "Well, Angie, I had a very successful day. A life-changing day, actually!" He closed his eyes and let out a soft moan. "I…I feel great! I came down to Portland with some big questions, but now I realize that I was being foolish worrying about such stupid things."

A grin spread across Angie's face that was so seductive and devilish that his scalp tingled along with the rest of him. Her right hand kept working on him and she leaned in to whisper into his ear, "Have you ever been blown in the back of a bus, Jamie?"

In fact, he hadn't. He'd certainly fantasized about it, but it had never happened to him. As he imagined such an event now, an idiot grin seized his face. While he was paralyzed by the pornographic movie playing in his head, Angie skillfully got hold of his zipper, eased it down, and placed her warm mouth upon him. Jamie gasped in pleasure, but his panicked eyes scanned the bus to see if anyone was watching. No one was. And as much as he knew that he should stop her, the throb of the bus's diesel, the whirl of the Maine scenery outside the windows, and the masterful workings of Angie's tongue on him made him just close his eyes and surrender to the pleasure of the moment. When he'd reached the point of no return, Angie sat back up and pulled some wet wipes from her purse. "For just these kinds of occasions," she whispered hoarsely.

The groping, caressing, and outright juvenile make-out session that followed lasted for the entire ride back to Kestrel Cove. When they exited the bus, they pretended they didn't know each other, but they made a beeline straight for her beat-up Subaru wagon and continued what they were doing. By the time they had driven the short distance to her trailer, neither of them was wearing underwear anymore. And, once inside the trailer, Jamie completely disregarded the voice in his head that warned him about making bad decisions, and he dove freely into the sexual pool that was Angie Williams.

That night's sex was done with reckless abandon and minimal time for recovery. For those times that Jamie couldn't get it up enough to satisfy her, Angie took matters into her own hands or used battery-operated toys that magically appeared out of drawers beside the bed. There was even a moment in the evening when she pushed Jamie out the door of the trailer to have an incredibly passionate session on the ground next to the parked Subaru. And even though he was very uncomfortable with doing this in a public place, Angie's orgasm outside seemed to be the most earth-shaking one of their entire time together. By the time they both were sated, it was past midnight and they fell into sound and blissful sleep.

Jamie awoke at four the next morning, but when he tried to wake Angie, she was dead to the world. He left her a note before heading out, and his pace was quicker than usual because he knew he had to get down to the wharf on time to put in a normal day's effort. If he didn't, Joe would grind him into powder for his ridiculous trip to Portland and his stupid questions about *lobstercide*. As he loped down the side of the road, an all-too-familiar pickup truck sped past him, squealed to a stop, and started backing up to where he stood. As the truck pulled up, Jamie knew he'd now have to answer a barrage of questions about why he was coming from the wrong direction at this time of the morning, and as the door flew open and Jimmy jumped out, he desperately tried to come up with a reasonable excuse. Joe smirked at him. "Need a ride there, college boy?"

"Yeah, I guess I took a wrong turn this morning," Jamie said, trying to sound convincing.

The guys exchanged glances before saying, "Uh-huh, that happens sometimes."

They rode in silence to the wharf, which unnerved Jamie. He had fully expected the inquisition to begin early, but Joe and Jimmy seemed comfortable to ride and not talk. After parking the truck, Joe said with bravado, "Well, let's go commit some lobstercide!"

Once aboard the boat, the three men began their regular preparations for a day of fishing, and no one talked too much. But even after they had fueled up, loaded the bait, and were steaming out of the cove toward the first string, neither Jimmy nor Joe seemed inclined to talk to Jamie. Because he'd fully expected an immediate interrogation about his day in Portland, he was not prepared for the silent treatment. Instead, he kept waiting for the exact moment the two of them would go on the offensive and attack him. But neither man did. It was like they were completely focused on having a normal day of fishing.

The assault finally came during the coffee break. After a brief conversation about the feel of the new propeller, the good fishing weather, and the TV show that Joe and Jimmy had watched that made a connection between the sexual prowess of several women in history and their obesity, Jamie was lulled into believing that he would not have to defend his trip to Portland or say anything about his day off.

"Hey, how's your Johnson this morning after all that sex with Angie Williams?" Joe casually asked. "I mean, does it burn when you pee yet?"

Jamie was tongue-tied. He'd been so fully prepared to defend his trip to see a rabbi, he had no defenses set up to protect himself against attacks about his secret tryst. He now just sat with his mouth open because he was unable to muster a decent reply.

"Angie Williams?" Jimmy clucked his tongue and shook his head. "Jesus H. Christ, college boy, if you were so desperate to get laid, all you had to do was ask us for help, and we would have set you up with someone easy, a real clean slut. Not the town whore!"

Joe's casual demeanor vanished, and he wagged his finger in Jamie's face. "All I gotta say is, you better have been wearing a jimmy last night, 'cause I'm definitely not paying for any treatment of the clap! And don't think that you'll get time off when you discover that Angie Williams gave you some kind of STD!"

Finally, Jamie found his voice, and he croaked, "Who told you?"

Jimmy and Joe looked at each other and burst into laughter. Jimmy was the first one to stop and be able to speak. "What, about her having STD's? Or about Angie Williams being the town whore?"

While the two men continued to laugh, Jamie's face flushed. "About me and Angie."

Jimmy cackled, "Omigosh! You get a hummer in the back of the Green Meanie, and you think no one would notice? Come on, Jamie, you might as well have called a meeting in the fish house and let her blow you there. I'll bet most of Kestrel Cove knew the exact moment you came on that bus ride!"

Joe snickered, "Yeah, and the way you two kept going at it like rabbits all the way to her place in her car—you must've known that *someone* was going to see that! You must be exhausted from staying up so late fucking."

Jamie's mouth finally slammed shut. "How do you guys know all this? Is someone stalking me?"

Joe's face took on a pinched look. "No one's stalking you, kid. If you choose to do all your sex acts in public, somebody's bound to see you!"

Joe stood up and went to the stern of the boat. He slipped the suspender of his orange overalls off to piss into the water. As he came back forward, he said robotically, "Well, as much fun as it is to torture the college boy, we've got to commit some more lobstercide to pay our bills."

Jamie jumped up and yelled, "You guys can't say all those bad things about my girlfriend! You should apologize—right now!"

Joe and Jimmy froze in place and stared at Jamie. Joe finally growled, "What did you just say?"

Jamie walked toward them. "You can talk badly about me all you want, but you can't say that kind of shit about Angie. She's my girlfriend now, and I won't let you say all that mean stuff about her!"

Jimmy started laughing, but Joe took a hard inquisitive look at Jamie's face before saying, "Jimmy, I think he's serious."

"Naw, he *can't* be. He's fucking with us."

"No, I think he's serious. He's as easy to read as a goddamn comic book, and he looks serious to me."

Jimmy shook his head. "Naw, there's no goddamn fucking way he could be that stupid!"

Jamie snarled, "I'm right here! Stop talking about me like I can't hear you. Of course I'm serious! No more talking shit about Angie, okay? You can ream me out about lobstercide or going to college or being a complete retard, but leave her alone. Please."

"For the love of Pete! He actually thinks she's his girlfriend now!" Joe said incredulously.

"No way! Nobody can be that stupid, can they?"

"Hello-o-o, I'm right here. Why are you still talking about me like I'm not here? I'm right here!"

Joe took a step forward. "Do you really think Angie William is your girlfriend now?"

Jamie shrugged. "Of course she's my girlfriend. When you do all those sexual acts together, it makes you something more than just friends, don't you think? We had sex...a lot...so, yeah, Angie's my girlfriend—"

"Did *she* tell you she was your girlfriend?" Jimmy interrupted.

"Well, not in those exact words..."

"Did she talk to you at *all* last night? Or was the only talking when she screamed out the most incredibly dirty directions you've ever heard while you were screwing?"

The truth in Joe's comment made Jamie's vision go red with anger. "Hey, I'm done talking about this!"

Joe pointed his finger at Jamie. "You know, if every moron from the peninsula who's dipped his Johnson into Angie Williams suddenly declared that they were her boyfriend, we'd have to wear name tags at the Angie Williams Boyfriend Convention!"

Jamie turned away and went to the baiting table. Jimmy looked eager to continue the pestering, but Joe waved him off because he could sense that the next comment would push Jamie over the edge. And although it would be wholly entertaining to watch the college boy crash and burn, they needed him to get another 300 traps hauled. So he quietly went into the wheelhouse and put the boat in gear. But Jimmy was like a puppy who was having too much fun to stop, and he came up with beseeching eyes to continue the fun. Joe shook his head and said, "Don't worry, we'll get him at lunch."

But they didn't get him at lunch. Jamie let his anger simmer and stew the rest of the morning so much that, by noontime, he was totally unapproachable. He sat apart from them and ate in an angry silence, and no amount of prompting or goading could get enough of a response to warrant the continuation of the game. So Joe and Jimmy began a conversation about designing different ways of running down suspects on the television show *Cops*. Jimmy's plan of rigging police cruisers with gruesome metallic cowcatchers that would catch and shred the perps was the most creative, and the two men enthusiastically talked about how much fun it would be to drive over people on city streets.

Jamie heard none of this. His anger was now so complete that he only saw the bait and lobsters in front of him. And to make matters worse, all of Joe's and Jimmy's comments had been so correct, his own mind was turning against him. He knew that no respectable girl would give a complete stranger a blowjob in the back of a public bus. And Joe was absolutely correct—after getting off the bus, the only talking that happened was when Angie had barked out specific and urgent instructions during sex. And if Jamie's declaration that Angie was now his girlfriend had seemed unbelievably foolish to the guys, he shuddered to think what other people in the Kestrel Cove community were now saying about him. Unfortunately, his fury at the guys had grown too big to admit any of this to himself yet, so he held onto his anger against Joe and Jimmy as tightly as a man clinging to a life ring.

Jamie refused to talk to them the rest of the afternoon. Even when they were steaming into the wharf to offload their lobsters, he wouldn't respond to any of their attempts at conversation. And as they walked up the ramp from the skiff dock, they simply let him walk away when he said he'd see them the next morning. They were unsure if he'd actually show up, but they hoped so. They really liked the kid, and they were bummed at the thought that he might quit over the likes of that whore Angie Williams.

The next morning, Jamie was waiting when Joe and Jimmy pulled up in the parking lot. While he was completely exhausted from another night of uninhibited sex with Angie, he couldn't help having a big grin on his face as the two men walked up to him.

"Jesus, he can't stop smiling, Joe," Jimmy said, stating the obvious.

"Yeah, well, he's getting laid. He can smile. Me, I *almost* got laid last night. 'Cept my old lady woke up and fought back. Damn bitch!" Joe said with a chuckle, "So I ended up jerking it instead."

Jimmy laughed, "I'm telling you, I've never jerked off more in my life than I have since I got married! Ain't that true with you, too, Joe?"

Joe rolled his eyes. "Oh yeah, that's so true. College boy, promise me you won't ask Angie to marry you, for several reasons. Mostly because, once you're married, you'll find yourself having to jerk off night after night!"

As they hauled their first string, Jimmy tried to tease Jamie a little about Angie, but he shut him down by shrugging his shoulders and smiling. The same responses kept the fun to a minimum during the breaks, and the day became another one of silence between the three of them. When they were done, Jamie didn't even pretend that he was walking to his campsite, but headed toward the trail that would lead him to the pipeline and back to Angie's. As the guys sped past him in the truck, Jimmy flipped him the bird, which made Jamie laugh out loud for the first time all day.

That night, Jamie began to realize that the energy of the relationship with Angie was already leaking out like the sand in an hourglass. He knew it was perfectly normal for a new romance to lose some of its initial luster, but he was surprised to feel such a deep sense of emptiness so quickly. He tried to ask her questions about herself, but she waved off every attempt. When he tried to have deeper conversations about their relationship, she just steered them toward having sex again. But she seemed almost bored. He tried to get her to go outside and have sex or bring out the toys, but she refused, and he knew that she just wasn't into him anymore. So when she asked to take the next night off, he wasn't surprised. In fact, he felt a sense of relief.

That next day on the boat was different. Jimmy and Joe seemed content to distance themselves from Jamie for the entire day. The routines of the job meant that the three of them no longer needed to speak to get everything done, and they only made small talk during the breaks. But over the course of the day, Jamie realized that Jimmy and Joe weren't mad with him, nor were they disinterested. Their quietness was only the type of space that friends gave one another to figure things out. So Jamie understood that there was a real friendship slowly germinating between the three of them, just waiting until he came to his senses again.

Sitting alone at his campsite that night, Jamie began to think about his situation. Summer was in full swing now, and he'd been lobstering enough to feel a confidence that he was doing a good job on the boat. He was working hard and he was making money. And even though his car wasn't fixed yet, at least Jerry had it up on jack stands nowadays, which was a clear indication he was going to start working on it sometime soon. The other fishermen, sternmen, and residents of Kestrel Cove all nodded or said hello to him these days, and he couldn't help feeling that they now thought of him as a part of the community. All in all, he felt pretty good about his life.

But, as he listened to the call of a barred owl and heard the wind whispering through the treetops, he had to admit that he wasn't sure what he really felt about Angie. He enjoyed the sex, but the truth of the matter was that he was dating the town whore—and that meant the entire affair was on borrowed time. His own stark acceptance of these facts surprised him. He knew that this fling with Angie would be over soon, and whereas this would've caused him some pain before, he was now calm and unemotional about it. He seemed to be fine with the knowledge that he'd be Angie's lover until she grew bored with him and switched to someone new. This admission didn't upset him because the truth was, he was happy enough.

But not completely happy. That beautiful girl at the store, Shelley Vanes, troubled him. Every time he was around her, he felt a twinge of excitement to see her and his stomach did a gymnastic floor routine. Whenever she talked with him at her register, he couldn't stop staring at her. And their eyes had met a few times and had even locked onto each other. No, there was no denying that he was deeply attracted to her—and he couldn't help but feel that she was attracted to him, too. And while it struck him as more than a little weird to be pining for another woman so blatantly while taking a night off from his current sexual partner, he knew that, before anything could develop with Shelley, his relationship with Angie would have to play itself out.

Angie took care of that when she requested yet another night off. As he ate dinner alone at his campsite, he enjoyed the solitude and quiet of the moment. Since it felt like the perfect night to watch the sunset from the wharf, he set off on the shoreline trail. Oddly, when he got to the wharf's parking lot, there was a car right where his Volvo had been smashed by Drake. As Jamie went closer to it to warn the people inside that they were parked in the notorious no-parking spot, he quickly realized that they were having wild sex. He smiled at their foolishness in picking the stinky wharf as the location for an intimate event, and he was about to continue on his way when the door flew open and the couple flopped out onto the gravel in what looked like a wrestling match.

Even before he got a good look at them, Jamie heard the familiar urgent barks of dirty directions and knew that it was Angie screwing another guy. As the couple writhed on the gravel, he felt the anger of betrayal come flushing through his system. His face and ears began to burn, but the sudden coolness of acceptance of a self-fulfilling prophecy washed over him and extinguished his rage. Since he'd always known that Angie was going to do this, he had already fully accepted it. So how could he be angry with her? He couldn't. And this understanding allowed him to view the awkward scene before him with complete calmness. All he wanted to do now was retreat without being seen.

But Angie saw him first. She stopped what she was doing and looked directly at him. It took a while for the guy to realize that she had stopped, and he continued to maul her body for some time before he stopped and noticed Jamie, who was standing there like a deer in the headlights. The couple disengaged and fixed their clothing. The guy finally asked Angie, "Um, is there a problem here?"

She gave a subtle nod.

"You know him?"

Another slight nod.

"Hey, buddy, I don't want any trouble."

Jamie did not recognize the guy and was neither intimidated nor angered by him.

"Sorry, Jamie," Angie said quickly.

Jamie had wished for just this kind of moment with Laura, but it had never happened. Now, here he was, catching Angie with another guy, and he had nothing to say because he felt nothing for her. When this truth hit him, it caused him more pain than what was happening in front of him. All Jamie wanted to do was turn and head back to his campsite, but he knew that response would evoke more drama than was needed. He simply needed to figure out how to make a gracious exit.

Jamie's silence was obviously unnerving the guy, who, in a voice crumbly with rising fear, croaked out, "Really, man, I don't want no trouble! We'll just leave, okay?"

"No, don't leave," Jamie finally said. "I know it's going to sound weird, Angie, but I'm very thankful to you for this."

"Wait—you're not mad at me?" Angie asked, sounding almost hurt.

"No. No, I'm not. Not at all. Actually, I needed this. I needed it all—the good and the bad. So, more than anything, I'm just feeling grateful. I'm going to head back to my campsite now. Don't let me put a damper on anything; just get back to whatever you were doing. But stay in touch, Angie. I'd like to hear about your beauty shop when that happens."

Angie seemed genuinely confused by Jamie's nonchalance. "Uh, okay, Jamie. I will."

He turned around and headed back on the path toward his campsite, but he heard the guy ask, "Was he your boyfriend or something?"

Angie said quietly, "Naw, just a guy I know from high school."

Jamie kept walking, but he momentarily wondered if, as this new guy groped and sucked and diddled her into a renewed sexual frenzy, she would think about Jamie at all. He doubted it. And he knew that was the way it was supposed to be. He chuckled to himself because his final thought about the whole event came right from Jimmy's and Joe's comments on the boat: he hoped the guy was wearing a jimmy—it's no fun when it burns when you pee!

15

As he brushed his teeth and got ready to walk to the wharf, Jamie had such an odd feeling of liberation that he wondered if it was similar to what the inhabitants of Petersburg, Virginia, had felt after that horrible siege ended in 1865. He was so relieved to be back to his regular and normal life that he didn't even dread how Joe and Jimmy would probably make him endure several days of "We told you so, we told you so!"

When he got to the wharf's parking lot, he glanced at where the car had been the night before and wondered at Angie and the guy's decision to have sex there. Joe's truck came flying down the hill. It spun into the parking lot with a spray of gravel, and Joe and Jimmy hopped out with more purpose than usual. They gathered their things and came right over to Jamie.

"'Morning," Jamie said, as always.

The two men exchanged a look, and then Joe said, "I was thinking we might want to take the day off. Go into town and do some shopping and some drinking."

"Hell, yeah!" Jimmy responded enthusiastically.

Jamie was surprised by this announcement because they hadn't missed a single day of fishing all summer, and he didn't know why they would do so this day. He peered out at the horizon for some sign of an approaching storm. "Is the weather going to turn?"

"Naw, it's supposed to be beautiful," Joe stated.

"Then why would we take an unscheduled day off?"

"Geez, boy scout, don't worry, your mommy won't spank you for playing hooky for one day!" Jimmy teased.

Jamie scratched his head. The two guys seemed to be staring at him, expecting him to say something. He looked at the water and then back at Joe. "Huh. Well, it's your call, right, captain?"

"Damn right!"

"It just seems a weird time to take a day off. The boat's fine. The weather's good. The lobsters have been thick the last few days. Why take a day off now?"

Jimmy now seemed irked by Jamie's questions. "Who the hell cares why? Let's just go into town and take the day off, college boy!"

Joe said calmly, "Hey, no reason to get pissy, Jimmy. Isn't this why we like the kid so much? Most sternmen would look for any excuse to not go fishing, but this kid's looking for an excuse *to* go. You gotta like his dedication."

"Yeah, but he's looking a gift horse in the mouth, ain't he? You're here, trying to help a guy out who's in a bad place, and he's asking why. I just don't think that's cool, Joe."

Jamie broke in with, "Why do you think I'm in a bad place?"

"What?"

"You just said to Joe that he's trying to help a guy who's in a bad place, and since you must be referring to me, I want to know why you two think I'm in such a bad place."

Joe cleared his throat and said, "Hey, we know that you found Angie over there fucking another guy last night, and we figured you'd be upset. It's never easy to get broken up with, but to catch the bitch doing it with another guy, that's gotta hurt. I mean, it's not like we didn't tell you that this was gonna happen, but it must have hurt like hell to have it happen that way. We thought it would be better for you to take the day off and do some drinking to forget about it all."

"Huh! How the hell does this kind of news get out?" Jamie asked in exasperation.

Joe shrugged. "How many times do we gotta tell you that news travels fast here?"

"Fast? It's like live streaming coverage!" Jamie said, and had to chuckle.

Joe lifted his baseball cap and used his knuckles to scratch his scalp before putting the hat back on. "So, what do you say, Jamie, wanna take the day off?"

"No, I don't. Look, thanks for thinking about me, guys, it means a lot to me. But I'm fine. You know, all those mean things you said to me the other day were the truth. I knew what Angie was and what our relationship was really about, so I'm not surprised at all how it ended. I'm a little bummed that she got bored with me and found someone new as quickly as she did, but the events of last night are not as hurtful as you might think. To tell you the truth, I'd rather go fishing and make some money—I think that'd make me feel better than goofing off and drinking today."

Joe grinned proudly at Jamie, but Jimmy seemed wholeheartedly disappointed. Joe looked out at the water, then clapped his good arm around Jamie's shoulders. "Atta boy! Spoken like a real lobsterman. Come on, let's go commit some lobstercide!"

Jimmy didn't quite say "Aw," but it was clear that he was more than a little disappointed with the decision and slightly angry at Jamie's determination to go fishing. Joe's good-natured grin disappeared when he looked at his ace man. "Come on, you big lush, the only fucking reason you're upset about going to work is that you have to wait another eight hours for your first beer! Buck up, little camper, let's go fishing. Afterwards, I'll get you a whole twelve-pack for yourself. How does that sound?"

This cheered Jimmy up, and he noogied Jamie's head. "Hey, don't tell nobody, but I found a girlfriend of mine fucking someone else once. It hurt more than you're letting on. Even cracking the guy's skull open and driving his car into the drink didn't make me feel any better…okay, maybe a little better."

"Yeah, but you didn't find her fucking in the wharf parking lot, now did you?' Joe said with a snicker. "That must have been a little weird."

Jamie said, "It does seem like a strange place to have public sex."

"Easier for the satellite to see her."

Jamie tilted his head to see if Joe was kidding. "What do you mean?"

"What time did you catch her?"

"I dunno."

"I can tell you," Joe said with a shrug. "It was just about eight o'clock."

"How do you know that?"

Jimmy put his hands on his hips as he explained, "You see, Jamie,

Angie's a classic exhibitionist. Now, exhibitionism is not automatically a compulsion, as some people think. There're just people who have a distinctive tendency to sexually expose themselves. When it becomes a compulsion, it's a condition sometimes called apodysophilia. Angie is an exhibitionist, but she does not require public sex to come to complete orgasm."

Joe said dryly, "I'm not even going to fucking ask what show you were watching to learn that one! But he's right: Angie gets off better when she's outside fucking exactly at eight p.m."

"Because she comes a lot harder when she thinks the satellite is watching her!" Jimmy added enthusiastically.

"Think about it. She begged you to have sex outside at night, right? You probably didn't check a clock at that moment, but I'll bet it was just before eight p.m. and that she came like a train to the station!"

"And how the hell would you two know *any* of this?"

"Hey, Kestrel Cove is a small town, bub."

"Yeah, but..."

Joe started walking away. "Well, if we're gonna commit some lobstercide, we ain't gonna do it flapping our gums here on the wharf. Let's hit it!"

Even though it was a very hot and hard day, working on the back of the boat was the wash cycle to clean out any dirt that had gathered between the three of them during the Angie Williams episode. Throughout the day, Joe and Jimmy kept checking on Jamie, but there was nothing to indicate that there was anything wrong with him. As a matter of fact, the college boy seemed more animated and more a part of the team than he had for some time. And during the breaks, they kept the conversations away from Angie, and Jamie was involved and even forceful in voicing his opinions.

When Joe declared that he thought the solution for all of the troubles in the Middle East lay in carpet bombing the area with nuclear weapons to turn the whole desert into one giant sheet of glass, Jamie calmly told him what a ridiculous idea it was to destroy the world to fix a problem that the United States had been so instrumental in starting and maintaining. Jimmy and Joe were incredulous, and lit into Jamie with a cruel combination of humor and ridicule, but the three of them enjoyed the scrap. The entire debate wrapped up with everyone involved being satisfied that they were all right and that Jamie was fine and didn't need any more pampering.

But the idea of doing something special for Jamie was crackling on the airwaves between other boats. Originally, it was Wiley's idea to throw him a party. Ever since the college boy had bested him at the fish house meeting, he'd taken a special interest in him. He'd personally cringed when it became common knowledge that Jamie and Angie Williams were sleeping together. And when he heard about Jamie catching that little slut with another guy, he'd almost gone out to look for him to kick his ass. Now he wanted to do something for Jamie to help him get over Angie, and what was better than a huge party? He'd asked Bobbie to talk on the radio with every boat to get commitments from the other sternmen and captains to come to Jamie's campsite to party hard that evening.

Joe had been listening to the conversations on the radio with keen interest. Although he knew that Jamie was fine, he was impressed and somewhat proud that the guys of the cove wanted to throw a party in his sternman's honor, and it made Jimmy and Joe beam like proud fathers. When the announcement was made that they were stopping a little early, Jamie furrowed his brow with suspicion. As he washed down the boat on the way to the wharf, he was surprised to see that many of the other boats in the fleet were also heading in early. With another five or six hours of sunlight left in the day, this seemed highly unusual.

At the wharf, everything and everybody was moving with a quickened pace. They unloaded the lobsters like it was a race, and even the wharf rats seemed in a hurry. As they came up from the floating dock, Joe announced to Jamie, "There's been a call for a party at your campsite this afternoon, so we need to go to the store and buy some beer."

"What?" Jamie asked in genuine confusion.

"Wiley's organized a party at your campsite."

"Why?"

"Good God!" Jimmy exclaimed. "Do you gotta ask that question about *every*thing?"

"I'm just wondering why someone would organize a party for a complete stranger, that's all."

Joe gave him a semiserious look. "I guess you ain't as much of a stranger as you think, Jamie. Wiley thinks you need something to get over the whole Angie thing, and he figures a big old party would do the trick. It usually does. It's actually an incredibly nice thing, and you should take it as the compliment it is. The radio's been full of plans for it all day, which is pretty cool, actually. There's a bunch of sternmen and even some captains who said they'll come to your campsite for a drink tonight. Granted, most guys from Kestrel Cove don't need much of an excuse to do that, but it still shows that you're becoming part of this place after all. You know, not every goddamn flunky who works on the back of a boat in this cove gets such special treatment after their ride on the Angie Williams roller coaster is over!"

Jamie smiled. "Well, then, I guess we should go to the store and buy a couple *cases* of beer! One for the guys and one for Jimmy!"

"Hey, fuck you, you little puke!" Jimmy said with a laugh.

Jamie had heard Joe loud and clear—it was an honor to have all the guys wanting to throw him a party—so it was crucial for him to embrace the idea and have fun. They climbed into Joe's truck and sped to the store. While Jimmy called Linda from the public phone outside to ask her to pick him up later, Jamie and Joe went inside to buy the beer and snacks. As soon as he walked by the registers, the dark-haired cashier clucked her tongue at Jamie. She obviously had a burning dislike for him, and every time she saw him, she glared menacingly. She now took the opportunity to say loudly, "I wonder who you're going to find your girlfriend fucking tonight!"

Joe sucked some air in over his teeth at this nasty comment, but Jamie acted as if he hadn't even heard it. Shelley, over at the other register, sent a silent signal for the other cashier to stop. But the young woman's scratchy voice broke the uneasy silence again. "Well, of course, with Angie, you'd have to check every hour, on the hour, to get a full roster of who's screwing her at that exact moment!"

Joe was about to turn around and say something, but he saw that her taunts were having no impact on his sternman at all. Jamie picked up the two cases of cold beer, and headed toward the front of the store. "Hey, Joe, should we buy some chips?"

Joe wondered at Jamie's nonchalance, but just said, "Uh, yeah, I guess that'd be good."

"Could you please grab a couple of bags, then?"

Joe shuffled off toward the chip aisle. The dark-haired cashier cackled, "Of course, the Angie Williams Fuck Club probably has more members than the goddamn Mickey Mouse Club! Instead of wearing those hats with the mouse ears on their heads, the members of that club would have to wear giant red plastic sore-covered cocks around their waists. How's that sound, college boy?"

Jamie ignored her. He walked up to Shelley's line and put his cases of beer onto the belt. Joe came up and wanted to pay for the chips and beer, but Jamie refused his offer. Shelley smiled sweetly at him and leaned forward. "Don't let her get under your skin. Veronica has a lot of good qualities, too. You know—"

"What the hell, Shelley? Don't talk to the little puke! Jesus, girl, he's scum!"

Jamie turned to face the dark-haired cashier. "Veronica?"

"Yeah, pecker head?"

"Well, from the intense anger you're displaying toward Angie Williams right now, I'd guess that she has wronged you at some time. Perhaps she took a boyfriend or girlfriend of yours, which can be heartbreaking. From your general outward appearance," Jamie gestured with his hands to point out some of her slovenly features, "I'd guess that you haven't replaced that special person quite yet. But don't worry; with the obvious positive qualities that you possess and the incredible charm and wit that are so elemental to your personality, you'll land another special person very soon—within weeks, months, or possibly a year or two, I'm sure. You reek of being a love magnet, Veronica—for either a dude or a chick."

Jamie turned back to Shelley, who was standing with her mouth open and his change in her extended hand. He reached out and took the money from her, but he made more contact than was totally necessary. She seemed to be waiting for the eruption of Veronica and didn't respond to his hand-touching. Jamie thanked her, grabbed the beer cases, and headed out the door of the store. He didn't turn around, but if he had, he would have seen three people—Veronica, Shelley, and Joe—all standing silent and stunned by his quick-witted rebuttal of Veronica's attack.

As Jamie put the cases of beer in the back of the truck, Jimmy cleared his throat to indicate that he wanted one. When he cleared his throat again, Jamie handed him a second one and they got into the truck. Suddenly, Joe came flying out of the store and hopped in. Without warning, he started the engine and threw it into gear, spilling some of Jimmy's beer as he backed up with the ferocity of a demolition derby driver.

"Hey, what the hell, Joe?" Jimmy barked as he wiped his shirt off.

The door of the store flew open and Veronica barreled out, her face red and twisted in rage. Shelley was trying to hold her back, but she was bellowing, "Where's that fucking little puke? I'm gonna kick his scrawny little ass!"

Jimmy saw Veronica coming toward the truck and he started hollering, "Joe, get us the fuck out of here! Hurry, hurry!"

Joe jammed the accelerator down, and the truck spun in a shower of rocks and shot out of the parking lot, screaming a little when the rubber met the paved road. The engine howled and the tires rumbled with their own primordial rhythm. They hadn't gone too far before Jimmy finally asked, "What the hell happened in there?"

"Jamie just told off Veronica."

"You're kidding me!"

"Well, I think he did. I mean, I've never heard anything like it! On the one hand, it sounded like he was being kind and caring, but on the other hand, I think he just called Veronica an ugly dyke who lacks charm. I ain't exactly sure, to tell you the truth. I don't think Veronica is totally sure, either. She certainly wasn't pleased with his comment, however, as you could see. Jesus, Jamie, you nailed the part about her losing a boyfriend to Angie! Holy shit, I don't think I've ever seen that girl so riled up!"

Jimmy polished off his beer. "You're just lucky the girl didn't have any weapons on her—we'd be driving you to the emergency room if she had."

Joe nodded. "I'd give her quite a bit of room for the next few weeks or months, Jamie. Maybe even more room than you give Drake."

When they pulled into Jamie's campsite, there were several trucks already parked near his tent, and a small group of men was standing around with beers in their hands. Jimmy barely waited for the truck to come to a stop before he jumped out, grabbed another beer, and enthusiastically joined the group. Jamie grabbed the cases of beer from the back of the truck and lugged them over to a fish tote filled with ice. Just then, another truck came flying down the driveway and skidded to a stop. Wiley jumped out, and with a raucous rebel yell, bounded over to Jamie with a half-drunk bottle of bourbon in his hand. He pumped Jamie's hand and smacked him on the shoulder, slurring a string of encouragements about recovering from heartbreak, and offering other advice about love. Jamie quietly leaned forward and said, "Hey, Wiley, I hear you're the guy who did all this. Thank you."

Wiley smiled bashfully, "Ah, I just needed an excuse to drink with the guys."

And as quickly as he'd come up, Wiley continued on and joined the group already drinking. Jamie felt hurt from this last comment, but he'd seen the twinkle in Wiley's eyes and knew that it had been said in good humor. He smiled, shook his head at this befuddling Kestrel Cove culture, and then sought out Joe to drink a few beers with him.

A fire ring was made with rocks from the shoreline, wood was gathered from the forest, and a large bonfire was soon blazing. A radio in one of the trucks was turned up and blaring country music. With the tunes, the fire, and the booze, the gathering quickly took on the roiling atmosphere of a party. By the time the sun had sunk lower in the sky and more and more men had arrived at the campsite, Joe had thoroughly circulated the story of Jamie telling off Veronica. This prompted many of the men to come and clap Jamie on the back with laughter and words of encouragement—and to quietly warn him to never turn his back on her in the future.

The beer supply didn't last long. With the men drinking hard and the energy of the party building, Joe caught Jamie's attention and showed him the nearly empty fish tote. "Somebody needs to go to the store to get more beer."

Jamie could see that no one was going to volunteer, so he offered to walk there to buy as many beers as he could carry in his backpack. Joe announced Jamie's trip to the store and asked if anyone needed anything. Jamie was suddenly inundated with so many orders and cash for cigarettes, cigars, chips, beer, and porno magazines, he had to make a shopping list before walking up the driveway with his empty backpack on his shoulders.

When he reached the main road, he was surprised to run into Bill Hand. "Oh, hey, Jamie. I was just on my way down to say hi."

"Hey, Bill, we're having a party."

The blasting country music and the sounds of drunken conversation, sprinkled with occasional shouts, made it abundantly obvious that a party was raging nearby. Bill Hand chuckled. "Uh, yeah, I know, Jamie. The entire peninsula knows about this party."

"Well, we're pretty much out of beer, so I'm headed to the store to get more."

Bill Hand frowned. "On foot?"

"There's not much sobriety down there, and the last thing I want is for one of those guys to get in a drunk-driving accident while buying more beer for my party! I figured it was safest for me to hoof it."

Bill Hand considered for a moment. "You know, I've been standing here for a few minutes, debating whether to make an appearance or not. You see, parties are not my thing, but I wanted to support you. But now, if you don't mind waiting just a minute, I'll run up and get one of my cars to drive you to the store. That way, I'll be helping, but I won't have to go to the party. What do you say?"

"Sure, Bill. I'll just head down the road a ways until you come up, okay?"

Bill Hand did not answer, because he'd already slipped into the forest and was gone. Jamie started walking and wondering if he would ever understand the elusive Bill Hand. Several cars drove past him, but none stopped. In his haste to leave and get the vehicle, Bill Hand hadn't told Jamie what kind of car he would be driving, so with each approaching vehicle, Jamie tensed up in case it was his ride. Then he heard a throaty whine that was unlike anything he'd heard before, and he knew that Bill Hand was coming. When the completely restored cherry-red 1928 Stutz BB Black Hawk Speedster pulled up next to him, he froze and mouthed the word "Wow!"

Bill Hand was sitting behind the wheel with a huge grin. "Well, hop in, Jamie."

"This is a killer car!" Jamie exclaimed as he took in the surprisingly simple interior.

"You're sitting in a piece of Kestrel Cove history, Jamie. This is the very car that made the fortunes of several important families from this peninsula. Drake's uncle, Oliver Muldoon, drove this during Prohibition to deliver illegal booze from the cove to the grateful drinkers of Maine and beyond. I had her completely restored, except I left the bullet holes in the fenders. The engine is pure magic. Oliver had her set up to go as fast as a jet plane. He was far ahead of his time, and with the booze money flooding in, price was no object. Legend says that he went down to the fair city of Boston and picked this beauty up, then drove her into a secret garage to make the necessary modifications to the engine. I haven't driven her in a dog's age, so I thought it'd be fitting to do so as we drive to get beer for your party. Pretty clever of me, huh?"

Jamie tried to nod, but Bill Hand hit the accelerator and the car leaped forward, sending him deep into his seat. The sound of the engine was almost feral, and Jamie struggled to see the speedometer—it was inching up to 100 mph. The store went flying past.

"Hey, Bill?" Jamie yelled over the engine noise.

"Yeah?"

"The store…we just passed it."

"Shit! Sorry! Once you get comfortable in this car, you want to drive to the moon and back. Hey, wanna buy your beer in Portland? We could do it in forty minutes!"

"Naw, Bill, I think the guys would rather me buy at the store so I can get back quick."

"Quite right. The host of the party shouldn't be gone too long, should he? Plus," Bill Hand said with a sneaky grin on his face, "Shelley's probably still working at the store. Perhaps you would impress her pulling up in this baby, huh? Oh, no! Veronica's still working, isn't she?"

"Probably. Why?"

Bill Hand clucked his tongue. "You really better let me drive you to Brementon. It'd be safer than going in to face the wrath of Veronica. She's probably still pissed from you calling her a lesbian without any graces. You really seem to know which characters to take on, Jamie. First Drake, now Veronica. Both of those people have the ability to make your life in Kestrel Cove incredibly uncomfortable."

"Does every citizen have a police scanner of Kestrel Cove scuttlebutt?"

"Life in a small town. Love it or leave it," Bill Hand responded coolly. He turned the car around and drove quickly back to the store. Before Jamie could get out, Bill Hand asked quietly, "Are you sure you want to go in there?"

"I need beer and they sell beer, Bill."

"Just stay close to Shelley. She'll protect you."

Jamie took a deep breath and opened the door. He wanted to walk in confidently to face the fiery and vengeful Veronica. But when he didn't see her at her register, he scurried to the beer section, grabbed two cases, and headed back to the check-out. Shelley's register belt was full of items, and she was standing there with a smirk on her face as he came up. "Well, hello again," she said.

"Oh, hello," Jamie stammered, still looking around nervously.

"Don't worry, she's gone home," Shelley said sweetly without looking up from scanning the items.

"Did I upset her so much she had to go home early?"

"Naw, she started her period today, and she's bleeding like a stuck pig."

Jamie had no idea how to respond to this, which made Shelley grin even more. He looked down at the pile of merchandise on the belt, and thinking that someone was checking out in front of him, he grabbed his cases of beer and held them back as the belt began to move.

"Oka-a-ay, you can let those cases come up here so I can scan them, too," Shelley said.

"But that's not my stuff!" Jamie blurted out.

"Wow, you *are* flustered, aren't you? Or maybe drunk?"

"What are you talking about?"

"The guys called ahead for me to pick out the items on your list."

Jamie missed most of what she said because he was staring at her again.

"Hello-o-o?" Shelley warbled, breaking him out of his spell.

"Oh, gosh, sorry. What were you saying?"

"I asked you if you wanted me to undress for you."

Jamie was flabbergasted. "*What?*"

"Well, you were just undressing me with your eyes, which seemed to be taxing you so much that you couldn't even answer my simple questions or pay for these groceries. And since I'd like to go home at some point tonight, I thought I'd save you the effort and just undress for you!"

"Oh…gosh…no, don't do that. Oh, I mean, I would love it if you…I mean, I'm sorry, I wasn't doing what you think I was. Sometimes I try to come up with just one word that describes the person I'm looking at. It's one of my most annoying habits, and I usually end up looking like an idiot as I do it. And that was what I was just doing to you. I'm terribly sorry."

"Oh, yeah?" Shelley asked skeptically. "And what word did you just come up with for me? Naked? Sexy? Boobies? Hmm?"

Jamie licked his lips. He couldn't think up a lie, but the truth sounded stupid. He exhaled and said it anyway. "Vitality."

"Vitality? Really? That doesn't sound too exciting," Shelley said with disappointment.

"Are you kidding? Vitality comes from the word *Vita*, which means *life*. When I think of you, I think of someone who has the bright light of life. You're so beautiful and intelligent, you literally shine." Jamie's voice trailed off because he realized he had said way too much. He had not only called her beautiful, but he had probably insulted her, too. He coughed and looked at the pile of groceries waiting to be bagged.

Shelley hadn't taken her eyes off of Jamie for a second. Her cheeks were flushed with the compliments he'd just uttered, and she suddenly felt the rush of possibilities between the two of them. She was grateful that Veronica was not here now, because this moment between her and Jamie was too personal and intimate for anyone else to see. But now the boy needed to hurry up and get back to his party, so she looked at the register display and automatically said, "That'll be seventy dollars and fifty cents."

Jamie muttered. "I'm having a party."

"Yeah, no shit, Sherlock."

He looked up into her eyes and saw nothing but mischievousness. He rolled his eyes. "Oh right, news travels pretty quick around here, huh?"

"Actually, I figure that any guy who comes in here and buys two cases of beer, five bags of chips, cigarettes, cigars, and…what are these?… porno mags! and *isn't* having a party, must have a major problem!"

Jamie chuckled as he handed over the money. "You know," he said quietly, "you could come to the party if you wanted to."

Shelley surveyed the store in a pantomime that she was working, and said, "Thanks, but if I were to show up, I'd get shit from all sides. The boys would think that you and me are an item, which ain't never gonna happen, college boy. And the girls, especially Veronica, would be after my hide for going to a party without them. So thanks for the invite, but I think I'll just finish my shift and go home. Okay?"

Jamie nodded. "I'll take the cases to the car and come back for the rest."

He headed out and put the beer in the backseat of the Stutz, which was purring like a cat as it idled. Bill Hand said, "You were taking forever in there. I almost came in to make sure Veronica wasn't beating the shit out of you. But when I didn't see her car anywhere, I figured she's not here. And if she's not here, then you and Shelley were all alone. And if you two were in there alone, I figured the beer purchase might take a little longer."

Jamie nodded. "And there are more groceries inside. I'll be right back."

"Take your time," Bill Hand crooned.

Jamie went back in and gathered up the groceries. Shelley smiled sweetly at him. "So, Mr. Hand's giving you a ride in the old Stutz, huh?"

"Yeah, it was kind of him to drive me. That way I don't have to carry the beer in my backpack."

"Uh-huh. Well, you better tell Bill to drive like a fury to get you back. Leaving those guys out there for this long was mighty risky. Booze and Kestrel Cove fishermen is a tough mix—it can get out of hand just like that. See you later!"

Jamie stopped to say something, but then her mild warning registered a tingle of alarm, and he hurried out of the store. As soon as he took his seat, Bill Hand raced the car out of the parking lot and shot down the main road. Jamie was quiet for a time, and finally Bill

Hand said, "Maybe you should ask her out."

"Shelley? Yeah, I should, Bill, but I still feel unclean from Angie Williams, and I don't want that to contaminate the next relationship I try to start. But there's definitely something about Shelley that makes me want to unabashedly ask her out. I just want it to be at the right time, that's all."

"Very logical."

Jamie sighed. "Matters of the heart are never logical."

When they got to the driveway, Bill Hand stopped the car and said, "I'd rather not drive down there. Do you mind lugging all the stuff?"

"'Course not. I wouldn't want you to get this beauty stuck down there."

"Well actually, this car made a career of driving the back roads and through muck and mud. Believe me, it's not the car getting stuck that I'm worried about."

Jamie understood. He grabbed the bags and set them on the shoulder of the road. He was about to reach for the cases of beer when the explosion of a shotgun filled the air, followed by a loud cheer. There was another concussion and another cheer.

"What do you think is going on, Bill?"

"One can only imagine," Bill Hand said with a shake of his head. He turned off the Stutz and slid out of the car. Jamie hoped he would grab a case of beer or the bags of groceries, but he walked past them and down the driveway without looking back. So Jamie grabbed everything and scurried behind him like a loaded Sherpa.

As they rounded the slight bend in the driveway, they came across the first white body of a dead seagull lying in the road with its bloodied wings sprawled in a way that looked like the earth had risen up and smacked into the bird in midflight. Bill Hand kneeled down and moved the bird's head. He stood up as if he'd been stung. "Ah, Jesus!'

Another concussion and another cheer.

Bill Hand took off like a rabbit, running down the driveway toward the party. Jamie left the cases of beer on the ground next to the dead gull and tried to keep up. They found another dead gull, stopped and looked at it silently for a moment, then continued on. They passed another one stuck in the low branches of a tree. Jamie could now see that the party had split into two groups, one around the campfire and one by the water. Bill Hand and Jamie ran directly to the group at the fire, and when Bill Hand yelled at them, his lispy voice was high-pitched. "What the fuck is going on here?"

Several of the men standing around the fire started to speak, but then they saw the fury in his eyes and remained silent. Finally, Ed Simmons came out of the shadows and staggered forward. "Well…uh…Bill, some of those young shits got pissed at the way the gulls were pestering us…and someone said they should shoot 'em."

"Shoot 'em?" Bill Hand echoed.

"Uh, yeah…shoot 'em…" It seemed that he might have more to say, but he closed his mouth and drifted back into the shadows again.

"Ah, Jesus!" Bill Hand breathed. Then he said in a tight voice, "Gentlemen, this party's officially over! Go home!"

Bill Hand didn't wait for anyone to debate his authority, he just turned and headed off toward the group on the shoreline. Jamie ran to catch up, passing several more bodies of dead gulls. At the water's edge, they found Wiley and other sternmen standing in a semicircle. Vernon Quigley's new sternman, Bob Freeman, was holding the shotgun. Wiley had a nearly empty bag of sandwich bread in his hand. In front of them, the waters were clogged with the floating bodies of dead gulls.

When Bill Hand and Jamie came up, Wiley asked, "Hey, where's the beer, dude?"

Bob Freeman echoed the question. "Yeah, where's the god-damn beer?"

But Wiley immediately saw how angry Bill Hand was as he looked at the dead birds, and he hung his head. "Sorry, Bill."

When Bill Hand spoke, his voice was brittle and dry. "Do you all know what you've done here tonight?"

The tone of his voice made most of the men wilt with the serious-ness of the situation. But Bob Freeman remained jovially unaware that he'd done anything wrong. "Yeah, we been shooting gulls. We're doing the community a public service. These fuckers won't get into anyone's trash tonight!"

Bill Hand snarled, "These *fuckers*, as you so delicately put it, are federally protected, you moron! They're as protected as whales and bald eagles! Do you realize just how much trouble you're all in? *Do* you? You can't shoot gulls, for God's sake!"

Bob Freeman still seemed to not understand the implications. "They're fucking gulls! There's millions of them!"

Wiley seemed to be cringing with embarrassment as he took a step forward and said in a forlorn voice, "Uh, we're sorry, Mr. Hand. We'll clean it all up, and no one will have to know. It'll be okay."

Bill Hand sighed loudly. "Oh, Wiley, you can't do something this stupid and just swipe it under the carpet. Not this time. This is gonna leave a mark."

"What do you mean?"

"You know that red cottage out there on Busters Island?"

The men collectively nodded.

"Well, who lives out there?"

"The MacAurthurs," Wiley said quietly.

"Yep, Eugene and Martha MacAurthur. Anyone wanna guess what they do for a living?"

There was silence.

"They are the heads—the *heads*—of the Maine chapter of the Ornithological Society of America. For those of you who are not familiar with that big word, *orn-i-tho-logical* refers to *birds*! So, at this very moment, pointed directly at you, is one of the most powerful bird-watching telescopes on the entire coast of Maine. Your little gull shoot has been seen and probably photographed by the head of the most powerful bird protection agency on the fucking East Coast. By now, they've made several impassioned phone calls to the local authorities, and if those were ignored, I'm sure they called federal sources of law enforcement."

Someone in the darkness whistled. Wiley shuffled his feet on the pebbled beach, making a sound like geological castanets.

But Bill Hand was not done. He turned to Jamie. "Remember how each time you've seen me puttering around this land, I've been searching for different birds?"

"Yes."

"The MacAurthurs study the birds that inhabit this land and call me to let me know where they all hang out. They've been more than a little peeved about you staying here, but I swore to them that you wouldn't hurt their birds. This little party of yours just cost you a place to live."

"Whoa!" Wiley yelped, waving his hands. "Jamie wasn't involved! He wasn't even here. He was buying beer when the shooting started. If the MacAurthurs are staring at us through their telescope and took pictures of the shooting, they'll know that Jamie just arrived with you. He's not in trouble."

Bill Hand assumed a conciliatory tone saying, "No, Wiley, he's in quite a bit of trouble, actually. You see, after they watched this massacre through that magnificent telescope, they've called their entire cell phone's address book for law enforcement. They may have even called the governor's office and the Coast Guard. And, depending on Sheriff Gus's attitude tonight, he may be on his way to escort Jamie off this land right this very moment. After watching this display of—" he glanced around at the carcasses of dead gulls and sighed, "idiotic carnage, the MacAurthurs will want blood. Jamie will be the villain, so they'll want his."

"*What?*" said Jamie in disbelief.

"Sorry, Jamie, but that's what happens at a party where dozens of protected gulls are executed and you're the reason for the party. Of course, it's going to all fall on you."

Jamie looked down at the ground and clenched his fists in frustration.

Wiley spoke up. "Okay, what can we do for Jamie?"

"Everyone needs to clear out of here *now*. If the sheriff does decide to make an appearance tonight, it would be worse to have a gaggle of drunken guys meet him."

"All right, you assholes, you heard the man, everybody go home!" Wiley bellowed.

"You too, Wiley."

"Aw, come on, Bill, I want to help. I'm the guy who got Jamie in trouble in the first place. This whole party was my idea. I gotta stay."

"If you really want to help out, Wiley, you need to make yourself scarce, too."

Wiley turned to Jamie and said quietly, "Dude, I'm so sorry. It was stupid to start shooting those gulls."

Jamie patted Wiley on the shoulder. "I know, Wiley. Sometimes good things have a way of spinning out of control, right? But, like the great Robert E. Lee said, 'Get correct views of life, and learn to see the world in its true light. It will enable you to live pleasantly, to do good, and, when summoned away, to leave without regret.'"

Wiley looked intently at Jamie and said with a shake of his head, "I have no fucking idea what you just said, college boy, but I sure hope it meant that you're accepting my apology for getting you evicted tonight!"

16

After Bill Hand helped Jamie take down his camp and clean up as much of the mess from the party as they could, he offered to put Jamie up in his gatehouse for the night. When they were back in the Stutz, Jamie suddenly remembered the two cases of beer and the groceries he'd dropped. He opened his car door again and said, "Hey, wait a minute, Bill. I'm going to get all that stuff we brought back from the store."

But of course, everything was gone. He didn't really want any of it, but the missing items put a cap on the catastrophic night. Losing his idyllic campsite and becoming the main culprit in an environmental massacre made him angry, but finding that one of the fleeing partygoers had stopped long enough to pilfer the beer and groceries made him close his eyes, clench his fists, and roar in frustration.

When he got back in the car and told Bill Hand that everything was gone, the man responded coolly, "To be expected, really."

Jamie's anger began to boil over. "Jesus Christ, Bill, who starts shooting seagulls at a party, for God's sake?"

"Ah, Jamie, the citizens of Kestrel Cove never disappoint. They're amusing from afar, but infuriating when you're in their midst. You have to understand, these men are like children—when you leave them to their own devices, they're bound to hurt themselves or someone else. And if alcohol's in the mix, even well-intentioned acts can go sour."

"I just can't believe Wiley would do this to me!"

Bill Hand's head swiveled quickly to look at him. "Jamie, before you pass judgment on that boy, I really want you to think about who was here to face the fire tonight and who had already skedaddled. In other words, who wasn't here when we got back and found the boys shooting? I think that as you think about the cast of characters who were still here when we returned, you'll find some specific people missing. Now, maybe they left before the trouble started. Or maybe they stirred things up and left before the shit hit the fan. If it's the latter, then someone really hung you out to dry tonight, but that person sure wasn't Wiley. Because, even with all his faults and foibles, he would never do that to you."

"Okay, you may be right, Bill. I won't be too hard on Wiley. But I'm still screwed! I liked that camping spot. It was convenient to get to work, and it was peaceful and quiet. But now I'm homeless again. What the hell am I going to do?"

Responding to the frustration in Jamie's voice, Bill Hand said kindly, "Well, you're set for tonight in the gatehouse. Tomorrow, I'm sure the guys will find you a new place. It won't be quite as lovely, but you'll be fine. Don't worry; these things have a way of working themselves out."

"I just need to get some sleep tonight," Jamie said through clenched teeth.

At the gatehouse, Bill Hand flipped his high beams on to illuminate the front door of the building. He walked over to a large rock, turned it over, and pulled the key out of its hiding spot. He unlocked the door, turned on the lights in the stairwell, and signaled Jamie to come in.

The gatehouse was a two-story brick building with a red tile roof. Although it was small, it looked and felt like it could survive a hurricane, a tornado, or a direct assault from any enemy invader. The stairwell went directly up to the apartment on the second floor.

"Is there anything on the first floor, Bill?" Jamie asked.

"Just storage," Bill Hand said with a shrug.

The apartment was almost luxurious. The shining hardwood floors, the crisp white walls, and the shining faucets, fittings, and appliances all made the gatehouse a smaller relative of the big house atop the hill. Jamie was feeling too blue to appreciate it all, and he looked at Bill Hand sadly and stated, "I'm just going to bed, Bill."

"Okay, Jamie. I'll go down and turn on the hot-water heater so you can take a shower."

"Before you go, Bill, I really want you to know how grateful I am for everything you've done for me. If it weren't for you letting me stay here, I'd be in jail or just wandering around in the woods tonight. Thank you."

"Don't mention it, Jamie. Just remember, you didn't do anything wrong tonight—it's just the way parties in Kestrel Cove tend to go. It'll look better in the morning. Good night."

"Good night, Bill."

Jamie heard him head down the stairs and then drive away, and the ensuing silence made him feel very out of sync. Before he got ready for bed, he explored the apartment. The main room was divided in two by a double-sided bookcase. On one side of the bookcase, a couch, a large comfortable chair, and a rocking chair surrounded a beautifully hand-carved coffee table, creating a living area that was small but cozy. On the other side, there was a dining room table and four chairs.

When Jamie browsed the books on the shelves of the bookcase, he noticed that most of the titles were familiar. He grabbed the hard-cover copy of *Catch-22*. He gingerly opened the cover and looked at the title page, and he was shocked to find that it was a first edition. And there was a personal inscription from Joseph Heller to Bill Hand on the title page. After reading this, Jamie put the book back and picked up another. It was a first edition of Kurt Vonnegut's *Slaughterhouse Five*, and he found another intimate message from the author to Bill Hand. Jamie replaced it and took a step back. This bookcase was not only full of classic first editions, but each one had a personal inscription from the author—it was the El Dorado of modern literature!

Then Jamie spotted a book by his idol, Shelby Foote. Hands trembling with excitement, he reached out to grab it. He flipped open the cover and found the title page. There, from his own personal idol to none other than Bill Hand, was the inscription. Jamie gasped as he read it:

> *To Bill Hand,*
>
> *You would have made your ancestor, William Jason Hand, very proud with your creation of the Civil War Battlefield Protection Fund. Just as William Jason Hand had dug in and faced Lee's Tigers on the top of Culp Hill in the battle of Gettysburg, so too have*

*you dug in and faced the forces that threaten these
precious sites of such valor. By protecting them, you have
stemmed the assaults that they face in this modern era.
William Jason Hand and all the men from that noble
war salute you!*

Sincerely,

Shelby

Jamie put the book back on the shelf as gently as if he were placing an egg back in its nest, and then he sat down heavily in the nearby chair. He'd had no idea that Bill Hand had started the Civil War Battlefield Protection Fund! When the CWBPF had singlehandedly battled developers to ensure that several Virginia Civil War battlefields were protected from the tsunami of sprawl that was threatening to engulf them, Walter Whetstone had actually cried tears of joy. Not once, in any of their conversations, had Bill Hand alluded to the fact that he was a Civil War buff and battlefield protector.

Somewhat reinvigorated by this discovery, Jamie got up and continued his inspection of the apartment. The kitchen was set up like a ship's galley, so the appliances, shelves, and drawers all fit together like sleeping dogs. When he opened the small refrigerator, the only items inside were twelve bottles of beer. He was ready to shut the door, but the odd lettering on the beer caught his eye. At first, Jamie thought it was Japanese, but then he realized that it was squarer and flatter than Kanji. He guessed it was Korean. Jamie had never tasted a Korean beer before, and he was more than a little tempted to crack one open and try it. But it was too late at night for that, and he didn't want to do anything that might anger Bill Hand.

He began a quick inspection of the cupboards to see if there were any other surprises. There were several boxes and cans of foods that had what Jamie guessed was Arabic writing on them. It seemed highly unusual for a small kitchen in a Maine guesthouse to have Korean beer in the fridge and Arabic food in the cupboards, and he was curious enough to want to think up some indirect way to ask Bill Hand about it all in the future.

When the alarm clock woke him up the next morning, Jamie set about making sure that the guesthouse was put back in order. He meticulously made the bed, then carefully made sure that the bathroom was clean. He put everything back in its rightful spot in the apartment before gathering his things at the stairwell, writing a note of thanks to Bill Hand, and heading down the stairs.

He walked over to his former campsite and looked at the scene in the dawning light. Dead gull bodies lay on the ground like petals from a giant chrysanthemum, and Jamie shook his head at the senselessness of the slaughter. Instead of the fiery outrage he'd felt the night before, he now felt a deep-seated melancholy about the whole event. It seemed to him that whatever the people of Kestrel Cove touched turned out badly. And it didn't matter if it all started with good intentions—it all ended shitty! Even his own emotional roller coaster of the last few weeks seemed to bear this out. The whole series of events, from his wild affair with Angie Williams to their awkward public breakup to the throwing of the party to the horrible gull shoot, and finally, to his being thrown off his campsite, pointed to the fact that his life among these people consisted of nothing but extreme highs and lows. And Jamie had to wonder, if the rest of his time in Kestrel Cove followed this pattern, would he be able to survive with his sanity intact?

As soon as Joe's truck pulled into the wharf parking lot, Jimmy started making faces and laughing at Jamie about the bulging duffle bags and backpacks in his arms. But both men helped him put his gear in the bed of the truck. Jimmy howled, "Whoa! That was one helluva party last night, huh?"

"Yeah, but with dire consequences!" Jamie lamented.

Joe said, "Aw, don't worry, kid, we'll find a new campsite for you this afternoon."

"Not as nice as the one I was just thrown off of, huh?" Jamie retorted.

Joe's face was expressionless as he said "Beggars can't be choosers."

The hard work on the boat made the day fly by. The mindless labor helped Jamie manage his thoughts, as the loose threads of anger, sadness, pride, hope, and defeat all wrapped around each other and wove a rope of discord within him. He let the harshness and heat of the day coil it into neat piles well below the surface of his consciousness. Joe and Jimmy fed off Jamie's intensity, and the three men worked with such fluid efficiency that they hauled through the traps well before the sun had even threatened to sink in the western sky.

As they walked away from the wharf and toward the truck, Joe announced, "All right, let's find the college boy another place to camp."

Jimmy agreed. "Yeah, if we can find you another campsite quick, we can drink a few beers there together and have another little party!"

Jamie grabbed his gear. "Naw. You know what, guys? I think I'll take care of this one on my own."

Joe cocked an eyebrow at him. "You can't just walk around the woods with your gear and plunk your ass down somewhere, Jamie. You'll get shot doing that! Come on, let's go cruising for a new spot. We'll stop by the store and get a twelve-pack or two, and then find you a campsite."

"No thanks, Joe. I've spent the day thinking about this, and I've come to the conclusion that I need to find this one on my own."

"It's not like you're gonna hide from us," Jimmy leered, "we'll find you eventually, college boy."

Jamie chuckled. "Oh, don't worry, I'm not going to live in some cave like an ascetic."

"Ass-*what*?" Jimmy said. "Did you really just say you're gonna be an *ass-septic*?"

"Never mind, Jimmy," Joe said with a snort as he got into the truck and started the engine.

Jimmy waved his hands in the air. "Come on, Joe, we can't let him just wander around looking for a campsite!"

"Yes we can. As you may be aware, our college boy here has an independent streak a mile wide, and we gotta respect that. It's one of his better qualities. We need to let him figure this one out on his own. So why don't you and me go and get some beer and do some shooting at my place?...We'll see you tomorrow, Jamie. Good luck finding a good spot."

Jamie waited for the roar of the truck's engine to fade as it went up the hill and disappeared before looking around and saying aloud to himself, "Okay, Jamie Kurtz, what now?"

His first idea was to sleep in the Volvo. But when he got up to the garage, he found, much to his surprise, that the car's doors had all been removed. So even if Jerry would let him sleep in the car, the mosquitoes would drain all of his blood during the night. He found humor in the fact that the good news that Jerry was finally beginning to work on the car was now bad news for his search for a new place to sleep. His life seemed like a bank of elevators all going in conflicting directions.

Jamie thought about walking over to Bill Hand's gatehouse to spend another night there. But by the time he hit the open space of the pipeline, he had decided against that plan. He couldn't keep letting his friends bail him out—he needed to start solving his own problems. And that's when he suddenly remembered the campsite next to the store that Bill had shown him on their walk together. It had a fire ring and privy, and its location was perfect for Jamie to be able to walk to and from the wharf each day. It would be as good a place as any to camp for the night, and possibly for the rest of the summer. So Jamie started walking the pipeline in that direction with a new sense of optimism.

When he heard the familiar whine of an oncoming dirt bike, he stopped. And as soon as Wiley saw Jamie standing there, he shut off the engine and let the bike coast up to him. As he came up, he smiled. "Hey, when I heard you were out here trying to find a campsite, I came looking for you. What the hell you doing, wandering the pipeline with all your shit like a homeless person? That just ain't right!"

"Hey, Wiley, you know that spot near the store—the one with the shitter and fire ring?"

"Yeah, sure."

"Well, that's gonna be my new campsite. I mean, if no one's there already."

Wiley grinned. "Don't worry about that. If anybody's there, they'll vacate it for you. I'll make sure of that!"

Wiley walked his bike alongside Jamie as they made their way in silence for a while. Suddenly Wiley pushed a big hand up against Jamie's shoulder and said, "Dude, I'm wicked sorry for the fucking gull shoot last night! I never meant to get you in trouble!"

Jamie shook his head. "I know, Wiley. Plus, it wasn't just you."

"Naw, dude, I started shooting them gulls…"

"Yeah, but after someone else suggested it, right?"

Wiley cocked his head. "Yeah, that's true."

"Yeah, something Bill Hand said made me think about some things that led up to the gull shoot. I didn't notice it at the time, but Joe was gone when I got back from the store. I'm figuring it was him who first suggested the shoot."

"Uh-huh, he did. He said something that made me think about getting the gun from my truck to shoot them gulls."

"Yep, that makes sense. And he was also the one who noticed the beer was running out and that I should go to the store to get more."

"Huh, that's interesting."

"It sure is, Wiley, it's *very* interesting. I think that behavior's called stirring the turd!"

"So are you pissed at him?"

Jamie considered this for a moment. "Naw, but I see Joe in a new light because of it, I guess. It's not that I don't trust him, but I don't *totally* trust him—if you know what I mean."

"Sure."

They continued in silence until they came to the campsite. No one was there, but they found several beer cans and bottles lying around the fire ring. Wiley helped Jamie clear the spot, then went to the store and brought back a six-pack. He handed Jamie a beer and said, "I told the girls at the store that you were camping out here now. They were both glad to know that. And I gotta say, Shelley seemed really intrigued by the news. I think she likes you, dude."

Jamie grinned and blushed. "Really?"

"Hey, look at that—you like her, too! That's cool! Me and Shelley grew up together. She's beautiful and smart—way too smart for me—and you, being a college boy, you just might be the right guy for her."

Jamie's smile faded. "Wait a second…Veronica knows I'm back here, too? Jesus, Wiley, she'll come in the middle of the night and slit my throat!"

Wiley laughed. "Naw, dude, I think she kinda respects you. I guess any guy who can dish it out as well as he can take it gains that girl's respect. I'm sure she'll still mess with you whenever you're in the store, but if you keep proving you're a worthy adversary, she'll fight pretty fair."

"Huh, that's good…I guess."

"Now listen, don't leave any of your stuff out and about during the day. This place gets too many visitors who might have sticky fingers, if ya know what I mean. I'll make sure this place is known around as yours, but you also need to play it safe, too, okay?"

"Thanks, Wiley."

"Oh, sure. Hey, I gotta get going."

"Well, thanks for the help."

Wiley looked down at his feet and wagged his head. "Aw, fuck, after getting you chased off the other place, it's the least I could do."

"See you around. And come on over and visit whenever you want."

"Oh, you're gonna have a shitload more visitors here, dude. As a matter of fact, I think your social calendar is gonna fill right up."

Wiley kick-started his bike and took off. Jamie made a fire and cooked some dinner, and, while he ate, he looked around at the new spot. It was a comfortable campsite that was a little more exposed than the last place, but he knew that, once Wiley passed the news around that he was camping there, it was going to be secure.

As he was cleaning up from dinner, Shelley came timidly into the campsite to say hello. Although he was excited to see her, he was suddenly quite aware that he was still wearing his smelly work clothes. But Shelley didn't seem to notice. "So, are you comfy out here?" she said.

"Yeah, I think this'll work just fine. I'm just worried that Veronica is going to do something really bad to me out here."

Shelley shook her head. "Veronica's got attitude and a real bad temper, but she's not a malicious person. She likes getting mad and yelling at you, but she wouldn't do anything really terrible. She seems to like the drama that you provide, so she isn't going to ruin that fun by doing anything that leaves you permanently disabled!"

"That's good, I guess. Hey, would you like a beer, Shelley? Wiley left a couple with me. They're not ice-cold anymore, but they taste pretty good. Everything tastes better when you're camping."

She smiled at him. "Naw, I'm still working. I'm just taking a smoke break."

"You smoke?"

"Not anymore. I quit a year ago, but they still let me take my smoke breaks, so I usually go outside and just hang out. Tonight, I thought I should come over and say hi. Actually, I'd better get back inside—if I stay out here too long, Veronica will start a rumor that we had time to fool around. I'll see you around, neighbor."

"Yeah, see you, Shelley," Jamie waved.

Watching her retreat, the realization hit him that he'd already had visits with both Shelley and Wiley at his new campsite, which had never happened at the old one. It was definitely clear that, in this more central location, many more people were going to stop by and visit him. And although he wasn't an overly social person, it felt good to have the company. Especially if it was Shelley! He smiled at the way things were working out.

"Thought you could hide from us, huh?" Jimmy's voice boomed out from the darkening woods. He stepped into the campsite, followed by Joe, and each man had a can of beer in his hand. As they sat down on the log by the dying fire, Joe pulled out another one from the pocket of his sweatshirt and handed it to Jamie. "Here ya go, college boy. We decided to come by to check out your new spot. Pretty nice, huh?"

"Yeah," Jimmy said, "when Wiley called and told us about it, we were happy for you. Not only did you find a good place, kid, you got one that's easier for us to visit—and next to the store, too. Good job!"

Joe gave Jamie a sly smile. "And you've already had a visit from Shelley, huh?"

Jamie tried not to let on that Joe's comment had surprised him. "Yes, she came by to welcome me to the neighborhood."

"The way I hear it," Jimmy chuckled, "you guys had plenty of time to fool around. Did you feel up her boobs?"

"Jimmy, I'm not even going to dignify that with an answer," Jamie said, chuckling himself.

Joe said, "Yep, keep that intimate stuff private, college boy. Hey, Jimmy, remember Shirley Bailey?"

"Ya mean, Stick-It-in-My-Ass-Shirley?"

"Yep. I gave it to her right here in this very campsite."

"No, you didn't! Did you really stick it in her ass right here?"

Joe rolled his eyes. "Well, what do *you* think?"

Jimmy guffawed, then turned to Jamie and asked, "Know what's the worst thing about fucking a girl in the ass?"

Jamie, completely dumbstruck by this new and disgusting direction of the conversation, answered without much enthusiasm, "What, Jimmy?"

"Your cock smells like shit!"

Joe and Jimmy broke into laughter and nearly fell off the log. Jamie just shook his head and put a pained expression on his face. But the more he thought about his current situation, the more he started to smile. Somewhere along the line, it had become normal to be sitting around a fire drinking lukewarm beer with some of the insane residents of this little fucked-up fishing town, talking about the most inane and potentially vile topics. And as much as he knew he should shudder with discomfort, he couldn't help feel that these moments were the warm beginnings of a subtle contentment in his life.

Joe took a sip of beer and noticed Jamie's thoughtful face. He smirked, "Now that you're behind the store, all kinds of new friends are going to show up for visits. You know, you just might end up being thankful that the gull shoot at the other campsite happened."

Jamie let the comment pass without a rebuttal, then he asked, "Should I send the thank-you note to your house, Joe, or hand it to you on the boat?"

There was silence between the three until Jimmy barked a hearty laugh. "He's a real goddamn smart-ass, ain't he?"

"Yeah, he is," Joe concurred. "But that's why we like him, right?"

17

As June began to surrender to July, the residents of Kestrel Cove were surprised to receive invitations to Bobbie Schmidt and Clara Vanes's wedding and reception. Because the couple had lived together for so long, most people assumed they were already married. In point of fact, it was Clara's announcement that she was three months pregnant that now mandated the need for an official ceremony. And while half the community immediately threw itself into the preparations for a grand wedding on July 31st, the other half began planning the biggest and baddest bachelor party Kestrel Cove had ever seen.

The only male on the peninsula who didn't know anything about these plans was Jamie Kurtz. He'd noticed that other captains and sternmen were treating him differently, but when he tried asking Jimmy and Joe about it, their excuses and stories were so preposterous, they reeked of blatant lies. When Jamie finally couldn't stand it anymore, he refused to step into the skiff to head out to the mooring one morning. He planted his feet, shook his head, and crossed his arms as he said, "I am not getting into that goddamn boat unless you two tell me what's going on around here. No one's talking to me about it, and I demand to know what it is."

Joe started with one of his stories, but Jamie cut him off. "That's bullshit, and you and I know it, Joe! I swear, if you don't tell me the truth right now, I'm heading right back to my campsite and taking a personal day!"

"Who the fuck ever said you get personal days?" Joe barked.

But then Jimmy muttered, "We really should tell him, Joe."

"No, Jimmy, we all decided it was best if we didn't."

"You *all* decided about not telling me something?"

Joe waved him off with his hand and continued his debate with Jimmy. "Remember?"

"I know, but he should be part of this. It ain't fair. Come on, Joe, he's as much a part of this community now as anyone. He deserves to know so he can get excited, too."

"Jesus, Jimmy, we all talked about this—"

"See you guys later. I'm done." Jamie turned and started walking away.

"Okay, okay. But first you have to promise you will not tell another living soul. And I mean *no one*!"

Jamie nodded solemnly as he put his hand over his heart. "I swear on my dead grandfather's grave that I will not tell anyone what you are about to tell me."

"Clara and Bobbie are getting married."

Jamie rolled his eyes. "Duh, the entire peninsula knows that. That's old news, even for me. People have been talking about it like it's the goddamn Super Bowl. But that's not what you guys are keeping from me. Come on, spill it!"

Joe exhaled through his teeth. "Okay, I'll give you some clues. What usually happens before a wedding?"

"I dunno—planning, buying flowers, writing vows?"

Jimmy shouted, "Think, college boy, think! What happens before every wedding?"

Jamie was still unsure what they were looking for. "I don't know."

"All right, let me try another angle. Imagine, if you will, that Wiley asked you to be the best man in his wedding. What would you have to plan?"

Jamie had never been a best man, but he closed his eyes and it came to him. "Oh, the bachelor party!" he exclaimed.

Joe hunkered down a little. "Shh! Jesus Christ, don't say it so loud! But, yes, the bachelor party!"

"That's it? Why is everybody keeping that a secret from me?"

"Because Clara's forbidden Bobbie from having one. She seems sweet on the outside, but she's still a Vanes, which means she's tough as nails. If that woman doesn't want anyone to throw Bobbie a bachelor party, woe to the poor man who goes against her wishes. But no fisherman from this cove, especially Bobbie, can get married without one! So we've all been secretly planning it. We all want to make it an epic night, but we're totally living in fear of Clara's wrath. If she finds out, guys will be found skinned and hanging from trees!"

"Okay, but why couldn't anyone tell me? You guys don't trust me?"

"Shelley," Joe stated evenly.

"Shelley?"

"Dude, you're practically dating her!" Jimmy hissed.

Joe came closer. "Everyone in Kestrel Cove has been following your little romance with quite a bit of interest. We all know that you go into the store every day to say hi to her and that she comes out on her smoke breaks to talk to you. You guys talk a couple of times every day."

"So what?"

Joe said, "She's Clara's sister, Jamie, so whatever Shelley knows goes right to Clara. We all decided that you two are talking and flirting so much with each other, that even an innocent slip-up with Shelley would go straight to her sister. We just thought that it'd be best if you didn't know anything about it until the moment we picked you up."

"So I'm invited?" Jamie asked excitedly.

"Of course!" Jimmy scoffed.

"Now, you *cannot* tell Shelley, okay?" Joe warned.

"Got it. My lips are sealed. I swear I won't utter a word to her!"

"You better not," Jimmy threatened, "We know where you live."

But even as the entire Kestrel Cove community tried hard to act as if nothing special was happening, underneath its calm exterior the excitement was building and growing so fast that it threatened to burst the seams of every relationship. Lobstering went on normally, but there were far more boats rafting up to one another for conversations about the epic parties of the past and the memorable drinking feats at them. And the more the fishing fleet talked, the more the anticipation about the bachelor party continued to swell, and swell, and swell.

When the day finally arrived, the fishermen of Kestrel Cove struggled to keep functioning. They were all exhausted from the month-long buildup, but they had to keep up the illusion that nothing out of the ordinary was going on. So even though the boats all headed out that day, very little fishing happened. And since every man in Kestrel Cove was keenly aware that Clara's friends were taking her to Portland for a girls' overnight of shopping for the wedding, they looked at their watches and at their battered clocks every fifteen minutes to calculate how much more time there was until the bachelor party was scheduled to begin. By four that afternoon, every single boat was in the cove, unloaded, cleaned, and at the mooring, and the wharf was completely lifeless.

Joe and Jimmy picked up Jamie at the store parking lot, and as they sped down the road, their nervous energy filled the cab of the truck. Jimmy tilted his head back and drained a can of beer. He threw the empty out the window, reached down to the twelve-pack under his legs, and took out a fresh one. After he'd opened it and taken a couple of sustained gulps, Joe growled, "Come on, Jimmy, pace yourself, man. It's gonna be a long night, right?"

"Hey, don't you worry about me, buddy. I'm like an athlete who's been training for his whole life and now he's finally made it to the Olympics. I'm in the fucking *zone!*"

Joe pulled in behind several other pickups that were parked along the side of the road outside Clara and Bobbie's house, and shut off the engine. Jimmy lifted his can of beer like a toast. "Well, gentlemen, let's go have some fun! And Jamie, for God's sake, don't embarrass us like you usually do, okay? Try to act like a normal human being, not a fucking college retard! Ta-ta, boys!"

Joe and Jamie watched as he bounded off and joined a group of men standing in the yard. Country music was blaring from speakers in the upstairs windows of the house, and the party seemed to be in mid-swing already. Joe was taking in the scene with a furrowed brow, and he suddenly turned to Jamie and said, "You've never been to something like this before, have you?"

"A bachelor party?"

"Naw, a fishermen's party."

"Does the gull shoot count?"

"Fuck, no. That was an afternoon tea compared to this."

"Well then, no, I guess I haven't. I mean, I went to a bunch of frat parties at Bridgewater."

Joe snorted, "This isn't gonna be a college frat party, Jamie. This is gonna be a whole new experience for you. Just keep your eyes open and watch your back."

"Jesus, Joe, sounds like we're going into battle, not to a party."

"Listen, I've been going to fishermen's parties since I was a teenager. You need to know that this party *will* boil over into chaos at some point tonight. They always do. When you combine a bunch of fishermen and an unlimited supply of alcohol, nothing good comes from it. I don't think it'll be too long before someone gets hurt and needs to go to the hospital. When the shit really hits the fan, just look for me. I'll be ready to leave, and we'll get the fuck out of here before it gets too bad."

"Okay, but what about Jimmy? Should we watch out for him, too?"

"Oh, don't you worry about him. He'll be passed out somewhere before anything gets close to boiling over!"

As they walked across the lawn, a group of captains called for Joe to come over, and Jamie knew the invitation was exclusive. He veered away and scanned the crowd for familiar faces. Drake was standing with some older men, and when he saw Jamie, he pursed his lips into such an unpleasant expression that Jamie was forced to look away. When he spotted Jimmy with a group of other sternmen who were tending a large bonfire on the lawn, he was now holding a humongous plastic mug that Jamie knew was full of beer. Jimmy smiled as he lifted his mug high into the air and walked away. It was the last time Jamie saw him all night.

As Jamie filled his own red plastic cup at the keg, he was punched from behind by a powerful shot to his shoulder blade. And, although there was no anger behind it, the blow was hard enough to knock him forward. He recovered quickly and turned to see Wiley standing there with his hands in a boxing stance. He had a big smile on his face, and after faking a vicious uppercut, he slapped Jamie on the back and yelled, "Well, howdy, *perfessor*! You ready for a helluva party tonight?"

"Yeah, it already has the feeling of something special, Wiley. With that big fire over there and all of this restless energy coming off everyone, it's kind of like those famous nighttime rallies that Hitler used to put on. I guess fires and excitement always bring out powerful primal emotions, huh?"

Wiley's face soured. "Whoa, bro, did you just call us a bunch of Nazis?"

Jamie waved his hands in front of him. "Oh God, no. I was only saying that tonight has the feeling of something almost supernatural."

Wiley laughed. "Aw, I'm only fucking with ya. But if you ask me, the Nazis didn't have it *all* wrong!"

Jamie was about to say something to clarify the conversation when Wiley asked, "Hey, what're you drinking there, bro?"

Jamie lifted his half-filled cup as evidence. "Beer."

"Aw, man, you need a real drink!"

"Got one right here, Wiley," he said, lifting the cup again.

"No, here, try this." He thrust forward a label-less pint bottle that was full with a clear liquid.

"Oh, no, I couldn't, Wiley. I'm just going to stick to beer tonight."

"Try this!" Wiley's tone was no longer a teasing request but a demand.

"Okay…" Jamie said, bringing the bottle to his lips. He said a silent prayer in hopes that he wasn't about to drink antifreeze or Woolite, and he took a swig. The liquid burned his lips and mouth, and singed its way down his esophagus and instantly set his stomach afire.

"Aghh! What the hell *is* this?" Jamie sputtered.

"Moonshine!" Wiley roared. "I made it myself! Well, me and Evan Kootcher made it. Kootch is a sternman from a boat over on the other side of Kestrel Cove. Anyways, this is our first batch of Kootch's Hootch. Pretty good, don't ya think?"

"It's real smooth," Jamie wheezed.

Wiley laughed again. "Hardy-har-har, you're a regular riot!" Then he threw a hard punch to Jamie's shoulder and another mock uppercut that would have knocked him flat in a real fight.

Jamie rubbed his shoulder. "Ow. Did you used to box?"

"Not professionally, dude. But me and my friends used to like to mix it up."

"Huh, you've got the punch for it."

Wiley jinked around like a boxer on the offensive. "I used to throw uppercuts, roundhouses, *BAM-BAM*. I was a knock-out machine. But then I had some of my tendons cut, so I can't throw my punches too hard nowadays."

"Cut?"

"Oh yeah, man. When I was stabbed the last time, some of the tendons in my arm got cut, right here. You can see the fucking scar." ·

"Wait a minute. You've been stabbed, Wiley?"

"Yo, bro, I've been stabbed, like, eight times."

"Eight times? With a knife?"

"No, with a piece of fucking bone! Of course, with a knife!"

"Eight times?"

"Aw yeah, man! I been stabbed here, here, and here! All over my fucking body. This one here on my arm, my best friend gave me that one."

Wiley was clearly serious, but Jamie asked incredulously, "Your best friend stabbed you?"

"Oh yeah. I was wrestling with him at a party. We'd both been drinking all day, so we were pretty fucked up. Anyway, I got him in a headlock and started to squeeze with all my strength. But he had a knife in his sock. As I squeezed harder and harder, he reached around and grabbed the knife. I never saw it. He just came around like this and put it into my goddamn arm right here next to the elbow!"

"Holy shit!"

"You got that right. And I gotta tell you, that knife was so fucking sharp I didn't feel it until it sliced up against the bone. I sure as shit felt it then! He had to drive me to the hospital, but then the pussy got sick in the emergency room. They had to do some surgery on me 'cause there's this air bag in your elbow and if it gets fucked up, you're whole arm's fucked. The nurse had her finger in there, wiggling it around! No shit, dude. She had her fucking finger up to the first knuckle in there, and my friend got all sick and had to leave the room. I said, 'You're such a fucking pussy! You stab me, then you get sick when they're stitching me up!'"

"Your best friend actually did that?"

"Aw, yeah. When he and me got a couple of beers in us, we'd get rowdy. We'd blow off some steam. See this scar right here on my eyebrow? He gave that to me, too. Him and me were drinking and we got into an argument. He said something I didn't like, so, *POW!*

I got a good punch to his face. His lip was all puffed up and bloody, but he punched me right back, *BAM!* right above the eye. Hardest punch I ever took, man, but I took it. I just stood there, seeing stars, and then the blood started flowing down my face. He'd split my eyebrow wide open, so I said, 'Oh shit, who's gonna take me to the hospital this time?'"

"He punched you so hard you had to go to the hospital?"

"Yep, and he had to drive me that time, too."

Jamie was shaking his head. "So I take it you guys aren't friends anymore."

"Of course we are. Why wouldn't we be?"

"Because he punches and stabs you, Wiley! You can't be friends with someone who routinely puts you in the hospital, can you?"

"Aw, dude, we get a couple of beers in us and fight—that's how we unwind. Get rowdy and rough—it's fucking awesome! We fuck each other up, then we're friends again. That's what friends do, ain't it?"

"It is?"

"Of course. Only people who are your friends can hurt you and forgive you when you hurt them back. I counted up one day, and I figure that my buddy owes me sixteen stitches. And that motherfucker knows that I'm gonna get them from him one day."

Wiley suddenly spotted some other young sternmen over in the woods smoking a joint, and he said to Jamie, "Hey, man, you wanna go and burn one?"

Jamie looked over and shook his head. "Naw, you go ahead, Wiley."

"Well, see ya later. There's burgers and hot dogs by the grill. You better eat—that way you've got something in your stomach when you puke! Ah, man, this night's gonna be epic!"

As Jamie watched him swagger off, he felt very alone. He knew that he couldn't hang with Joe or the other captains and he couldn't go and be with Jimmy and his hard-drinking friends, so he felt as if he didn't fit into any group that was here at the party. This realization made him want to leave, but he knew he couldn't do that, either. So instead, he went back to the keg to refill his cup.

A black man was there pouring himself a mugful of beer, and

Jamie knew he had to be the guy everyone referred to as Nigger Bob. The man smiled a toothy smile. "Hey, Jamie, you need a beer?"

"That sounds great, Bob. Want me to pump the keg? Looks like we're losing pressure."

"Sure."

As Jamie pushed down on the black plastic pump, Bob stated calmly, "You seem to be searching for a group to hang with tonight."

Jamie nodded. "Yeah, I was just realizing that I can't hang with the captains or the sternmen tonight. It's something I guess I'll need to figure out as the evening unfolds."

"Yeah, you just have to wait for an opening or an invitation. I'm used to not totally fitting in here sometimes, too. "

"Do you mean because you're black?" Jamie asked hesitantly.

"I'm *black?!* Aw, Jesus, no one told me!"

Jamie blanched with embarrassment, but the other man laughed. "Ah, I'm just fucking with you, kid!"

"If you don't mind me asking, how *do* you put up with being the only African-American around here?"

"Actually, there are several black families on the peninsula. We aren't as invisible as it seems sometimes. That being said, I don't think anyone else has the word 'Nigger' attached to their name."

Jamie pulled back. "You know about that?"

"Of course! You think I wouldn't know that the entire area thinks my name is Nigger Bob?"

"I just…I never…I, uh, I'm sorry," Jamie sputtered.

"Hey, don't be. At first I was angry, but this skin ain't only dark, it's thick. It has to be. Plus, whenever I'm visiting some family members down in Roxbury, they say *nigger* every other word when they're speakin' to you. It sure seems everybody likes to use that damn word. 'Course, it's different to hear a bunch of white people use it. But I've come to realize that no one in the Cove says it in anger or hatred—to them it's like Hairy Frank, Little Al, or Stick-It-in-My-Ass-Shirley Bailey—it's just a description of the obvious to differentiate one from another."

"Well, I hope you know that I never call you that, Bob. I think it's offensive."

The black man chuckled quietly. "Well, Jamie, it's nice of you to say that, but I gotta tell ya, if you don't call me Nigger Bob when you're talking about me, all you're gonna do is create a helluva lot of confusion. You'll start talking about just Bob, and everyone will be wondering which Bob you're talking about. There's Scary Bob, Crazy Bob, Stupid Bob, Pedophile Bob, and there's Nigger Bob. No one will know which one you're talking about if you just say Bob. So I know you may not want to say it, but remember, to these guys, it's just my name."

Some men on the other side of the yard started yelling for him to come over and join them. He raised his cup in acknowledgment and turned back to Jamie. "Well, my adoring fans are calling me. Hey, good talking with you, Jamie. Get yourself some of the chicken on the grill. My wife marinated it for the whole week. It's so tender, it'll melt in your mouth! Better get some before it's all gone!"

"Thanks, I will."

Jamie watched him get swallowed up by the group like a piece of coal falling into a snow bank. As he scanned the yard to see where the grill was, his eyes met Drake's again just as he mouthed the words *Pussy…college boy* to someone standing near him. Jamie rolled his eyes. Maybe he wasn't as different from Nigger Bob as he'd thought.

Several older men were tending a vast number of hamburgers, hot dogs, chicken parts, ribs, and other unidentifiable pieces of meat on the massive charcoal grill. They were moving quickly and constantly to monitor all the meat cooking in the flames, and the sweat ran down their faces onto their shirts. After they loaded up his plate with food, Jamie started to hunt for a place to sit and eat. Bobbie Schmidt and Vernon Quigley, his best man and organizer of the party, happened to walk past him. Jamie lifted his cup and said, "Congratulations, Bobbie!"

The fisherman looked Jamie over before speaking. "Thanks, college boy. I hear everyone was sure you were going to spill the beans about this party to Shelley, huh? But you didn't, did ya? Good man! But when are you gonna finally ask that girl out on a date? She's dying for you to do it, and she's not gonna wait forever, you know."

Jamie spilled some of his beer. "Really?"

"Duh. She's been talking about you since you first arrived in Kestrel Cove."

"Really?"

"Jesus, for a college boy, you're kind of dumb, ain't ya?"

Jamie smiled grimly. "Jimmy thinks I'm retarded."

Bobbie let out a loud laugh, and then he said, "Well, just promise me you'll ask the girl out soon!"

"I definitely will. I would love to go out and have dinner with her."

"Yeah, but don't try anything! As her soon-to-be brother-in-law, I'd be the one who'd have to shoot you if you misbehave in any way with her. So, ask her out soon, but don't try anything. Got it?"

"Yeah, sure," Jamie said with a nod. "Congratulations on both the wedding and the baby."

Bobbie slapped him hard on the shoulder, "I'm starting to see why Joe speaks so highly of you, college boy."

After Bobbie and Vernon walked off, Jamie felt a flush of satisfaction that his captain was saying nice things about him to the other captains. And then he felt a twinge of foolishness for caring what Joe said about him.

There was a sudden surge of energy at the party. The men in the yard got skittish and loud for a moment or two before quieting down and speaking in whispers. A cry went out that it was nearly eight o'clock, and everyone started mechanically heading toward some kind of cover. Some shuffled into the house, while others scurried over to their cars to continue drinking and smoking inside them. Jamie wasn't sure what to do, so he joined the group of men herding into the house like cattle. After twenty minutes of awkward standing around, the all-clear was given, and the men headed back onto the lawn to resume the party. Once outside, everyone now seemed licensed to let loose and party hard, and the yelling and laughing became louder and cruder. To Jamie, it felt like those prophetic divinations that Joe had delivered at the truck were now about to come true.

But before things had a chance to get too wild, a big SUV rumbled up the driveway. The doors swung open and a short man dressed like a pimp escorted three strippers inside the house. Vernon made a dramatic announcement that the night's entertainment had arrived, and there was an instant chorus of primal grunts and howls as the men formed a ragged, jostling line at the hurricane doors to the basement. By the time Jamie found a spot inside, the entire subterranean space was crammed full, and the smell of smoke and liquor was only over-whelmed by the metallic aroma of lust and testosterone as the men eagerly awaited the entrance of the strippers.

The manager came down the stairs with an air of importance and toughness. Because of his diminutive size, some of the fishermen scoffed at him, but he confidently strode right into the middle of the basement. An old Barcalounger chair had been set up there for Bobbie to sit in, and the manager stood behind it and looked around the room coolly. Then he shouted, "Good evening, gentlemen! You're in for a night to remember. My girls are some of the best dancers in the entire state of Maine! But we have one rule, gentlemen, and if it is not fol-lowed, we will instantly leave and you won't have any more entertain-ment tonight. My girls and I have zero tolerance about this rule—as soon as anyone comes close to breaking it, we're out of here! My girls can touch you, but you cannot touch them. If anyone grabs or pinches or bothers any of my girls in any way, we're done here. Got it?...Good. Let's get on with the show!"

Seated in the Barcalounger, Bobbie held up his cup of beer and the men in the crowd whooped excitedly for him before turning their attention back to the staircase. The manager turned on a CD player, and a rhythmic dance tune started blaring.

"From Presque Isle, gentlemen, please give a rousing welcome to Candi!"

The men in the basement hooted and whistled as the woman paraded slowly down the stairs and over to the Barcalounger. She was a very tall and beautiful brunette who posed regally next to Bobbie. She was so attractive that the manager had to yell louder to get the leering eyes of the men off of her and onto the next stripper coming down the stairs. "Gentlemen, I present Susie from Augusta!"

This second woman resembled the quintessential redheaded girl next door. She moved with a prancing step to stand next to the first stripper, and she struck a pose that was both provocative and cute. The two women exuded confidence. They were beautiful and they knew it, and the men in the basement were in awe of them. Bobbie Schmidt looked up at the two strippers and smiled contentedly. To Jamie, who had never been in this kind of environment before, it seemed at first that these women were in danger to be in the midst of so many lustful men. But he quickly realized that they were completely safe because they were the ones in control of the situation.

"But, gentlemen, let's not forget our third girl! From Lisbon, here's Margarite!"

As soon as the third stripper came down the stairs, Jamie gasped because he knew that she was going to be the source of all the trouble that was to come. Whereas the first two women were so cocksure that they had instantly overpowered the animalistic urges of the audience, Margarite walked awkwardly over to the Barcalounger, and it was painfully obvious that she lacked confidence. Like a pack of dogs that sense weakness, the men surged forward with naked aggression at this third stripper. Jamie found himself pressed forward by the men around him hurling cat-calls and rude comments at her. And as she posed next to the other strippers, her eyes betrayed the fact that she was petrified—and the entire room knew it.

The manager shut off the music and barked out his next set of directions. "Okay, gentlemen, the girls are going to individually dance for the groom now. After they dance for Bobbie, each one will pick a corner of the room to dance for a group. At that point, you can go over to where your favorite girl is and request them to do a dance for you!"

The men applauded. While Candi and Susie looked coolly at the men with distant smiles, Margarite's eyes continued to flash her fear. The manager turned on the CD player again, and Candi began to dance. Being tall and lanky, she moved her arms and her legs suggestively, and when she put her foot onto the headrest of the comfortable chair, her long, muscular legs commanded so much attention, the men around the room strained forward to see. As each piece of clothing came off, the men groaned with anticipation, until she finally lowered the last strap holding up the lacy teddy and slid it down to her ankles. As she stood there with her breasts bared, a collective sigh of satisfaction came from the audience.

Before the music started again, Susie made several quick pelvic movements that seemed designed to break the trance from Candi's dance. Being smaller and more compact, she danced with her hands close to her torso. Occasionally she put one of her hands into her panties, and this caused a shared groan to course through the group. When she was finally topless in front of Bobbie, Susie's full bosom heaved with exertion, and the men applauded and whooped with appreciation.

But as the manager started the music for Margarite's dance, a malevolent cloud started to settle in the basement. Her dance moves were so forced and fake, the men began a guttural guffaw that sounded like a chain saw. She pushed her pelvis out and shook her breasts, but this was as seductive as watching the gyrations of a washing machine. And when she took her top off for the finale, the final piece to the misfitting puzzle fell into place—right across her left breast was the tattoo of someone's name done with such poor quality that it looked like the writing of a felt-tipped marker. When she stopped her dance, the audience broke into cruel laughter and booing.

As the women now spread out to do their separate dances, the manager reminded everyone of the no-touching rule, and told them that the dances would cost a dollar each. The men around Jamie began rustling in their pockets for their cash, and several were moving purposefully toward their favorite dancer. It was clear that many of them had fallen in love with Susie or Candi, but Jamie could sense a more sinister element around him, too—men who wanted to get closer to Margarite to scare her and feed off her fear. Like a pack of sharks led by the trail of blood to a struggling animal, these men swam menacingly through the agitated crowd to get to her.

Jamie wanted to leave the basement, but he felt compelled to witness what was going to happen next. The manager turned the music up very loud, and this seemed to ignite an already unstable situation. Instantly, each stripper had a ring of men around her, and the small, enclosed space seemed to compress. Jamie could see that the large groups of men who had encircled Candi and Susie were like a group of children who did not want to ruin a good thing, and, other than carefully reaching over to stuff their money into the women's thongs, they respectfully kept their distance.

But when he looked over to where Margarite was dancing, he saw that everything was quite different. While she continued to dance in a manner that was not erotic, the half dozen or so drunken men in her audience were anything but respectful. They hurled insults and made rude comments about her breasts and her dancing style, and Jamie noticed that her thong was completely empty. He felt so badly for her, he contemplated giving her a dollar. But one glance at her audience, and he knew that he'd be beaten up if he tried.

Then it happened. An old man Jamie had never seen before broke the circle, staggered forward, and actually grabbed Margarite's breasts. She pushed him away and continued to dance halfheartedly, but then she made a quick movement to get closer to the stairs. The circle of men began to close in on her with their hands out like a bunch of zombies in a '50s monster movie. She continued to dance, but she was now like a pinball bouncing from one groping man to another. Jamie tried to push forward to rescue her, but someone elbowed him in the stomach and knocked the wind out of him.

The gunshot silenced the entire room. Most of the men were too stunned by the concussion in the enclosed space of the basement to react right away, and they stood dumbly staring back at the manager. He now stood by the base of the stairs with a small smoking handgun pointed up at the floor above him. He screamed, "All right, you motherfuckers! I clearly explained the rule and the consequences to you all before! No touching means *no touching*! You assholes over there touched Margarite, I saw you! So, we're out of here! Come on, girls!"

The men who had been watching Candi and Susie looked at one another and then at their retreating dancers, and had an almost child-like reaction of disappointment. But the manager wasn't looking at them; he was concentrating on Margarite, who was still encircled by her menacing audience. One man said something under his breath to her, and her eyes flashed again with pure terror.

The manager yelled, "Hey, dickwads, make some goddamn room for her to pass or I won't be putting a slug in the ceiling with the next shot!"

No one moved. They continued to block Margarite's way and mutter things to her. The manager cocked his gun dramatically. "I ain't gonna say it again! Move out of the way, motherfuckers!"

Grudgingly, the men opened their ranks and Margarite ran toward the other dancers, and then the three of them raced up the stairs. The manager, gun still cocked and pointed at the men in the basement, looked ready to say something profound, but then he just muttered, "Assholes!" and went up the stairs.

The basement immediately exploded into violence. Those who were enamored with either Candi or Susie were so enraged at the men who had ruined their fun by touching Margarite that they attacked them. Complete mayhem ensued. The lingering smell of gunpowder and the sounds of pandemonium made Jamie panic and scan the basement for Joe. When he finally saw him in the opposite corner and caught his eye, Joe shook his head, lifted his plastic cup in a mock toast, and cocked his head at the hurricane doors of the basement. Jamie carefully edged his way around the pockets of violence, headed up the stairs, and went right to the keg on the lawn.

When Joe found him there, he had a casual smile on his face. "Well, that was certainly exciting, huh?"

"Insane is more like it!" said Jamie.

"So," Joe smirked, "do you think it's time to go home now, college boy?"

"Yes, Joe, I do. This party is totally out of control!"

Joe glanced over at the doors leading to the basement and seemed to savor the sounds of chaos coming from them. "Well, Jamie, it's not completely out of control. As a matter of fact, it's gonna calm down here in a minute or two."

"And then what, Joe?"

"Then a party happens. Everyone is going to start drinking and just having fun again. But eventually it'll get bad again. And when it does, it will be worse than what just happened. Much worse. And when you're sure that it's as bad as it's going to get, find me like you did this time, and we'll leave."

Joe turned and walked toward another group of men, and Jamie was left alone again. The brawls in the basement were over, and the combatants were being placated with booze and were making up with one another. But the premature departure of the strippers caused a sour mood to descend on the whole party as the crowd's disappointment was now amplified by the darkness of the yard. And as this feeling began to overwhelm the lights from the house and the campfire, there was now something even more disconcerting and ominous about the party. The night shadows seemed to swirl and change, and the men at the party drifted in and out of view like ships in a fog. Jamie could tell by the way the conversations and laughter were becoming more jagged in nature that everyone was getting drunker by the minute, and that an unhealthy anger was starting to fester. He worried about the explosion of violence that seemed imminent.

When Jamie saw that the trees on the edge of the yard were now entirely engulfed by the shadows, he made his way over there. Standing alone in the sheltering darkness, he felt safe and protected for the first time all night.

"Psst."

Jamie whirled around to see who was signaling him, but he couldn't make them out in the thick darkness. He inched forward and hoarsely whispered, "Who's there?"

"Me, dumbass."

"Shelley?"

"No, it's Eleanor Roosevelt. Just back from checking on the U.N. Charter! Yes, it's Shelley."

"What are you doing here?"

"*Shh*, not so loud!" She whispered as she moved close enough for Jamie to see her. "I was just curious about how everything was going, so I came by to see for myself."

"You knew about this party?"

"Everyone on the peninsula knows about this party, Jamie."

"Even Clara?"

"No, she doesn't know. But only because all the Kestrel Cove women have been working hard so she wouldn't find out. Because we all knew that this party was going to happen no matter what, we needed to get Clara off the peninsula and far away. We couldn't have her completely pissed off at Bobbie and every other fisherman in the cove over this—after all, it's better when a new marriage starts off on a good foot, right? I mean, she'll find out eventually, but by then the damage won't be as bad."

"So why aren't you in Portland now?"

"I've got to open the store in the morning. Plus, my mom needed me to come home tonight. Clara has her friends, so I knew she wouldn't miss me too much if I slipped out early."

"Oh, I see."

"So, it's just barely nine o'clock, and there's already been gunfire, huh? I'd say that means it's been a successful party!"

Jamie shrugged and said halfheartedly, "Yeah, I guess so."

"Are you having fun, college boy?"

"Yeah, sure," he croaked.

"Yep, I can always tell when a guy is truly having a great time at a party when he drifts off to some dark trees to stand alone. So how come you're not over there mixing it up?"

Jamie relaxed a little and chuckled, "I guess this just isn't my cup of tea. I feel a little…"

"Out of place," Shelley finished for him.

"Yes."

"Have you been drinking? That always helps. Social lubrication and all."

"I'm supposed to drive Joe home, so I can't get too drunk."

"Always the responsible one, huh, college boy?"

"I guess."

Jamie looked at Shelley's face and smiled. Talking to her now was the most fun he'd had all night. Being this close to her made his insides rumble.

Shelley clucked her tongue. "I was just about to leave, but then I heard the gunshot. That certainly got my attention. Then the strippers came flying out the front door and hopped into their car and drove off in a cloud of dust! It was wild!"

"That's one way to describe it."

Shelley put her hand on Jamie's arm, which set off sparks inside him and made him shudder with latent excitement. "Well, I gotta go. If anyone catches me here, I'll never hear the end of it! I just came over to check on the boys…and on you. It's obvious that this party is about to hit its stride. Soak it all in, college boy. Just be careful, okay?"

"Yeah, Joe warned me things could get dicey tonight."

"Yep, this is the time when the pack mentality comes into play. Just keep your wits about you."

Jamie shook his head. "Actually, I was just wondering if I

should slip out now and go home."

"What?" Shelley's voice was honed to a fine point. "You wanna leave *now*?"

"Yeah, you know, avoid all that bad stuff we know is coming."

"Yes, 'cause life is all about slipping out early to miss the bad stuff, right?"

Jamie was confused by her sarcasm. "Like you said, the shit is definitely going to hit the fan tonight. Why do I need to stay to see any of that?"

"Oh, college boy, you have so much to learn! You can't run away from everything because it's a little scary! Life is all about experiencing everything, the good things and the bad things. You just have to pick the right time to carefully make your exit before the bad things suck you in and swallow you. This party is going to be talked about for years, and you're right here in it. Don't miss anything just because you're scared."

Jamie could not stop himself from saying, "Well, I'm really glad I didn't miss this chance to talk with *you* tonight. I like talking with you, Shelley Vanes."

"I really like talking with you, too."

"Do you want to go out with me sometime? For dinner and a movie, perhaps?"

"Are you asking me out on a date?"

Jamie laughed nervously. "Yep, I guess I am."

"Here? Now?"

"Well, when you were just saying that I shouldn't let my fears rule me, I realized that, even though I've wanted to ask you out, I haven't because I've been too scared to. It's time to confront that fear right here, right now."

Shelley purred, "Yes, I would really like to go out with you!"

A voice suddenly called out of the darkness for Jamie. It was Wiley, and he was drunkenly staggering in their direction.

"Oh shit, it's Wiley!" Shelley hissed.

"Hey, what's up, Wiley?" Jamie asked loudly.

Shelley grabbed Jamie's shoulders tightly. "If he finds me here, I'm toast. I'll not only be the girl who crashed the bachelor party, all kinds of rumors about you and me will be spread around Kestrel Cove! I won't be able to show my face on the wharf!"

"I jush wanna know if you want s'more of this 'shine," Wiley slurred as he staggered closer.

"No, no, Wiley, I don't need any more drinks, buddy. Thanks, though."

"Don' need any more drinksh? 'Course you do, man! C'mon, have a little drink. Hey, what the fuck you doing over here anyway?"

Jamie hesitated because he could not think of anything to say. Then he blurted out, "I'm taking a dump, Wiley."

"What?"

Shelley giggled, but Jamie shielded her from view with his body. "Oh yeah, I have this thing where I have to shit on the lawn of any party I go to."

Shelley was wracked with laughter and pressed closer to Jamie's back.

"No kidding, bro? Tha's a little twisted."

"Oh, yeah, it is twisted, Wiley, but I can't help it. Every time I go to a party, I have to crap."

"But you're over in Clara's flower bed, dude. You like shittin' in a woman's flower bed, too?"

Jamie whispered over his shoulder to Shelley, "I am?"

Shelley whispered back, "Yeah, we're right next to Clara's bed of pansies. They're her pride and joy."

"Oh yeah, Wiley," Jamie yelled back, "that's the other part to my thing, man. I…uh…also like to jerk off in a woman's flower beds."

"Jesus! At the same time?"

"Yep."

"For real?"

"Oh yeah, I get a good crap going and then I choke the chicken at the same time. It's very cathartic."

Shelley was now heaving with laughter, and she squeezed Jamie's arms to keep from laughing out loud.

"Jesus Christ, dude, that's totally wacked! You might need to go see a fucking shrink about that!"

"Oh yeah, well, I'm almost done now. Stay right there, and after I finish, we can go back to the party."

"No, dude, I think I'll just go right back by myself. Jesus H. Christ, shittin' and jerkin' off into a woman's garden? I knew you were a little off, man, but wow, you're *way* off!"

Wiley staggered away, and when he had disappeared completely from view, Shelley doubled over with laugher. "Shitting and jerking off on Clara's garden? Really? That's the best you could do, college boy?"

"I panicked, okay?"

"Well, you're gonna get quite the reputation from that one!"

"Hey, it's not like he'll remember any of that."

"What?" Shelley stopped laughing and stood up.

"He's drunk as a skunk, Shelley. I could have told him I was fist-fucking a beagle over here, and he wouldn't remember it in the morning. Hell, I'm sure he's forgotten everything I said already."

"Uh, Jamie?"

"Yeah?"

"You know all those crazy stories he's always telling you?"

"Yeah?"

"Are they about when he was sober or drunk?"

Jamie scoffed, "Drunk, of course."

"Uh-huh."

"So what?"

"The boy ain't that drunk right now, not for Wiley."

"But he's slurring his words!"

"He does that when he's sober. He's been hit in the mouth so many times, his upper lip looks like it has elephantiasis."

"But he was staggering and weaving all over the place."

"He has an inner ear problem from being punched in the side of his head, too. He walks like that even when he's been drinking orange juice!"

"So exactly what are you saying, Shelley?"

She took a deep breath. "I'm saying that your assumption about his lack of memory function due to alcohol consumption is completely faulty, Jamie. Wiley has one of those memories that holds onto things, even in the fog of alcohol."

"So he'll remember all that bullshit I made up?"

Shelley giggled. "Oh, you're gonna hear a lot more about shitting and jerking off in gardens in the future."

"From Wiley?"

"From everybody!"

"What?"

"You just seemed to really surprise Wiley with the admission that you need to defecate and masturbate in a woman's garden at parties. I've grown up with that boy, and I didn't honestly think that he could be surprised by anything. But you sure just did! That's why I'm quite positive that he's gone right back to his buddies to tell them everything you just said."

"You're not helping, Shelley."

"Sorry," she said warmly as she laughed again.

Without warning, Jamie leaned in and gently kissed her on the lips. They kept kissing in the darkness of the night until Shelley pulled away and smiled. "I think you need to head back to face the fire now."

"Yep."

"You gonna be all right?"

"Yep."

"They're gonna make fun of you."

"Yep, and I couldn't care less. I'm thinking of something else right now."

Shelley pointed her finger into his sternum. "You need to call me and properly ask me out."

"When?" Jamie asked with a grin.

"Just call me."

◇◇◇◇

Jamie headed back toward the bonfire and the keg. Darkness hid the expressions on the faces of the men who passed randomly across the lawn near him, and he went over to refill his cup with beer. As he stood alone in the midst of the milling drunken revelry, he was smiling with what would have best been described as a shit-eating grin.

Just then, a low-slung sports car screeched to a stop in the driveway, and a tall blond woman in a full-length fur coat and a huge man in an old fedora got out and went in the front door of the house. It wasn't too long before word was excitedly passed along that she was the replacement stripper. Once again, the men quickly herded back down into the basement, leaving Jamie alone with his thoughts about

Shelley. The new silence brought him to attention, and he hurried to join the crowd down in the basement.

The environment was electrified, but it was different from the first round of strippers. There was an air of mystery to it now. Even though the men were definitely more drunk and rowdy now, they all seemed to be wondering about what type of stripper would volunteer to come in the middle of such an obviously dangerous situation. Bobbie was seated back in the comfortable chair in the middle of the crowded basement, and then every single man watched intently as the huge muscled manager came slowly down the stairs. His bulging arm muscles rippled as he spoke in a booming voice. "If any of youse do anything to Mary that she don't like, I will kill you."

The threat was so real, no one in the basement uttered a sound. The manager bent down and turned on the music for his stripper, and out of the boom box came the howling scream of Guns N' Roses' "Welcome to the Jungle." The stripper came bounding down the stairs, two steps at a time, and ran across the basement floor like she was storming a beach. She wore only a thong and a chainmail halter that allowed her nipples to poke through, and the men in the crowd watched in shock as she leapt into the air, landed on her knees on the armrests of Bobbie's chair, and grabbed him by the hair to jam his face into her breasts. She began gyrating madly and bucking wildly as if possessed by demons.

Bobbie had not been expecting any of this, and the woman was hurting him with her movements, which felt more like an assault than any kind of erotic dance. When she painfully raked his face on her halter for a second time, he'd had more than enough. He stood up with the woman still attached to him like a starfish, and swatted her to the concrete floor. The crowd breathed a collective "Ooooh!" and looked toward the muscled manager, who remained motionless on the stairs.

There was a momentary silence as everyone watched to see if the woman had hurt herself, but she was instantly up again and grinding and bucking as if the swatting had been part of the act. She reached out and grabbed the nearest guy, a sternman from a lobster boat on the other side of the peninsula, and yanked him by the hair into the comfortable chair and began her attack on him. The crowd was so stunned by her energy and her ferocity, they barely noticed that Bobbie was angrily making his way toward the hurricane doors to leave the basement.

When Bobbie reached the steps to the outside, Jamie asked, "You okay, Bobbie?"

The groom's face was twisted by his anger, and he had a trickle of blood coming from his eyebrow. "That fucking bitch nearly ripped off my goddamn face!"

He lumbered on up the steps and out onto the lawn. When Jamie turned back to the room to see what was happening, the stripper was standing on the arms of the Barcalounger pounding the seated sternman's face into her crotch. The loud music continued to blare, and the crowd, ever mindful of the muscled man's threat, was quickly comprehending that there wasn't much that Mary the stripper didn't like to do, and their energy began to surge again. When she took off her thong and thrust the sternman's face back into her bare pubic region, the men pushed forward to see. As soon as Jamie saw the man's pink tongue come out, he knew he had seen enough. He scanned the crowd, and there was Joe looking right back at him, clearly giving the signal that it was now time to leave. Jamie made his way up the steps and out onto the lawn.

When Joe found him, all he said was, "Ready?"

"Yep."

"Let's get the hell out of here."

"What about Jimmy?"

"Don't worry about him—he's passed out somewhere safe," Joe deadpanned. "He's fine."

A man came out of the cellar and ran around Joe and Jamie like a small dog. "She's letting guys lick her! She's letting guys lick her!"

"And you're missing it, Fergus?"

"Aw, I don't got any more money!"

"Here," Joe said, handing the man some ones.

"Aw, Jeez, thanks, Joe!" The man rushed frantically back into the basement. Light, loud music, and shouts spewed forth from the opening like an aperture to hell.

"You're driving, college boy," Joe said as he tossed Jamie his keys.

They rode in silence. Jamie was still digesting the events of the night. It had been too full an evening with too many layers to easily process. When they got to the house, Joe said, "You gonna be ready to fish hard tomorrow?"

"Yep, you know it."

"Bring extra food, 'cause I want to move some gear around, and I don't think we'll be in as early as we've been lately."

"Okey-dokey. Do you think Jimmy'll be able to fish hard tomorrow?"

"Oh, don't you worry about him. That boy's got a gift for drinking fast, passing out, and then working hard the next day."

"That's a real gift," Jamie chuckled.

Joe started to walk off, but stopped and put his good hand on his hip. "Did you really shit and jerk off in Clara's flower bed, college boy?"

"Oh, Jesus Christ!"

18

Jamie could not stop thinking about Shelley. The events of the bachelor party the night before were so unreal, trying to sort them all out was like unraveling a complicated hallucination. But their brief encounter only made him want to ask the girl out on a date as soon as possible, and he decided that he would call her right after he got done with work. Instantly, the day took on the feeling of a mere task that had to be endured before he could make his all-important phone call.

But Jamie found himself in the midst of a battle on the boat. While Jimmy was trying to work off a major hangover from the bachelor party, Joe was attempting to punish him by making work harder than usual. And since they were so preoccupied with one another, neither one seemed to notice Jamie's existence at all. While Jimmy tried to use nicotine to cancel out the effects of the residual alcohol in his system and smoked more prolifically than ever, Joe countered this by repeatedly asking him to use the deck hose to wash various things on the boat This always resulted in a dampened cigarette and a sour expression of scorn from the ace man, both of which made Joe grin devilishly. By the time the morning coffee break rolled around, both Joe and Jimmy bore the chagrined expressions of couples who've been married too long.

After lunch, Joe announced that they were going to shift some gear from areas where the fishing was slowing to an area where it would be better. They hauled up a string of traps and left them on the deck of the boat. Then they hauled another set, and stacked those traps atop the first string. They did this four more times, until the deck of the *Bobbie C.* was piled high with traps and covered with a spaghetti plate of lines. As they steamed to the new area to set the gear out again, Jamie banded lobsters and baited bait bags as the wall of wet traps loomed menacingly in front of him.

In his continuing effort to punish Jimmy, Joe set out the gear faster than usual. During the second string, Jimmy's sluggishness caused him to make a mistake. One of the lines streaming off the boat wrapped around his ankle and nearly pulled him down. He managed to shake off the noose without being hauled overboard, but it was obvious that, although Joe saw all this happen, he didn't take the boat out of gear or back down. After the whole string was set, Jimmy stalked up to the wheelhouse and poked Joe in the chest. "Hey, you motherfucker! Why don't you slow the fuck down before someone gets hurt or killed out here?"

In a steely voice, Joe said, "If you can't keep up, maybe it's time for you to find another job."

Jimmy lit another cigarette. "I nearly went over that time, you asshole! And you didn't even slow down. If you're pissed at me for getting drunk last night, just say so. Don't be a prick and try to kill me!"

"If you can't handle the heat, get out of the kitchen."

Jimmy shook his head and exhaled a huge plume of smoke toward Joe. "Goddamn, you can be such an asshole sometimes!"

Joe just grinned. "Get ready, we're here. Put this set in the water. And this time, Jimmy, don't almost die doing it!"

For the rest of the afternoon, the boat was tightly wound. Jimmy was pissed at Joe, and Joe was thoroughly enjoying punishing Jimmy. Meanwhile, Jamie only wanted time to go faster so he could call Shelley, so he was hyper-focused on making the most efficient use of his movements. The boat was like a big Bavarian clock with pop-out figures that twirl and spin in their own little circles, as if dancing with their own personal demons.

As the three of them walked up the floating dock at the end of the day, they did so in edgy silence. Then Joe stunned them by announcing that the next day would be a half day to let the gear soak and the crew recover. Upon hearing this news, Jamie realized he'd now have enough time to get ready for a date with Shelley, and the urgency he'd been fighting all day to call her and ask her out on a date surged out of control. Without explanation, he blurted out his goodbye to the guys and started jogging up the trail toward his campsite.

Joe and Jimmy watched him go, and when he'd disappeared from view, Joe muttered, "He's gonna call her for a date, isn't he?"

"Yep," Jimmy concurred.

The two men stood silently by the truck for a few uncomfortable moments. Finally, Joe asked, "Hey, you wanna drink some beer?"

Jimmy looked warily at Joe, but the man seemed sincere in his peace offering. He pursed his lips and nodded, "Sure, that sounds good. Hair of the dog might be just what I need."

"It always is, Jimmy."

◇◇◇◇

Jamie sped right to his tent, changed out of his work clothes, and then headed over to the pay phone to call Shelley. As he put his quarters in, a sweet voice sounded behind him. "Who you calling, stud?"

Jamie turned around and there was Shelley smiling at him. He hung up the receiver. "Actually, I was just about to ask a girl out on a date."

"You don't say."

"Oh yeah, I was going to ask her if she wanted me to pick her up tomorrow at five o'clock."

"Now, if this girl happens to work a job that goes until five p.m., she'll need a little more time to shower and get all pretty for ya."

"Oh, so you're saying I should ask to pick her up around five thirty?"

Shelley smiled. "Uh-huh, that sounds much better, college boy. But I gotta ask, how in the hell are you gonna pick this girl up and drive her anywhere when your car is dismantled and in pieces at Jerry's? On your bike?"

Jamie said ruefully, "Uh, I don't even have a bike."

Shelley giggled. "Well, that's gonna cause a little problem, don't you think?"

He puffed out his chest. "Nope, this girl's so special, I'll beg, borrow, or steal someone's car to go on a date with her!"

"Why don't you just let the girl drive her own vehicle?" Shelley cooed as she moved a step closer.

"No way, I'm a traditionalist! I think the boy should provide the transportation, especially on the first date!"

"Oooh, you were calling this girl for your first date?"

"Uh-huh."

"Well, that *is* special, isn't it? And what are you proposing to do on this first date with this girl?"

"Well, I haven't seen a movie since I started working here in Kestrel Cove, so I thought that I'd ask her to go to the Corners with me to eat dinner and catch a movie."

"What movie?"

"I like historical movies, and there's one playing about the Civil War that I think would be good."

Shelley took another step forward and got even closer to him. "Uh-uh, not a war movie. A romantic comedy is much better for a first date."

"Romantic comedy?"

"Oh, yes, a much better genre to select for a first date. No girl wants to get all gussied up to watch a movie about boys killing one another."

"They don't?"

Shelley moved in until their bodies were nearly touching. "Naw, they want to get romantic. Come on, what's the real point of a date? It's sure not to talk about campaigns and casualties of war!"

"Oh, okay, romantic comedy it is. After the movie, I thought that this girl and I could grab an ice cream somewhere."

"And then what?"

"Then? Well, it'll be pretty late, so I was figuring on taking the young lady back to her house at a reasonable time."

Their bodies now touched and he could feel her warmth and his heart began to beat faster. Shelley leaned in close to Jamie's ear and whispered, "A first date is no time to be reasonable."

Jamie was tongue-tied. He tried to think of something suave to say, but his brain couldn't function properly. He struggled to string letters together to form words to make a semi-intelligent sentence, but all that came out was something that sounded akin to Goofy's dumb laugh, "Aw, shucks."

Shelley pulled back, and Jamie wondered if he'd just obliterated the moment. Then she started to laugh. It was as if barn swallows were flying out of her mouth as she laughed, flittering and swooping around the early evening air. He looked into her eyes to try to read what she was truly feeling as she laughed so wildly. He fully expected to see pity or ridicule, but there was a twinkle in them that was nothing but amusement. "You are too funny, Jamie Kurtz! I like being around you 'cause you make me laugh! Once you figure out your car situation, come by and pick me up at five thirty tomorrow, okay?"

"Well, okay, but I'll have to call this other girl and reschedule our date first."

Shelley punched him hard on the shoulder and they both laughed. Suddenly her face took on a serious look. "Hey, I do have a special request. I know it's gonna sound a little weird, but you'll have to trust me on this one, okay?"

"Okay," he replied.

"My family can be a little overwhelming, so when you come to pick me up, honk the horn and stay in the car. I'll come out to you."

"But don't you want me to—"

"No, it'll be better if you stay in the car, okay?"

"Okay, Shelley, I'll stay in the car and wait."

She kissed him on the cheek. "Don't be late."

"You gotta be kidding me! I'll probably be sitting in your driveway most of the goddamn afternoon!"

Shelley laughed and headed back into the store. Her laughter bubbled around him like effervescence. He felt like he was floating as he walked back to his tent.

Jamie awoke with a frenetic urgency the next morning. If Joe was being truthful about only fishing for a half day, he'd have more than enough time to get ready for his big date with Shelley. But if Joe had changed his mind, Jamie would have to be ready to hit the shore running to get ready for it. He had to be prepared for both scenarios, so he packed his backpack with the essential clothes, his ditty bag, and towel and headed off for work early.

When he got to Jerry's garage he left a note taped to the front door that read:

> *Hey Jerry,*
>
> *I need to borrow a car REALLY, REALLY BADLY for something I have to go to tonight. Since my Volvo isn't ready yet, is there any way that you can loan me a working vehicle for the night? We've got a half day of*

fishing, so I'll talk with you after lunch.

Thanks,

Jamie Kurtz

When Joe and Jimmy pulled up to the parking lot, they saw that Jamie was waiting for them like an expectant father. Since they had completely forgiven one another for any of the sins of the day before, they were now completely united and ready to torture the college boy again. Jamie didn't know it, but Veronica had overheard him and Shelley making date plans at the store, and she had immediately disseminated this news to the airwaves. The entire community of Kestrel Cove now knew that Jamie and Shelley were going on their first date, so as they saw the boy's nervousness, Jimmy and Joe nodded to one another and got ready for the fun of teasing the college boy.

"Hey, Jamie?"

"Yeah, Joe," Jamie wearily replied.

"Jimmy and me were just discussing something. If we went up to Rockland today to get some supplies to work on the boat, we could make a whole day of it, and come back tonight after dinner. It'd be a helluva lot more fun than fishing half a day. What do you say?"

Jamie's mind went into panic mode. "Naw, I think I need to make some money today, Joe. So I think we should definitely go fishing!"

Jimmy chimed in, "Yeah, me too."

"Really?" Joe asked with some surprise.

"Oh yeah," Jimmy continued seriously, "I think we should shift those other traps to deeper waters today. Instead of taking the day off or just fishing a half day, I say we spend a really long day getting that gear in the right place. We could work until six or seven because tomorrow is Sunday and we have it off. I say that we put in a *really* long day today and work until it gets dark!"

Jamie couldn't believe his ears. "No, that doesn't sound like a good idea, either! Let's just fish a shorter day today like you talked about yesterday."

"Well, you won't make much money that way," Joe said coolly. "Jimmy's right. If we fish a long, long day, it would mean that you would be making *more* money, college boy."

"Hey, money for half a day is better than no money at all, right?" Jamie responded too quickly.

Joe and Jimmy looked at each other, but they didn't crack even the slightest traces of a grin. Joe scratched his head. "I dunno…"

Later, when Jamie figured out that they were just toying with him, he'd think about this moment and muse that Joe and Jimmy were two of the most straight-faced liars he'd ever met in his entire life. But for now, he was purely panicked and trying to figure out a way to not miss his date with Shelley.

Joe finally acquiesced and said that they'd only go fishing for half a day, as planned, but he and Jimmy took every opportunity to make up chores and propose time-consuming jobs to do while out on the boat. After toying with him all morning, Joe even faked an engine failure just before coming in. As he calmly described how he and Jimmy were going to have to take the boat's diesel engine apart to find the "flux capacitor," Jamie's heart crawled up into his throat. He watched as Joe and Jimmy calmly opened the engine box and started fixing the fictional ailments, and he tried to look over their shoulders, but he couldn't see the wicked grins they wore as they pretended to work on the engine. When it appeared that the boy was going to faint with panic, Joe nodded at Jimmy to put the engine box back on and said that they'd give it another try. Of course, it started up without issue as soon as Joe turned the key. As they steamed toward the wharf, Jamie scrubbed the gunwales and deck like he was scouring a heavily encrusted pan.

At the floating dock, Joe made one last attempt to play with Jamie. He said nonchalantly, "Oh, hey, Jamie, my old lady wanted me to invite you to come over for dinner tonight."

"Jesus Christ, I work for you for, like, forever, and your old lady never asked *me* to dinner!"

"You ain't college educated!" Joe snapped.

"Well, if I was you, kid, I'd take that offer—it ain't likely to be repeated."

"Sorry, Joe, but I can't. Not tonight."

Joe smiled a crocodile's grin. "Oh, really? Why not?"

"I…I'm sort of busy," Jamie replied quickly.

"Oh, really? How could you be busy, living in a tent and all?" Joe asked with feigned interest.

"Well, I'm going to eat dinner with my old college professor tonight."

"Huh, how are you getting there?" Jimmy inquired.

"Where?" Jamie asked nervously.

"To your dinner with your college professor, dummy!"

"Uh, he's coming to pick me up."

"That's nice of him," Joe said slyly. "Do you need to take a shower beforehand?"

Jamie sensed a trap. There'd been no overt reference to homosexuality or pedophilic teachers preying on former students, but he felt, for the first time all day, as if he was being baited. He responded swiftly, "I'm going to clean up at Bill Hand's gatehouse."

"Well, okay, if you're all set," Joe said with a shrug.

Jamie didn't wait for any more comments, but instead nearly ran up the gangplank of the floating dock to the wharf. He yelled over his shoulder, "See you guys on Monday!"

Jamie ran directly to Jerry Shute's. The three garage doors were open, but no cars were in the bays. Country music blared from a grease-coated radio. He found Jerry under the front end of a Trans Am in the parking lot, and he cleared his throat to announce his presence before speaking. "Uh, hey Jerry, it's me, Jamie Kurtz."

"Yep."

"Well, I was wondering if you got my note. I left it on your door."

"Uh-huh."

"So what do you think?" Jamie asked with some excitement.

The mechanic scrambled out from under the car and sat up. He wiped his hands on his filthy rag and looked up at Jamie. "About what?"

Jamie exhaled impatiently. "About me borrowing a loaner from you for tonight!"

Jerry Shute chuckled and kept wiping his hands. "Oh, *that* note. You see, I ain't Hertz, Jamie. I'm just a local peckerneck who repairs cars. I'd give you one if I had one, but I ain't got no loaners!"

"But I need a car!" Jamie exclaimed. "It's important!"

"Sorry, kid, all the cars that are here are here 'cause they don't run. I ain't got nothing running to give you. Call a car rental place in Brementon."

Jamie looked up at the sky in frustration. "Jerry, I need the car this afternoon. It's really important!"

"I don't know what you want me to do, kid. None of these cars are in working condition. I'm sorry. The only vehicle here that would start and drive is my tow truck."

"Your tow truck?"

The look on Jerry Shute's face went sour with regret, like he wanted to find those last words and re-swallow them. "Oh, I can't let you take my tow truck."

"Why not?"

"'Cause what happens when someone calls for a tow?"

"How often does that happen, Jerry?"

"It could happen…today."

"But it doesn't usually?"

"It hasn't happened yet, but it could."

"I'll tell you what, Jerry," Jamie said with emphasis, "I'll leave the radio on, and if you get any calls tonight, I'll bring the truck right back and you can pick up the tow."

"I dunno. I've never let my tow truck be borrowed by anyone."

"Come on, Jerry, I'm begging you. I'm so frigging desperate, Jerry! I need a vehicle badly tonight. Come on, please, do me this one favor!"

Jerry blew out his breath out with a kind of snort. "When do you need it?"

"At five p.m., after you close the garage!"

Jerry exhaled again. "I guess if you keep the radio on and listen for any calls, it wouldn't hurt nothing if you were to borrow it tonight. But when I come to the garage tomorrow morning at six, I want that god-damn truck right here, fueled up and in one piece! Got it, kid?"

"Oh, hell yes, Jerry!" Jamie boomed.

Jerry renewed the rubbing of his grimy hands on the rag. "Keys'll be in it."

"Thanks, Jerry! I owe you!"

"Just make sure that you get her back in one piece, okay?"

"I promise!"

This solution to his transportation issue made Jamie feel confident in his ability to figure out the rest of what needed to happen before his date. And as he walked up the trail toward the pipeline, he felt good because he thought he now had a good chance to actually make his date with Shelley live up to his lofty expectations.

19

Jamie didn't want to bother Bill Hand, so he went directly to the gatehouse, found the hidden key, and let himself in. He hadn't asked for permission, but he figured Bill wouldn't mind if he took a shower and cleaned up. But, as he reached the middle of the stairway, he heard strange voices coming from the apartment. He immediately wanted to turn around, but he could hear chairs being overturned and loud shouts in a language that was not English. He froze. Suddenly, the door flew open at the bottom of the stairs, and there stood Bill Hand, ghostly pale and out of breath. The fear in his voice made his lisp more pronounced. "Jesus H. Christ, Jamie, what the hell are you doing here?"

"I came to take a shower, Bill! I've got a date with Shelley tonight!" Jamie shrieked back.

A dark-skinned man in a suit was now standing at the top of the stairs with an automatic pistol leveled at Jamie, and he barked something in a gruff voice that resonated off the walls of the stairwell. Bill Hand said something back in the same language that sounded much more soothing. The man in the business suit spoke again, but with less force, and Bill Hand retorted with another cool response. When Jamie looked back at the top of the stairs, the man was no longer there. "Bill, what the hell's going on here?"

"We need to go outside, Jamie. *Now!*"

Jamie immediately apologized. "I am *so* sorry, Bill. I needed to take a shower and I didn't think anyone would be here and I just thought you wouldn't mind if I let myself in. Then, as soon as I heard people, I knew I had made a terrible mistake. Why was that man pointing a gun at me? Who was that? Were there other men there? I heard other voices. Who are those people, Bill?"

"Businessmen, Jamie."

"What kind of businessmen carry automatic pistols and come ready to shoot people without provocation?"

Bill Hand sighed. "The kind who fear for their lives, that's who. Businessmen are targets of assassinations and kidnappings all around the world, and these men just happen to be prepared for those kinds of things. I'm just glad you weren't hurt, Jamie, but you must leave right now."

"Was he speaking Arabic?"

"Persian, actually."

"You speak Persian?"

"I do business with people from a bunch of different countries, and it pays to have a rudimentary understanding of their language to facilitate negotiations."

"What could you possibly be negotiating with a bunch of armed thugs? Definitely not computer stuff."

Bill Hand glanced up at the windows of the gatehouse and pushed Jamie by the shoulders. "Just head up to the big house and take your shower there. Congrats on asking Shelley out, by the way. I'm glad you didn't drag your feet too long. After you're clean, take the back trails down to the pipeline and just keep going. Don't come back here."

Jamie took notice of both the severity of Bill's message and his acknowledgment of his date with Shelley. "Thanks, Bill. And again, I'm sorry!"

"Ah, don't worry; it'll all be fine, trust me. Go up to my house and clean up. And Jamie?"

"Yeah?"

"Try to have some fun tonight."

Unnerved by the events at the gatehouse, Jamie rushed through his shower. The way that Bill Hand had seemed flustered and scared was so out of character, it betrayed the seriousness of the situation. Jamie hurriedly toweled off, got dressed in his good clothes, and headed down the trail without stopping.

Once he was back at his tent, he realized that he still had a few hours to waste before it was time to pick up the tow truck. He tried reading, but couldn't concentrate. He nervously paced around his campsite, but when he heard gunshots nearby, he knew that Joe and Jimmy were spending their free afternoon drinking and shooting. He couldn't bear to be tortured by them anymore, so he set off for the wharf to waste time down by the water.

Soon he heard the characteristic whine of Wiley's dirt bike far behind him. As the boy came racing around the bend and saw Jamie, he drove over and killed the bike's motor. He boomed out, "Hey, man, shouldn't you be getting ready?"

Jamie chuckled. "So you know, too, huh?"

Wiley looked a little sheepish. "Um, know about what? Naw, I weren't saying nothing about anything. I was just wondering what the hell you're doing walking around the pipeline in the middle of the afternoon all dressed up."

Jamie made a grand gesture. "I'm bored, Wiley, and I'm trying to figure out what to do."

"Whoa, bro, then I'm just the guy you need right now. Hop on! I need your help, and we'll be done in plenty of time to…do whatever you're gonna be doing later."

Jamie hesitated. Getting on a motorbike with Wiley wasn't the most prudent thing to do. The boy was an agent of trouble, that was for sure. But maybe going for a motorbike ride would be just the distraction he needed, so he hopped aboard. And it sounded like he could help Wiley with something, too. Win-win.

As they sped away, kicking up a shower of rocks and dust, Wiley adjusted to the extra weight on the back of his bike. Jamie hung on with a death grip around his waist as they bounced and jumped through the ruts of the pipeline like a motocross track. They flew past the trails that went up to Bill Hand's, and Jamie wondered if the Persian thugs had calmed down yet. The warm summer afternoon air coursed over them and bugs smacked into their faces as they barreled down the pipeline, and whenever it crossed the main road, Wiley would slow down long enough to ascertain if a car was coming and then gun the engine. The bike would catch air, and Jamie's stomach would fly up into his throat each time. The force of each landing made them both grunt heavily.

The pipeline came to an end at a gate with a large UNITED STATES NAVY—NO TRESPASSING sign on it. There was a field of tall grass on the other side of the gate that led down to the abandoned fuel dock. As they sped past the gate and headed out into the field, Jamie tapped hard on Wiley's back with his chin. He stopped the bike and snarled, "What the hell, dude?"

"We're not supposed to be on this field, Wiley! That giant sign back there said so!"

"They never stop nobody. Believe me, I've ridden here too many times to count! Relax, man."

With this, Wiley gunned the bike and raced toward the water. The field was uneven and the bike jiggled and bounced like a bucking bronco. Even though he had to hold the handlebars tightly as the bike tried to spring free, he kept the throttle wide open. When they got to the shoreline, he shut off the engine.

"Phew, we were really speeding right along there, huh?" Jamie said, inspecting himself for dirt or mud.

"Aw, yeah, man. This bike can really move! Even with us two on it, she screams!"

"Uh-huh," Jamie said, glancing at his watch. "So, it looks like it's about four thirty. We need to head back pretty soon so I can go over to Jerry's for my ride."

"Uh, just a second. I lost something on the beach here earlier, and I gotta find it."

"You lost something on *this* beach?" Jamie asked incredulously.

"Oh, sure. I saw it when we steamed past here this morning. It's black and about yay big," Wiley said, making an object with his hands the size of a football.

"Wiley, I don't really have too much time."

"No worries, man, this'll only take a second. With you helping, it'll take even less time!"

They walked down onto the rocky shore. Jamie looked around the rocks, but he couldn't stop looking at his watch. Suddenly Wiley yelled, "Ah, here it is!"

He scooped up the object, which was bound tightly in black plastic, and started walking back toward the bike. Jamie tilted his head and warily asked, "Uh, Wiley, what is that?"

"Come on, dude! Hop on; we need to hurry and get you back in time."

The new urgency in Wiley's voice told Jamie that they were doing something that was both illegal and dangerous, so he quickly scuttled over to the bike without another question. As he jumped on, Wiley jammed down on the kick-start, and the bike roared to life.

Wiley thrusted the black object into Jamie's stomach. "Hold this between us, okay?"

The black plastic was wet and smelled like the ocean. It soaked Jamie's shirt as he leaned forward. Jamie yelled into Wiley's ear, "Hey, Wiley, what the hell is this, for real?"

"Pot, bro!"

"Pot?"

"Oh, yeah. This is the way my dealer delivers it to me. He drops the bundles in the water from his boat and they float onshore, and I go and get them later. This little rascal here got away from me. Had to get it before someone else stumbled on it."

The bike shot forward and they sped back across the grassy field. They were nearly to the gate when they saw the black SUV with the blue and red flashing lights over on the main road. A loudspeaker bellowed, "You on the bike, stop now! You're trespassing on government land! Halt! We've got you blocked in! Stop now!"

"*Hold on!*" Wiley yelled as he gunned the engine.

"Wiley, what the hell?"

"I dunno, dude, this has never happened before!"

"My date!" Jamie hissed.

"Don't worry, they'll never catch us. They never have so far!"

"But you just said this has never happened before!" Jamie pointed out.

Wiley stared straight at the gate ahead of them. He seemed less worried about the vehicle in pursuit on the road, and he grinned knowingly as he saw their path free of any obstacles. Suddenly, his grin melted as another black SUV pulled up and blocked the way to the pipeline. They were now, in fact, trapped by the two vehicles.

"Oh God, there goes my date!" Jamie moaned.

"Hold on, man!"

"Wiley, what the—?"

The bike shuddered as it skidded into a sharp turn, spewing grass and dirt. When it straightened out again, it was pointed directly toward the woods. Nothing but crowded trees and rocks were in front of them now, and Jamie squeezed the bale of pot tighter to Wiley as he screamed, "I really, really don't want to die today!"

Wiley laughed out loud. "Whoa, dude, no one's dying today! I'm just trying to get you to your date on time! Just hold on; we're gonna be airborne in a second or two."

"Airborne!?"

"*HOLD ON!*"

In front of the bike, there suddenly appeared a rock shaped like a gigantic rhombus with one side sloped gently like a ramp. They hit this at full throttle, and the bike flew up in the air and over a small clump of trees. As the back tire gently brushed the tops of the pine saplings, Jamie closed his eyes. When they landed, it felt like the bike was going to snap in half, but Wiley kept it upright and accelerating down a narrow path that wound through the trees. As the trunks whizzed by, Jamie sensed that Wiley had done this all before, and this gave him the confidence to loosen his death grip somewhat. They went through a grove of tall ferns and then the bike jumped back onto the pipeline.

As if it had been expecting them, the black SUV came speeding up from behind.

"You on the bike, stop this instant! Stop or we'll shoot!" a voice from the black SUV blared.

"Don't worry, man, they never shoot!"

The sound of gunfire made them stiffen with tension. "Jesus, Wiley!"

"Just hold on!"

When they came to the first place that the pipeline crossed the main road and Wiley didn't even pretend to slow down, Jamie knew how high the stakes actually were, and he squeezed in tighter.

Wiley yelled over his shoulder, "Dude, we've got to stay ahead of that other SUV on the road! They're gonna try to get ahead and trap us. We're gonna not let that happen!"

Then Wiley saw the mud puddle that Rickie Hughes had gotten stuck in during their race the previous weekend, and he steered the bike toward the school bus–size obstacle. But he got too close to it and lost control of the bike in the mud. As it slid completely sideways and Jamie began screaming, Wiley barked for him to hang on. Mud sprayed them both from head to toe as he struggled to keep the bike upright.

The government SUV was not as lucky. It hit the puddle squarely, and, just like Rickie Hughes, immediately sank up to its axles in mud and stopped instantly. The driver, dazed by the impact, now tried to reverse out of the mud trap, but the wheels just churned up a mixture that looked like café au lait. The agents inside the SUV slammed the dashboard in disgust and radioed to the other SUV.

Somehow Wiley had recovered the bike from it cockeyed slide, and now he gunned the engine again and took off down the pipeline. At some point during their slide, Jamie had closed his eyes, and when he reopened them, he saw nothing but a mud-covered world. The bike, Wiley, the black ball of pot, and he himself were all coated thickly with it, and the realization that his date with Shelley was now completely sabotaged hit him harder than the landing of the bike off the ramp. Even if he and Wiley survived this chase, there was absolutely not enough time for him to get back to his tent, clean up, and get ready for the date. And, as they sped around Mt. Buxtor and headed toward the main road again, he was trying to come up with what he'd say to Shelley by way of explanation.

That was when they came right up on Bill Hand and his Persian guests picking raspberries. The bend in the pipeline had shielded the sound of the motorbike until it was too late, and it was clear that they'd surprised the group as the same large man who had confronted Jamie on the stairwell at the gatehouse pulled out his automatic pistol again and leveled it at them. Wiley and Jamie instinctively ducked low on the bike as they went past, and the spread of fire the man let off was wide because Bill Hand knocked into him, causing the bullets to whiz harmlessly into the woods.

But as Wiley and Jamie came to the crossing of the main road, they nearly collided with the other black SUV as it screeched to a stop. The occupants of this vehicle jumped out and took aim at the fleeing motorbike as the Persian businessman, now free from Bill Hand's interference, fired again. These shots kicked up geysers of dirt near the SUV, so the armed government men took up defensive positions behind their doors and radioed that they were under attack from a new target. But Bill Hand forcefully escorted his guests back up the trail to the safety of his property, and later described the experience as "herding a fucking flock of pissed-off goats!"

Now that they were no longer being pursued, both Wiley and Jamie relaxed a little. But when Jamie looked down at his mud-spattered watch and saw that it was 5:05 p.m., he groaned loudly, "Aw, what the hell am I going to do now, Wiley? I'm totally covered in mud and it's too late to get cleaned up!"

"Trust me, dude, I've got an idea."

The bike slowed and turned onto a trail that led to a trailer. Wiley turned off the bike and told Jamie to get off. He grabbed the black plastic bundle and put it safely away inside a small shed behind the trailer. He came back and wheeled the bike behind the shed and left it there. "All right, let's get you cleaned up and ready to go on your date!"

"Where are we, Wiley? I mean, I know we're near the wharf, but whose trailer is this?"

"Alfred's."

"Wiley, how in the hell is Alfred going to be able to help me? I'm soaked through with mud. I don't have time to shower, go back to my camp—"

"Just trust me, okay?"

"Okay."

When Alfred opened his door, he was wearing a pair of tattered shorts and a wife-beater T-shirt. He didn't seem too surprised to see either Wiley or Jamie on his stoop, and calmly looked both of them over before saying, "Wow, look at the two of you! I don't even want to know what you've been up to or why you just put that black plastic bundle in my shed and your bike behind it, Wiley. The less I know the better, I think. But I am wondering why you're now banging on my door."

"Alfred, we've got an emergency here."

"We do?"

"We've got to get Jamie cleaned up and ready for his date with Shelley."

"*We* do?"

"Come on, Alfred, be a sport and help me help Jamie. Look at him, Alfred, he's about to shit himself 'cause he thinks he's gonna miss his date. He needs a goddamn shower and a fucking clean outfit."

"How come you don't take him to your place and get him a goddamn shower and a fucking clean outfit there?"

Wiley snorted with frustration. "Come on, Alfred, he's in a rush. We'd never make it to my place and back to Jerry's to borrow his truck in time for him to pick up Shelley."

Alfred turned his stern gaze onto Jamie. "How could you be so dumb to get involved with this yahoo a few hours before your big date?"

Jamie shrugged. "He said he needed my help."

"Uh-huh," Alfred said with a faint smile, "he gets more suckers that way."

Alfred was shaking his head so vigorously that Jamie was prepared for him to say no, but then Alfred wagged his index finger. "I had a friend just like Wiley when I was your age, and you'll never guess who it was. It was Drake! He'd ask for my help and get me in so much goddamn trouble. But when a friend like that asks for help, you go and help him, huh? All right, strip those muddy clothes off, college boy, 'cause I don't want you messing up my trailer. Then get your ass in the shower and clean up. Don't waste too much time, and don't jerk it while you're in there. Wiley and me will get you an outfit from my closet. What size shoe do you wear?"

"Ten and a half."

"You'll have to survive with an eleven and a half."

Jamie stripped and hustled into the trailer in his boxers. He found the bathroom and went straight for the shower. The trailer was surprisingly clean, although it smelled strongly of cigarette smoke and whiskey. A TV was blaring in the living room, and something fragrant was cooking in the kitchen. Jamie turned the water on and showered quickly, scrubbing the mud out of his hair and off his skin. He found the towel that Alfred had left while he showered, and dried off with it. He wrapped the towel around his waist and came out of the bathroom. Wiley called him to come down to Alfred's bedroom. He walked the carpeted hallway hopefully and found the two men staring down with proud smiles at an outfit they'd laid out on the bed. Jamie looked at it doubtfully. There was a cream-colored *guayabera* shirt with embroidered tunas swimming up and down the front from the lapels to the waist. Under the shirt was a pair of blue pleated polyester pants with a wide white belt. Under the hanging pant legs were two white patent leather shoes. Jamie's smile dropped, dragging Wiley's and Alfred's along with it.

Wiley looked down at the floor, but Alfred cleared his throat. "Well, maybe next time you're all covered in mud and need help just minutes before your big date, you should stop at a house where the person has more fucking fashion sense!"

Jamie heard the hurt feelings and quickly recovered from his initial disappointment enough to say, "Naw, it's not that, Alfred. I just realized that, with this freaking powerful outfit, I'm going to have to fight Shel— my date off with a bat!"

Wiley and Alfred beamed with pride over their selection. Alfred wagged his finger at Jamie again. "We all know who you're going on this date with tonight, college boy. Just know that I've watched that girl grow up, so don't try anything with her tonight or I might be smashing *your* skull in with a baseball bat!"

"He'll be a perfect gentleman, won't you, man?" Wiley offered proudly.

"Well, you better be, that's all I'm saying. Go ahead and get dressed now."

After Alfred and Wiley left the bedroom, Jamie looked at the ashtray full of cigarette butts that sat atop the *Playboy* magazine on the bedside table and shook his head at the ridiculousness of his situation. He grabbed the pants and put them on. They were a little tight around the waist, since Alfred was much slimmer than Jamie, and they were a few inches too long, so he rolled them up a little. The polyester itched his legs and scratched his loins. He cinched the belt and then put on the shirt. The shoes completed the outfit, and he looked at himself in the mirror and chuckled at the silliness of his reflection.

As he opened the bedroom door, Wiley jumped him with handfuls of cologne that he rubbed over Jamie's ears and neck. The overwhelming aroma of Old Spice enveloped him and tingled on his skin.

Jamie howled in surprise, "Oh, man! Wiley, you bastard!!"

"Can't have you smelling like ass for your big date, man!"

At the door, Alfred patted Jamie on the shoulder. "Better get going, college boy, we don't want you to be late!"

Wiley smacked him on the back. "Good luck, stud!"

Jamie smiled foolishly. Being chased, shot at, and dressed up in this ridiculous outfit all combined to make him feel high, but a wave of concern hit him enough to turn back toward Wiley and ask, "Hey, is the earlier…uh, excitement over? Do I need to avoid certain roads tonight?"

It took Wiley a few moments to grasp what he was trying to say, but then he nodded with a knowing look. "Naw, they're looking for two kids on a bike. They ain't gonna spend too much time canvassing the area looking for a fancy-pants in a tow truck. Plus, I doubt they got a real good look at our faces—just our asses!"

"Okay," Jamie said halfheartedly with a wave of his hand. As he hiked the trail that led to the garage, he heard the music inside the trailer get boosted up in volume, and he smiled at the thought of Alfred and Wiley partying together. He just hoped Wiley wouldn't stab Alfred.

The tow truck had the keys in it as Jerry had promised. When Jamie started it, the CB radio that hung from the dashboard blared out as other tow truck operators chattered about how a black SUV needed to be extracted from the mud on the pipeline. He doubted that Jerry would be upset if he ignored this one call. Plus, it sounded as if the situation was under control.

As he drove out of the lot and onto the wharf road, the tow sling swung and the chains and wires jangled loudly. Jamie drove straight to Shelley's house, and he was actually a few minutes early when he parked in the driveway behind her pickup and a tricked-out SUV. After he honked, he stayed in the truck as Shelley had instructed him to do.

The white two-story cape-style house looked the same as a lot of other places on the peninsula, and the house and lawn were well kept. Because he didn't know any specifics about Shelley's family, he tried to use the items he saw outside the house to provide some clues about the people inside of it. The plastic toys strewn around the yard indicated that there were several youngsters in her family, but the snowmobiles and dirt bikes that were parked under the trees along the driveway revealed that there were older kids, too. Jamie hoped that Shelley would tell him more details during their date to see if his detective work was any good.

It was as his eyes scanned the yard again that he first saw the burly man with the baseball bat approaching from the side door of the house. He was wearing gray shorts and a T-shirt, but no shoes, and he had the bat up like he was looking for the perfect pitch. Dark rings around his eyes seemed to accentuate his jet-black hair and mustache. Since they could easily see one another, Jamie rolled down his window and said hello.

The man stopped and puffed out his chest. "For a repo man, you sure ain't too quiet."

Jamie was unsure what he was talking about, so he said, "Uh, this is where Shelley Vanes lives, right?"

"You can't repo Shelley's truck, asshole, she owns it outright!"

"No, no, I'm Jamie Kurtz. I'm Joe Quinn's sternman. Shelley and I are supposed to go out tonight."

"Sheee-it, you're Shelley's big date? I didn't *think* you were a repo man, but I couldn't figger out who else would drive around in a tow truck and just sit in the driveway."

"I had to borrow Jerry Shute's truck because my car is being worked on—"

"The way I heard it," the man interrupted with enthusiasm, swinging the bat down to rest on the ground, "Drake nearly stove the side of your car in with his bait truck!"

"Yeah, that's about right."

"You shouldn't a pissed him off, huh?"

"Guess not."

"Well, why the hell are you just sittin' out here? Come on inside."

"Um, Shelley told me to honk the horn and wait for her to come out."

The man chuckled. "Aw, she ain't ready yet."

"She's not?"

"Naw, she had to stay at the store to restock the bread aisle. She just got home and came in like a goddamn Tasmanian devil! She's ta-kin' a shower right now. Come on, get outta the truck and come in-side—Momma wants to meet ya."

The man started walking toward the house and glanced over his shoulder to make sure Jamie was coming. He wasn't. Shelley had told him to wait in the car for a reason, and he didn't want to start this date off by making her mad at him. When he'd hesitated a little too long, the man snapped, "Come on now, kid, don't make me come over there and drag your ass outta the truck!"

His threat trumped Shelley's, so Jamie got out and followed him. At the door of the house, he turned and said, "My name's Leon, by the way."

"Nice to meet you, Leon."

The inside of the house smelled of cinnamon. Somewhere a television played loudly, and as Jamie and the black-haired man made their way toward the room the sounds were coming from, two small children came up to them and started shouting, "Shelley's date is here! Shelley's date is here!"

A rasping woman's voice sounded over the TV and kid noises, "Well, bring his ass in here. I want to meet him!"

When Jamie entered the TV room, he found a rotund woman lying on the couch in a flowery muumuu with five children sitting around her like the midget courtiers of a royal queen. They all seemed to be somewhere between five and ten years old, and they sat so close to the woman that they looked like barnacles on the sides of a ship's hull. They all simultaneously looked up at Jamie with expectant eyes. But no one spoke.

The television volume was very loud, so Jamie had to nearly shout, "Hello, Mrs. Vanes. My name is Jamie Kurtz."

"Oh, I've heard all about you! Our Shelley is as excited for this date with you as she's been about anything in quite some time. So, you're summering here in Kestrel Cove, huh?"

On the TV screen, a talk-show host was trying to start a fight between the lesbian lovers of his bisexual guests. Jamie found the commotion somewhat distracting, especially in light of the implications of the last question. He responded quickly, "Uh, I'm not sure that I'd call myself a summer person, Mrs. Vanes. I'm sterning for Joe Quinn until the season is over."

"Sterning? Hmm, what cottage does your family own?"

"Cottage? My family doesn't own a cottage, Mrs. Vanes. I camp in a tent near the store."

As the children lost interest and turned their attention back to the fracas on the screen, Mrs. Vanes continued to stare at Jamie. "Huh, I musta heard Shelley wrong. I swear she said your family owned a camp down by the water and you were here for the summer."

Jamie cleared his throat. "Maybe she was talking about someone else."

"Whatever. She does tend to exaggerate. Hmm, she also didn't say that this was a date to a costume party!"

Jamie looked down at his outfit. "I had a small wardrobe malfunction."

"So you ain't dressed up as a spic pimp on purpose?"

"No, there's actually a funny story behind this outfit," Jamie started to explain, but Mrs. Vanes had also lost interest in him, and she shifted her body to face the television. Out the side of her mouth, she said, "Just be a gentleman on your date tonight, young man. Shelley's special to all of us. If she gets hurt, there'll be hell to pay. Leon can still swing that bat like nobody's business. Almost made it to the Majors 'cause of it."

Jamie thought about responding, but no one seemed to care that he was still in the room. He heard the thunder of feet coming down the stairs, and there was Shelley in a beautiful flowered summer dress with her hair pulled back in a ponytail. She sounded frantic when she yelled, "Is he out in the driveway? Is he here? Has he been waiting long?"

When she saw him, she froze in her tracks. She blinked several times as her mind processed the fact that he was standing in the hallway of her house. She finally whispered, "I thought I asked you to stay in the car until I came out."

Jamie shrugged his shoulders. There was too much to explain to get it all out in a rational way. Before he could say anything, Leon went by them with a Budweiser bottle in his hand, on his way to the TV room. "Aw, cut him some slack, Shelley. Momma wanted to meet him, so I invited him in—with my bat."

Shelley rolled her eyes and whispered into Jamie's ear. "I'm sorry. Like I said, my family can be a little crazy."

Jamie inhaled as much as he could of her ambrosia and whispered back, "It's okay. No worries. Truth is, I've been counting the seconds all day until we could go out."

"Really?"

"Thirty-six thousand, eight hundred and fifty-four at the current moment. I'd really rather not get to thirty-seven thousand!"

With a warm smile for Jamie, she turned and hollered toward the group that was now completely entranced by the fist-fight on the TV screen, "See you guys later!"

"Don't be too late. I might need some help tonight."

"Sure, Momma."

"Goodbye, Mrs. Vanes," Jamie offered.

"Uh-huh."

Suddenly Leon boomed out, "Jeez, that dyke punches like a dude, don't she?"

Shelley grabbed Jamie's arm and led him quickly out of the house. When they were outside, she sighed and said, "I was trying to protect you from them. I'm so sorry that you were exposed to that. Don't worry, I don't think it's contagious. And I'm adopted, I swear!"

Then her eyes flicked back and forth between Jamie and the tow truck. Finally, she said, "There's a story behind all of this, right?"

"You mean the outfit?"

"Yes, Jamie, I mean the outfit, the reek of cologne, and the tow truck in the driveway!"

"Ah, yes, there is a story."

"Well?"

"You really want to hear it now?"

"Yes, I should think so."

"Okay, while I was impatiently awaiting our date, Wiley came by and convinced me to go on his dirt bike to pick up his pot delivery at the fuel dock. Several black SUV's came out of nowhere and chased us down the pipeline! Then they started shooting at us, but we ran into some Arabic gun-toting businessmen who were with Bill Hand, and they all got into a gun fight and—"

"Wiley? Dirt bike? Pot delivery? Shooting? Arabic businessmen?"

"Uh-huh," Jamie said with a knowing nod.

"What about this outfit?"

"Well, my date clothes got all muddy, so Wiley took me over to Alfred's and he let me clean up and borrow some of his clothes."

"Alfred?"

"Yep."

Shelley grinned mischievously. "Is that why you look like Guido the Killer Pimp?"

"Yep."

"And the tow truck?"

"Well, I had to borrow Jerry's truck because he didn't have any other vehicles to lend me. It was this tow truck or nothing."

"You look like Tubbs from the old *Miami Vice* television show."

"Yes. Yes, I do."

Shelley giggled softly and stepped up to him. She kissed him sweetly on the lips. "You see, Jamie Kurtz, like I told you the other night, you make me laugh. Come on, let's go. I'm starving."

"Allow me, madam," Jamie said gallantly as he opened the passenger door of the tow truck. Several beer cans clattered to the ground, and Jamie cursed, "Oh, Christ on a crutch! I *did* try to clean up the truck a *little*!"

Shelley giggled again and kissed him again. This time, Jamie saw the curtains of the house swing shut and he announced, "I think they saw that one."

"Good. Maybe it will get them away from that goddamned TV!"

"Your mother seemed to be under the impression that I'm a rich summer person."

Shelley rolled her eyes. "My mother hears what she wants to. When I said that you were here for the summer and camping out, she assumed you were a Richie Rich at one of those fancy cottages. Ever since my dad died, money's been a little scarce. My mother's under the illusion that if I marry a rich guy, everything will be fixed."

"Hate to disappoint her, but I don't think it works that way."

"My mom has money on the brain because she doesn't want any of us to end up like her. Now do you see why I didn't want you to meet them?"

"Leon came out with a baseball bat because he suspected me of being a repo man."

"Aw, that figures," Shelley said gently.

Jamie shut the door, walked around to the driver's side, and climbed in. He backed the truck out onto the main road and headed toward the Corners. The tires were loud, so he had to raise his voice when he said, "Well, I'm *glad* I got to meet your family, Shelley. I don't really know all that much about you. I mean, I know that you work at the store and I know that you grew up around here, but I didn't have any idea that you've got younger siblings."

"Well, I don't know that much about you, either, college boy. I guess that's the purpose of a date, isn't it?"

Jamie smirked. "So that's the only purpose of a date, hmm?"

"Oh, don't you think that anything physical is going to happen on this date, mister. You're going to work a helluva lot harder than you did with Angie Williams!"

Jamie visibly deflated at this comment, and when Shelley noticed, she was angry. "Oh, don't be such a pussy, Jamie Kurtz! I was just kidding, for God's sake! If you're gonna do the crime, you've got to be able to do the time. Don't wilt whenever I razz you about her."

"But I'm embarrassed about that whole thing! I can't believe I went out with that girl!"

"Like I said to you at the party, life is about experiencing *everything*. You've got to take chances if you're going to get the most from it."

Yeah, but I don't see how Angie fits into that category!"

"If you learn the lesson from it, you'll become a better person because of it."

"I just don't want it to ruin things with you."

"It won't. But you acting like a wimp whenever I try to kid you about it—now *that* could be a major turn-off."

Jamie swallowed hard. "Okay, I'll try. Just lay off the Angie jokes a little, okay? To me, it was all an embarrassing mistake that I hope won't ruin my chances with you. The truth is, I really like you."

No one spoke in the tow truck for a moment, and Jamie suddenly feared he'd been too honest. Out of the silence, however, Shelley said quietly, "I really like you, too, college boy."

Jamie cleared his throat. "Well, tell me about your brother Leon. He seems interesting."

"Brother? Leon's not my brother, Jamie, he's my stepfather."

"He's your stepfather?"

Shelley giggled, "Of course. He and Momma have been married for about five years now."

Jamie glanced over at Shelley. "Well, anyway, he seems nice enough."

"He's been pretty good to me, even when I've been somewhat of a devil. What I like about Leon the most, however, is that he knows that he's my mother's husband, not my father. I give him major points for that. Now, don't get me wrong, the man's as useless as tits on a nun. He works like a banshee at the landscaping company he works at, but around the house, he doesn't lift a finger to help out with the little ones or help with Momma. I guess he think that's my job."

Jamie shook his head. "So what's going on with your mom?"

"You mean health-wise?"

"Yeah."

"Oh, she's a sick woman. Diabetes. Emphysema. Broken heart. You name it, she's suffering from it. Been lying around on the couch like that for the last couple of years. She's always in front of the television!"

"Are all those kids from Leon?"

"Naw, only the two youngest. The older ones are Leon's from an earlier marriage."

"Jeez, he doesn't seem old enough to have children that old!"

Shelley clucked her tongue. "They start early around here. Anyway, those kids are all pretty good, for little kids."

"So your mother had two children after she had you?"

"Yep, Momma is a regular baby factory. My parents were married early and they had Clara, Scotty, and then me. Three children in six years! When my dad died, Momma just sat around in mourning. Then she met Leon and found some happiness. She pumped out a couple more kids, then her body and heart gave out on her."

"Scotty? I haven't heard about him before. Does he live in Kestrel Cove?"

"No, he got out of here as soon as he could and headed to Portland. He owns a rug cleaning business there. He has a nice house in the suburbs and a wife and three kids of his own. He's sailing right along in life and doesn't come back here too often. Now that Clara's getting married and having a baby, she's all set, too! Bobbie's a high-liner, so she'll never have to worry about wanting anything. So that leaves me to take care of Momma. I guess I'll be stuck here in Kestrel Cove forever."

Jamie reached across the seat and touched her hand. "No way! I can't see you getting stuck *any*where, Shelley!"

"Sometimes the *have-to's* in life become like those fly strips that hang down from the ceiling. They snag you and won't let you go!"

Jamie started to laugh, but when Shelley shot him a hurt look, he stopped. She spoke with an edge to her voice. "Just what the hell do you think is funny about what I just said?"

"Because you, my dear Shelley Vanes, are a beautiful butterfly, and I've never seen a butterfly on one of those fly strips—not ever. You're far too beautiful and smart to ever get stuck anyplace that you don't want to be!"

Shelley's face softened and she purred as she caressed his hand. "Flattery will get you everywhere, young man."

"Oh, yeah?"

"Hey, where we eating tonight?"

"Omigosh! What time is it? We have six o'clock reservations at the Hungry Rancher!"

Shelley gasped, but then saw that he was kidding. "Very funny, college boy. For real, where are we eating?"

"You'll see."

When they pulled into the parking lot of the hamburger joint called Rickenbacker's, Shelley smiled happily—the place was one of her favorites. They got out of the truck and, as the headed toward the front door, Jamie felt brave enough to offer his hand to her. Without hesitation, Shelley took it and they walked hand in hand into the restaurant.

There was a good weekend crowd inside, but they didn't have to wait long for a table. Once seated, they started talking, and their conversation flowed nonstop through the meal. By the time they got to dessert, Laura's name finally came up. Jamie didn't want to talk about her, but Shelley kept asking for more details about the relationship and the breakup. He felt embarrassed to be revealing what he saw as his failures, but she kept encouraging him enough that he felt safe telling her everything. When he got to the part about working at the Hungry Rancher, living alone in the apartment, and getting evicted, Shelley shook her head sympathetically. He concluded with, "And that's how I got to Kestrel Cove."

Shelley grabbed her coffee mug and came over to Jamie's side of the booth. She snuggled next to him and whispered, "Sounds like it's been a bit of a rough ride for you, Jamie Kurtz, but I'm wicked glad you landed here in Kestrel Cove."

When the waiter came back with their bill, Jamie attempted to pay the whole thing, but Shelley refused to let him do that. They each paid their part, then they walked back to the truck. There, Shelley suddenly said, "I know you said that you haven't seen a movie in a while, but would you be too bummed if we skipped it tonight?"

"Skip the movie?"

"Uh-huh. I'd rather go somewhere with you to hang out and talk some more."

Jamie grinned. "That's sounds really good to me!"

"But just not here."

"If not here, where?" Jamie asked with a shrug.

Shelley smiled an impish grin. "I know just the place. Come on, let's go."

As they chatted and laughed about his misadventures on the boat, Shelley scooted over and snuggled closer to Jamie. She looked up and said, "Oh, take the next left."

"Huh, I've never been down this way before."

"A night of firsts, huh?" Shelley said as she started caressing the back of his neck. He was concentrating on the headlight-illuminated road ahead, but his insides were tingling with excitement. The warmth of Shelley's body, the smell of her perfume, and the massaging motions of her hand on his neck made him want to stop the truck and dive into her. Shelley suddenly spoke again. "See that bridge up ahead? Count four mailboxes from it and then turn onto that dirt road."

Jamie did as instructed. The road seemed to disappear into the darkness and he brought the truck to a stop and turned on the dome light. "Hey, are we trespassing on somebody's land? I've already been caught doing that!"

"Jeez, don't get your panties in a bunch, college boy! I know who owns this place and I have permission to be here," Shelley said with authority.

"Oh, yeah? Who is that?"

"Bill Hand. And he told me that I can come here anytime I want."

"Wow, you know Bill Hand that well?"

"No one knows Bill Hand that well, Jamie. But I told him once that I was interested in birds, especially shore birds, and that gave me an in with him."

Jamie stared at her. She went on, "I took an art class and got interested in drawing and painting shore birds. When I told Bill about it one time, he said I could come to this place to bird-watch anytime."

"But we can't exactly use that excuse tonight. I mean, I've already messed things up with Bill Hand enough today. I don't know how he'd react if he found out that we came here for non-ornithological reasons!"

Shelley moved away a little and looked at him with a stoic expression. "Okay, Jamie Kurtz, I'm gonna give you a moment to collect yourself. A very short moment. You're in a tow truck with a cute young woman who has the major hots for you and wants to show you her favorite desolated and private spot on the whole damn peninsula—a spot that she's never shown anyone else—and she wants nothing more than to let what's going to happen, happen. Take your moment to decide whether you're up for that. If you are, put this truck in drive and head to the end of the road. If you aren't, throw her in reverse and take me right home!"

A millisecond later, he drove the truck down the dirt road into the darkness of the forest. He was pretty sure he heard Shelley say under her breath, "Good boy."

The spot was truly breathtaking. The road just seemed to end at the shoreline, as if there were plans for a bridge that was never built. Out in front of them, a small bay opened expansively under a full moon. The lunar light gilded the rippling top layer of the water, and as soon as the truck was turned off, the silence of the woods pressed up against them. In a whisper, Shelley told Jamie to roll down his window. The sounds of the night—the gentle lapping of the water, mixed with the drone of traffic far away, and the sounds of their breathing—created a subtle rhythm that was purely magical.

Jamie exhaled and said, "Uh, wow…"

But Shelley raised her index finger as if she were pointing at the roof of the tow truck. After they had sat in silence for a few moments, she slid over and nestled against Jamie's shoulder. She whispered seductively, "I'm sorry for shutting you down, Jamie, but I just wanted to be with you and soak in this silence and peace; I haven't gotten any of that for some time. So what do you think?"

Jamie wanted to say and do so much, but when she placed a warm hand on his knee, he stiffened.

She laughed at his response. "You're scared shitless right now, aren't you?"

Jamie chuckled and admitted, "Yes, I'm scared of making the wrong move with you."

Shelley thought he meant that starting anything with her was a bad move, and she was about to say something defensive when Jamie continued, "I'm having the most amazing time on this date with you, Shelley Vanes, and I don't want to ruin it by trying to jump your bones. Even though I really, really, *really* want to!"

Shelley let out a breath and started laughing. "You see? That's why I'm smitten with you. Most guys would be thinking about nothing but getting my clothing off, but you're sitting over there doing a risk assessment with what *not* to do! You really *are* a funny bird."

"So I've been told."

"So let me help you in your quandary, okay? Just relax, 'cause you can't make a wrong move with me tonight. We are not going to have sex tonight, Jamie, but I'm dying for you to pick a path and follow it as far as it takes us."

Jamie couldn't wait any longer, and he planted a kiss on her. It was one of those kisses that baffles both participants with its depth and scope, and they held tightly to one another and let it saturate them. When she finally broke it off, Shelley said breathlessly, "See? You definitely can't do any wrong moves tonight."

When the tow truck turned around and drove back up the dirt road again two and a half hours later, they were lovers. Even though Shelley had been true to her word about not having sex, they'd savored and sampled each other in so many intimate ways that the power and energy of their new relationship scared both of them a little. Their good-night kiss was so passionate, they nearly headed back to the point to finish what felt like unfinished business. But Shelley eventually went into her dark house and Jamie drove off to return the tow truck to the garage. He left a short note of thanks to Jerry on the front seat and then strolled back to his tent, humming all the way.

20

Joe and Jimmy were waiting for him at the wharf that Monday morning with coyote grins on their faces. It was the first time they had ever gotten there before Jamie, and he was extremely surprised to see them. He nodded as he walked up, but they stayed in the truck, smiling at him. He looked around to see if he was missing some kind of joke, then he asked, "Are we heading out today?"

Joe rolled his eyes. "Did you have a good weekend?"

"Yes, I did. Did you guys?"

Both men nodded, but neither spoke. Finally, Jamie said, "Well, are we going to commit some lobstercide or not?"

Joe and Jimmy chuckled at his comment, then grabbed their stuff and got out of the truck. Joe said, "I hope you two clowns are ready to work hard today. We need to get some more gear moved, and I promised Sally I'd get home early today. I'm gonna really crack the whip!"

And they did work hard. But they were now such a well-oiled team that they made quick work of the extra tasks that Joe wanted to get done. Jamie kept waiting to face the inquisition about his date, or to have to dodge assorted inappropriate sexual innuendos, but neither Joe nor Jimmy mentioned the date or Shelley all day.

At the end of the workday, Joe invited them over to his place for some drinking and shooting. While Jimmy enthusiastically accepted, Jamie declined by saying that he wanted to head over to Bill Hand's to apologize for a misunderstanding. Without asking for any clarification, Joe and Jimmy drove off in a cloud of dust and blaring country music, leaving him standing alone in the wharf parking lot.

"Hey, lover-boy, how was the date?" a voice sneered from the shadows.

Jamie hadn't seen the wharf rat Vincent standing there, so he was startled by his question. He turned to face him. "Good, I guess, Vincent. It was really fun."

"Hee-hee, I bet it was, college boy. Getting laid always is," the skinny man tittered.

Jamie didn't like Vincent because he spent his days scurrying around the wharf and hiding in the shadows trying to avoid Drake. He was a lazy mooch, and he definitely did not have the right to talk that way about Shelley. Jamie took a step forward and said, "What did you just say?"

"The way I heard it, Jerry had to clean the pecker tracks off the seat of his tow truck! Har-har!"

Jamie took a few more determined steps toward Vincent. He wasn't sure exactly what he was going to do when he got to him, but he certainly wasn't going to let him say any more bad things about Shelley. He grabbed Vincent's shirt and pushed him roughly up against the wharf building. The boldness of his sudden attack startled Jamie almost as much as it did Vincent, who was now cringing and whining, "Hey, what're you doing?"

A different voice thundered, "Nobody talks that way about Shelley Vanes on my wharf!"

Jamie and Vincent spun their heads and saw Drake standing there, a snarl on his face. "I don't give a rat's ass if you talk trash about the college boy, Vincent, but nobody talks about Shelley Vanes like that! Not on my goddamn wharf!"

"Sorry, Drake. I didn't mean nothing by it."

"Let him go, college boy, so he can get back to whatever it is that he does on my wharf."

"Sure, Mr. Muldoon, no problem," Jamie said as he released his grip.

"Vincent, you fucking rat, get back to work!" Drake barked.

"Okay, Drake, I'll head back and empty them trays, okay?"

"Yeah, sure, sure, Vincent, you do that. And Vincent?"

"Yeah, Drake?"

"Next time I hear you saying any crap about Shelley, I'm gonna let college boy here kick your ass like he was aiming to do. I might even help him. Got it?"

"Yeah, sure, Drake."

Vincent scurried off and disappeared from sight. Drake watched him go, then turned to face Jamie. There was a pregnant silence. Drake pointed a meaty forefinger at Jamie. "Just remember, college boy, that girl's sacred around these parts. You hurt her in any way, there'll be a line around this wharf of guys who will hurt *you*. Got it? I'm watching you. We're *all* watching you!"

"Got it, Mr. Muldoon. Uh, thanks."

"It's Drake, goddammit! Mr. Muldoon was my fucking old man!"

With that, he turned suddenly and walked away. Jamie had been in Kestrel Cove long enough to know that something momentous had not only just taken place between him and Drake, but with the entire peninsula. And, as he walked up the hill and away from the wharf, the implications of the changes left him lightheaded and inebriated with both excitement and fear.

21

Now that Shelley and Jamie were officially an item, he had an intimate view of the preparations for Bobbie and Clara's upcoming wedding. Seeing how the whole Vanes family was throwing itself into this event made Jamie start to think about his own family. He hadn't talked to either his mother or father since coming to Kestrel Cove, and he realized that he missed them. Since it was Sunday and he was lounging around his campsite, he decided to call his father from the pay phone outside the store. When his father picked up, he sputtered with concern and anger. "Goddammit, Jamie! Why the hell haven't you called? Your mother's been worried sick about you!"

Jamie instinctively straightened up and gripped the phone tight before saying, "How are you, Dad?"

"Where the hell are you? Do you know how many phone calls I've made to try and find you? I've had to talk with that useless landlord, who, by the way, was a whirling hornet's nest from the little presents you left him—and we'll talk about those later, young man. Anyway, I called Professor Whetstone to see if he knew where you were, but he didn't. I even had to speak with that thug who runs that awful restaurant you worked in—and the Cro-Magnon had the balls to threaten me! Your mother was convinced that you were in jail, in the hospital, or worse! She hasn't slept well in over a month; she's a wreck!"

"Dad, if you remember, during our last phone call, you made it clear that you were done with me."

His father backed off a little. "Well, you should have at least called your mother, Jamie, to let her know you were fine. It was selfish of you not to do that."

Jamie looked up at the sky. "I'll call her as soon as we hang up."

"Good. Now, where the hell are you?"

"After you and Ezra Jackson evicted me, I quit the Hungry Rancher and got a new job."

"Where?"

"In the small coastal town of Kestrel Cove."

"Oh, I can only imagine what you're doing now. I mean, what could be lower than being a fry-o-lator bitch at a third-rate steakhouse? "

"I work on a lobster boat, Dad."

His father snorted. "Good God, Jamie! When will this downward spiral end and you finally reach your nadir?"

"Hey, Dad, I'm doing just fine. Thanks for asking. The work is hard, but I like my captain and his ace man. I'm really enjoying lobstering. I have a good place to live and a new girlfriend. I'm actually very happy these days."

His father disregarded everything Jamie had just said. "Well, don't call me to clean up this goddamn mess this time!"

"What?"

"I've been cleaning up after you for these last few years, but no more. Now that my lawyers and I are done with that idiot of a landlord, this teat is dry. You can beg me all you want when this little adventure of yours turns sour, but you're not getting a goddamn cent from me. Do you hear me? Nothing. Absolutely not another goddamn penny."

Jamie's grip tightened on the phone. He clenched his teeth, and said tersely, "If you curse at me one more time, Dad, I'm hanging up."

"What did you say to me?"

"I've listened to you bully and belittle me for long enough, Dad, and I'm not going to take it anymore. I've done exactly what you asked me to do—I've gone out on my own and I'm succeeding."

"Jamie, you've been nothing but a disappointment since you graduated from Bridgewater. And now you're wasting your talents working on some goddamn lobster boat."

"Give my best to Mother," Jamie said as he calmly hung up the phone.

The silence that followed made him feel more alone than ever. But just as fast as it had come, the sense of loneliness was flushed out of him. Nearby, Wiley was resting on his motorbike and sipping on an icy drink as he talked to some other sternmen, and Jamie looked over at his good friend and wondered what he was talking about. Inside the store, his girlfriend Shelley was working the busy Sunday shift, and he was aware that he was counting down the time until she was done and they could be together again. And when he heard the gunshots in the distance, he knew that Joe and Jimmy were out in the yard shooting together. He wasn't alone—he was a part of this community. And that meant that he now had a new family.

22

Summer slammed into the peninsula with the force of a hockey check. As if the tropic-like heat and the seemingly eternal sunlight weren't enough indication that it had arrived, the flood of summer residents was clear enough proof. Cottages that had been boarded up and lifeless now boiled over with parties and suntanned children running through the yard. And roads that had been deserted and lonely now had such a steady stream of cars on them that small traffic jams erupted all over the peninsula. Jamie kept waiting to hear someone bitch and complain about this invasion, but the residents of Kestrel Cove not only remained impassive about it all, they seemed excited about the changes.

But there was an unusual buzz to this summer because of the fast-approaching wedding between Clara and Bobbie. The entire community was bracing for it, and the collective anticipation was building to an unsustainable level. From the lowly wharf rats to the leaders of the community, everyone was gearing up for that party at the reception. Dresses and good outfits were being brought out of the closets and cleaned, wedding gifts were being purchased, and appointments at the beauty salons and barbershops of Brementon and the Corners were being made. To Jamie, the level at which everybody was primping and preening was similar to the preparations for a royal wedding, and he made several ill-fated jokes about this. From the sternness of the rebukes to these, it was clear to him that that was exactly what the people of Kestrel Cove were preparing for.

It troubled Jamie that he still did not get it. But he knew that he couldn't talk to Joe or Jimmy about it all because whenever he brought up the topic, they either belittled him unmercifully or got downright mad at him. So he decided to bite the bullet and ask Shelley about the importance of this one event. So one night, right after she had arrived for her usual visit to his tent after closing up the store, he quietly inquired, "Hey, I need to ask you a question about Clara and Bobbie's wedding."

"Sure, what about it?"

He hesitated slightly. "Well, I don't understand why the people of Kestrel Cove are getting so excited about it. After all, only the family is invited to the ceremony at the church. I know it makes me sound like an insensitive boob, but I just don't get why people are getting so worked up over what amounts to just another party at the reception in the Community Center. Can you explain it to me?"

Shelley giggled. "You're not an insensitive boob, you're just still an outsider. You have to remember that Clara and Bobbie have both grown up here, so their wedding is something special to Kestrel Cove. And while it's true that most people are gearing up for the party at the reception, they're really excited for one of those events that's going to unite our community and bring us together to witness something that's bigger than just the individuals who make up this place. It's not a royal wedding, but it's something akin to that, I guess."

"Wait—I'm still an outsider?"

She stroked his jaw. "Oh, come on, Jamie, don't sound so hurt! I mean, how long have you really been here? Two months. It might seem like a long time to you, but that's a very short amount of time to be part of a community. Think about Bridgewater. How long did someone have to be around there to be considered an insider? Not two months, I can tell you that! Maybe two years. Well, it's the same here. You're gonna have to live with us for a lot longer before you're considered more than a glorified visitor. Plus, we all know that you're going to leave Kestrel Cove right after the lobstering season ends."

"Whoa! Who says that's going to happen?"

Shelley looked at him strangely for a moment. "No, you'll want to leave by then."

"What if I don't?"

"You will."

"What if I become so happy here that I never want to leave?"

She pulled back further. "I think that when lobstering winds up, you're going to need to make some choices, that's all I'm saying."

Jamie grinned. "Maybe we'll all have to make some choices then, huh?"

"Yes, maybe we all will. And that's a good segue to something I wanted to ask you!"

"Oh, really? And what would that be?"

She responded by crawling on top of him and pinning him down. He struggled a little, but she was strong and easily straddled him. She leaned down toward his face and whispered, "I want to move into the tent."

Jamie stopped struggling. He was genuinely stunned. "You want to move into my tent?"

Shelley cuffed him playfully on the forehead. "No, there's another goddamn tent around here that I thought about moving into! Yes, I want to live with you in this tent."

"You want to live with me?"

She cuffed him again. "What are you, a goddamn parrot?"

"No, I'm just startled that you want to move in here, that's all. I mean, it's tiny, and there's no shower. Plus, what will your family think?"

Shelley laughed, "Hey, I'm not a complete dummy! I'm not going to move out of my mom's house completely. I'll need to take showers, do my laundry there, and I still need to help my mom out from time to time, but I just want to spend more time with you!"

Jamie smiled. "I would *love* to have you in my tent, Shelley! And we could look for an apartment together, if the tent's too small."

"Hey, one step at a time there, cowboy! I think just living in a tent together will be adventure enough for the moment. Getting an apartment together would be taking it to a whole other level. Okay?"

"Yeah, sure."

And that was that. The next day, Shelley brought some of her things into the tent. The news seeped into the entire Kestrel Cove community like dye. Although it was common knowledge that the two were dating, Shelley's moving into his tent changed everything. Their relationship immediately took on such an official status that most people began to refer to them as the single entity "Shelley/Jamie," and even Jimmy and Joe now treated them like a married couple.

They even began using the terms "Jamie's old lady" and "the old ball n' chain" when talking about Shelley.

◇◇◇◇

The summer sun was relentless, and the stifling heat not only made the work on the boat more challenging, but much more odiferous. With the bait baking into an unholy ripeness and the three men sweating buckets, Jamie could barely stand his own smell by the end of each day. This would have been intolerable if he were alone, but now that he was sharing the tent with Shelley, he was desperate to figure out a way to clean himself up. He didn't want to be an imposition on any of his friends, so he tried to figure out another solution to this dilemma on his own. But after his initial attempt to take a cleansing swim in the ocean after work left a saline dust on his skin that made him more itchy and uncomfortable than he'd been when he was filthy, he felt like he was out of options. It was Wiley who solved his problem for him.

During one of his usual daily visits to drink a beer with Jamie at his campsite, Wiley crinkled his nose and sniffed the air. "Phew, dude, you smell like shit!"

"Gee, thanks, Wiley."

"Naw, man, I mean it—you reek!"

"Jesus Christ, Wiley, I don't know what to do! I've tried swimming in the ocean, but that's like rolling in salt, for God's sake! I'm totally chafed down there, if you know what I mean. I can't ask anyone to let me use their shower every damn day—I can't be a pain in the ass like that! But I don't know what else I can do!"

"I don't know either, dude, but you smell like the inside of a bait barrel."

"I know, but what can I do? I'm so freaked out that Shelley is going to stop dating me because of my smell!"

"You could shower at my place."

Jamie smiled. "Thanks, buddy. But it would get old for you, too. I just can't figure out where I can find fresh water that's in walking distance."

"Holy shit, man! What about Wright's Folly?" Wiley bellowed.

"Wright's Folly? What's that?"

"Hey, grab your soap and shampoo—we'll head right over there!

I know how you can get cleaned up any time you want."

Wiley drove his truck down a dirt road near that store that Jamie had never noticed before and parked the truck on the side of the road. With no explanation or instruction, he bounded out onto a faint trail. Jamie followed dutifully, but he struggled to keep up. The trail staggered its way through the forest until it came to the stone edge of a small quarry. Wiley spread his arms wide and exclaimed proudly, "Welcome to Wright's Folly!"

"What the hell is this, Wiley?" Jamie asked in amazement.

"I guess there was an old stonemason from Massachusetts by the name of Marcus Wright who moved onto this peninsula around the Civil War. After ignoring the advice of the people around here, he decided that he could supply the world with the purplish granite you see at our feet."

"Did he succeed?"

"'Course not!" Wiley said as he reached down and picked up a loose rock. When he squeezed it, it shattered into pieces. "It's fucking fragile as an eggshell and cracks under pressure, which ain't too good for construction projects, right? After his venture completely failed, Wright left in disgrace. But he left this huge hole in the ground. Over the years, it filled up with water, and now it provides us locals with a hidden and secluded swimming spot. It'll be perfect for cleaning you up! And it's close enough that you can walk here every day!"

Now that Wiley had shown him the quarry, Jamie expected him to leave and let him bathe in private. But the boy stood where he was and looked out at the water. "Damn, this is the best swimming hole on the whole area!"

"Thanks for showing it to me. It's perfect, Wiley. "

"Yeah, it is," Wiley stated bluntly. In a blur, he whipped off his shirt and started undoing his belt to slip his pants off.

"Um, what are you doing?" Jamie asked nervously.

Wiley looked at him as if he'd spoken gibberish. "I'm going swimming, bro."

Before Jamie could respond, Wiley got completely naked and jumped in. The water was so clear, Jamie could see the whiteness around his friend's farmer's tan. He looked like an iceberg. When his head popped back up, he called out, "So, are you gonna swim in your clothes? I mean, it probably wouldn't hurt them none to be dunked underwater."

Jamie slowly peeled off his smelly clothes. As he uneasily tried to cover himself and move toward the rim to jump in, Wiley hollered, "Jesus H. Christ, dude, you're as white as the fucking snow, huh?"

Jamie let out a little yip of embarrassment as he jumped into the water. When he came back up to the surface, he found himself all alone. Wiley had swum out to the middle of the quarry and was crawling his way over toward the other shore. So Jamie swam back to get his shampoo and soap. He needed a place to wash, but the quarry had been cut with sheer edges and there was nowhere to stand. Jamie swam along the edge until he finally found a rock he could stand on, and he immediately began to furiously wash himself. The soap was foaming up wonderfully, and he squeezed some shampoo into his hand and started scrubbing the herring scales out of his hair. He was nearly in ecstasy as he started to feel cleaner.

The cacophony of girlish screams from behind him almost knocked Jamie over with their force. When he looked for the source of the noise, some of the shampoo got into his eyes and started to burn them. He teetered and moaned like some kind of old-time horror-flick monster, and the screams were joined by angry words. He jumped in the opposite direction from the outbursts and into the cold water.

When he came up again, Jamie saw that there was a group of six preteen girls in camp uniforms being consoled by two young female counselors on the rim of the quarry. One of them was now wagging her finger angrily at him. Wiley had swum over next to Jamie, and he bellowed toward the counselor and the shrieking girls, "Aw, calm the fuck down! Who the hell are you guys?"

The counselors seemed affronted by Wiley's cursing, and one of them glanced back toward the group of girls and said quietly, "We're from the Whitter Yacht Club's summer camp."

Jamie had heard about the place. Whenever the residents of Kestrel Cove spoke about the yacht club, they always used a snotty rich-person's accent to make fun of the members. Drake sneered the most because he hated the way they kept their incredibly expensive boats over at the fancy club, but came around the peninsula to find the cheaper diesel fuel at his wharf. Unfortunately, they expected the same amount of service there as they received from the club's uniformed dock boys, and Drake took particular pride in saying to them, "If you want cheap fuel, you're gonna hafta pump the damn stuff yourself."

"Well, what the hell are you all doing here now?" Wiley barked.

"We come here to teach our sailing class lifesaving techniques."

"Here? In Wright's Folly? At this time of the day?"

The counselor put her hands on her hips. "The sheer sides of this quarry make it a similar experience to getting someone over the gunwale of a boat, and the water temperature is warmer than in the ocean. Plus, it's secluded and private at this time of day. We come here a lot, but we don't usually find two naked men bathing together."

Wiley looked at Jamie and Jamie looked back at Wiley. The last comment was loaded with enough innuendo that neither one knew what to do with it. Deny such a statement with too much vigor, and it looks true. Ignore such a statement, and it also looks true. The last thing either of them needed was for the guys at the wharf to hear that they were bathing naked together in Wright's Folly! After all, being known as the guy who jerks off and shits in a woman's flower garden was a tame reputation in comparison to men who like to bathe together in abandoned quarries, and both Wiley and Jamie felt their scrotums tighten with fear.

Finally, Jamie said calmly, "Excuse me, but if you all could just go back a little ways into the woods while we get out and get dressed, you can have the place to yourselves."

"No."

"No?"

"I don't know what you two queers were doing in the quarry, but we're not going to walk our already traumatized campers back into those woods just to let you get out."

"You're kidding me, right?" Jamie asked incredulously.

"No, I'm not," she responded as she crossed her arms in a defiant gesture.

"Come on, Mimi! Let's just let them get out," the other counselor said nervously.

"No, we've all endured enough today! We're not going back into those tick-infested woods just so these two lovebirds can get out!"

"Ah, for fuck's sake!" Wiley shouted. "This is such a cluster. I'll tell you what's going to happen. I'm going to count to five, then I'm getting out. I don't know what ol' Jamie has hanging between his legs, but God gave me a schlong that dangles. When I get out, I'm gonna take my time, and I'll tell you what, your little girls are gonna get a healthy look at my glorious meat, and I don't give a rat's ass if it causes them to have nightmares."

With that, Wiley swam to the edge of the quarry. The counselors looked down at him, and it was abundantly clear that he was not bluffing. They began barking directions. "All right, girls, let's go back and give these two men some privacy."

But it was already too late. Wiley had started to pull himself up onto the edge of the quarry before the two counselors could usher their campers back into the woods. As he stood naked on the side of the quarry, Jamie could see that he hadn't been idly boasting—he was hung like a goddamn horse! Jamie got out of the water and quickly dried and dressed in one almost continuous movement. As they walked past the camp group on the trail back to the road, Wiley said something to the counselor that Jamie could not completely hear, but her reaction—shouting a string of insults—gave him a hint.

That night, when Shelley came into the tent and lay next to Jamie, she giggled as she said, "So now I hear that you like to hang out and swim with naked boys, huh?"

"Oh no! That isn't going around town already, is it?"

Shelley waited longer than she needed to, then pinched his leg and said, "Naw, Wiley told me."

"Why the hell would he do that?"

"Oh, he wanted to make sure that the rumor that got out was not about you two bathing together in Wright's Folly, but that *you* were bathing on one side and *he* was swimming on the other side. I told him that I wouldn't tell another soul—except you, of course."

"Phew, that was close, huh?" Jamie said, shaking his head.

"I can only imagine what would have happened if that story had gotten out to the boys at the wharf. You got lucky, and

I hope you learned a lesson today."

"Don't get naked with Wiley in public again?"

"No, I was gonna say, always wear your bathing suit when you swim at Wright's Folly."

Jamie blurted out, "I also learned something else today—Wiley's hung like a horse."

Shelley laughed. "Hey, he isn't that big! You're almost as big as him!"

The ramifications of her statement stopped Jamie's heart, and he was about to ask for clarification when she grabbed him as if to verify the anatomical size of his manhood. She nuzzled his ear. "Plus, you smell clean, for once. Come here, lover!"

23

The nearer Bobbie and Clara's wedding date got, the more stressed Shelley became and the more Jamie wondered about what his role was in the whole show. Initially, he'd figured that since the ceremony was only for immediate family, he was in the same boat as most of the peninsula—invited to the reception, but not the church service. But now that he and Shelley were living together in the tent, he wasn't sure if his status had changed or not. He knew that he shouldn't bother her by asking directly, so he kept lobbing subtle questions about what he should wear or where he would sit at the reception. But Shelley was too focused on her own responsibilities to pick up on his hints. Which meant that Jamie was flying blind, and he didn't like that at all.

Whether or not he was invited to the ceremony, he still had to make sure that he looked nice. But one look at his reflection in the store window told him that he was in dire need of a haircut. The only barbershop he'd heard people talk about was in Brementon, and he couldn't get there without a car. So he asked Joe and Jimmy who cut their hair. They both said that their wives did, and from the terse tone of their answers, Jamie understood that neither of these women was a solution to his dilemma. In desperation, he turned to Wiley at the campfire and asked, "Hey, Wiley, who cuts your hair?"

Wiley took a big sip from his beer and smacked his lips. "My old lady."

Jamie was somewhat stunned by his answer because he had no idea that Wiley had a steady girlfriend. So as Jamie digested that bit of information, he said, "I didn't even know you had a girlfriend."

"Sure. Who the hell do you think I've been rushing off to every night?"

Jamie scratched his head. "Actually, Wiley, you sit around this fire pit with me until I tell you to go home."

"Well, my old lady works weird hours, so I don't want to be in her way."

"Oh, what does she do?"

Wiley squinted at Jamie and his voice came out cold. "Don't you fuck with me, college boy!"

Jamie heard the menacing tone and he said soothingly, "I'm not, Wiley, I'm not. I didn't know that you had a girlfriend until a couple of seconds ago, and I honestly don't know what she does for a living."

"Joe and Jimmy haven't told you?"

"Wiley, those two haven't said anything about you at all, actually."

Wiley didn't look convinced. "She's a telemarketer of sorts."

"Oh, really? What does she sell?"

Wiley gave Jamie another severe look. He took a slow swig of his beer, but finally said in a low voice, "She's a phone sex operator."

"She is?"

"Yeah, for now. She wants to open her own hair salon someday, but she makes a lot of money talking dirty to guys—and girls—on the phone. There's serious money in it, dude!"

"Are you okay with her doing that?"

"Sure. I mean, she's not doing nothing to nobody, 'cept talking, right? I mean, she doesn't do the things she *says* she's doing, most of the time."

Jamie let that last comment float off into the night. He didn't know what else to say, so he took a drink of his beer to stall for a moment and think up something encouraging and nonjudgmental. He searched the Rolodex in his brain for what he should say. When nothing better came up, he settled on, "Well, the money sure sounds too good to pass up."

Wiley grinned. "You bet it is! She's gonna have saved enough to open her salon in the next couple of years. She might even partner with your ex, Angie Williams. It would be stupid to open two beauty shops here at the same time, right?"

"Yeah, I guess so," Jamie responded with a shrug. "So, you think your old lady could give me a haircut? I need to look my best for the wedding."

"Oh, sure, dude! Tomorrow, go to the quarry and take a bath and get cleaned up. I'll pick you up at the store and we'll head to my place. Vicky will make you look all perdy again, okay?"

"Okay, that's sounds good, Wiley." After a slight pause, Jamie added, "So Vicky gave you that haircut you've got now?"

Wiley's eyes widened. "Uh…naw, she was too busy to cut my hair the last time, so I had to go to town to get this."

Jamie stiffened. "But the haircut before that? She did that one, right?"

"Yeah, that's right, that's right. She gave me *that* haircut. She's really good with hair—her teachers at the beauty school called her gifted. You just tell her what you want her to do, and she does it to you."

The sexual charge of that statement was too much for either of them to address, and they finished their beers in silence with the plan for the next day's haircut set.

When Shelley came into the tent later that night, he didn't mention his haircut appointment with Vicky. He figured he'd hint around with Joe and Jimmy on the boat the next day to find out if Vicky was any good, but he fell asleep wondering which was worse—showing up to the wedding with shaggy hair or with a horrible hack job. It was not a pleasant last thought and he slept a troubled sleep.

However, he was just as confused the next day. When he asked the guys about Vicky and haircutting, the two didn't say much, either good or bad. Instead, they became obsessed with the woman's overall mental state. Since Wiley was well known to be totally crazy, the guys figured that Vicky must be even crazier to live with him. This prompted a long discussion about whether they would ever stay with a woman who was certifiably insane. Both Joe and Jimmy agreed that they would, but only if she was really good in bed. Jimmy added, "I'd live with a retard if she could give good head!"

Jamie left the conversation when it became specific as to what exact sexual acts would make it acceptable to live with a mentally challenged woman because he didn't want to imagine any of the visions that Jimmy and Joe were conjuring up, and he didn't bring up Vicky for the rest of the day. The two didn't notice his retreat from the conversation, and they continued delving into the topic with frightening tenacity.

Later, as Jamie waited for Wiley to pick him up at the store, he felt totally conflicted. He had not found out anything definitive in terms of Vicky's ability or inability, so he knew that he was in no position to refuse the haircut offer at this point. If there had been even one semi-genuine justification for backing out, he could. But without one, he was bound by the oral agreement he'd made with Wiley the night before. The fact was, there was no turning back now—he'd have to live with the consequences, whatever they were going to be.

Soon Wiley's truck came racing into the parking lot and slid to a stop. He didn't say anything as Jamie jumped in, but he nodded with purpose. After making a few attempts to initiate conversation as they rode along, Jamie had the uncomfortable feeling that Wiley was too nervous to talk. They sped down the main road and then turned off on a dirt driveway that ended at a tiny green cottage. Jamie looked at the building and wondered how two people could live in what amounted to a shed, especially through a long, cold Maine winter. Just as he was about to say something, Wiley announced proudly, "Welcome to my palace, dude!"

"You own this, Wiley?"

Wiley looked at Jamie with instant reptilian distrust. "Yeah, why?"

"I just didn't know that you were a homeowner, that's all."

"For fuck's sake, college boy, first you didn't know that I had a girlfriend, then you don't know I own my own house! How can we be good friends when you don't know anything about me? What'd you think, that I live alone in the goddamn trees and swing from vines?"

"Naw, Wiley, you seem like such a carefree guy, I guess I just didn't think that you would have such important commitments in your life."

"Harrumph."

With that, Wiley headed off toward the front door of the cottage. He opened it quickly, not checking to make sure that Jamie was following him. Jamie knew that he'd ruffled Wiley's feathers, and he was nervous about that. Even though he was confident that their friendship was sound, he didn't want anything to threaten their relationship.

The inside of the cottage was so dark, it took some time for Jamie's eyes to adjust. There was a bar with three stools that separated the big room from the small kitchen. In the corner, a toilet sat like an outcast. It had a shower curtain that swept around it, and Jamie did a double-take when he saw this, for it meant that a person who was on the throne, taking care of business, as Jimmy liked to say, was only separated from the other people in the room by a flimsy piece of fabric that would not dampen any noises. The thought of this made Jamie cringe, and he quickly scanned the rest of the space to get away from looking at the overly exposed bathroom. The bedroom was up in a loft that could only be reached by a dark wooden ladder, and there was a black metal woodstove with a stovepipe that fed into a crumbling chimney. The whole room smelled of smoke, and even though the smallness of the building created a sense of comfort, Jamie could not help feeling a little trapped, too.

But the one thing that Jamie did not see was where Vicky would even be able to cut his hair. The cottage was so small, he could not believe that anything could be hidden from view. But he didn't see anything that would serve the purpose of a styling chair. Wiley must have sensed what his friend was looking for, and he removed a white sheet from an obscure shape in the corner. There, bolted right into the pine planks of the floor, was a beat-up stylist chair.

"There she is, the Throne of Doom!" he belted out gleefully.

Jamie gulped, but couldn't speak. Vicky came down the ladder from the loft holding a cigarette in one hand and a can of beer in the other. "Yeah, fucking funny, Wiley. Way to scare the customer! Why don't you just tell him it took me three times to pass the beauty school course, too? I'm sure that would make him feel even better!"

Jamie gasped as he turned to Wiley, who waved him off. "Naw, I didn't tell him about that, Vick. Anyway, this is my buddy Jamie."

"Nice to meet ya," she said, extended her cigarette hand toward him. "Wiley's told me lots of good things about you."

Vicky was not at all what Jamie had expected. For one thing, she was much older. She seemed clearly twice Wiley's age. As a matter of fact, if Jamie had met the two in town together, under different circumstances, he'd have thought that she was his mother or an older aunt. That's not to say she was unattractive—she was quite pretty—but she had a face that betrayed the fact that she had seen too much in life, and it was creased with distinctive wrinkles. She also had a gravelly voice that Jamie found instantly sensuous.

"So what kinda cut do you want?" she purred.

"Just a trim, really. I've got to look good for a wedding."

"*The* wedding, you mean."

Jamie nodded. "Yeah, Bobbie and Clara's."

"Is there any other? The whole stupid peninsula is getting itself ready for this damn thing, but I don't see why! I mean, no one gets to go to the ceremony. We, the poor peons of the kingdom, aren't invited to attend! So all the rest of us schlubs are getting primed and ready for the party afterwards, and who the fuck cares about that?"

"Jesus, Vick, ease off a little! Jamie dates Shelley Vanes, remember?"

"Hey, I'm sorry. Didn't mean no disrespect. I'm just saying that everyone's getting so worked up about this party. But why? We're all gonna to be so drunk afterwards, we won't give a fuck about what anyone looks like! But you, being family and all, I guess you need to look good, huh?"

"Actually, I'm not sure if I'm invited to the wedding or not. Like you said, it's only for family, and Shelley and I aren't married or anything. Boyfriend status might not be enough to get me through the door of the church."

"But you still want to look good, huh?"

"Oh, definitely! I want to make a good first impression. My hair's longer than Stonewall Jackson's these days."

Vicky gave him a blank look. "Who's he? A musician?"

"Naw, Vick, he was a Confederate general in the Civil War," Wiley chimed in.

"That's right, Wiley!" Jamie said with a note of shock in his voice.

"He got his arm shot off by his own troops."

"Yes, that's absolutely correct! When he was inspecting the lines at Chancellorsville, his men accidentally shot him, and then his doctors had to amputate his arm. Wow, Wiley! Stonewall is a personal hero of mine."

"You admire people who get shot by their own troops?" Vicky asked with a snort.

"Naw, Vick, he was the best general the South had. His death really hurt their cause, babe. Probably changed the outcome of the whole war," Wiley responded confidently.

Jamie said, "Holy shit, Wiley! I'm really impressed! You never told me you knew about this stuff!"

Wiley shrugged his shoulders uncomfortably. "It's in this graphic novel I'm reading."

"Comic book," Vicky added.

"Fuck you, Vick, it's a goddamn graphic novel! The character's a history buff—like you, college boy—and he tries to find the missing arm of Stonewall Jackson to keep it from killing people."

"Oh," Jamie said quietly.

"There's our genius—gets all of his information from a fucking comic book!'

"It's a graphic novel, goddamn it, Vick!"

"Whatever."

"I'm just impressed that you know anything about Stonewall Jackson, Wiley. He was a really interesting guy—a bit of a religious kook, but a fantastic general! His death *did* change the whole Civil War."

"Yeah, well, if there was a comic book series about American History, Wiley'd be a goddamn historical scholar by now instead of just a sternman!" Vicky sneered.

Wiley shouted, "*Fuck you, Vick!*"

The volume of Wiley's yell was so high, Jamie backed away a step, just in case this verbal argument became a physical one and weapons were drawn. However, neither of them seemed overly upset by his outburst. As a matter of fact, Vicky acted as if nothing bad had been said at all. She went over by the styling chair and grabbed a clump of magazines while Wiley walked casually to the refrigerator and opened the door. He stuck his whole head and shoulders in, then stood up and put his hands on his hips. "Hey, Vick, where's the fucking twelve-pack I bought yesterday? There's like three beers in here now!"

"We drank them, butt-head."

"What's this *we*—you and the turd in your pocket? 'Cause I've only had one of those beers. One, Vick! Now there's hardly any more left."

"Jesus, Wiley, what's the big fucking deal? When you take college boy back home to his tent at the store, just buy another twelve-pack, okay?"

Wiley shook his head, grabbed two of the beers, and shut the door of the fridge. He walked over to Jamie and gave him one without asking if he wanted it. When he tried to hand it back, Wiley said, "Naw, dude, you're gonna need that!"

"So, Junior, what kinda haircut do you want today?" Vicky grumbled.

Jamie knew that he was now at a crossroads. Enough about the visit so far had put him on edge, but having Vicky suddenly call him Junior, a name that no one in his entire life had ever entertained calling him before, made him nearly panic with the urge to run away. Vicky and Wiley were staring hard at him, so he said meekly, "Um, just a trim off the front and back, I guess."

"Well, pick a magazine."

"Excuse me?"

"Hey, they told me at beauty school that I'm a visual learner! I need to look at pictures first, then I can make the cuts. Look through them magazines and figure out who you want your hair to look like."

"Seriously?"

Vicky exhaled a puff of smoke toward the rafters of the cottage and her warm, husky voice purred, "I'll make you look like anyone you want. Just look at them pictures and I'll do anything you want me to."

Vicky's last raspy statement made Jamie's testicles tingle, and he clearly saw that she was probably a star in the phone sex world. "Okay, I guess."

The phone rang somewhere up in the loft and Vicky said, "Sorry, boys, I just need to go up there to answer that call, okay? Get comfortable and pick out a picture, Junior, and I'll be right back."

"I thought you were off duty today, Vick," Wiley said with a grimace.

"I traded this phone call with Trisha. He's a strange one, and she's tired of taking his calls."

Jamie began to page through one of the magazines. He'd hoped that Vicky would be skilled enough to give him a haircut that would make him look presentable. He didn't need to look like a celebrity, but he browsed through the magazines anyway in hopes that he'd find someone acceptable. Since it was too late to flee the scene, he just needed to stay calm, take his time, and make the best of the situation. Even as he could hear Vicky start to moan and pant up in the loft, he felt the walls of the shed close in a little on him.

"She can't give you a nigger's haircut," Wiley blurted out.

"Pardon me?"

Wiley leaned in. "Don't pick a photo of a nigger for her to imitate, dude, 'cause she can't do those kinds of cuts."

Suddenly, sounds from the loft reached Jamie's ears. "Omigod! Oooh…aah…just like that. Honey, you keep going without me for a second, okay? My microwave timer just went off and my anal probe is nice and warm. I'm gonna go get it so we can continue, okay?"

And then Vicky was hanging her head down toward them. "Ya know, I can hear you, Wiley! Don't fill the boy's head up with negative thoughts. Just 'cause Nigger Bob weren't happy with his cut don't mean that I can't do that kinda haircut. He could've just been a particularly choosy customer. Besides, if the boy wants to look like Eddie Murphy or 50 Cent for this wedding, let him choose that for himself. He's his own man."

Wiley leaned closer and whispered, "Dude, don't choose any nigger haircuts."

Jamie flipped the page and saw Matt Damon looking back at him. The haircut was nothing too complicated, and the wholesome actor looked dashing and handsome. That was a helluva lot better than the boy bands and freaks that he'd seen so far. Hadn't Shelley even commented recently that she had a crush on Matt Damon? It wouldn't be so bad to look just like him!

Vicky's phone orgasm reached a violent and loud crescendo, and Jamie had to admit that it sounded very authentic. He even felt somewhat aroused by it. When she came down the ladder, noticeably smelling more like alcohol than when she went up, Jamie smiled and said that he wanted to look like Matt Damon.

"I don't know none of their names, Junior. Just show me the goddamn picture."

"Come on, Vick! You know Matt Damon! He was in *The Italian Job, Ocean's Eleven,* and the *Bourne Supremacy.* Remember? We've watched his movies together."

"Uh-uh, don't know him. Just show me his picture."

Jamie leaned forward to point out the photo of Matt Damon, but

Vicky grabbed the magazine out of his hands so fast, he wasn't sure if she knew which picture he had meant. So he added, "The white guy in the green shirt."

"Yeah, yeah. Got it. Okay, Junior, hop into the chair so we can begin."

"Uh…what about washing my hair?"

"Washing your hair?"

"Yeah, you know, most barbers or stylists wash the hair before they cut it?"

Vicky looked over at the sink and exhaled more smoke. "Oh, that. Nope, can't do that 'cause my sink's full of dirty dishes. Numb-nuts over there hasn't done his one job here at home in, like, six days."

Wiley shrugged. "I've been busy, babe. You know, making the money and all."

Vicky looked right at him. "Hmm, I don't see too much of that money, do I?"

"When you drink my whole goddamn twelve-pack, Vick, you've seen most of that money."

The exchange between Vicky and Wiley was lost on Jamie, who was still mourning the fact that he wasn't going to get his hair washed.

Suddenly, Vicky commanded, "Come on, Junior, hop up there!"

As Vicky put the itchy sheet around his neck, he prepared himself for the disaster that was coming. Up to this point, he'd held out some hope that he'd get some kind of pleasure from this whole experience, be it satisfaction with the haircut, the sensuous rapture of a good hair washing, or even the thrill of meeting his friend's girlfriend, but now the whole event had become so sour, he closed his eyes to surrender to the inevitable.

"Hey, dude, I gotta go and work on my truck. That damn tailpipe came loose during the last pipeline race, so I gotta secure it so it don't wiggle free. I'll be back in a little, okay?"

"Sure, sure, he's in good hands now, ain't ya, Junior?"

"Oh, sure, Wiley, I'll be right here."

Vicky forced Jamie to look straight ahead. And that was when it hit him that there was nothing on the wall except paneling. There was no mirror. How could that be? There was no way for Jamie to check what she was doing and see the damage. His apprehension swelled and started choking him. He closed his eyes tight and listened to the snip of the scissors and the buzz of the clippers.

This all took him back to when he was seven years old. In spite of an untold number of warnings from both of his parents to not climb onto the table to reach the metal cabinets where his mother hid the candy and cookies, Jamie had defiantly done it again. When the table tipped and he struck the side of his head on the sharp edge of the cabinet, the blood had flowed so red and so profusely that he had nearly pissed himself in fear. His mother had rushed him to the hospital, where he received eight stitches in the emergency room. His father had shown up as the doctor was finishing, and he'd casually said that if he'd been there when they started, he would have requested that no anesthesia be used. He argued that anyone who was stupid enough to disregard so many repeated warnings did not deserve to have the pain numbed. Later, when the bandages were finally removed and Jamie could see the stitched wound in the mirror, he was shocked at the puffy pink gash that was held together with heavy black thread. It was not what he had expected to see, and he never stood on that table again—he'd completely learned his lesson.

"Vick, what the fuck are you doing?!"

Wiley's loud outburst shattered Jamie's flashback. He turned toward the voice, almost impaling his eye on a pair of scissors that hovered in Vicky's hand near his ear.

"Jesus, Wiley, you just scared the shit outta me! You can't come in here and yell like that! Not when I'm working on a customer!"

"Vick, what the fuck are you doing?" Wiley repeated.

Aggravated, Vicky shifted her weight to one leg and said sarcastically, "Giving your friend a haircut, numb-nuts, what the hell do you think I'm doing?"

Jamie heard Wiley's steps across the small space and his body tensed for the impact that seemed imminent.

"Vick, that sure as shit does not look like Matt Damon! That looks more like some kind of a goddamn punk band haircut!"

"He said the white dude in the green shirt, and that's what he's getting."

"Lemme see that goddamn magazine!"

Vicky swatted Wiley across the stomach with it. "Here you go."

"This looks nothing like Matt Damon, Vick!"

"He said the white dude in the green shirt."

"Are you trying to tell me that Matt Damon looks like that in this photo right here?"

There was hesitation in the time it took Vicky to answer, then she declared, "That wasn't the picture he pointed to."

"That's fucking Matt Damon, Vick! Who'd you think he was pointing to?"

"Not that picture. Flip the magazine over."

Jamie heard the rustle of paper, then he heard Wiley gasp, "Aw, Jesus, Vick, you gave him a haircut that looks like Malcolm Headrush, the lead singer of the Dead Pregnant Kittens!"

"I told you, I don't know who the fuck Matt Damon is! Junior said the white dude in the green shirt, and that dude right there is wearing a green shirt!"

"That dude is a *freak*, Vick. For the love of Christ, does Jamie look like the kind of guy that would want to look like Malcolm Headrush at a family wedding in Kestrel Cove?"

"I don't know this guy—I just met him. I mean, he's your best friend, not mine."

Jamie finally spoke up. "Could I please see a mirror?"

"Naw, dude, you don't want to see this. Let us just figure out what to do next, okay?"

"No, Wiley, I need to see myself. Please."

"Yeah, he might like it, Wiley!" Vicky shrieked.

"He ain't gonna like it, Vick! He asked to look like Matt Damon, and you made him look like Bozo the fucking Clown! He ain't gonna like it."

"Wiley, I need to see it."

"Naw, dude. Trust me. You don't."

"I need to. Please."

Wiley came back with a large wall mirror, and walked up in front of Jamie. Reflected back was clearly Jamie's face, but the rest of the image was so foreign, it looked like Vicky had glued a photograph of someone else's hair onto the mirror. He turned his head and the reflection reciprocated. A swath of his hair was buzzed down to the skin and circled the back of his head from one ear to the other. Over this, like some kind of upturned bowl, sat the rest of his hair, untouched. His bangs had been shaved down to the skin as well, and his face looked out from the hair with a shocked expression. "Oh my God! I've never looked so horrible in my entire life!"

"Don't worry, dude, we'll fix it."

Vicky punched Wiley hard. "Fix it? It's a fucking great haircut! It may be my best work ever! Look at that picture, then look at his head. It's dead-on for that guy."

"Yes, Vick, but he didn't want to look like that freak coming out of rehab; he wanted to look like the clean-cut heartthrob that's standing right here! You've got to try and make him look like this guy now."

"Can't be done."

"Come on, Vick, you gotta try. He can't go to the wedding looking like that!"

"He'll be the coolest dude there, Wiley. People will be filled with envy."

"Yeah, after they laugh their asses off. Come on, Vick, how can we make *this* haircut look like *this* haircut?"

Jamie sat with his head down. He had fully expected this whole thing to end in disaster, but now that it had, he felt nausea welling up in his stomach. He would certainly make an impression on Shelley's family if he showed up looking like the lead singer of the Dead Pregnant Kittens, wouldn't he? The entire peninsula would be talking about it for years. Forget losing Shelley; he'd be laughed out of town! Or worse—tarred and feathered! Jamie's palms moistened with fear.

"All right, all right, we'll see what we can do to make you look like this *other* white dude in the green shirt."

The scissors clipped and hair fell on the floor. Wiley hovered too closely, and his sound effects betrayed the losing battle that was being waged. Even Vicky was now sighing and grunting in such a way that Jamie knew it was a lost cause.

Finally, he'd had enough torture. "Okay, that's it. Just buzz me!"

"Naw, Junior, I can do it. Let me try—"

"Nope, no more. Buzz me, Vicky! I can't sit here anymore. Buzz me now!"

"Dude, you sure?"

"Yep, buzz me."

"Junior, I can do this."

"I know you can, Vicky. I'm not saying you can't. Let's just cut our losses, okay? Buzz me," Jamie said forcefully.

"Okay, Junior. Here we go."

The electric clippers scraped across his scalp, shedding balls of hair onto the floor. The tingle of his newly naked scalp made Jamie shiver. It was over quickly, and the pile of hair on the floor was large. When the clippers were shut off, the silence that followed worried Jamie more than looking like the lead singer of a punk band. Images of concentration-camp survivors and lice-infested victims shot across his mind with alarming clarity.

Finally, Wiley spoke. "Huh. You know what, dude? You look good like that. Naw, I ain't kidding you. You just lost your fluff and got some gruff. If I met you on the street, I'd leave you alone. I mean it. If I didn't know that you're a soft, pansy-ass, sensitive college boy, I'd give you a wide berth. You look good, dude. You look kinda tough."

Jamie wanted to see. "Get that mirror again, Wiley."

Vicky patted Jamie's shoulder. "Just get up and go see for yourself, Junior. There's nothing more I can do to you."

Jamie stood up and more of his hair tumbled down his front onto the floor. He walked slowly toward the mirror and looked at himself in it. And, after the initial shock of seeing himself with a bald head, he had to agree with Wiley. Not only was the warm and fuzzy college student gone, there was a new toughness in his appearance. His eyes were clear and sharp, and there was no hair to offer protection or places to hide. The strength of his face was now out there for everyone to see. He turned his head different ways, nodded approvingly, and said with some bravado, "You know what, Vicky? I like this! It isn't half bad."

"'Course it isn't, Junior. We aim to please."

Jamie chuckled, "How much do I owe you?"

She put her finger to her lips. "Well, seeing that I really had to give you two haircuts, I may have to charge you twice."

Wiley waved his fist in the air. "Aw, Vick, for God's sake! You made him look like Malcolm Headrush! He didn't ask for that! Nobody would ask for that!"

"Oh, calm down, numb-nuts, I'm only kidding…kinda."

◇◇◇◇

The ride back to the store was done in complete silence. As Jamie got out of the truck, Wiley leaned over and said, "Dude, sorry about the mess-up with the Matt Damon haircut. But I gotta say this new look makes you look as tough as nails. I think Shelley's gonna be turned on when she sees you—she likes the tough guys."

Jamie nodded, but his heart was heavy with the worry that she would not only not like it, but her whole family would not like him because of it. He walked past the store with his head down. He wasn't going to go in there to show off his buzz cut to Shelley now. He'd wait until she came to bed that night. Maybe it would be too dark to see him then. But as he got closer, he heard noises that indicated his campsite was not vacant. He looked up and saw a group of teenagers sitting on the logs around the small fire they had started in the fire ring. When he saw that his tent was open, he clenched his fists and hollered, "What the hell is going on here?"

The teenagers were clearly unnerved at being discovered, but one of them stood up. "What's the matter, man? Is this place yours?"

Jamie didn't recognize them, so he knew they were summer visitors. "You're damn right it is! This is my campsite, and I'm staying here."

The young man, wearing what Jamie was sure was an Abercrombie & Finch outfit sneered, "But you don't own it, right?"

"Nope, just staying here."

"Then it really isn't yours, huh?"

"No, the campsite isn't, but the tent is. I don't mind you sitting around my fire ring, but you shouldn't have opened my tent!"

"It was open when we got here!"

"That's bullshit! I never leave it open because of the bugs! If I find anything out of place or missing from my tent, there's gonna be hell to pay!"

The other teenagers stood up and tensed for battle. Jamie stalked past them to his tent and looked in. "Why is my stuff all over the place? Have you been rooting around in here? Well, now we've got ourselves a problem, don't we?"

He went back over to the leader of the group, who finally said the one thing that Jamie had been dreading all along: "And what the hell are you going to do about it, bub? You're a little outnumbered here. So why don't you just pipe down, huh?"

Jamie's face twisted with such rage that the other teenagers began to shuffle and whisper. "I'll tell you what's going to happen, asshole. You and you fucking friends are going to get out of my goddamn campsite and let me get some sleep. If I find anything missing from my stuff, I'm gonna make a call."

"Oooh, are you gonna call the sheriff? We're scared!" the boy mocked.

"Naw, I'm not going to call the sheriff, asshole, I'm going to call my buddies. They've got anger issues and they usually walk around with loaded guns!"

The teenagers, for the most part, stood rooted to their spots. One or two couples slipped away, but the main core of the group did not move, although their faces showed the fear that they now felt. One girl nervously looked at the leader and said, "Come on, Tony, let's just get out of here. Let's let this guy go to sleep."

"Shut up, Nancy, we've got as much right to stay here as he does. He doesn't own this goddamn place. He's a squatter. And he's in no position to be ordering us around."

Jamie saw the group gain confidence, so he added, "I sure hope your daddies have good dental plans and health insurance because, even if I lose this round, I'm gonna fuck a couple of you up in the process! Some of you are gonna be missing teeth or at least an eye, that's all I'm saying."

Jamie was never sure where any of that came from, but it worked. Glances shifted toward the leader, all looking for the needed support. When he hesitated to offer any kind of rebuke, Jamie took the opportunity to move as quickly as he could and landed a punch squarely on the boy's jaw. It was the second punch Jamie had ever thrown in anger. The speed with which he'd moved and the force of his punch surprised the teenager, and he was knocked down. The rest of the group was too stunned to respond. If Jamie had been a real fighter, he'd have landed a few more punches and finished the job. Instead, he stood over his fallen opponent with his fists clenched, threateningly solid as a statue. He spit the words out between gritted teeth: "Get the fuck out of my campsite *now*!"

Jamie had waited a fraction too long, and another one of the kids had snuck up from behind to get a clear shot at him. But just as he was about to pounce, he was intercepted by a blur that jumped in from the woods. The jumbled ball of humanity rolled toward the trees, and then Wiley rose up over the other boy and knocked him out cold. When he added three more punches to the unconscious boy's face, several of the others begged him to stop. He threw one more punch, just to spite them, then stood back up crouching like a panther.

When he was tackled from behind and knocked him to the ground, Jamie's reaction was primal—he sent his elbow into his attacker's nose, smashing it into a bloody clod. The boy groaned and let go of him, and Jamie stood up. As his wounded opponent now got slowly to his feet, gripping his bleeding broken nose, Jamie saw him reach down, grab an empty beer bottle, and smash it against a tree trunk. He then waved the jagged edge at Jamie and growled, "Come on, asshole, it's your turn to bleed now!"

With the brandishing of a weapon, several others in the group retreated into the darkness and headed toward the parking lot of the store. Jamie felt curiously confident. In spite of the threatening weapon before him, he actually started to take a step forward. But Wiley came beside him and put his hand across his chest to stop him. He looked straight at the boy and smiled a wolfish grin. "Naw, dude, this fucker's all mine. Come on, peckerwood, let's dance!"

Wiley advanced on the boy, pulling a large fishing knife out of a sheath on the back of his belt. He waggled the knife at the boy, and Jamie felt the first real pang of fear. He had so much adrenaline running through his system that even the broken bottle hadn't scared him, but seeing Wiley with the knife now made him realize that someone was going to get seriously hurt or killed. He was about to speak up when the shotgun went off behind him.

"Put the knife away, Wiley!" Joe bellowed. He was holding a smoking sawed-off shotgun with the pistol grip in his good hand.

He glared at Wiley with fire in his eyes.

Wiley didn't blink. "Naw, Joe, these little fuckers went into Jamie and Shelley's tent and pawed through their goddamn stuff!"

"I know, Wiley. We'll take care of it—put the knife away."

"But I ain't finished with 'em yet, Joe."

Joe leveled the shotgun at Wiley. "Yes, you are. Nobody's getting carved up out here tonight!"

Wiley looked at Jamie, who nodded at him and said, "Come on, man, I want to be able to party with you at Bobbie's reception, not visit you in jail!"

Wiley smiled at the comment. After a moment of hesitation, he slipped the knife back into its sheath and backed away.

"Now, you drop that broken bottle, kid."

The frightened teenager stared at Joe. He held tightly to the bottle and seemed unsure about what to do. Joe repeated his command.

The boy did as he was told, but there was defiance in his eyes.

Sheriff Gus burst through the trees on the path, gasping for breath. "Jesus, Joe, you didn't shoot anyone, did ya?"

Joe smirked. "Not yet, Gus."

"For Christ's sake, Joe, I thought we'd agreed that you'd not shoot that damn thing off!"

"The kid had a broken bottle in his hand," Joe said with a shrug.

"Oh, he did, huh? Well, that certainly sweetens the pot, doesn't it?"

The pack leader found his voice. "Sheriff, we didn't do anything wrong here! That guy doesn't own this place, and the tent was open when we got here. He must've left it that way! He hit me first and then his friend pulled the knife on me. I know my rights, Sheriff. I have the right to defend myself."

Sheriff Gus holstered his gun and gestured for Joe to lower the shotgun. He walked up to the boy and said, "What's your name, son?"

"Reggie. Reggie Harper."

"Where do you stay?"

"*The Commons.*"

The Sheriff scratched his neck. "Yep, know the place. I guess your father is none other than Vincent Harper, huh?"

"Yes, that's right. So I guess I might know the law as well as you do."

"Well, son, being a lawyer and all from the big city, your father would be the first to tell you that trespassing upon another man's land instantly forfeits several of your rights."

"But that guy doesn't own this land!"

"Nope, you're right, he sure doesn't. A man named Drake Muldoon owns this land. Does that name sound familiar?"

"The guy who owns that dump of a wharf?"

"Hmm, interesting description. Yep, Drake Muldoon owns the wharf and he owns this land, too. And guess who he gave permission to camp on it."

"That guy?"

"That guy. And his girl. And guess what else: he told me to personally look after the two of them while they were guests on his land. So, when I get a report that there's a gaggle of teenagers drinking at his campsite, I start heading this way. Turns out, there's a civilian corps to this protection detail, too. So when the neighborhood watch comes upon you bothering this young man or his girl, you've got some real trouble."

"Hey, he punched me first! Then that guy over there attacked my friend and drew a knife on me! Jesus, they're the real troublemakers here!"

"Well, actually, the defense of a person's property from trespassers is a mighty sticky thing, as your father will explain to you when he gets here."

"My father's coming here?"

Sheriff Gus chuckled, "Oh, yes. He's very interested in getting your side of the story as to why you and your friends are trespassing on Drake's land, bothering his guests, and drinking beer and other alcoholic beverages even though it's clear that you're not old enough to buy yet. He'll probably want to talk with the other parents I've contacted—you know, the folks of the kids I had to put in handcuffs when they started fleeing the scene. It's gonna be one big social ball out there in the parking lot! I didn't have enough room in my squad car, so I had to call for a parent volunteer driver, so to speak. So, let's say good night to these nice people, Reggie Harper, and head out to the parking lot to wait for Daddy so we can talk about everything that's happened tonight."

The teenagers began to shuffle in the direction of the parking lot. They eyed Jamie and Wiley maliciously and gave Joe and his shotgun a wide berth, and then they hung their heads like prisoners being escorted to jail. Sheriff Gus raised his hand and the line of people stopped. "Oh, yeah, I almost forgot. Drake wants you all to know that the consequences will be much more severe if you ever come back and trespass on his land again."

None of the kids needed clarification on what he meant. Some of them looked at the sheriff and understood the legal ramifications that another infraction could mean, and others looked right at Wiley, Jamie, and Joe and clearly knew there were other kinds of consequences, as well.

The campsite was quiet for a few minutes, and then Wiley started babbling praises to Joe about Jamie's performance in the fracas. He was as enthusiastic as a puppy, but Jamie noticed that Joe kept the shotgun close to him, as if he didn't fully trust the boy's exuberance. When Wiley discovered that the teenagers had left an unfinished case of beer, the party was on, and the three of them sat around the fire and drank until it was all gone. Even Sheriff Gus came back after the chaos in the parking lot was settled, and he sat by the fire and talked with them for a while. He found the entire incident amusing, and he especially relished the scene that had unfolded as the rich parents came to pick up their delinquent children.

Jamie was tired, slightly drunk, and ready to go to bed when Sheriff Gus, Joe, and Wiley suddenly stood up and announced that they had to go home. They'd not been gone long before Shelley arrived—it was as if they had known exactly when she was coming. She ran her hand over the stubble that covered Jamie's head and cooed, "Hey, sexy, you're looking tough tonight. Did I hear it right that you actually slugged a Richie Rich?"

Jamie nodded proudly. "Yes, I did. When I saw that those little fuckers had gone through our stuff, I was so pissed, I attacked him! I got one punch in and then didn't know what to do next. Luckily, Joe and Wiley were watching out for us."

"Oh, believe me, we're part of several people's daily security routines. I'm actually surprised that those kids even made it to have a party here. I hear Wiley pulled a knife on one of them."

"Yep. But Joe showed up and stopped him."

"It seems like you've been a good influence on Wiley. In the past, he'd have stuck someone anyway. But I think you've mellowed him, Jamie. And I think he's spiced you up. How many times have you ever slugged someone?"

"Oh, I dunno for sure," Jamie shrugged.

"Liar, liar, pants on fire."

"This makes two times."

"See? I think Wiley is helping turn you into a regular ol' rough-neck! Now you even got the haircut to go with it. It's very sexy!"

"Really?"

"Oh, yes. And why don't we discuss just how sexy in the tent?"

24

When Clara and Bobbie's wedding day finally arrived, the whole community of Kestrel Cove dropped everything it was doing. Hand-drawn signs were posted on the wharf, the post office, the store, and the other businesses to let people know they'd be closing down at noon. Summertime residents, day-trippers, and pleasure boaters around the peninsula were forced to find the next closest place to get their supplies and services. And whenever anyone inquired why, the pat answer was, "The wedding's today."

Jamie still wasn't sure whether he was invited to the wedding ceremony, but instead of being paralyzed by uncertainty, he decided that he needed to get clean, dressed up, and ready to offer his services to help—no matter what his role. And, as the entire fishing fleet was taking the day off, he had made arrangements with Bill Hand to use the shower in the gatehouse and get dressed there before heading over to Clara and Bobbie's house to help out there.

He knew exactly what he was going to wear—his standard good outfit consisted of a blue blazer with golden Union officer buttons, khaki pants with pleats and cuffs, a starched white shirt, and his silk necktie with the Mathew Brady image of Robert E. Lee on it. He was convinced that this outfit had been the key to winning the internship in New York City, and he protected it inside a Bridgewater College hanging garment bag like it was a fragile religious icon.

He left his campsite after breakfast to head over to the gatehouse. Even though it was open and he had talked to Bill Hand to arrange his visit, he called up the stairs several times to make sure that no one was inside. He felt ridiculous doing it, but he went up the stairs shouting, "Don't shoot! I'm unarmed!"

Afterwards, Jamie walked up the driveway to the main house. The old Stutz was parked outside, and it had been washed and polished to a lustrous shine. Bill Hand was standing on the porch admiring the car, but he shifted his gaze to Jamie as he came closer. "That's quite a look, Jamie."

"What, not good?"

"No, no, you look very handsome. I just hadn't seen your new haircut yet."

"I got it from Wiley's girlfriend, Vicky."

"Ah, that explains it. Well, it certainly makes you look more rugged," Bill Hand said as he continued to scan Jamie from head to toe. "You're certainly dressed up."

Jamie took a step back. "Oh, am I overdoing it?"

"No, that outfit looks good on you. Very clean-cut. You may be overdressed a tad for this event, but that might be a good thing for today. I'm sure someone is going to show up in flip-flops, cargo shorts, and a Hawaiian shirt, but...um, are you wedded to the tie?"

Jamie caressed the tie. "I love this tie, Bill!"

"It's a nice tie, Jamie. And if I'm not mistaken, that image is the infamous photo by Mathew Brady of Robert E. Lee after his surrender at Appomattox."

"That's right! I forget that you're a Civil War buff, too."

Bill Hand shook his index finger. "The tie is quite nice, Jamie, but it's going to attract a lot of...uh, attention."

"It is? Why?"

"Well, since the frame of the photograph is repeated all over the tie, it kinda makes it look like an old man trapped in a box or a jail cell. This audience isn't going to care if it's a Mathew Brady photo or a Marcia Brady photo—they're going to obsess about why the old man is trapped in that box. And that image of Robert E. Lee is a spitting image of Shelley's great-uncle. I've never noticed it before, but that looks exactly like Vernon Vanes in a jail cell. It's going to catch a lot of eyes in that family."

"But I like this tie, Bill, and it's the only one I have."

"I've got a lot of nice-looking ties if you want to wear something that will attract less attention."

"But I like this one," Jamie said stubbornly.

"It does fit your personality. I'm just trying to prepare you for the fact that it's going to get a lot of attention at this event."

"Nobody's going to notice my tie."

"No pun intended, Jamie, but suit yourself."

They chatted a little longer, then Jamie said goodbye and headed over to Bobbie and Clara's. He knew their house was the supply depot for everything pertaining to the wedding, and he hoped that he could help out there and see Shelley before the ceremony. As he approached the house, he encountered Clara in the yard. Her hair was coiffed and her face was made up, but she was still in her bathrobe, and she was clearly doing some of the last-minute tasks before the wedding. She looked up at Jamie with an icy stare. "What, are you here to shit and jerk off in my garden again, college boy?"

Jamie sputtered, "No, oh God, no, Clara. I'm here to lend a hand."

Her face softened into a devilish grin. "Hey, I'm only fucking with you. It's pretty cool that you came here to help. Now I see why Shelley's been talking my ear off about how great you are. If you want to help, it looks like my grandfather could use a hand moving the booze from the garage to his truck."

Jamie looked around and spotted the older man struggling with some boxes. He turned to go, but Clara called out, "But don't get dirty. You're all dressed up and look so nice. I hope everyone has the class to dress up like you…but…hey, is that old man trapped in a box?"

"What?"

"On your tie. Is that old man trapped in a box?"

"No, it's a famous photo of Robert E. Lee."

"You know what? That old man looks just like my great-uncle Vernon."

"Naw, it's Robert E. Lee," Jamie replied. When Clara's face didn't register any recognition, he said, "The famous Confederate general? You know—Robert E. Lee."

"Uh-huh," Clara mused distractedly.

"Well, I'll go help your grandfather. If you see Shelley, could you tell her that I'm around? See you later, Clara. And congratulations, by the way."

"Thank you, college boy. It looks like the weather's gonna hold for us."

"That'd be nice."

"Yeah. Hey, make sure you have a good time tonight. Ya know, it ain't a bad thing to let loose every once in a while. Shelley says you need to do that more."

"Oh, I'll try." Jamie waved and started to walk away, but Clara called out, "Oh, hey, my grandfather's name is Winston. Talk to him in his left ear if you want him to hear you!"

As Jamie came up, the elderly man recoiled and looked at him with distrust. When Jamie announced who he was and what he was doing, Winston smiled a broadly. "Oh, I've heard of you! My granddaughter Shelley has talked all about you, that's for sure. She's gone on about you so much, I've had to turn down my Miracle Ear so I don't have to listen to her!"

"I guess that's good news, sir."

The old man grabbed Jamie's hand with a warmth and strength that caught him off guard, "Young man, you better pay attention today. If you don't do nothing stupid in the near future, you and Shelley just might be in Bobbie and Clara's shoes sometime soon!"

Jamie attempted to address the grandfather's prognostication, but before he could muster any kind of response, the old man began staring down at his tie. "Um, why do you have a picture of my brother Vernon in a box on your tie? Are you trying to be funny, young man?"

"No, sir. It isn't a picture of your brother; it's actually a famous photo of the Confederate general, Robert E. Lee."

The old man nearly put his nose on Jamie's tie for a closer look. "Naw, that's Vernon."

"No, sir, it's Robert E. Lee, the famous Confederate general."

"Well, it'd be damn weird if you were to wear a tie that not only had a picture of my brother on it, but had a photo of him in jail. Ya know, Vernon weren't too proud of the time he spent in there, and if he were to hear that you were wearing a tie that made fun of him, there might be some problems that could arise."

The old man turned a deaf ear to him and started working on the boxes again. When Jamie went to take one from him, he looked as if he was personally offended by the offer of help. He shook his head. "I ain't so old that I can't carry a damn box of booze! If you really want to help, grab another box and let's get them all into the truck and take it over to the Community Center!"

Jamie didn't have to be told twice, and they worked in a comfortable silence as they loaded the pickup truck. Just as they were closing the tailgate, Shelley came out to find Jamie. She whistled a catcall and kissed him passionately on the lips. She was wearing jeans, a T-shirt, and no bra, and he could feel her breasts against him as he hugged her. Shelley pushed him away to look at his outfit and gave him an approving grin. "Jamie Kurtz, you sure do clean up pretty damn good! If you're not careful, you're gonna be the handsomest guy at this thing today. And I can't believe you came over here to help out! You look so—um, what's with that tie?"

"It's not your great-uncle Vernon, and he's not in a box or in jail!" Jamie said with exasperation. "It's the famous Mathew Brady photograph of Robert E. Lee! Bill Hand, Clara, and your grandfather have all told me that it's weird."

Shelley looked closely at the tie. "I don't know, sweetie. It's a spitting image of Great-Uncle Vernon, and it does look like he's back in the clink."

Jamie threw up his hands. "Okay, okay, I give up! I won't wear the goddamn tie!"

"Well, don't have a hissy fit, Jamie. Don't you have another one?"

"You know, Bill Hand offered me some of his ties. Maybe I can go back and get one from him."

Shelley nestled up against him and ran her hand over the stubble on his head, which completely defused the anger that was welling up. She virtually purred into his ear, "You can do whatever you want, Jamie Kurtz. Just know that you're gonna be the hottest guy at this whole wedding! I'll see you at the church, stud. Don't be late!"

As he watched her walk seductively back into the house, it dawned on him that Shelley had just officially invited him to the wedding ceremony. The implications of this stunned him, but the spell was broken when Winston suddenly called out, "Hey, college boy, you coming with me to unload these boxes, or are you just gonna stare off into space like an idiot?"

The Community Center was deserted when they pulled into the parking lot. From the outside, the gruff cinder-block exterior looked as foreboding as ever. Inside, however, lavish decorations of tissue paper streamers and buntings made the space inviting and festive. The dining tables were covered with white tablecloths and floral arrangements, and the buffet tables were aligned and laden with ruffles and paper puffs. The bar stood out like a beacon in the corner of the room, and Winston and Jamie set out to stack all the boxes of booze behind it. When they finished, Winston filled two plastic cups from the tap. They touched their cups together quickly and drank down the very cold beer in refreshing and satisfying gulps before heading back to the truck.

As they were about to pull out of the parking lot, Bill Hand came flying up in the Stutz and slid to a stop. He got out and nodded at the old man. "Winston."

The old man nodded back. "Bill."

Bill Hand had something colorful in his hand as he walked straight to Jamie's window. "I know I said that you could make your own decision, but I really think you should take one of my ties to wear to this thing."

Winston spoke up. "Thank God! I don't know if I could have handled an entire day with those pictures of my brother in jail on his tie!"

"I tried to tell him, Winston, but he's a bit stubborn."

"Well, that ain't a bad quality to have in life—especially if he wants to keep dating my granddaughter."

Bill Hand nodded knowingly. "That's certainly true, Winston. Okay, Jamie, I've picked out three that I thought would go well with your outfit. These are all Charvet silk from one of the first shirt shops in France, which I thought might appeal to your historical passions."

He held up the three ties. There was a bright orange one, a golden one, and a navy-blue one that seemed to have light-blue waves on it. The brighter ties caught Jamie's eye, but the blue one seemed to be more his style, and when he reached for it, Bill Hand nodded his approval. "You're a person who knows himself, aren't you, Jamie? Good choice. That tie is beautiful and attracts all the right attention."

"Thank you, Bill."

As Jamie knotted the new tie, Bill Hand and Winston talked

about the small details of the wedding day—how the weather was good but not too hot, how the Community Center was decorated nicely, how the bride seemed calm and ready, and how the whole day should be one hell of an event. By the time they had run out of things to say, Jamie was ready. The two older men nodded their approval as he carefully rolled up his Robert E. Lee tie and put it in his blazer pocket. Bill Hand hopped back into his car, revved it, and sped away in a cloud of dust.

Back at Bobbie and Clara's house, Jamie was kept busy with small but essential pre-wedding jobs. And in the process of putting the giant wicker gift basket and the guest book into the car that was going to the Community Center, getting the right bouquets to the right brides-maids, taking the foil-covered macaroni salad from the fridge and put-ting it onto the backseat of another car, zipping Shelley's dress, and washing all the dishes that sat around the kitchen like hurricane-stranded shipwrecks, Jamie met all the members of the Vanes family and they, in turn, got a chance to meet him. Working side by side and getting all of these tasks accomplished planted the seed of mutual re-spect, which took root and grew strong by the time their caravan head-ed toward the church.

Naturally, Jamie had been under tight scrutiny. There may have been a few family members who grumbled when they first heard he had been invited to the wedding, but after all his work at the house before the ceremony, everyone seemed to consider him a bona fide family member. They even insisted that he sit up in the front pew next to Winston.

As he waited for the ceremony to start, he studied the interior of the church. Like most Congregational churches in Maine, it was quite utilitarian. None of the windows were stained glass or ornate, but their large clear panes let the warm summer sun bathe the sanc-tuary, the earth-tone walls, and the deep maroon carpeting that cov-ered the aisle. The pews were simple and supremely uncomfortable. Even the raised wooden pulpit where the minister led Sunday ser-vices was a plain-looking box, but it was framed between two doors, which helped to create a certain visual symmetry. A large wooden cross on the wall behind the pulpit appeared to be made from two stained 2 x 2's, and the entire church had an unassuming atmosphere that was warm and friendly.

At one o'clock sharp, Bobbie and his two groomsmen took up their position in front of the altar. The congregation quickly settled down and got ready for the ceremony to begin. The minister came out and stood right next to Bobbie. He was a very large man with a head of wavy white hair and an Amish beard, and he looked like a man who might have been a sea captain or a fisherman in the past. He whispered something in Bobbie's ear, which made the groom laugh out loud, and then the organ began to play the processional hymn.

The first bridesmaid was Bobbie's younger sister, Carmen, and she walked confidently and regally. Her light-green dress was tight, but it was obvious that the tightness was due to her musculature. Jamie remembered hearing the stories of how she'd left the peninsula to go up to Alaska to work on a fishing boat, and the set of blue anchor tattoos on her forearms reflected her strength and toughness.

When Jamie saw Shelley start to walk down the aisle, she quite literally took his breath away. She was awash in the sunlight, and her blond hair and green dress energized the entire room. Jamie locked his eyes on her and sighed audibly. Winston leaned over and whispered, "You gonna be all right over there, young man?"

Without taking his eyes off of her, Jamie responded quietly, "She's the most beautiful thing I've ever seen in my whole life, sir."

Winston seemed prepared to add something sarcastic, but when he saw the way his granddaughter returned the boy's gaze, he smiled in the way that old men sometimes do when they know a secret that only they can understand.

When Shelley took her position at the front of the church, the organist instantly stopped playing. After a momentary lull, Wagner's famous Bridal Chorus emanated from the organ, and Jamie smiled. He knew all about the opera *Lohengrin* because it had been written in 1848, the same year that the last slave-owning president, Zachary Taylor, died. And since it was this man's death that led to the Compromise of 1850, one of the main factors in the inevitability of the Civil War, Jamie could never forget the connection. He laughed at his own geekiness now, and turned his attention to the very beautiful and pregnant Clara as she processed down the aisle toward Bobbie.

The wedding photographer's camera continued to click after the organist stopped playing, and the sound was like pebbles being thrown into a metal culvert. The minister whispered something to Clara that made her giggle, and then he faced the congregation. His booming voice was warm and powerful, and everyone in the room was enveloped by it as he said, "Most of you know me, but some of you may not. My name is Joshua Clements, and I'm the minister of this church. I'm supposed to start this ceremony with some reference to the Wedding at Cana and the sanctity of marriage, but I'm not going to say anything about that because I figure we're all here to celebrate the union between Bobbie and Clara, not to hear a bunch of history lessons. And I'm also supposed to say that if anyone knows of any reason why these two should not get married…blah, blah. But I'm not going to say any of that, either, because, mostly, I find that to be a rude leftover from a less informed age, *and* I know for a fact that if any of you had had any bad things to say about these two, you would've told it to their faces a long time ago. This is Kestrel Cove, after all!"

The congregation had a good laugh about this. The minister quieted the group by continuing, "Now, as some of you might know, before I became a minister, I was the captain of the *Janet Calliope*, a thirty-eight-foot gillnetter out of Rockland. When the fish were thick, I made good money. Matter of fact, I put two kids through college with that boat!

"Then the storm of '86 changed all that. We don't need to rehash the story of my boat sinking or how long me and my crew waited in that cold water to be rescued, but the event changed my life. And Clara and Bobbie, I know that there are many ministers out there who could say what I'm trying to say more eloquently and beautifully than me, but one of the biggest lessons I took away from that experience is that a married couple should be like a good crew on a boat. In the good times, a good crew makes it all better. In the bad times, a good crew supports one another. Why? Because they realize that they're dependent on each other and that they're working toward a common goal. A married couple needs to recognize this, too, 'cause it's gonna get stormy and it's gonna get rough. But it's also going to be as good as it can possibly be and everything is going to go your way. And if you are good crew members to one another in all kinds of conditions, you'll never have to face life alone."

Bobbie and Clara were staring straight into the minister's intense blue eyes and nodding their heads. The minister looked up and addressed the congregation. "And you all out there, you need to really listen to the words of this ceremony today. These two have planned a straightforward service with not a lot of bells and whistles. But you're all witnesses, and you need to hear the words as clearly as you can. I celebrate a lot of weddings, and it always seems that, because the words are so familiar and people are more excited about the reception than the ceremony, we tend to rush through all the important stuff. That's a damn shame, since what we're going to say here has the most power that we, as Christians and human beings, can utter to each other. So, make it your goal to really listen to the words today."

And Jamie did just that. As the ceremony went on through the lessons and the vows, he kept staring straight at Shelley. She was absolutely and breathtakingly beautiful, and as he focused on her, the words that were spoken fluttered around the room like butterflies. And it was while Bobbie, his strong voice wavering with emotion, made his vow—"I, Robert Fulton Schmidt, take you, Clara Ruth Vanes, to be my wife, to have and to hold from this day forward, for better or for worse, for richer, for poorer, in sickness and in health, to love and to cherish; from this day forward until death do us part"—that Jamie realized he was crying. He tried to stifle the tears, but Winston hoarsely whispered, "Aw, hell, college boy, do you really need a tissue?"

The end of the ceremony marked an abrupt change, as the simplicity, peacefulness, and purity of the wedding got shoved aside when the bride and groom walked down the aisle and stepped outside. Almost immediately, it seemed as if the event itself was resigned to being carried away on different rails as new agendas took it over. The profound words of the service were now replaced by the agitated and frenetic barking of commands from the wedding photographer as she posed and photographed the bridesmaids and groomsmen. The throb of the party could now be heard coming from the Community Center, and Jamie knew that part of the photographer's urgency came from the fact that she saw, all too clearly, that the wedding party wanted nothing more than to slide right over to the reception and join in. Regardless, she meted out her orders like an invading general.

And once the wedding party entered the Community Center, the event took on a new speed and force. With the knowledge that most of the people attending the reception would be too drunk later in the evening to enjoy them, all of the traditional elements were jammed together to be done as quickly as possible. The couple was introduced, danced their first dance, danced with their parents, did the garter and bouquet tosses, crammed wedding cake into each other's mouths, and did the dollar dance, all within the first twenty minutes. And Jamie saw how Bobbie and Clara went through the motions of each ritual as if they were walking through the rehearsal of a play. What they were doing was required, not enjoyed, and it had to get done and out of the way so the real fun could start.

However, the bouquet and the garter tosses provided a moment of amusement. Once Bobbie had seductively slid the garter down off of Clara's leg, the single men were cajoled into forming a group to catch it. Not only were most of them acting like prisoners being led to the firing squad, but, as Bobbie got ready to fling the garter like a giant rubber band, they all ducked and flinched. While many of their girl-friends in the crowd found this humorous at first, they grew visibly annoyed as their boyfriends continued their evasive maneuvers. As for Jamie, it wasn't that he didn't *want* to catch the garter; he just didn't want to embarrass Shelley trying to do so. He stood casually off to the side of the main group, but when Clara hissed something into Bob-bie's ear, he instantly shot the garter right at Jamie's heart. The group scattered like it was an incoming RPG round, and he had no choice but to catch it when it struck him. He held it aloft and smiled sheepishly at the catcalls and laughter that followed.

But the bouquet throw was completely different. Several of the single women were overeager, and some even appeared to be doing warm-up exercises to get themselves ready for the moment. The bachelorettes crowded close to one another and jockeyed for a better position. Shelley was in the midst of the pack, but she was well aware that, since Jamie had caught the garter, she shouldn't attempt to catch the bouquet. She wouldn't avoid it if it came her way, but she certainly wasn't going to go after it like a cornerback going for an interception, as some of the girls seemed ready to do. When Clara turned around and got ready to heave the bouquet over her shoulder, no one noticed that she was using a Moosehead Beer mirror on the wall to find the exact location of her young sister. Without warning, she threw the bouquet with the velocity of a fast-pitch softball toss directly at Shelley, who barely had time to recover from it hitting her squarely in the bosom. Some of the other women lunged for it, but Clara had threaded the needle and they were too late. There was a call for Jamie and Shelley to kiss, which they did to shut up the chanting.

That was the last complete and coherent memory Jamie had of the reception. When he awoke the next morning, he had no idea where he was or what had happened the night before. His brain felt like a lava dome that was achingly expanding and threatening to burst apart the seams of his skull, and, although it pained him to move his eyes, he needed to try to ascertain exactly where he was. On his third attempt, he spotted a large photo on the wall of Mr. and Mrs. Vanes standing with their three children in front of them, which told him that he was in Shelley's mother's house.

Figuring out what had happened at the reception proved to be much harder. The images and events were so blurred and comingled in his mind that he was unsure what was fact and what was imagined. It was pretty clear that while he and Shelley were drinking with Vicky and Wiley, the four of them had gotten rip-roaringly drunk. But although he was far from certain about the rest of the details, he could piece together enough fragments to make a few educated guesses. He knew that he had been offered a permanent job on the *Bobbie C.* by an equally drunk Joe; he and Wiley had used the throw-away cameras to take pictures of the crotches of other guests; he had had wild sex with Shelley in the backseat of Bill Hand's car; he had declared his undying friendship with Wiley; and, quite possibly, he had made an impassioned speech from the stage of the Community Center to the whole crowd.

When he sat up in the bed, his stomach heaved. He moaned and looked around the room in a panic for a wastebasket to throw up in. But the nausea passed, and he held his aching head in his hands. He could hear noises coming from downstairs, and he knew that he needed to make his way there. Getting his feet down to the floor and standing erect were harder than he'd expected, and he kept stopping to vomit, but it never came. He got to his feet, and the floor felt more unstable than the deck of the boat. He groped for the doorjamb, not only to steady himself, but to reassure himself that it was actually there. After a moment or two of standing there to regain his balance, he opened the bedroom door.

A flock of young children was seated on the floor there, and when they saw him, they yelled and screamed with excitement, causing bombastic echoes to ping and pang inside his cranium like a gong. He closed his eyes and held onto the door. As he began shuffling toward the stairs, the children, acting like criers announcing the arrival of a dignitary, ran in front of him, screaming at the top of their lungs, "The college boy's finally awake! The college boy's finally awake! Here he comes!"

At the foot of the stairs, he clung to the banister for a moment, then slowly made his way toward the sound of the voices in the living room. As he walked in, he was so bent over and shuffling that he looked like an elderly usher at an old theater. Some teenagers seated nearby yelled out, "Hey, it's the college boy!"

Jamie winced, but then his vision cleared enough to see that there was an entire room of people, including Mrs. Vanes, all her children, and several of Shelley's cousins, staring up at him. He croaked, "Where's Shelley?"

"She had to open the store. It's, like, midafternoon, ya know," Mrs. Vanes said with a chortle.

"Is she okay?"

"She's in much better shape than you!" one of the teens said gleefully.

Jamie was thoroughly embarrassed, but when the unmistakable taste of bile floated up in the back of his throat, he asked in panic, "Oh, my God! Did I throw up?"

"Buckets," Mrs. Vanes answered with a shrug.

Jamie closed his eyes. Mrs. Vanes continued, "In a garbage can outside the Community Center, sweetie. You did it once, and then you were through."

He clutched his neck like a garrote was around it. "Oh, no. Tell me I didn't get anything on the tie!"

"Jeez, what is it with that tie?" one of the older kids asked. "When it was definite that you were going to blow chunks last night, you just *had* to get the tie off before you did. Shelley had to untie it and put it in her purse before you emptied your guts into that trash can!"

"It's Bill Hand's tie."

This explanation seemed to justify his actions, and everyone nodded with understanding. Winston suddenly walked into the room and spoke directly to Jamie. "Shelley wanted me to come over and get you, young man."

"Aw, no, he hasn't had any coffee or eaten anything yet!" Mrs. Vanes exclaimed.

The mere mention of food and coffee made Jamie's stomach flip-flop again, and he shook his head slowly. "No, thanks. I don't think that eating or drinking would be too good for me right now."

Leon came into the room wearing ripped shorts and a wife-beater shirt. "Hey, look, it's *the damn torpedoes* guy!"

Jamie groaned. If he'd made a fool of himself in front of the whole community and in front of her family by getting drunk and acting like an ass, he knew that Shelley was going to be absolutely furious with him.

Winston wagged a finger. "No, Leon, he didn't say *the damn torpedoes*! He said *damn the torpedoes*."

"What's the difference?"

"Well, I think Jamie was saying that, even though life has a lot of obstacles that can be scary, he's learned that you have to throw caution to the wind and steam headlong into whatever life has to throw at you."

"Naw, I don't think that's what he was saying at all," Leon said with snort. "He was saying that marriage and children are like torpedoes that hit us as we sail through life. That's why he said *the damn torpedoes*!"

"Oh, Leon, you totally heard him wrong!" Mrs. Vanes said loudly. "He was clearly saying what Winston just said. Remember, he went on and proclaimed his undying love for Shelley despite the torpedoes that life might send their way. That's when he started yelling *damn the torpedoes!* over and over."

"Hmm, I don't know," Leon said with a shake of his shaggy head. "I think I'm right. Which one is it, college boy?"

It hurt Jamie's head to have everyone stare at him, and he licked his lips. "David Farragut, the Union admiral in the Civil War who uttered that famous quote, was trying to urge his fleet into Mobile Bay no matter what dangers lay ahead. If I was making a wedding speech and talking about me and Shelley in front of the whole community of Kestrel Cove, Leon, I'd say that I meant that you need to move ahead and disregard the fear of obstacles."

"Huh. I'm still not sure that's what you actually meant," Leon said stubbornly.

"For the love of Pete, Leon, the boy should know what he was trying to say!" Mrs. Vanes said.

One of the cousins then came to Jamie's defense, saying that the speech was one of the most beautiful things she'd ever heard. Winston noticed that Jamie was getting paler, so he leaned over and said very quietly, "Let's get out of here, college boy."

"Okay," Jamie replied.

"But I think you want to put some pants on first," Winston said with a grin.

◊◊◊◊

The way the scenery blurred outside made Jamie's eyes ache, so he closed them and rested his head against the truck window. Just as they were pulling into the store parking lot, he knew that he had to ask Winston the one question he most dreaded. "Winston, just how much did I humiliate Shelley last night? How mad is she at me for making an ass of myself?"

The old man brought the truck to a stop, put it in park, and turned off the engine. He snickered to himself. "I ain't gonna lie, college boy, you had one helluva night. You got drunker than a skunk, and then you had yourself some fun. I know that you've got a headache that feels like your skull is going to split open, but don't beat yourself up—you didn't do anything but endear yourself even more to me, Kestrel Cove, Shelley, and the entire Vanes clan. All Shelley kept saying was that she hoped you would loosen up and have fun. And guess what? You did. In the process, you were a lovable drunk, a fabulous dancer, and you truly made the best speech of the night. That shithead, Vernon Quigley, made a speech that was just plain awful! But you got up there and hit all the high points about love and life. Puking in a garbage can and having to be driven home are only badges of honor at a Kestrel Cove event!"

Jamie grimaced, but he was relieved. "Oh, good! I wouldn't be able to bear it if I'd done anything to embarrass Shelley."

Winston said, "Oh, I don't think you need to worry about that. But I gotta say that when a young man gets up on a stage in front of the whole community and confesses that he loves Shelley Vanes more than anything else in the world and that he wants to marry the girl, people around here are going to take some notice. And when that same young man goes on to say that he's found a home and a new family here in Kestrel Cove, he may have to deal with some feedback in the future."

"Oh, God, Winston, I think I'm gonna be sick again."

25

The entire month of August was as close to perfection as Jamie had ever experienced. The weather was nearly ideal for lobstering. The sunny, warm, and windless days and the quantities of lobsters they were catching made working on the lobster boat so much fun that Joe, Jimmy, and Jamie were all a little disappointed each afternoon when it was time to head in. But the good times continued well after the boat was back at the mooring. Not only did the guys usually go back to the campsite to drink beer, but it was common for Wiley and others to join them and sit around the fire ring laughing and telling stories. And when Shelley finished her shift, she often brought food and more beer so the party could continue until the wee hours of the night. After everyone left, Shelley and Jamie would go into the tent together, but they rarely went right to sleep.

But now that summer was in full throttle, it seemed as if everyone was too busy to fully acknowledge that this month actually signaled the end of summer. Chilly, foggy mornings and trees that were no longer verdantly green were the subtle hints that colder and less comfortable times were fast approaching. The summer residents were aware that they needed to hurry up and enjoy what was left of their vacations, and their movements and activities took on more desperation as they tried to suck everything out of the idle days before they had to go home. For the year-round residents of the peninsula, however, having fall begin to nudge summer out of the way was like being able to see the light at the end of the tunnel. And, like weary marathon runners who continue to grind their way toward the finish line, they were all determined to get in all of their good times before winter came.

On one particularly clear and warm August day, the *Bobbie C.* headed in early after another good day on the water. Although the job lacked any shred of variety or notoriety, Jamie felt a deep sense of accomplishment that he was doing his job aboard the boat very well, and he was proud of himself for helping the boat succeed. The baiting and banding responsibilities were now his entirely, and the baiting table and lobster tank were his domain, and Jimmy and Joe no longer double-checked his efforts or offered to lend a hand. The college boy had things in hand, and the men had the confidence in him that allowed them to completely focus on their own tasks. So, as they motored toward the wharf to unload the lobsters, fuel up, and get the bait for the next day, they were cocky with the certainty that they were one of the very best crews in the entire cove.

After they tied the lines to the pilings, Drake came over and looked down at them with his hands on his hips. "What the hell do you guys want now?"

Joe looked up. "In a bad mood, Drake?"

"Who the hell wouldn't be? We've been invaded all day by *tourons*. I've got assholes milling around my wharf, poking their noses into my office and touching lobsters. Then there's them rich yachters demanding to be treated as if they're the only people in the whole goddamn world. And to top it all off, I've got a bunch of useless idiotic oafs laying around my wharf, sleeping and slacking. Who wouldn't be a tad bit grumpy with all that going on?"

Jimmy and Jamie had already emptied the lobster tank and put the lobsters into ten totes that were on the deck, and while Joe and Jimmy winched them onto the deck of the wharf, Jamie went to pitch the bait for the next day. Drake sneered at him as he walked by, then continued talking to Joe. "Well, what do you got for me today?"

"About seven hundred pounds. Maybe more."

Drake whistled and raised an eyebrow in surprise. "Two pounds per trap?"

"Looks like it," Joe said with some pride.

Jamie had the fishing totes ready. He wanted to get them filled quickly so they'd be ready to load as soon as Drake and Alfred had processed the lobsters from the boat, so he didn't see the BMW convertible pull into the parking lot or Laura and her muscular boyfriend get out and start walking toward the wharf.

"We need some lobsters," Alex Pettingill announced grandly as they came up to Drake.

Drake looked up from the *Bobbie C.*'s lobsters and said, "Someone'll be right with you folks. Vincent, take care of these people!"

Vincent appeared from the shadows of the office. His sudden appearance startled Drake, who said gruffly, "What the hell you been doing back there, Vincent, sleeping?"

"Naw, boss, I was stacking pallets."

Drake looked him over suspiciously. "For a whole hour?"

"Well, first I had to take a dump, but when I went over to the shitter, the door was locked, so I—"

"Never mind! Jesus Christ, we don't need to hear all those goddamn details—just help these nice people get their lobsters."

"Right-o, boss."

Drake shook his head at Vincent, then turned his attention back to sorting the lobsters with Alfred.

Alex proudly informed Vincent, "We need eight—no, ten lobsters—each two pounds or more."

"Right-o."

Alex puffed up and said more loudly than was necessary, "No, make it an even dozen. A dozen two-pound lobsters!"

"Did all these lobsters come from one boat?" Laura asked sweetly, pointing down to the totes of lobsters on the wharf deck.

Drake's eyes slowly scanned the brown and muscular legs up to the short tennis skirt, up over the flat stomach and onto the curving bosom, up the slender neck, and smack into the brown eyes of Laura. He grinned an alligator grin at the attractive young lady. "Why, yes they did, ma'am! From that boat right down there."

The moment Laura spoke, Jamie's head whipped around. Like a seal pup who finds its mother on a crowded beach by the sound of her call, his body twisted to see where the voice had come from. When he saw Laura standing right behind him talking to Drake, his guts rumbled with anger, shame, and grief. And next to her was that bastard, Alex Pettingill! Jamie quickly looked back down at the bait in the bins, hoping that the redfish heads would give him some feeling of solace, but they didn't. With their open mouths and bulging eyes staring back at him, Jamie felt more vulnerable than ever. He moved his back more squarely to hide himself from Laura and Alex and hoped they would just get their lobsters and leave.

While Laura allowed Alex to take care of supervising Vincent, she wandered over to the edge of the wharf to look down at the lobster boat. She said sweetly to Joe, "Are you the captain?"

From his vantage point down on the deck of the boat, he had a wonderful glimpse up Laura's skirt. He smiled coyly. "That's right."

"Do you fish alone?" she inquired.

"No, I've got some help."

She looked over her shoulder at Jimmy at the winch. "Oh, the two of you?"

Jimmy was staring at her now, too. She was good-looking and he liked her attention. But before he could answer, Joe yelled up, "Naw, we've got a third guy, too. He's getting bait up there somewhere. Hey, Jimmy, isn't Jamie right there?"

Jimmy looked past Laura to Jamie, who had his back to the girl, and he called over, "Hey, Jamie, wave at the nice lady over here!"

"Jamie?" Laura muttered.

Jamie turned reluctantly and felt his face flush. "Uh, hey, Laura."

"Jamie Kurtz," Laura declared with a slight gasp, "is that you?"

"Wait—you know her?" Jimmy asked loudly.

"Um, yeah. This is Laura. I knew her at Bridgewater College."

Jimmy's eyes widened in recognition of the name from the stories of Jamie's past. He smiled at the woman, then motioned for Joe to come up.

"What are you doing here, Jamie?" Laura asked.

"I work on that boat."

"Wow! Since when?"

"June."

"Well, you seem like you're doing good."

"Oh, yeah, very good, actually."

Alex came out of the lobster shed with two damp white-and-blue paper bags of lobsters in his hands. Laura gestured toward Jamie. "Hey, Alex, look who I just bumped into."

"Jamie Kurtz? Omigosh! Well, doesn't that beat all? Ha-ha, I can't believe it!"

"Uh, hi, Alex. How's it going?"

"What are you doing, Kurtz? You don't work *here*, do you?" Alex asked derisively.

The scene had now attracted Alfred's and Drake's attention, and the tone of Alex's voice made them square their shoulders in a defensive posture. Joe came up the ladder and stood next to Jimmy, who whispered clarifications into his ear.

"No, I don't work here on the wharf. I work on that lobster boat down there, the *Bobbie C.*"

"I've often wondered if we'd ever run into each other again," Laura admitted, "and what we'd do when we saw one another. Now that we're here, I don't know what to do. I mean, I would give you a hug, but you look a little too messy for that."

Jamie looked down at his mud-and bait-splattered bib, and felt a sense of relief. The worst thing—even worse than being discovered pitching bait by his ex-girlfriend and her new boyfriend—would be to have to hug Laura right in front of this audience on the wharf.

"Uh, yeah, I guess so, huh?" Jamie responded uneasily.

"I just can't get over you working *here!*" Alex said as he chuckled again.

"He don't work here," growled Drake. "He works on that boat. He already said that!"

"Oh, how the mighty have fallen, huh?" Alex continued, ignoring Drake's comment and addressing his growing audience on the wharf. "You wouldn't believe this guy in college! He was a superstar, at least for one professor! I thought you were going to be adopted by Walter Whetstone, Kurtz—or married to him. Ha-ha! Does he come down here to buy lobsters and talk to you about the good old Civil War days?"

Jamie wanted to shrink away to nothing. His tongue was tied, his eyes were avoiding Laura, and he stammered to respond to the nasty put-downs from Alex. Out of the corner of his eye, he could see Bobbie and Wiley motoring in toward the floating dock in their skiff, and he wished that Laura and Alex would just go away.

"Jamie, how come you aren't at the Hungry Rancher anymore?" Laura asked.

"Well, I—"

"Can you guys believe that? This guy graduates from one of the best colleges in the world and then goes to work at some horsemeat grill! You can't make that kind of stuff up, can you? Ha-ha!"

"I quit," Jamie said softly.

Laura smiled at him and said, "Well, it looks like the change did you good, Jamie. You've got lots of color, like you've spent some time outdoors. And it looks like you're beefier, too."

"Oh, yeah," Alex snorted, "you're a regular ol' bodybuilder, Kurtz!" He smirked at Jamie, then continued in a loud voice, "Anyway, we've rented that yellow cottage with the tennis courts that overlooks the ocean at the end of this road for the weekend, and we're having some of the gang over. Norm Johnston, Craig Benson, and Harpie Anderson—you remember them, all Chi Rhos. We're having a lobster bake tonight. You should come over for shits and giggles."

Jamie had no problem remembering those three. They had teased him so badly at a frat party that he had foolishly taken a swing at one of them. His feeble punch had missed, but theirs hadn't. They'd picked him up and tossed him out onto the lawn. Laura had been so embarrassed by the whole scene, she'd left him out there and stayed at the party. And it was then that Alex and Laura made it official that Jamie was out and Alex was in. He'd often wondered if that fight had caused her to give him the heave-ho. Of course, deep down, he knew that it really didn't matter. But the day that Jamie Kurtz showed up at a lobster bake with those three Chi Rhos and Alex and Laura was the day that Satan was wearing long johns and a fleece sweater!

Bobbie and Wiley came up the gangplank and joined the group. Alfred leaned over and quietly filled them in on what had been going on.

"Do you still live in the apartment in Brementon, Jamie?' Laura asked.

"No, I got evicted."

Alex jumped on that. "So lemme get this straight: you quit your dead-end job at the Hungry Rancher, got evicted, and you landed *here*?"

Jamie became painfully aware that everyone was staring at him, almost imploring him to strike back and defend himself, but he still didn't want to make a scene. Hadn't Alex been saying the truth? Jamie was the academic star who'd not only lost the girl, but given up the future with the golden road to do a menial job that served the likes of Alex! There was no way to defend himself against the truth, so he just remained silent and wished for this whole episode to be over.

It was at this awkward moment that the final ingredient of this improbable mix was added—Shelley came flying into the parking lot in her pickup truck. The dust settled as she turned off the engine and slid out of the truck, slamming the door behind her. Her noisy arrival caught Jamie's attention, and he struggled to maintain his composure. Everyone followed his gaze toward the parking lot and saw Shelley marching toward him.

"Well," Alex announced, looking around the group of people on the wharf, "as absolutely titillating as all this has been, we've got to get home to start cooking, Laura. You know Chip, he'll have drunk seven beers by now and be running naked around the neighborhood! Ha-ha!"

"Hey, Jamie!" Shelley said loudly as she sidled up and planted a firm kiss on his lips.

"Um, hi, Shelley. What are you doing here?"

"Heard you guys came in early, and I was wondering what you were doing. Oh, excuse me; am I interrupting something? Who are these people?"

"This is Laura. And this is her boyfriend, Alex," he said matter-of-factly. "This is my girlfriend, Shelley."

She waved her hand at the newcomers. "Nice to meet you two. Did you go to college with Jamie?"

"Uh-huh, we did," Laura said softly. "We just came down to buy some lobsters and ran into him."

"Yeah," Alex sneered, "this is the *last* place I'd've thought we'd ever run into Jamie Kurtz!"

"How so?" Shelley asked innocently.

"He's a Bridgewater College grad, for God's sake! And now he's working on this ratty old lobster wharf? We're just surprised that he'd land here."

"You don't say." Shelley's voice had an edge to it. "Where did you think he would land?"

"Oh, I guess everyone knew he wasn't going to be a major success or anything. I mean, he studied the Civil War. Not a lot of mul-timillionaires know Gettysburg from Pearl Harbor. But I never thought he'd end up working on some rotting old lobster wharf, dating one of the local girls, and up to his armpits in rotting fish in Bumfuck, Maine!"

"Alex!" Laura hissed.

"What the fuck did you just say, you ass-wipe?" Jamie snarled with a ferocity that surprised everyone, especially himself.

Alex noted how everyone was glaring at him. "Oh, hey, I'm sorry, I didn't mean to say anything insulting. I just thought you'd do better than *this*, Kurtz! I figured you'd be teaching high school history or working at a podunk community college somewhere by now, that's all."

"First off, Alex, the thing with you is that you never *mean* to say anything insulting, it just happens naturally. You're kinda like a skunk who doesn't *want* to stink, it just does! You can't help being ignorant and insulting because as soon as your mouth opens, nothing but shit comes out of it. Secondly, you need to apologize to Shelley and to Drake! You can insult me all you want because truthfully, I couldn't care less what you think about me. But when you go and insult my girlfriend and my friends—now, *that* I won't stand for!"

Alex puffed up his chest to take Jamie on, but when he saw the anger simmering in the group's eyes, he put his hand up as if fending off an attack. "Hey, now come on, I didn't mean to insult—"

"You keep saying that, you fucking moron, but you just repeatedly insulted this wharf and then you pretty much just called my girlfriend a slut. You better apologize and take it back, or there's going to be a *big* problem here."

"With who?"

"With me, you douche-bag!"

"Oh, is that right?" Alex sneered. "And what the hell are you gonna do, Kurtz? Do you really think that you'd last even a second going head-to-head with me?"

"God, you're such a moron! Take back those fucking insulting things you said about this wharf, Kestrel Cove, and Shelley!"

Alex snarled at the crowd, "Hey, I didn't mean to insult nobody but Kurtz. If I insulted anyone else, I didn't mean to. Come on,

Laura, let's get the hell away from this place!"

"Before you leave, Alex, let me tell you something that I've wanted to say for a long time. You know, I've always let you and your friends walk all over me because I really thought you all were better than me. But guess what? You're not. As a matter of fact, one of the best things I've discovered since living here is that I'm *way* better than you! I'm smart, funny, and I'm a pretty good guy most of the time. You, you're none of those things!"

"Yeah, right! Look at you! Look at me. You, you're living in the middle of nowhere working on a lobster wharf. Now look at me. I'm a successful banker in Boston and I drive a BMW. And don't forget, when we did go head-to-head, Kurtz, I got the girl!"

Jamie shook his head and chuckled. The stupid shallowness of Alex's comments almost meant that he didn't need to respond, but he couldn't pass up the opportunity. In a clear voice, he said, "Hey, Alex, are you a retard or something? I've said at least four times that I don't work on this goddamn wharf—I work on that lobster boat down there! Do I need to get you a flowchart with a lot of pictures so you can finally understand that concept?

"And as for the other stupid drivel you just uttered, battles and wars, buddy, battles and wars. The Confederates won a lot of battles during the Civil War, but they ultimately lost the war. Oh, yeah, that's right, you don't know the difference between Gettysburg and Pearl Harbor, do you? Well, you see, if you lose a battle, you can always come back. But if you lose the war, you're just a loser. So yeah, you won the girl, but in the end, you're nothing but a big, stupid loser. Your job? Your fancy car? I'd bet my left nut that your rich daddy gave you both of them—you didn't earn any of it. So, what does that say about you? You're nothing but a selfish, self-absorbed asshole no one really likes—except other self-absorbed assholes. So sure, I lost the battle for Laura, but in the end, you've lost the war, buddy. Battles and wars."

Alex looked around at the spectators and saw that they were not only enjoying Jamie's oration, they seemed to be laughing at *him*. He clenched his jaw angrily when he spoke. "Ya see, Kurtz, this is what I'm talking about! You spout shit from the Civil War to defend yourself. You know, you could never fit in with normal people at school, and now I see that you'll never make it with normal people in the outside world, either!"

Laura gasped. "Alex!"

"God, you're such a dumb-ass! Well, guess what, Alex? I like it here in Kestrel Cove. And I really like these people here. I trust them. And they like me—or at least tolerate me—just the way I am. I'll take any of these people over you and your circle of friends anytime! So, go on now, take your lobsters up to your fraternity brothers and drink your beers and laugh at everybody you think is less than you. You're all the kings of the whole world, and we're all just the peons! But just know that you've embarrassed yourself here on this wharf. And, what's worse, you've embarrassed Laura with your big mouth and your pea brain. I've got more work to do now, and since I don't work on this wharf, I don't get paid to talk nice to moronic tourists like you....Nice to see you again, Laura. Take care."

Jamie smiled at Laura, then turned and looked at Shelley as if no one else existed. Alex was ready with another rebuttal, but Jamie had ended the conversation so convincingly that he knew it would look futile and stupid to say anything more. He stood there with a red face, glancing around for an ally of any kind, but he couldn't find any, even in Laura. When he tried to grab her arm to escort her off the wharf, she threw his hand off and started walking angrily toward the car.

Jamie cooed, "Are you up for a movie at the corners tonight?"

Shelley smiled. "Why, Jamie Kurtz, of course I am!"

"Historical fiction? You know how I love history!"

"How about a romantic comedy? You know how I love romance!"

"Right. Romantic comedy it is."

Joe smiled proudly at Jamie and then nodded at Jimmy to indicate that they needed to get back to the job of winching lobsters up to the wharf. Drake and Alfred grumbled toward Alex, but went back over to the totes of lobsters to continue their sorting.

Alex turned and mumbled, "You people are all freaks!"

Everyone on the wharf seemed to have forgotten about him when they went back to their chores, and they missed his parting shot. Except Wiley. He followed Alex with a stealthy gait and intercepted him before he reached the gravel of the parking lot. He looked the *dumb-ass* up and down as if studying him to buy him, then he said menacingly, "I'll see you around, right, bub?"

Alex was ready to discount the smelly, bait-smeared fisherman standing in front of him, but when he looked into Wiley's eyes and noticed the pure and effortless malice in them, he felt a shiver of fear go through him. "Uh, yeah, sure, whatever you say."

"Good day, ma'am," Wiley said sweetly to Laura with a fox-like grin.

He watched as they got into the convertible. Alex was too obvious about avoiding eye contact as he backed the car up and started to drive away, but Wiley stood like a statue, staring after them as they drove up the hill and out of sight.

Jamie finished pitching bait, pulled the totes over to the edge, and then helped Jimmy winch them down to the deck of the boat. He was about to climb down, but Joe said, "Don't worry, Jamie, we can take her out to the mooring without you. You stay here and keep Shelley company. Throw your 'skins down here and we'll put them away. We'll see you tomorrow."

"Really?"

"Yeah."

"Okay, sure. Thanks."

As the *Bobbie C.* pulled away from the wharf, Jamie and Shelley stood for a moment and watched it go. Finally, Jamie asked, "So Shelley, what are you *really* doing here?"

"I heard you were having a bad scene with your ex on the wharf."

Jamie shook his head. "You heard that, all the way over at the store!?"

Shelley scrunched up her face. "Come on, you know how news travels in these parts."

Jamie rolled his eyes and nodded. "Well, it wasn't Laura who was the problem. All in all, she was fairly nice. It was that asshole, Alex."

"Uh-huh, the way I heard it, he was running all over you and you weren't defending yourself."

Jamie threw his arms up in the air. "Now, come on, how the hell do you know that?"

Shelley smiled and looked around. Jamie followed her eyes. He saw the people on the wharf, the fancy B&B at the top of the hill, and the clam diggers working the mud flats that the low tide had exposed, but he didn't quite see what she apparently wanted him to see. "Yeah?"

"You're part of this community now, Jamie! And whenever someone in this community is seen as needing help, we all come running."

"Wait a minute! You thought I needed help?"

"Yep, I sure did. That asshole was being mean to you."

"And you figured you needed to come here and protect me, huh?"

"Hell no!" Shelley bristled with attitude. "I figured I'd bring something to you that might make you care enough to defend yourself."

"You thought that Alex would insult you?"

"Yep, I did," Shelley said with a nod.

"And you were right."

"Yep. About that and about you finally fighting back. I was impressed with what you said, and I think everyone on the wharf was too, even Drake."

"You think so?"

"Oh, yeah! You're a virtual Daniel Webster!"

Jamie leered and said in a sensuous voice, "Oh, my sweet, you know what historical references do to me!"

"Yes, I do. So kiss me, my geek."

Jamie and Shelley kissed passionately right there on the wharf. The kiss was too big and too long, and, although the wharf rats, the captains and sternmen, and Drake, Alfred, and Wiley all knew that the young couple was in love, when they saw that momentous kiss, there seemed to be a collective enlightenment within all of them—this was no longer just a summer romance between Shelley Vanes and Jamie Kurtz; this was something much deeper. With this sudden and new understanding, some of the men smiled and some of them grimaced. Things were going to get very complicated soon.

From the moment they parked their car and started walking toward the wharf, everyone knew that the two men wearing sunglasses and overly casual clothing were federal agents. Some of the wharf rats chuckled as they watched the men's forced nonchalance, but a few others dropped to the ground and crawled out of view. Either way, as the two visitors approached Drake, who was unloading Hai's boat, they became the center of focus for the entire wharf.

"What can I do for you, agents?" Drake asked without looking up.

The two men glanced at each other with surprised looks. "Ah, sir, we were wondering if we could ask you some questions."

"Ain't that the damnedest thing?" Drake continued, keeping his eyes on the lobster tote he was weighing.

"How's that, sir?"

"You know, asking a question to ask permission to ask a question. Sorta chicken n' the egg kinda stuff, ain't it? I mean, I could deny you permission to ask me a question, but then you've already asked a question without my permission. Weird."

The men standing nearby on the wharf snickered, which caused the agents to grimace. The red-haired agent flashed his badge and talked in an overly loud voice. "All right, let's start over. I am Agent Murphy and this is Agent Timmins. We're from the Federal Bureau of Investigation. We'd like to ask you all some questions about two strangers that might have come to this very wharf recently. Maybe just a few days ago."

"We get a lot of strangers around here."

The blond agent said, "Well, these two men may have looked innocent, but we think they're more than a little dangerous."

"Ya don't say," Drake crooned. "I look around this place and all I see are morons!"

The men on the wharf snickered again, but the red-haired agent continued, "Have you noticed any strangers around here lately?"

"Well, Agent Murphy," Drake said slowly, "it's August on the coast of Maine. So, you know, we're kinda in the thick of our tourist season here. So there's been a whole host of strangers on my wharf lately."

Although the two agents had been trained extensively at Quantico on how to conduct an interview, and were veterans at doing so, they'd been forewarned by the Boston office that a bunch of Maine fishermen could be a hard bunch of nuts to crack. Initially, they had scoffed at the insinuation that they'd be challenged by *anyone*, but now they looked at each another with growing frustration.

"You would be hard-pressed to miss these guys," Agent Murphy hissed.

"Yes, that's right," Agent Timmins said with a nod, "they'd stick out like a sore thumb—they're Asian."

Drake stopped his work and turned to face Hai, and he smiled as he asked, "Hey, Hai, have you seen any slanty-eyed bastards around here lately?"

Without making eye contact with either Drake or the agents, Hai merely shook his head silently and kept unloading the lobsters from his tank.

The agents had somehow missed seeing him standing there, and now their faces flushed with embarrassment. Agent Timmins sputtered, "What we meant was that these two men weren't locals, and they would have come around asking questions before disappearing again."

Drake continued, "Asians, huh? Now, Alfred, do you remember them Jap tourists that came by a couple a weeks ago?"

"Yeah, sure, Drake. About fifty of the little buggers came down here on a bus."

"Yup, they piled off so thick that we was wondering if they sat three to a seat, since they're so little. Anyways, they came flying off that bus with their cameras clicking! I swear I was photographed about a thousand times that day!"

"Oh, yeah!" Alfred chimed in. "I figure there are three dozen photos of my boots and four dozen of my ass floating around the streets of Tokyo right now!"

Drake and Alfred started everyone laughing, except the agents, who remained stone-faced and serious. Their questioning was not only going nowhere, they were being made fools of. And they had long ago lost their patience and their sense of humor.

"No, goddammit, these weren't Japanese tourists on a bus!" Agent Murphy suddenly barked. "They were two Asian men in a rental car who probably asked for directions or some other unimportant information. After they got whatever they needed, they drove off and didn't come back. Come on guys, cut the crap! We're trying to find these two individuals before they do something bad. It's a matter of national security. So, do you remember them?"

"Well," Drake said slowly while scratching his chin, "them Jap tourists headed off in their bus and didn't come back."

"We've already said, sir, that these two men were not Japanese!" Agent Timmins said.

Drake grinned. "Weren't Japs, huh? I gotta tell ya, I've never been too good at telling them Asians apart." He turned back to Hai and said, "Sorry, Hai!"

The men on the wharf chuckled, and then Hai said something softly in Vietnamese to his sternman, who grinned with a quick burst of humor.

The agent pointed at Hai. "What was that you just said, sir?"

Hai, looking down, said softly, "I said that I have the same problem with Caucasians."

The men on the wharf now roared with laughter. The agents looked at one another, signaling that it was time to leave. They both knew that they were not going to get the information they needed from this bunch.

"I wonder," Alfred suddenly interjected, "are Arabs considered Asians?"

Drake looked up from the lobster he was measuring. "Now, Alfred, why in the hell would you ask a dumb-ass question like that? These men were just asking about some Japs, and you go and start asking a question about Muslims."

"They weren't Japanese," Agent Timmins reiterated with a sigh.

Alfred scratched his chin and continued, "Well, I didn't ask about

Muslims, Drake. Arabs live on the Arabian Peninsula and speak Arabic. Muslims, on the other hand, are any people who worship Allah and his prophet Muhammad. Most Arabs are Muslim, but most Muslims are not Arab. See?"

"Excuse me, gentlemen, we've gotta leave now. If you remember anything about any unusual visitors, please call the FBI office in Boston."

"Alfred, what in God's green earth are you talking about? You're rambling like a drunken washerwoman!"

"It'd be like saying that Americans and Christians are the same. Sure, most Americans are Christian, but not all Christians are American. They live in Europe, Asia, Africa, and even Australia."

"Don't forget South America and Latin America!" one of the wharf rats enthusiastically added.

"Well, we'll leave our card in the office," Agent Murphy said in exasperation.

Drake waved his hand as if he were swatting at a bumblebee. "I'm completely goddamn stunned here! What the hell are you talking about, Alfred?"

Vincent stepped forward. "Ya know, Alfred's right. I was watching the Discovery Channel last night about Muslim pilgrims going to Mecca and they were from Indonesia, Russia, and even America. Hell, with most of 'em, ya couldn't tell they was Muslims just by looking at 'em!"

Drake swiveled his head like he was watching a tennis match. "I can't believe my goddamn ears! First, Alfred starts asking bone-head questions about the difference between Muslims and Arabs, then you start spouting information from the Discovery Channel, Vincent. I thought you were homeless and living on my wharf! So how the hell are you watching cable television in the first place? Jesus H. Christ, I'm surrounded by a bunch of imbeciles! No wonder nothing gets done around here—you guys are all brain damaged!"

"Aw, Drake, come on now. I was only saying that, since Arabia is technically part of the continent of Asia, Arabs must be considered Asians. So when those two FBI agents just asked about some Asians coming here, we all had images of Japs or Chinks or Gooks—no offense Hai—in our minds, but these guys they're pursuing could've been Middle Eastern. That's all I was saying. Maybe we misunderstood the original question. Maybe they're looking for Arabs. Is that what you're looking for? Hey, where'd those guys go?"

Everybody turned and saw that the agents had started back toward their car. The wharf rats were smiling because they'd been successful in frustrating the federal agents, but Drake's face clearly showed that he was not done arguing with Alfred and Vincent quite yet.

"They were North Koreans!"

Heads swiveled toward the shouted words—which had come from the direction of Hai's boat. Hai stood against the gunwale of the boat, looking up at the men on the wharf and twisting his baseball hat in his hands. The two agents had frozen in their tracks at the sound of those shocking words, but now they turned and nearly *ran* back to the edge of the wharf. "What was that you just said, sir?"

"The strangers were…North Koreans," Hai said with a bowed head.

The agents exchanged a knowing look. "And what did you say your name was again?"

"I didn't."

"What is your name, sir?"

"Hai Hien Ngo."

"Well, Mr. Ngo, when did these men come to the wharf, and how could you tell they were North Korean?"

Hai shuffled his feet and looked at the men staring intently down at him. His answer was visibly painful to him, and he coughed nervously before he spoke. "I grew up outside the city of Hanoi in the People's Republic of Vietnam. When I was inducted into the army, we had many foreign advisors around to train us. Some were Russians. Some were Chinese. And there were a few North Korean advisors, too. Once you've been around North Koreans, you never forget how to spot them. The strangers who came to the wharf the other day were definitely North Korean."

"So, Mr. Ngo, you're from Vietnam, huh?" Agent Murphy pulled out a small notebook and started to write in it. "That's a very interesting detail."

Drake stiffened. "Hey, wait a goddamn minute here! You can't talk to this man with that tone on my goddamn wharf! Hai has lived here in Kestrel Cove for over twenty years now. That means he's lived here as long as he lived over there. He's a red-blooded American as much as you and me, except he has slanty eyes, eats raw fish with rice, and has a house full of monkey-like nephews and nieces and cousins and God knows who else. So put that goddamn notebook away, Agent Murphy, and listen to what the man has to say."

The FBI men shrugged and Agent Murphy put away his notebook. Hai smiled a quick warm smile at Drake, and then continued talking to the agents. "They came here around noon last Wednesday. I was at the wharf early because I was going to sell my lobsters to Mr. Drake early. My wife want to make *Pho* and I had to go to Portland to get the ox tails and spices."

"*Fuh?*" said Agent Timmins.

"*Pho*," Alfred corrected. "It's Vietnamese beef soup."

The agents looked at one another and then at the rest of the wharf rats nodding their heads. Agent Timmins put his palms up. "Oh, come on now! How do you all know that *Pho* is Vietnamese beef soup?"

Alfred answered for the group. "Like Drake said, Hai's been here in Kestrel Cove for over twenty years. Every Vietnamese New Year, he invites us all over to his house for the Tet celebration. He and his wife serve up *Pho*. It's wicked delicious! I even tried to get the recipe from his wife one time, but she wouldn't give me her secret ingredient. I tried to drink it out of her, but she drank me under the goddamn table!"

The men on the wharf laughed, including Hai and his sternman.

Agent Murphy quickly continued, "So, it was noon when you saw these North Koreans…"

"Yes," nodded Hai, "I saw them ask for directions."

"To what?"

"Don't know."

"Who did they ask?"

"Don't know."

"Is he here right now?"

"Don't know. Didn't see his face. Saw North Koreans."

"Did you approach these strangers to talk with them?"

"No."

"You saw a bunch of North Koreans on this wharf and you

didn't go up and say anything to them?"

"I keep to myself. No talk to strangers."

"Even when you knew they were North Koreans?" Agent Murphy quizzed with an uplifted eyebrow.

"If you had not talked to me and others on the wharf today, I would never have talked to two FBI agents."

The men on the wharf nodded in unison, further angering the two agents. Agent Timmins wagged his finger at Hai. "Seems like you know more than you're saying."

"No, that is all I know. Two North Koreans came to wharf asking for directions. That's all I know, truly," Hai said, still working on the baseball cap.

"I dunno," said Agent Timmins with a note of suspicion. "Maybe we should bring you and your whole family in to talk about this some more."

"You'll need a small fleet of school buses to transport his family," Drake sniped.

The wharf rats chortled at Drake's joke, but Agent Timmins pointed his finger at Hai again. "Oh, yes! Once everyone's in different rooms and we start asking the tough questions, Mr. Ngo, I'm sure that we'll find out what we need to. We'll check everyone's immigrant status, and then we'll see how your financials add up. If there are any holes, we could even send some of your people packing!"

The murmurs on the wharf were accompanied by the shuffling of rubber boots on the wooden planks. When Agent Murphy looked around, he saw that the men were now edging closer to them and that the pathway back to their car was blocked. Several of the men held sharpened ice hooks in their hands, and while he wasn't actually nervous, he didn't like the way things were escalating. "Aw, I don't think there's a need for all that, do you, Bob? I mean, if Mr. Ngo says that's all he knows, I believe him. Don't you?"

Agent Timmins caught the concern in his partner's voice, and as he scanned the scene, he quickly grasped their situation. He nodded. "Yeah, that sounds good to me. But listen, if anyone wants to tell more of what they know, come and talk to…uh, sir, what's your name?"

"Mr. Drake Muldoon. Are you gonna bring me and my family

into your offices and audit our asses, too? 'Cause if you do, you'll be bringing in the sheriff and some other important people from around here. It'd be a mighty interesting event."

Agent Timmins chuckled. "No, Drake, we don't need to do that!"

"Only my friends call me Drake!"

"No, Mr. Muldoon, we don't need to do anything rash," Agent Murphy said calmly, "but if anyone comes forward as their memories clear, could you call us at this number? If someone remembers what they were asking directions to, please let us know. I cannot stress to you enough—these men are potentially dangerous, so knowing where they wanted to get to would help us stop something bad from happening. No names, just info. Okay?"

Drake took the business card from the agent and examined it. It was nothing but a business card, but he studied the front and the back as if there might be a secret message somewhere on it. He held it high up in the air. "Okay, if anyone remembers anything about those North Korean strangers after these two agents leave, let me know and I'll call it in and tell them, without any names!"

The agents looked satisfied. But when they turned to go back to their car, their path was still blocked by some of the wharf rats. Drake roared, "What the hell? Get out of the way and let these nice federal agents get back to their car!"

A pathway opened like the Red Sea and the FBI agents headed straight to their car and drove up the hill. It wasn't until they were out of sight that Drake finally hollered, "What do you think I pay all you slackers to do—just stare up the road? Get back to work!"

Within a minute, the wharf appeared deserted again, except for Alfred and Drake, who resumed unloading Hai's boat. When Drake bent down for a tote of lobsters, Hai said quietly, "Thank you, Mr. Drake."

"Yeah, yeah. But I got a word of warning for you, Hai."

"Yes, Mr. Drake?"

"Next time you see two FBI agents, keep your head down and your mouth closed. They may be from the government, but they're nothing but fucking pricks, all of them. I know you like to tell the truth and all, but that can be twisted and woven into a better net than those mackerel nets drying over there. Got it?"

"Yes, Mr. Drake. I thank you anyway."

"Hey, what are friends for?"

Just then Vincent came out of the shadows and made his way over to Drake. "Aw, Vincent, what the hell do you want? To tell me more about the goddamn Muslims on the Hajj?"

The skinny man looked around nervously. "Naw, Drake, I gotta tell ya something."

Drake looked at him like he was an alien. He waited, then finally said, "I ain't got all day, Vincent. If you can't get your brain to work right now, why don't you go back to your nap and think about it some more, okay?"

"It was me those North Koreans talked to," Vincent said, his eyes darting left and right.

Drake stopped measuring lobsters. "Yeah?"

"Hai was covering for me. It was me he saw talking to them, but he didn't rat me out."

"Hai's like that—he's an honorable man. What do you remember about your conversation with them North Koreans?"

Vincent rubbed his hands together. "They asked for directions. I told them how to get there and they left."

"Where did they want directions to?"

Vincent cleared his throat. His eyes shifted away from Drake's as the big man raised his eyebrows. "*Where*, Vincent?"

"Bill Hand's place."

"The North Koreans asked for directions to Bill Hand's house?"

"Yeah."

"And you told them?"

Vincent cleared his throat again. "Jesus, I didn't know! They looked just like they were some Chinks who were lost. I've had lots of other people ask for directions to Bill's place over the years, and I've never thought to not tell them. I mean, he's kind of a celebrity, right? Lots of foreigners want to meet with him. I didn't know these guys might be North Korean terrorists!"

"Aw, keep your halter top on there, Vincent! You didn't do anything wrong. Thanks for comin' and tellin' me."

"Are you gonna call the FBI?" Vincent asked with wide eyes.

Alfred looked at Drake with the same question on his face, but Drake's answer was quick and short. "We take care of our own first here in Kestrel Cove. I'll call Bill Hand to let him know that two FBI agents came here today asking about North Koreans looking for directions to his house—just to warn him and all. But we'll just keep all that other stuff to ourselves. Bill Hand's business is his business, got it? So, now go away and sniff some more glue and forget all that other stuff, okay?"

"Okay, Drake."

Vincent slid away and disappeared into the shadows. Drake watched his retreat and shook his head before beginning to measure lobsters with Alfred again. After they worked a little more in silence, Alfred finally said, "Well, that's kinda interesting, huh, Drake?"

"What's interesting?" Drake deadpanned.

27

The month of September remained similar enough to August to fool some into thinking that summer would never end, but then October came in cold and dry, and everyone had to admit that the herald of true fall was blowing its horn, loud and clear. Morning frosts were now common, and the woods were now fully committed to their transformation into a patchwork of oranges, browns, and reds. More than a few leaves had already fluttered to the ground. The summer residents had all gone home, and the roads were now empty and the tracts of summer cottages were dormant again as the peninsula took on the comfortable feeling of the off-season.

Because Shelley was spending the long Columbus Day weekend with Clara to help her plan and prepare for the arrival of the baby, Jamie woke up alone in the tent. He shivered as he got dressed, and then hurried into the store to grab a cup of warm coffee. And, even though they were taking the day off from fishing, he headed down to the wharf. This trip was partly out of habit and partly because he enjoyed walking through the autumn woods, but as he trekked along the pipeline, Jamie thought about how the lobstering was starting to slow down. There were fewer lobsters in each trap and in the lobster tank at the end of the day, and since the days were getting noticeably shorter, they were having to work just as fast to get through the gear before the early dusk. Jamie was unsure what all of this meant for him in terms of keeping his job, but he'd already decided to just keep working as hard as he could, and let Joe make those tough decisions whenever he needed to.

The wharf was deserted. During the previous week, Drake had hoarsely commanded the wharf rats to get everything ready to shut down for the winter. The ancient industrial power washer was rolled out of the storage shed, and several men had worked the hose like firemen to blast the dirt, scales, and grime off the decaying wooden structure. Once he was satisfied with the cleaning and organizing, Drake had quietly laid off some of the men. Jamie was hard-pressed to figure out exactly who was missing, but there were definitely fewer men working on the wharf these days. Joe had told him that Drake either found them menial jobs around the wharf or just quietly slipped them enough money to keep them in food or beer through the challenging winter months.

Jamie's moment of solitude was shattered when Joe's truck came down the hill and pulled up next to him. When Joe rolled down his window and beckoned him closer, he was surprised to see Jimmy sitting in the passenger seat. His captain grinned. "What the hell are you doing down here, college boy? You get the day off, and you still come down to the wharf?"

"I keep *tellin'* y'all, he's retarded!" Jimmy said.

Jamie gave him the finger, but then he asked, "What are you guys up to?"

"We've been looking for you! Now that we've found you, we're all going treasure hunting."

Jamie smiled. "Really? Should I get a shovel and make a map?"

"Just hop in, shithead, we're late."

"You're serious?"

Jimmy leaned across Joe and bawled, "Oh, shut your goddamn trap and hop into the fucking truck!"

Jamie shook his head as he walked around the truck and climbed in. They roared back up the hill, and Jimmy tousled his hair. "You know, college boy, we wouldn't fuck with you so much if it weren't so much damn fun!"

Joe smiled devilishly. "Yep, that's definitely true."

The two men laughed and elbowed Jamie in the ribs from both sides. He fought them off and then asked, "So, where are we *really* going?"

"The dump," Joe declared.

"Why in the hell would we go there?"

"'Cause that's where the treasures are—duh."

"I'm not sure I follow you."

Joe exhaled loudly. "When the summer officially ends, those

Ritchie Riches who own all the summer cottages close them down for the winter. As part of the process, they throw out things they don't want anymore. But since they've got more money than God, their trash is pure treasure to us. So every Columbus Day, everyone gathers at the dump as soon as it opens so we can pick through it all before it gets destroyed. We're late to the party already 'cause we had to drive all over the place to find you!"

"*Really?* People go to the dump just to pick through the trash?"

"It ain't all trash, college boy!" Jimmy said as he cuffed Jamie on the back of the head. "Most of it's in cherry condition. I heard that Clyde Simmons furnished an entire room of his trailer with what he picked last year. Inside his falling-down double-wide, he has a living room with an expensive Italian leather couch with only a few scratches on it, a nice big TV, an older DVD player, and a rocking stereo system."

When they got to the dump, there were several cars parked outside the gate. Joe clucked his tongue and nudged Jamie. "Ya see? 'Cause of you, we're late. We probably missed all the good stuff."

"Oh, bite me," Jamie said quietly.

The two men laughed at his response, and then the three of them got out and started walking toward the recycling and transfer station. There was an aluminum trailer on blocks with a hand-painted OFFICE sign on the door, and a man came out and greeted them as they approached. Jimmy boomed out, "Any good shit this year, Marty?"

The man smiled and said, "Oh yeah, there're some real treasures back there, that's for sure. What're you guys looking for?"

"Ah, you know, the usual—electronics and furniture," Joe said.

"Yep, well, there's a lot of that stuff back there. Good dining room table that needs a little refinishing, but the wood's solid. There's an amazing set of cabinets. Some really good DVD players on the other side of the compactor. There's even a car this year!"

"Bullshit!" Joe scoffed.

"Naw, I'm serious. A nice little rice-burner that's a bit rusty, but it runs real good. I guess the owners didn't want to be *inconvenienced* with taking it all the way to the junkyard in town."

"Hey, Jamie, you know anyone who needs a car? Heh-heh," Jimmy joked.

"How many trucks has Drake filled so far?" Joe asked with a snicker.

"I think he's on number two right now. Well, good luck, gentlemen."

They continued on toward the compactor, and when Jimmy saw something that caught his attention, he peeled away with an excited skip. When Jamie hesitated, Joe pointed at him. "Do you really need a shopping list, college boy?"

Jamie nodded. "Yeah, I guess so. I just have no idea what I need."

"Appliances, dude. When you and Shelley move into your new place, you're gonna need new appliances."

Before Jamie could challenge Joe's "new place" comment, Bill Hand came around the corner with several coils of cables and wires wrapped around his shoulder. Joe slipped away silently as Jamie sputtered, "Wait, Bill. *You're* at this thing?"

"Damn right! I've been waiting for that Patterson chap who owns that compound with the giant antennas to bring his trash to the dump. He's an electrical engineer from Boston and he just rewired his whole place, and I knew the bastard would dump it all here!"

"What do you need wire and cable for?"

"Oh, you know, I always have little projects going on here and there. Nothing beats free wire, Jamie. And, if I didn't take it, it would just be rotting in the dump or be burned up in the incinerator. This way, I'm getting some good stuff for free and helping clean up the planet. So, you must be looking for stuff for the new place, right?"

Jamie chuckled. "Everyone seems to know something I don't."

"Shelley asked me about renting the gatehouse the other day, but I told her that I've got too many guests staying there this fall. I put her in touch with a lady who rents her property really cheap. The owner's a little crazy, but she lives away in Florida. From what I've heard, Shelley talked with her and you guys have it if you want it. The place is small and furnished, but it has crappy appliances. So if I were you, I'd look for some of those today. See you later."

Jamie watched him walk away, and he thought about how it was still a little flummoxing that everyone learned about things going on in his life before he did. But when he saw something in a pile that was on his new mental list, he forgot all about that, and headed over to get it.

When their picking was finished, the three men had so many items that Joe needed to back the truck right up to the gate so they could put their booty into the bed. Joe had found a couple of good televisions, a nice DVD player, and some perfectly good hand tools. Jimmy had himself a complete set of handcrafted hickory cabinets that were perfect for the kitchen rebuild he was going to do during the winter. As for Jamie, he'd found a coffeemaker, a blender, a pasta maker, a knife set, and an electric skillet. All of the items appeared to be barely used, and he gingerly put them into back of the truck. A worried look came over his face. "Geesh, I don't know if I have enough money for all this!"

Jimmy shook his head. "Are you *sure* you're not retarded? We just picked this stuff out of the dump, shithead! It's free!"

Joe added, "You probably would have to pay for the car if it has a title, but the rest of the stuff is free. You see—it really *is* like finding treasure!"

They drove along for a while, obviously not toward the wharf or the campsite, and Jamie started to squirm. "I know you hate my stupid questions, but where are we going now?"

Jimmy and Joe looked at one another. Finally, Joe said, "He's friggin' adorable, ain't he? I'm going to miss having him around this winter."

"I know, right? He's so innocent and naïve, but it works for him. Like a helpless puppy.

"Oh, fuck you both!" Jamie laughed. "Just tell me what we're doing next."

Jimmy clamped his hand onto Jamie's shoulder. "You see, college boy, Columbus Day marks the beginning of the end for us."

"What do you mean?"

Joe spoke evenly. "I know that you've noticed that the lobster season is winding down, right?"

Jamie nodded. "Yep, there seems to be less of them in the traps each day."

"Yeah, well, that's what happens. The bugs start to migrate offshore to find the warmer water, so the places that we've been fishing successfully get abandoned. We've put enough gear out in the deeper water, but it's going to be harder to get out there as the fall weather gets worse and worse. And, after the initial run, the fishing out there will continue to quiet down until it stops altogether. Pretty soon, we'll stop going fishing every day, and it'll be just a couple of times a week, maybe. Then we'll start to haul the gear out of the water to store it for the winter. When all the gear is out, the boat comes out. That usually happens after Christmas."

"Okay," Jamie said uncertainly, "but we still have the rest of October and all of November before that happens, don't we?"

Jimmy cuffed him on the head again. "What happens every year in November in Maine, college boy?"

"Thanksgiving?"

"Think, boy, think! What happens during November and December? Come on, think about it."

Jamie had no idea, so he just shrugged. Jimmy roared with frustration and pantomimed the shooting of guns. Jamie was confused. "Civil War reenactments?"

"Hunting season, you moron!"

"Oh."

The guys rolled their eyes at each other. Joe growled, "Oh, I forget that you're a tree-hugger. You probably think hunting's bad and we shouldn't shoot Bambi, huh?"

"No, I don't really care one way or the other. I've never been hunting in my life and I probably never will."

"Oh, you're gonna go this year!" Jimmy said eagerly. "You ain't got much choice."

"Whenever the weather makes it too hard to go out lobstering, we're gonna go hunting. Most of the next two and half months we'll be hunting, hauling, and then hunting again."

"Okay," Jamie with a shrug.

Jimmy slapped his hand back down onto Jamie's shoulder and said in a patronizing voice, "And then, when the snow starts flying and the boats are out of the water, what do you think the people of Kestrel Cove do to enjoy the winter?"

"Ski?"

Joe couldn't help but laugh. "Now *there's* a fucking image! Can you just picture Drake on skis? Or Hai? Or Nigger Bob? Oh shit, that's funny! No, dummy, as soon as the snow's thick enough, we all go snow-mobiling. Using the pipeline, we can head past the Corners and hop onto the trails under the power lines up there. You can go almost any-where, even all the way up into Canada! We did that a few years ago. That was fucking awesome! We got so rip-roaring drunk and ended up at the strip joint with that hottie from Ottawa—what was her name?"

"Monique," Jimmy said, exhaling cigarette smoke out the window.

Joe grinned at the memory. "Monique! What a bod on her! Ah, that woman had talents! Anyway, the point I'm trying to make is that today is the day that things begin to really change for us. Now that we've all got our treasures, we spend the rest of the day scouting the best places to shoot a deer during hunting season and then we go shopping for snowmobiles."

"But don't you both already have snowmobiles?" Jamie asked.

Jimmy poked Jamie with his elbow. "'Course we do, retard."

Jamie tried to smack him on the knee, but missed. "Then why do we need to go *shopping* for snowmobiles?"

Joe, who was smirking at the way Jimmy continued to mug Jamie, said in exasperation, "You never know when you'll find a better ma-chine at a good deal. Just 'cause you've got something doesn't mean you don't always keep your eyes open!"

"That's right, *estupido*. You should never stop with just being sat-isfied; you have to keep looking for something better."

The double meaning was not lost on Jamie. "Hey, we're still talk-ing about snowmobiles, right?"

Jimmy mussed Jamie's hair again and turned up the radio, and Joe punched the accelerator enough to push them back into their seats. Jamie couldn't help but notice that his question had gone unanswered.

After they had driven around the peninsula to find good hunting spots, it was clear that what the two men were really looking for was any place where Joe could park his truck, roll the window down, and still have a shot at a deer in a clearing or meadow. Jamie was almost certain that hunting from a vehicle was probably illegal, but he re-frained from asking about this to avoid additional teasing and abuse.

By the time they were headed into town for lunch, Jamie was completely disoriented. All their meandering on the seemingly aimless and irrational back roads of the peninsula had gotten him so turned around, he was pretty sure he wouldn't be able to find his way home. They stopped at a diner for a bite to eat, then spent the rest of that afternoon stopping at each and every snowmobile they saw for sale on the side of the road. By the end of the day, Jamie had been completely schooled about snowmobiles and snowmobiling—the different makes, engines, seats, suspensions, repair costs, fuel additives, clothing options, helmets, and trails. Even Joe and Jimmy were impressed with the amount of information the kid had absorbed.

Back at the store, Jamie put his spoils from the dump in the back of Shelley's truck before going inside to see her. She was reading a copy of Edward Abbey's *Desert Solitaire* at her register, and she dog-eared the book and put it down when she saw him coming. She smirked at him. "So, did you buy a sled?"

"So you knew what we were going to do today, huh?"

She shrugged. "This isn't my first Columbus Day in Kestrel Cove, ya know."

"You could have told me," Jamie said with a smile.

"And ruin the surprise?" Shelley grinned back. She leaned forward and gave him a kiss on the lips. "So the guys didn't convince you to buy one, huh?"

"No, of course not. I'm not going to buy a snowmobile."

"Which one was your favorite?"

Jamie pursed his lips. "I know you're thinking that I'm going to say the 1964 Ski-Doo we saw near the Corners because I love historical stuff so much, but I was more impressed with the Polaris Indy 500 that we saw near the post office."

"Were they asking more than two thousand for it?"

"Just a hair."

"Yep, that's too much."

"Yep. I wouldn't have offered more than nineteen fifty."

Suddenly it hit Jamie that he was talking with his girlfriend about snowmobiles, of all things, and that made him smile. He had to admit that she was sexier than ever at this very moment.

She took a sip from her drink. "Did you find a good spot to shoot deer?"

"Yeah, Joe and Jimmy had some good places all scoped out."

Shelley nodded. "What did you notice about that clearing near the old McClintock Farm?"

Jamie remember the spot very well. In the clearing was an overgrown ancient orchard of gnarled and craggy apple trees that each had a pile of mealy and rotten apples on the ground around them. The guys got very excited because they were convinced that the apples would bring the deer right in like bait. And it was within easy reach of the road and had a nice place to park the vehicle with a good view of it all. But Jamie began to wonder why Shelley seemed to be testing him. He paused for a moment, then answered truthfully, "It was one of the best places we scouted. It had bait, the excellent possibility for ambush, clear sight lines, and a great place to park a vehicle. It was the perfect spot. If I were a hunter, I'd definitely camp out there."

"Yeah, that's all true, but the people who own that old farmhouse don't like hunters, and they're real quick to call the game warden."

"Yep, Joe and Jimmy said they're real assholes. Uh, I didn't know that you hunted, Shelley."

She smiled coyly. "There's a lot of things about me that you don't know, Jamie Kurtz."

"Do you want to know what I got at the dump?"

"What treasures did you find?"

"I got a coffeemaker, a blender, a pasta maker, a knife set, and an electric frying pan."

"Ooh, that sounds good. But you didn't pick up a TV and a DVD player?"

Jamie shook his head sadly, but Shelley smiled at him. "That's okay. It's just that winters in Kestrel Cove can be so long and dark, having something to watch makes the time go faster. I guess we'll have to find other ways to amuse ourselves, huh?" She winked.

Jamie responded with a smile, but then looked at her with a serious expression. "You know what else I got at the dump?"

"No, what?"

"The information from everyone that you and I have picked out a nice cottage to rent."

"Oh, shit, I forgot to tell you about that, didn't I?"

"Kinda. I mean, we've talked about the fact that we need to move into a place together this fall. I just didn't know that we were actively looking."

"Oh, I totally spaced and didn't tell you about any of that. After I talked to Bill Hand last week, everything started to fall into place fast. I guess I've been distracted helping Clara get ready for the baby. Oh, Jamie, I'm so sorry!"

"No, it's okay, Shelley. Bill told me that our place is owned by someone who lives away, and that it's really nice."

"Oh, it's so cute! It's private, but it isn't too far from everything."

"I can't wait to see it. When can we move in?"

"Next weekend."

"Next weekend?"

"Too soon?"

"No, of course not. Is there any way that I can see it before then?"

Shelley stood up abruptly. "You know what? I'm closing the store down in about twenty minutes. Why don't we head over there then?"

"That'd be great. The stuff I scored at the dump is in the back of your truck. We could leave it all in the cottage and not have to tote it around with us."

When they turned onto the driveway of their new place, Jamie got excited. As Shelley had said, it was far enough from the store and the center of Kestrel Cove to have some privacy, but close enough to the pipeline that he could still walk to work and get around. The gravel roadway went across a large open field, and Jamie felt compelled to say, "We're gonna need someone to plow us out this winter. The wind is going to whip across this field and pile the snow high and deep."

"Plow?" Shelley responded. She hadn't thought about that.

The driveway ended at two small, low-lying cottages. Both looked like they might only contain one room, but it was clear as they got closer that they were bigger than they'd first appeared. Shelley pointed to the cottage on the left. "That's ours! The other one is the landlord's, and she only comes here in the summer. We'll probably never see her. We just need to send our rent checks to her every month, and make sure that we keep an eye on her cottage, too."

"How much is it?"

"Only four hundred dollars! And that includes the electricity! It's also furnished, so we can live comfortably without spending too much."

"Wow, why is it so cheap?"

Shelley looked sheepishly back at him. "Well, mostly because we're earning our keep by watching the other place."

"And the other reason?"

"Well, the insulation isn't great, so we might be a little cold. It does have a fireplace that works, but we don't have any firewood. It'll be cozy for just the two of us, you'll see."

Once inside, Jamie saw that it actually *was* as small as it looked from the outside. There was a tiny kitchen, a living room that had a large couch and a couple of recliners that took up most of the space in front of the fireplace, and a teeny bedroom that barely held a double bed. Jamie was surprised to see the bed already made up and several boxes on it. Obviously, Shelley had brought all of this over to the cottage earlier. He pointed. "So you've started moving in, huh?"

She looked at him apologetically. "I was so excited when Mrs. Watson said yes, I couldn't help myself! I know I should've asked you about it all before, but I was so damn excited, I couldn't stop myself!"

Jamie smiled and said, "Well, it's perfect! I can't wait to move in. It's going to be an awesome place to spend the winter with you, Shelley Vanes. Oh, hey, why don't I bring those appliances inside now?"

"Sure, and while you're doing that, I'll get some things ready in the bedroom."

As he made several trips in and out, Jamie noticed that the kitchen floor actually slanted. He found an empty beer bottle on the counter, and when he laid it down on the floor, it instantly rolled toward the living room. He repeated this experiment a few times, and was surprised at the velocity the bottle gained each time. "Wow, this kitchen floor leans, huh?"

"Uh-huh," Shelley responded halfheartedly.

"I mean, any water that gets on the floor is going to run right into the living room."

"I guess."

Jamie was perturbed by her apparent indifference, and he walked over to the entrance of the bedroom to confront her. He didn't notice the shimmering candlelight coming from the room until he'd turned the corner and stood in front of Shelley. She was on the bed and completely naked, and she was smiling a devilish grin. "Hey, stud, wanna christen our new place?"

Jamie did not need to think about that offer at all, and he began to disrobe with wild abandon. But just before he was about to jump onto the bed, Shelley said, "Why don't you make sure the front door is latched. With your luck, college boy, half of Kestrel Cove might show up here at just the wrong moment!"

As Jamie and Shelley began to move their stuff into the cottage, they both realized for the first time that their new place had no closets. They were at a loss for what to do with all their clothes until they found a pair of antiquated wheeled coat racks hiding behind the curtains of the living room windows. When they located a small bureau next to these racks, Jamie smiled impishly. "Well, since our clothes will all be out here, it just means we'll have to get dressed and undressed right here in the living room. And you thought we were going to be bored without a TV this winter!"

Taking down the tent and leaving the campsite proved to be more sentimental for Jamie than he'd anticipated. So much had happened there. He'd fallen in love with Shelley, had the infamous fistfight with the summer kids, and enjoyed the nightly parties with his friends around the fire ring. And even though the site looked overused and dirty, he felt a funny lump in his throat as he walked away from it. Their little cottage was going to provide much better protection from the elements, and moving in together for the winter certainly upped the status of their relationship, but Jamie had to admit that he was sad as he got into Shelley's truck and they drove toward their new home.

When they got to the cottage, they were surprised to see a huge pile of firewood lying across their driveway. The wood, all nicely split and cut to length, formed a gigantic pyramid before their front door. It smelled oddly of bait. On it was a handwritten note that said:

> *Here's a housewarming present for you, Shelley*
> *—both literally and figuratively!*

We hope you have a warm winter of good memories.

Love,

Drake and the boys at the wharf

"Wow! I can't believe Drake did this!"

Jamie shrugged. "That's why it reeks, I guess. He brought it over in the bait truck."

Shelley tilted her head. "It's amazingly thoughtful. I can't believe he cut and split that for us."

"Not really 'us,' Shelley. The note is only to you."

"You're implied in several places."

"Can I also be implied when it comes to stacking it all?"

"In your dreams, college boy!"

The end of October was marked by the onset of some ugly weather, and Jamie knew that its arrival ushered in the beginning of the scenario that Joe had forecast on Columbus Day. The seas became so rough that the rolling deck made all of their jobs unpleasant and frustrating, and the entire mood of the crew began to sour. Each morning, it took longer and longer for Joe and Jimmy to get motivated enough to get out of the truck to go fishing, and at the end of each hard day, it was now common for Joe to announce loudly when they were back on dry land, "Well, that supremely sucked."

One morning, Jamie arrived at the wharf to find the wind howling and the bay raging white with surf. The air was cold and raw, and the stiff breeze was biting, so when Joe and Jimmy told him to join them inside the cab of the truck to discuss options, he gladly got in. As soon as Jimmy shut the door, however, he realized he was trapped. Joe drove back up the hill and announced that they were going hunting instead of fishing, and Jamie glumly submitted to the fact that he'd have to spend the entire day sitting in the truck near one of the spots they'd scouted just waiting for a deer that would never come.

Afterwards, when Joe and Jimmy invited themselves in for a beer at the cottage, they discovered that the college boy was in a foul mood. He wasn't in the right frame of mind to entertain them or put up with their usual razzing, and he snapped, "Are the rest of our days going to be like this one?"

Joe noticed the acid in his tone. "Nope, not quite. But we did warn you that these days were coming."

"Yeah, well, I didn't make any money today."

"None of us made money today, dummy!" Jimmy said. "Joe and I both get paid only when we catch lobsters. We didn't catch any today, so we didn't make any money, neither. So—no pun intended—we're all in the same goddamn boat."

Jamie backed off a little. "Hey, I'm sorry for sounding like such a dink. I'm just trying to figure out what I'm going to do now that the season is ending, that's all. I'm not used to having rent payments to make, even if they are pretty small."

Both men nodded their acceptance of his apology, but Joe started shaking his head. "Truth is, I'm done. Normally, the weather changes much more gradually and the lobsters stay pretty good for a couple more weeks. But the weather's gotten nasty right quick, and the lobsters seem to be ahead of schedule on their retreat. I've come to the decision that we're going to start winding things down right now. So whenever the weather's shitty, we're going hunting. And when the weather is halfway decent, Jimmy and I will start pulling up the gear."

"Wait—you and Jimmy? Not me?"

"Nope, we won't need you out there on the boat. I'm going to take the bait table and even the lobster tank off the boat to free up the deck space. We'll put all the keepers in bins and Jimmy can band them later. We'll bring the gear to the wharf, and we'll need your help then to put them in the truck and stack them to the trap yard by my house."

"What will I do while you're out hauling the gear?"

Jimmy snorted. "You could always help Jerry finish working on your car! Har-har!"

Joe sat up and his eyes were electric. "Naw, you know what, Jamie? That's not the stupidest idea! If you offered to help him on it, you just might get it back in time for next summer!"

Jamie rolled his eyes. He'd pretty much given up hope that his car would ever get fixed. Since he'd grown so accustomed to walking everywhere, he only truly missed the Volvo on those nasty days when the rain and wind made his journey to the wharf particularly unpleasant. Another troubling thought came into his head. "So, again,

I don't want to sound like a whiny baby—"

"Too late! You opened your mouth!" Jimmy cackled.

"—but if you two are going out to get the gear and I'm staying on shore, how do I get paid? I mean, I know you guys won't be making much money, either, but, like I said, I'm just trying to figure out how I'm going to pay my rent."

Joe said, "I'll pay you for the time that you're working on land for me—from the time we load the truck and drive it to my house, and all the time it takes to stack the traps there. It won't be much, but you can piece together the work with me and some other sources."

"Like what?"

"There's always odd jobs that guys need done around here. Plus, it's about time for Danny McGovern to bring his mussel boats into the bay again. You could always lump for him."

"Lump?"

"Don't fall for it, college boy!" Jimmy interjected. "That's the worst fucking work on the planet! It ain't worth no amount of money."

Joe shook his head. "Don't listen to him, Jamie, he's just a big fucking baby. Dan brings two big, sturdy lobster boats down here from Down East, and they drag the bay with a heavy metal rake for mussels. When the boats are full, they drop the bagged mussels off on the beach at high tide, and go back out and fill the boats up again. Then they come in to the same beach and drop off the second load. When it's dead low tide, a semi backs up to the beach and the lumpers gather all the bags onto pallets and load them into the truck. It's good money and it's all over before bedtime."

Jimmy chimed in again. "You make it sound great, Joe. Maybe you missed your calling as a military recruiter, huh? Don't listen to none of that bullshit, Jamie! Just imagine lifting heavy, muddy, and sharp-edged bags and slogging them through the mud to load a truck in the middle of the fucking cold night. I listened to Joe once, but I ain't never gonna do that again. You couldn't pay me enough!"

"Don't worry kid, we'll find ways for you to make money enough to pay your rent!" Joe said confidently.

The next day's weather was so atrocious that Joe called Jamie at the cottage to tell him that it was a no-go for the day. Jamie walked the pipeline over to the garage to talk to Jerry, and, much to his surprise, he discovered that his Volvo had been moved inside the building. And even though Jerry wasn't working on it at the moment, the mechanic stopped what he was doing and listened to Jamie's offer to volunteer his services. The man's face did not change expression throughout his spiel, and Jamie was sure that Jerry was going to veto the plan. However, the mechanic immediately began to catch him up to speed with what had been done and what still needed to be done, and provided him with a quick training session on the use of the tools necessary for the repair.

Jerry had taken off all the crumpled body panels to reveal the damaged frame of the vehicle. Not only was it slightly bent, but the front axle had completely snapped. He'd made some phone calls to his favorite junkyards and auto shops and found an odd assortment of salvaged parts to rebuild the car. He'd even talked with a mechanic in Portland who specialized in repairing older Volvos, and he had given him a lot of good tips and advice. But the truth was, Jerry was not eager to jump into the repairs because he knew how much work it was going to be. So he was especially thrilled to hear that the college boy was volunteering to do it.

Due to the variable weather, Jamie's work routine became completely unpredictable. He had no idea what to plan for each day until he met with Joe and Jimmy in the wharf's parking lot to discuss their options. And, after they had trapped him into going hunting with them several more times, he made it a point to decline all offers to even get close to the truck. He tried to become more adept at assessing the weather to predict what was going to happen, but the guys' plans had less to do with the overall conditions and more to do with the general lack of motivation and the primal call to go hunting. At first, this all maddened him, but Shelley helped him with his frustration by making it into a game. Every morning, they evaluated the weather at the cottage, and then they'd make their predictions as to whether it was a hauling day or not. Whoever made the incorrect prognostication had to do the dishes or cook dinner, while the prizes for the correct guesses were so provocative, made both of them eager to get back home at the end of the day.

Watching Joe and Jimmy head out on the boat without him pained Jamie every time. He hadn't enjoyed the roughness of hauling traps in the stormy seas, but he hated the feeling of being left behind. He especially disliked the way it felt to no longer be a member of the team. So, after they steamed out of the cove and disappeared from sight, he would go right to work on his Volvo at the garage. But all the time he was there, he had to keep a close lookout for the *Bobbie C.*'s return. Usually, he heard her first, but as soon as he saw the boat coming into the cove, he knew that he had just enough time to stop whatever he was doing and run down to get the truck and start working for Joe.

He quickly learned how to properly stack traps. After putting the base traps running parallel to the truck bed, he put the next layer of traps perpendicular to those. He made sure to put them with their kitchens in the center and their runners on the side rails of the truck bed. The way that the traps slanted in allowed him to stack a second layer going the same way. He then put another layer of traps going parallel, and crowned the whole pile with a few single traps. Then he took the coils of rope that were already tied to the bed of the truck and threaded them through the traps to cinch down the entire stack. Each time he drove a load up the steep hill, he was so sure that all the traps were going to fall off, he found himself clenching his ass muscles. But they never did, and once he'd crested the hill successfully, he relaxed a little because all he had to do the rest of the way was drive slowly with the flashers on and avoid any sudden stops or starts. At the trap yard outside Joe's house, he unloaded the truck and stacked the traps just like Joe and Jimmy had showed him, with the rope bridles of the traps all facing out in the same direction.

Because the job of moving the traps was solitary, Jamie actually found himself enjoying his time at the garage with Jerry. Not that the man talked much. He'd worked alone for so long that the blaring country-western music from the radio, the sounds of the grinders and pneumatic wrenches, and the peal of his hammer on metal were now the only companionship the mechanic seemed to need. But Jerry was thoroughly impressed with Jamie's enthusiasm and his ability to learn quickly. The college boy had not only sat down and read all the Volvo manuals, but afterwards he didn't seem overwhelmed by the long list of tasks that the repair of the car required.

◇◇◇◇

The day that Jamie shot his first deer, the wind was blowing fiercely and riling the waters of the bay into malicious whitecaps. There was absolutely no doubt that they weren't going fishing, but Joe and Jimmy lured him into the truck by saying that they wanted to get out of the weather to discuss some important tax information. As soon as he hopped in and was between the two men, he knew that he'd been duped. And as they sped past the garage and the bent frame that he'd planned to straighten that day, he became downright pissed at the guys for kidnapping him. He was still fuming when they parked in the grove of trees off the road with the clear view of the orchard on the old McClintock farm, but he knew better than to break the silence with some kind of temper tantrum.

So as Joe and Jimmy rolled down their windows, lit up new cigarettes, and stared intently at the clearing, Jamie remained absolutely motionless for nearly five minutes. The others could feel the rage emanating from him like a red-hot coal, so Joe said in a hoarse whisper, "I know you're pissed, but the truth is, me and Jimmy have been missing you, college boy. Between not having you out on the boat, you working on your car all the goddamn time, and you and Shelley moving into that love shack, we haven't gotten a chance to hang out as much."

Jimmy blew smoke into Jamie's face. "Yeah, it ain't as much fun out there without you. There's nobody to fuck with."

Jamie had been missing them, too, and the anger he was harboring instantly thawed and dripped away. He relaxed with a sigh. "Is this where you two have been hunting this whole time?"

"Naw, we've been mostly at some of the other places. We've been waiting for this spot to get hot. Today's the day," Jimmy said. He reached behind Jamie and took a rifle off the rack in the back window. As he put a round in the chamber, his stomach made a loud gurgling sound.

Joe looked down. "Holy fuck! What the hell was that?"

"My stomach," Jimmy replied mournfully.

"No shit, Sherlock. That sounded like some bad stuff heading down the pipes there, bub. You gonna be okay?"

"That goddamn Linda! One of her coworkers gave her a recipe from a snooty food magazine and she cooked it last night."

Jamie was intrigued. "Really? What kind of recipe?"

"French."

"And?" Joe inquired.

"And it's got my guts all rumbling this morning."

"What was in this recipe?" Jamie asked with a sly smile. It was clear to him that Jimmy was avoiding something.

"Pork tenderloin."

After another loud rumble from Jimmy's stomach, Joe yelled, "Oh, for crying out loud, Jimmy! What the hell is making your stomach to sound like you're about to shit yourself?"

Jimmy closed his eyes and winced. "The pork tenderloin was cooked in brandy and prunes."

"*Prunes?* Wow! You really *are* going to shit yourself!" Joe said with glee, coughing out his cigarette smoke. "Are you telling me that you ate a shit-ton of prunes the night before we were going to sit in a truck all day and go hunting?"

"Linda didn't tell me what I was eating until I'd eaten everything. Then she said that those little black blobs were prunes. It was hard to tell with all that brandy in it."

"Meaning that you were drunker than a skunk when you ate, huh?" Joe said with a sneer.

The three men settled into a humorous conversation about erratic bathroom behavior. Then Jimmy surprised Jamie by asking if he'd ever even held a gun before. When he told him no, the initial mocking tone of his response was quickly replaced with a more instructive and helpful lesson. That led to an intimate discussion about all the strengths and shortcomings of each of their fathers. Jamie kept expecting one of them to mention something wildly inappropriate, but the conversation remained honest and genuine until it seemed that everyone was embarrassed about exposing too much about themselves.

A bottle of bourbon was brought out and they took turns sipping from it as they gradually grew vigilant for any activity in the orchard.

And although he was bored, Jamie found himself enjoying his time with Joe and Jimmy on this ridiculous hunting excursion. He knew it had less to do with shooting a deer and more to do with drinking and hanging out with his two buddies, and he fully embraced it.

Right after lunch, Jimmy's eyes began to reflect the conditions in his gut. His stomach, which had continued to gurgle throughout the morning, now groaned in such a way that he began to panic. He squirmed uncomfortably and said, "Joe! Do you have anything in this truck that I could use for toilet paper? Like a fucking roll of paper towels, maybe?"

Joe chuckled. "You're gonna shit yourself, aren't you?"

"Not if you give me some fucking paper towels and let me take care of this over in those woods!"

Joe found a scruffy roll of towels under his seat. It was clumped together from some kind of moisture, but Jimmy grabbed it like it was the baton in a relay race, threw open the door, and sprinted for the woods.

While Joe and Jamie were laughing about Jimmy's predicament, Jamie spotted the deer as it came out of the thick woods around the orchard and began to feed on the brown and rotten apples. He pointed at it and whispered, "Joe, there's a deer over by that apple tree."

Joe had eyes on it instantly. He hissed, "Jesus H. Christ, I knew this was going to happen! I just knew that a huge buck was going to show up when Jimmy took his dump! Okay, college boy, pick up that rifle and shoot the fucker."

Jamie was surprised by the weight of the rifle, but he carefully pulled it up and aimed it out the window, using the door frame for support. His heart was beating wildly. "What do I do?"

"Just aim the gun and pull the goddamn trigger!"

"I've never done this before, Joe."

Joe was about to lose his patience, but he took a deep breath and said, "Just like an arcade game, Jamie. Look through the scope and line the crosshairs up on the shoulder of that beast. Then shoot it!"

The explosion was deafening inside the truck, and Jamie was sure that he'd closed his eyes. But when the deer leaned forward and fell to the ground, he knew that he'd hit it. He looked over at Joe, and the man's mouth was wide open and his eyes were huge. It took several seconds for him to get his voice back, then he started barking orders for Jimmy to pinch off the loaf and get back in the fucking truck, and for Jamie to hang on because they had to get that damn deer before the old coots in the farmhouse snagged it. He turned on the engine and revved the accelerator just as Jimmy ran up, fumbling with his belt buckle. He'd barely gotten onto the seat of the truck before they shot forward and raced toward the orchard.

"Jesus, Joe! Don't get us killed, dude!"

"The college boy just shot one of the biggest goddamn bucks I've ever seen! We got to get to it before those old people call the game warden!"

The tires squealed as they caught traction on the pavement, and the truck fishtailed. Jamie saw the speedometer heading up past 60 mph, and he realized that he wasn't wearing a seat belt. It appeared that Joe had no intention of slowing down as they approached the farm's dirt driveway. As a matter of fact, as the truck bounced and bucked onto it, he punched the accelerator down.

"Uh, Joe, let's not kill us all over a stupid deer, okay?" Jimmy said with a note of fear in his voice.

The truck was quickly bearing down on the Subaru wagon parked near the house, but Joe swerved without slowing onto the lawn of the farm. The wet grass was as slick as ice, and the vehicle slid sideways before Joe got it pointed directly at the deer. An elderly man with a shotgun came out of the farmhouse, and Jimmy yelled, "Oh, for fuck's sake, Joe, did you see that? That old coot Henderson is coming at us with his goddamn shotgun! We need to clear out of here before someone gets shot!"

"Don't get your panties in a bunch there, Sally! We're almost on it now."

"But it's moving!" Jamie pointed out.

"Oh, Christ on a crutch, Joe, the fucking thing ain't dead. How we gonna get it into the truck before we get shot?"

If he heard any of this, Joe didn't register it. Even the first shotgun blast didn't seem to take his attention off of the stag struggling to get to its feet. The truck bore down on it with increasing speed, and when Jimmy and Jamie glanced over at him just before the vehicle struck the animal, his face had a small smirk on it. Before either of the other two had time to react, Joe was out the driver's seat with a hunting knife in his good left hand. He slit the animal's throat in one fluid motion, and spun around to yell at Jamie and Jimmy to help him get it in the truck. They seemed too stunned to move, but the sounds of buckshot hitting the side of the truck woke them out of their trances, and they came flying out to join him at the deer. Joe had the animal around its bloody neck, and Jimmy and Jamie grabbed the still struggling animal around the middle and rear end, and the three men moved quickly to heave it into the bed of the truck and scramble back inside the cab.

Joe pushed down on the accelerator and the truck remained motionless momentarily while the tires struggled to get a grip in the grass and dirt. The next shot from the approaching and angry Mr. Henderson resulted in the unmistakable sound of taillights shattering. The truck responded like a spurred horse, and bucked forward and headed toward one of the apple trees. They avoided this, but the back of the truck smashed some of its lower branches. Joe got the truck under control, and continued to accelerate through the orchard.

"Holy shit, Joe! Where are you going?"

"Up to that old farm road we snowmobile on. It runs into the power lines and we'll have a lane back to the main road!"

"That works with the sleds, dude, but I don't think this truck will fit."

Jamie craned his neck to look out the back window to see what the old man was doing now. They had gotten out of his shotgun range, so he was getting into his car to come after them. The imminent danger of being shot was over for the time being, and Jamie swiveled his head to look in front of the truck at the scant dirt tracks that marked the road Joe was talking about. He glanced at Joe and then at Jimmy, and they were both covered in the deer's blood. He looked down at his own chest and lap and saw that his clothes were in the same condition. He let out an insane laugh. "This is so fucked up! And so much fun!"

Joe didn't take his eyes off the road, but Jimmy looked over at Jamie with incredulous eyes. He had a cigarette dangling out of his mouth. "You're right about the fucked-up part, college boy!"

The truck turned into the clearing underneath the power lines, and Joe disregarded the stones and puddles in it and drove faster toward where they could see a road crossing up ahead. They skidded to a stop to look for approaching traffic. Nothing was coming from the left, but from the right a Subaru wagon was bearing down on them. Joe shook his head. "That goddamn old man isn't giving up this time, huh?"

After Joe punched the accelerator and the speedometer nosed toward 80, they started putting some distance between themselves and the Subaru. Suddenly, Joe jammed on the brakes and turned the wheel, and the truck responded with sideways skid. Joe masterfully hit the accelerator at the right moment, and the vehicle sped right onto the pipeline. They bounced and pitched on the rough terrain, carefully avoiding some large puddles that covered most of the roadway, and then the truck began to slow down. "Ooh, that was close, huh? We're good now. Old Henderson ain't gonna push his little old-man's car too hard on the pipeline. And you were right—that *was* fun, Jamie!"

Jimmy yelled, "Well, jackass, I hope you've got a plan. 'Cause while Old Henderson was shooting at us, I bet his old lady was calling the game warden with the make and model and license plate of this truck. Even if we get to your driveway, we're in for a world of trouble! There's gonna be a real shit-storm from this one, I'm tellin' ya!"

"Jimmy, Jimmy. When have I ever gotten into too much trouble without a plan?"

After taking a deep drag on his cigarette and holding the smoke for a moment before releasing it forcefully at the ceiling of the cab, Jimmy said, "Well, dude, I sure hope you have one. I can't afford to take another hit on my criminal record!"

When the Maine Game Warden's green pickup pulled into Joe's driveway later, he found Sheriff Gus there, talking with the three men. Before the vehicle had stopped, an agitated Cliff Henderson popped out of the passenger-side door and began to berate them with accusations and threats. The old man became even more irate when he saw that his outbursts were amusing Joe and Jimmy, and he had to be restrained by the game warden. When he finally quieted down, the warden approached the sheriff. "Hey, Gus."

"Jason."

"So, Mr. and Mrs. Henderson witnessed these three men shoot a deer from their truck at the old McClintock Farm. These guys disregarded the signs of private property and tore up the place to get to the deer, Gus."

"Jeez, you don't say? I wasn't called about any of this."

The warden shook his head. "It was a real mess up there, Gus. The scene unfolded so quickly—Mrs. Henderson called me first about the deer being shot from a vehicle and then Mr. Henderson began chasing them."

"I even got some shots off at them!"

"He shot at them?" said Sheriff Gus.

"They were only warning shots!" the old man protested.

The game warden looked reproachfully at the old man, then he addressed the sheriff. "Actually, I'm surprised to find you here with them, Gus."

"Well, these three boys alerted me that they'd hit a deer on the road and that they stopped and took it to the vet to save it. According to Doc Johnson, they pulled up there with a mortally wounded deer, and unfortunately, he had to put the animal out of its misery."

The game warden rolled his eyes. "That's quite a story, Gus. But I'm going to have to see the animal to see if it all checks out."

Sheriff Gus shrugged. "Well, Jason, after it was put down, Joe called me to fill out the proper paperwork to claim the road kill. They all signed the documents, and the deer was taken right over to Howard Peltzerbun's for processing. The good news is that most of the venison is going to be donated to needy families here on the peninsula."

"Liars! Murderers!" Cliff Henderson shouted, pointing at Jamie, Jimmy, and Joe. "My orchard is ripped to hell! There's tire tracks all over the place from those lying sonsabitches over there. Let's go and look at those, shall we?"

The game warden acknowledged the old man's comments with, "I guess there's quite a mess there, huh?"

Sheriff Gus said, "What? You didn't see it for yourself, Jason?"

"I had to track down Mr. Henderson before he hurt someone, Gus. I didn't get a good look at the yard. But both Mr. and Mrs. Henderson saw Joe Quinn's truck driving through there."

"That's right," the old man hissed. "We're witnesses! We saw the whole thing!"

"Was it this truck you saw?" Sheriff Gus asked, jabbing his thumb at the truck parked behind him.

"Naw, it weren't that one. That ain't his truck! I know what his truck looks like 'cause the missus and me have watched him and his goon there scoping out our orchard before. We've let the game warden know every time that we've seen his truck. And that ain't it!"

"Nope, it isn't. It's a friend's," Sheriff Gus reported with a nod. "His truck's been over at Jerry Shute's since last week to be repaired. The brake lights quit working and the tailgate was all messed up. You know Jerry, he'll be fixing that until next year!"

The game warden chuckled, but then his face grew serious. "Let me get this straight, Gus. These men were not driving the truck that Mr. and Mrs. Henderson saw tear through their orchard to get to the buck that they shot on private property. But they hit a deer in this truck, and then they filled out all the necessary paperwork and are donating much of the meat to charity. Is that what you're telling me?"

"That about sums it up, Jason."

"That's sure pretty tidy, Sheriff."

"The truth usually is."

"Oh, you're not going to believe them, are you?" howled Mr. Henderson. "It's clear as day that they're lying and they have all their friends covering their asses! Even you can't be stupid enough to be fooled by this all, Jason!"

The warden's head bobbed from the insult. "Well, Gus, it sounds to me like a case of mistaken identity, and that these men were not involved. I guess Mr. Henderson and I will keep looking for the truck he and his wife saw. Sorry to trouble you all."

The old man began jumping up and down. "This is ridiculous! This is unacceptable! I saw those men do it! Oh, right, I hit their truck with one of my shots! I took out their taillight!"

Sheriff Gus tilted his head. "You said they were warning shots, Mr. Henderson. If you aimed a gun at people, it weren't warning shots."

The warden said, "Get in the vehicle, Mr. Henderson!"

"I will not! Those men did everything I said they did!"

Sheriff Gus took a step toward him. "If you don't want to get involved in a bigger fish fry that involves discharging a firearm at another person and a whole big bad ball of legal wax, you'll kindly shut up, sir, and get in the truck!"

Mr. Henderson climbed in, and he was still yelling and cursing as the truck turned around and drove out the driveway. When it disappeared from view, Sheriff Gus turned to the three men. "That was close, Joe. Even for you three morons, that was stupider than usual!"

Joe chuckled. "Thanks for your help, Gus."

The sheriff shook his head and smiled at them. "Just remember, boys, there are needier families on this peninsula than yours!"

"Oh, don't worry. We've got some nice tenderloins and back-straps with your name on them. And some for Jerry, Wiley, and Doc Johnson, too."

29

A few days before Thanksgiving, Jamie and Shelley were shopping at the big grocery store in Brementon, and as they turned a corner, their cart smashed right into one pushed by none other than Walter Whetstone. When the professor recognized Jamie, his whole face lit up. "Jamie Kurtz!"

"Professor Whetstone!"

He was a tall man with snow-white hair impeccably combed, and his full beard and mustache were neatly trimmed and brushed. And while he didn't have a top hat, he appeared to be wearing a complete outfit from the Victorian age. Over his woolen vest and pants was a long overcoat that had black fur at the cuffs and down the lapels. Shelley found herself staring at the dapper old man and his shiny black patent-leather shoes.

"Oh, I've been so worried about you, Jamie! After your father called me to ask about your whereabouts, I went to your apartment and then to that horrendous steakhouse to check on you. At both places, I was told in the most colorful language that you had skedaddled. But no one knew where to. I imagined the worst. Now that I see you, I know those fears were greatly unwarranted. You look absolutely wonderful!"

"You do, too, sir. Very Stonewall Jackson."

The elder man lifted his chin and stroked his beard and mustache. "Good eye, young man. I started out trying to be J.E.B. Stuart, but the disheveled nature of my facial hair irritated Maggie and me equally. After enduring all that itchiness and discomfort, I now appreciate that cavalryman's impulsiveness—he wasn't disregarding Lee's orders and acting like a prima donna, he was just trying to get relief from the mangy animal on his face!"

The two laughed heartily, but then Jamie noticed that Shelley was staring at them. "Oh, Professor Whetstone, this is my girlfriend, Shelley Vanes."

"Girlfriend? You don't say! Well, it's terribly nice to meet you Ms. Vanes!"

"Nice to meet you, too. Jamie has told me all about you," she said as she shook his warm, soft hand.

He turned to face Jamie. "So you're not only alive, but doing quite well, I see. That's very good, for now Maggie and I can stop worrying. But we need to have you two over for dinner right away. I'm sure the woman will cook up something delectable. How is this Sunday at five forty-five?"

Jamie looked at Shelley. "Are you done with work by then?"

"Yes, I'll be done at five o'clock on Sunday."

"Excellent! I look forward to catching up with you, young Jamie Kurtz, and hearing about your studies. And I cannot *wait* to hear more of *your* story, lovely Ms. Vanes! Till we meet again."

After they finished shopping and put all the groceries in the back of the truck, Shelley said, "I'm not sure that my whalebone corset and my evening gown are back from the dry cleaner's, but I guess dinner with the Whetstones should be fun, nonetheless."

"Oh, it will be, Shelley! Don't let his archaic exterior fool you—he's not trapped in the past as much as he appears. You have to remember that he's consistently one of the most popular professors at Bridgewater. He dresses funny and speaks very properly, but he has a heart of gold and a terrific sense of humor, and he connects well with people our age. His wife, Maggie, is an amazing lady, and I think you two will get along great. We'll all have fun, I swear."

When Sunday came and they pulled up in front of the imposing Federal-style house on a side street in Brementon, Shelley needed a little reassurance on that point. Jamie leaned over and kissed her on the neck. She had come home a little early from the store and had spent more time than usual getting ready for this dinner. Now she was breathtakingly beautiful, and he struggled not to get too frisky with her in the truck. Shelley pinched him hard on the leg. "Hey, I don't think it would be in the best taste to get caught making out by the Whetstones!"

"You're just so darn beautiful! I can't help myself."

"Jamie, are you sure you want to take me inside there?"

He pulled back and looked at her. She was returning his gaze with a seriousness that made him take notice. "Of course I do, Shelley. I want you to know Walter and Maggie! They're important to me."

"That's just it, Jamie. You talk about them more than you do your own mother and father. I know how important they are to you, and that's what's making me nervous—the Whetstones are practically family to you. What if I embarrass you? What if I say something stupid about the Civil War? What if I don't pass this test?"

Jamie gasped. "It's not a test, Shelley! It's nothing of the sort. These are people who mean a lot to me and I'm super excited to be introducing them to you! You are incredibly beautiful and intelligent, and I know you're going to sweep them off their feet. Just relax and try to have a good time, okay?"

Professor Whetstone greeted them at the door with a warm smile. He took their coats and hung them up in a nearby closet, and, as Shelley looked around the interior, she was momentarily transported to another era. The furnishings were straight out of the nineteenth century, and she was caught up in the magic of the portraits on the walls and the Victorian splendor of the hallway and parlor. She was overwhelmed with emotion as she said, "This is an absolutely beautiful house, Professor!"

"Oh, thank you, Ms. Vanes! It was built in 1853 by the ship captain Archibald Munston. He married his first cousin, who was, at the time, barely fifteen years old! He knew that he would be sailing around the globe for years at a time, and he wanted her to have a world of luxury and comfort to keep her busy and happy during those times. He even had a widow's walk built on the top of the house, though it's too far inland to see the water. The very construction of the house is ship-like. The oak crossbeams—"

"Oh, don't get him started talking about this house, young lady, he'll be going on and on for the next two hours, and we'll all be asleep—well, you and I will be. Jamie seems to have an incredible tolerance for his blab. Some would even say he enjoys it. But, for most normal people, it would be a slow death by narcotic ingestion."

With these words, Maggie Whetstone emerged from the kitchen. Her short hair had the look of a downy white dandelion head. She was wearing brown corduroys, a light tan plaid flannel shirt, and a woolen herringbone vest. Her face was lightly creased by wrinkles, which gave her a kindly and grandmotherly appearance. She was drying her hands on a white dishtowel as she came up to Jamie and hugged him. She turned and gave Shelley a quick but warm hug, as well.

"Maggie," Professor Whetstone crooned, "there's no need to insult me in front of our guests."

Maggie Whetstone's eyes twinkled. "They're not guests, Walter, they're family!"

"Harrumph. Just the same, remember we are meeting Ms. Vanes for the first time, after all. We don't want her to leave here thinking that I'm an old blowhard and you're a '*countrified*' old woman!"

Maggie beamed at Jamie and Shelley. "I think what Walter is saying is that we don't want you to think that he's a college professor or that I'm a lesbian. I mean, one of those two facts is true, but we'll leave it up to you two to figure out which one."

Professor Whetstone glanced at the ceiling and said, "Oh, Maggie!"

"So, Jamie, what do you have under the foil?" Maggie asked with a humorous expression.

He looked down in surprise, as if someone had tricked him and put the platter in his hands. "Oh, right. These are boiled venison and wild rice meatballs called *gagoonz* or Little Porcupines. It's either an Ojibwe or Cree recipe that I found online."

"Do your balls need to be warmed up?" Maggie asked with a devilish grin.

Shelley giggled, and Jamie answered with a flushed face, "No, they should be warm enough as they are."

"Maggie!" Professor Whetstone snapped.

She waved him off good-naturedly. "Just hand 'em over, Jamie. I'll bring them into the kitchen and take the foil off. You still drinking beer?"

"Yes, ma'am."

"You too, Shelley?"

"Yes, thank you, Mrs. Whetstone."

"*Maggie*, darling."

"Do you want some help getting that together…Maggie?" Shelley asked.

"Yes, that would be most helpful, dear. Hey, Mr. Blowhard, I guess you'll be wanting your usual snort of Old Crow!"

Jamie and the professor watched the two women chat their way through the swinging door into the kitchen, and then they moved into the front parlor. There was a modest fire crackling in a white marble fireplace, and the room was both warm and fragrant. The professor shook his head as they sat down. "Well, as you can see, Maggie hasn't changed a bit since you've been gone. The same old embattled and maddening mother hen!"

Jamie chuckled, "You wouldn't have her any other way, right?"

Professor Whetstone rolled his eyes. "As if I had any choice in the matter. Quickly, while we're alone, do tell me how you ended up with such a lovely creature at your side! The last time I saw you, you were still heartbroken from that horrible Laura. I never expected you to show up looking so healthy and so happy with a new love interest!"

Jamie nodded. "She's incredible, Professor! I keep pinching myself to make sure that I'm not dreaming. I mean, I don't know what the future holds, but I hope that it includes Shelley Vanes!"

"Okay, you intellectual dorks, stop talking about the impact of slavery on the creation of labor unions or the sexual confusion of George Armstrong Custer—it's time to pretend that you can function in normal society," Maggie announced as she came in with the meatballs arranged on a beautiful china platter.

Shelley came behind her with a tray holding three beers in tall crystal glasses and a crystal cocktail glass with three fingers of bourbon in it. Jamie saw as she set the platter down on the small table in the middle of the parlor that Maggie had put toothpicks in all the meatballs to make eating them easier. Shelley carefully presented the tray to Professor Whetstone first, then turned and offered Maggie one of the beers. She put down the tray and brought the other two beers over to the couch and sat next to Jamie.

Professor Whetstone lifted his glass and offered the toast. "'A house divided against itself cannot stand,'" he quoted. "'I believe this government cannot endure permanently half-slave and half-free. I do not expect the Union to be dissolved—I do not expect the house to fall—but I do expect it will cease to be divided. It will become all one thing or all the other.'"

Jamie smiled, but Shelley and Maggie were blank-faced. Finally, Maggie grumbled, "I think what Walter just said by ridiculously quoting Abraham Lincoln is that we're damn glad to know that Jamie Kurtz is doing bully well, and we're very excited to get to know you, Shelley!"

They clinked glasses and drank. When the professor took a meatball and popped it into his mouth, he exclaimed, "Oh, my! These are delicious! Did you say they're made of venison?"

"Yes."

"Where on earth did you get venison?"

When Jamie seemed too embarrassed to answer, Shelley did it for him. "Jamie shot a buck!"

"You *hunt?*" Professor Whetstone asked with shock.

Jamie shrugged, "I did that day."

"You shot a gun at a deer?"

"Well, I'm no Sergeant Grace, but I aimed the rifle and shot it."

Professor Whetstone started laughing with Jamie, but neither woman cracked a smile. After letting the two men giggle over their inside joke, Maggie explained with a sigh, "You have to get used to this, dear. These two Civil War dweebs tend to crack themselves up all the time. This time, they're giggling like schoolgirls because Jamie made an obscure reference to a Confederate sniper who killed an important Union general—Sedgwick, I think—at Spotsylvania."

"Oh, I see," Shelley said, all innocence. "And did this sniper shoot with his eyes closed and then get chased by an irate old man with a shotgun?"

Maggie guffawed. "Oh, I can tell there's a story behind this! I gotta hear the rest of it."

Shelley launched into the tale, leaving out none of the colorful details. At the end of her story, Professor Whetstone had a pained look on his face, and could only say, "Shooting a deer on private property from a vehicle without a proper hunting license seems rather reckless, doesn't it?"

But Maggie howled a warm laugh that filled the room. "That's the most wonderful and funny story I've heard in ages! Haw-haw! What I want to know is what you did with the blood-covered clothing?"

Jamie shook his head. "When we got to Joe's house, we all stripped out of our clothes and put on sweatpants and sweatshirts belonging to Joe and his wife. Neither of them is as tall as Jimmy or me, so we put on rubber boots to cover the high-tide levels of the pant legs, and we rolled up the sleeves to hide how short they really were. No one checked too closely, so we got away with it."

Maggie slapped her knee. "Oh, I wish I could've seen that, Jamie!"

The woman's hearty laugh was infectious, and Jamie and Shelley joined in. But Professor Whetstone wasn't laughing, and he kept saying, "You could have all gone to jail!"

◇◇◇◇

Dinner was a deliciously roasted capon with fall vegetables and a green salad. The food, the beer, and the warm comfort of the house loosened Jamie's lips, and he unabashedly regaled them with stories of his time in Kestrel Cove. Although their reactions to his wild adventures differed, both Whetstones were anxious to hear more and to learn about Shelley. At one point in the dinner, Jamie looked up at Shelley as she was describing her sister's wedding. He smiled because all of her previous anxiety about the evening had evaporated and she was expressive and bright in her retelling of the epic reception. The candles on the table illuminated her hair and her face, and she moved her hands gracefully as she spoke. He found himself staring intently at her, unable to tear his eyes away.

Both Walter and Maggie Whetstone observed this, but, as with other events of the evening, their reactions were quite different.

Right after Shelley concluded her story, Professor Whetstone sat forward in his seat and addressed Jamie. "About your future—"

"Walter!"

He put up his hands to silence her. "I've not mentioned it all night, Maggie, but we all know that I have to say something."

"For goodness sake, Walter, not now! Why don't you make an appointment with Jamie, and the two of you can meet in your office some other time to discuss that. We're all just having a wonderful dinner that doesn't involve that stuff. Leave it be."

"Now, Maggie, I'm not going to be like his callous and insensitive father on the issue. I just want to talk about the boy's future, that's all....So, Jamie, now that the internship is a thing of the past—"

His wife stood up angrily. "Damn the torpedoes, Walter Whetstone! Why don't you just scuttle the entire goddamn evening!"

Husband and wife locked eyes and stared at one another, and there was a palpable feeling to the static in the wordless conversation that transpired between them. Finally, Maggie slumped her shoulders and exhaled loudly. "Shelley, my darling, do you want to help me clear the table, or do you want to hear my dear husband try to drag your wonderful boyfriend down from the ethereal adventures he's been having with you and back into the sodden and unreal world of academia?"

"Maggie! I am doing nothing of the sort!"

"I think I need to stay for it," Shelley stated evenly. "Stand by your man and all that."

The older woman nodded and sat back down. "Yes, quite right. Let's both stand by our men. You can help protect yours, and I'll help deflect mine!"

Professor Whetstone sighed deeply. "All I was going to say to Jamie is that the New York internship was a one-time deal. By choosing to give it up and come back to Brementon, you shut that door forever. However, the door to getting your PhD is wide open, just waiting for you to take the steps to get through it."

There was an awkward silence, then Jamie spoke softly. "I'm not sure I want to jump into a doctoral program right away, Professor Whetstone. I'm really looking forward to finishing up the lobstering season, witnessing the birth of Bobbie and Clara's baby, celebrating Christmas, New Year's, and Tet, and then experiencing a winter in Kestrel Cove."

"But you could fill out your applications to graduate schools during the winter and be ready for the next fall, Jamie."

"Maybe he doesn't want to do that, Walter. Have you ever thought about that? Not everyone wants to drop everything and hop onto the track of becoming a professor," Maggie asserted.

"Well, Jamie does...or he *did*."

"Maybe he doesn't anymore."

Professor Whetstone looked at his wife in shock, then aimed his gaze directly at Jamie. "Is that true? You don't want to study the Civil War to become a professor of it anymore?"

Now everyone's eyes were on Jamie. Even the portraits on the wall were staring him, and he coughed nervously before answering. "When I graduated from Bridgewater, Professor, I thought I knew how everything in my life was going to play out. I was like one of those foolish politicians who thought that the Civil War was going to last only a few weeks, but nobody could have foretold the amount of time or the colossal loss of life it was really going to take. I thought I knew what love was. I thought I knew what being part of a community was like. I thought I was on the moving sidewalk to my destiny. I know now that part of this false sense of confidence was because I'd never really experienced much of this world. These last six months in Kestrel Cove have taught me that I need to see more and experience more before I can make some of these big decisions."

"Bullshit!"

"Walter!"

"No, Maggie, he needs to hear me out. We both know what Jamie is, and we know his potential. We know where he's going to excel and change this world, and it's not in some little fishing village like Kestrel Cove, that's for sure!"

Maggie was shaking her head. She spoke dryly. "Oh, my dearest husband, do you hear the arrogance coming from your mouth right now? Who are you to determine what this young man is and what his impact should be on this planet? You're not a god, Walter Whetstone, even though you need frequent reminders of that detail."

Professor Whetstone pointed at his wife. "And *that*, apparently, is your main job these days, my dearest Maggie. But stop and think about something. How many decades have I been a professor of American history? And, in all that time, how many times have you heard me get excited about a student's talents and potential in this field? How many?"

There was a silence that went on just a moment too long to be comfortable. Maggie closed her eyes. "Three times."

"Exactly. There have only been three times that I've come to this conclusion in the last two score years. Who were the first two?"

"I'm going to clear the table now, Walter."

"No, you're not! You're going to sit right there and tell these young people the names of the two previous students who I raved about as much as I do about Jamie Kurtz. Come on. What were their names?"

"Carl Jermanton and Cyrus Kronus," she replied with a grumble.

Professor Whetstone looked directly at Shelley. "Maggie and Jamie know these names, but you might not, dear. They're the heads of the American History Departments of their universities, and the unparalleled leaders of the modern study of the Civil War. They are not only preparing the next generations to investigate the topic, their research defines that very investigation. So, if Jamie is mentioned in that pairing of individuals, it means that he needs to take his rightful place in the study of the American Civil War!"

"So the boy has no choice, Walter? He's like some kind of Dalai Lama of the Civil War—his destiny is to sit in the grand pantheon of the academic ivory tower, whether he wants to or not?"

"Yes!"

"I find that disagreeable and completely wrong," Maggie said firmly, "and I will not stand for it to be the truth! I hate to put you on the spot, Shelley, but what's your take on all of this? You've been very quiet over there as my husband anoints Jamie as the Second Coming of Christ."

Shelley shook her head thoughtfully. "I'm sorry, but I believe that a person makes their own destiny. There are times when conditions can appear to suck you down and keep you spinning in eddies, but inevitably it is up to the individual to decide what they really want to do. Either they'll accept their situation as the truth and not fight it, or they will do whatever it takes to fight for what they really want."

Maggie slapped the table. "There it is! Damn right, young lady!"

When Professor Whetstone started to sputter, his wife pointed fiercely at Jamie. "I hope you listened to her words and really, really heard them, young man. And I hope to God you realize just what a treasure you have in your life, sitting across from you at this table. If you're half as smart as my jackass of a husband thinks you are, you won't ever let her go! Now, I've made flan, so who's ready for dessert and a cup of coffee with chicory in it?"

30

The Atlantic hurricane season was officially over, but a tropical depression that was building in the waters off Venezuela caught the eyes of the weather forecasters at NOAA. It was behaving enough like a developing hurricane that they gave it the unofficial name Nemo. And as the storm continued to intensify and seemed destined to follow a path straight up the eastern seaboard of the United States, a weather warning was issued from Florida to Maine for an almost historically devastating winter storm. The weather models all indicated that Nemo would be like a giant swirling top as it picked up moisture, and then it was going to head northward and plow right into a massive pocket of arctic Canadian air that was pushing in from the opposite direction. This sinister union was going to create a megastorm with such power and ferocity that it might completely disrupt the Christmas holiday.

The fishermen of Kestrel Cove, who had to be amateur meteorologists to begin with, saw the weather maps and knew exactly what was coming their way. A storm this intense could destroy all their gear in the water and smash their boats, so they began a frantic push to get everything out of the water before it hit. Overnight, the entire town became like a stirred-up anthill to get those tasks completed. Because time was of the essence, it was understood that there could no longer be any distinctions or disagreements between the boats, captains, and crews—everyone was in the same situation, and they all needed to come together to get everything done in time.

Even the old-timers said they'd never seen anything like it. All the boats were pulling their gear and bringing it to shore, dropping it anywhere they could find space. If the wharf was full of boats unloading traps, other captains started dropping theirs on the beach by the concrete ramp at the end of the cove road during high tide to be picked up later. Pickup trucks clogged the area and confusion reigned. It became obvious that, if all these traps were going to get to the right trap yards, someone was going to have to coordinate the process. And this role fell to Jamie.

As the new trap foreman for the entire cove, he began to lead teams of wharf rats to load the trucks and take the traps to the right houses. It didn't matter if they belonged to Drake, Hai, Bobbie, Vernon Quigley, Ed Simmons, Nigger Bob, or Matt Jay—if there was a pile of traps on the beach or on the wharf, they had to be gathered, transported, and stacked as quickly and efficiently as possible. And even when nerves became frayed during those times when the fishermen had to wait for the teams to get back, everyone understood and appreciated the way the community was pulling together. And they all appreciated the college boy's willingness to take the lead.

The week of nearly constant movement was exhausting. Just when it seemed like there was time for a break, another boat would come into the harbor with a load that needed to be dealt with. And because the urgency of the situation meant that the wind, weather, and daylight could no longer influence the process, the boats kept creeping in to dump their traps, and Jamie and his teams kept loading the trucks and driving off from sunup to sundown. Even the end of the day gave no respite, as the last loads usually consisted of huge coils of soggy and algae-covered lines. These not only taxed the already tired workers with their sodden weight, but smeared a greenish covering on all the clothing that came in contact with them. Jamie was so exhausted that he slept on the couch in his dirty clothes the whole week.

When the last load was finally stacked and no one had any lobster traps left out in the bay, a collective sigh of relief went up from Kestrel Cove. The hardest task was now completed, and the next one of pulling the boats did not require such large teams of support. As Nemo had moved north to start tickling the Florida peninsula and Drake had made contact with the boat hauler to come and get all the boats out of the water, most figured that they had a few days to rest up before they began the process of getting everyone's boat up on land and out of danger.

Jamie was more deeply fatigued than he could remember ever being. His arms, back, neck, and legs all hurt to move, and he wanted nothing more than to rest up. With Shelley now pretty much living over at Clara's to prep for the imminent birth of the baby, he was looking forward to a few days of solitary inaction and sleep. But after taking a hot shower and settling down on the couch to read while he drank his morning coffee, the phone rang. When Jamie picked it up, Jimmy's voice thundered from the other side, "Hey, college boy, where are ya?"

"Obviously at home, Jimmy."

"Well, we need you down at the wharf."

"Why?"

"Someone had the good idea to check the tide charts, and to-day's the very best day to take all the boats out of the water before the storm gets here"

"Oh, come on! I just got comfortable and was relaxing."

"Wah-wah! Get your ass down here—we need your help!"

The phone went dead, and Jamie heaved a loud sigh. He got dressed and headed out. When he arrived at the wharf, he found the whole harbor astir with activity on both land and sea. A big semi was lined up at the top of the cement ramp, and there was a group of men standing around it. The truck had a normal tractor cab, but its low-slung trailer looked like a giant tuning fork with two sets of padded arms coming up from its sides.

As Jamie started in that direction, Jimmy intercepted him. "You certainly took your sweet time, huh, college boy?"

"Fuck you, Jimmy. I put on clothes and started walking right after you hung up on me."

"Harrumph. Then you must walk slower than Winston Vanes!"

Jamie could see that he was just kidding around, so he shrugged his shoulders and asked, "So, where am I needed?"

"You're gonna drive Joe's truck in front of the boat hauler and lead him to each fisherman's house, and then you'll help with the stands and blocking. I know it don't sound like much, but having your help will make things go faster, and we might even get all the boats out before the tide changes."

"Okay."

"They'll start with the smaller boats first. The bigger boats have deeper drafts, so they need more water. Drake and the truck driver have already worked out the order. Hai's going first. The *Bobbie C.* will be somewhere in the middle. Once I'm done talking with you, I'll head out to the mooring. Joe's already out there, getting things straightened up. Hopefully the weather will hold and this won't suck too much. See ya later."

Jamie brought Joe's truck down and parked near the ramp. The driver and Drake seemed to be in the middle of an intense conversation, but this ended when Drake whistled loudly toward the moorings and twirled his index finger over his head in a big circle. Upon seeing the signal, Hai pulled his boat away from its mooring and steamed toward the ramp. The driver backed his truck up until the wheels of the trailer were under water. After setting the air brake and blocking the cab's wheels, he climbed onto a metal cage-like platform at the head of the trailer and grabbed a yellow control box. With the push of a button, an extra set of wheels unfolded underneath the front of the trailer and lifted it up enough to unhook it. Using the control box again, the driver started letting out cable from a winch on the back of the cab, and the trailer descended down the ramp and into the water. When the upper set of padded arms was just above the surface and looked like loving hands to guide the boats onto the trailer, the driver stopped and waited for the approaching lobster boat.

Hai motored in slowly until the bow of his boat was right between the padded arms, then the truck driver gave him a series of hand signals to get the boat perfectly lined up. The lobster boat inched forward toward the front of the trailer, and when the truck driver was happy that it was on straight, he signaled Hai to give the throttle some power. The boat hesitated at first, but then it slid up until its bow was nearly touching the driver. Hai's sternman was up on the bow, and he handed the driver a line from the bow bit to be tied off onto the trailer. The second set of padded arms came up from under water to cradle the stern of the boat. When the driver whistled and clenched his fist, Hai shut off the boat's engine. Slowly, the winch began to pull the trailer and boat out of the water, and, when the trailer was re-hitched to the truck, the driver hopped back into the cab and pulled the rig forward. He got out again and did a quick survey to make sure the boat was securely supported, then he nodded to Jamie before climbing back into the cab and starting to rumble toward the hill.

Jamie had been to Hai's house before, but he was always disappointed that it looked like almost every other fisherman's house on the peninsula. He knew it wouldn't have Vietnamese roof lines or slate shingles or Buddhist shrines around, but he wished it didn't look so ordinary. Now he parked off to the side of the driveway and walked up as the semi was getting ready to back up into an open space beside Hai's trap yard. There were six blue metal boat stands with wooden heads painted orange and several scattered piles of short and thick wooden blocking nearby on the lawn. Jamie was unsure what to do, but Hai called down to him from up on the lobster boat, "Jamie, see ladder against house? Please get it so Trai and me can get down from boat. Then we can help Mr. Jones back up."

As soon as their feet touched the ground, the Vietnamese men began chirping directions to the driver and to Jamie, and within fifteen minutes of building cribbing piles underneath the boat's keel and positioning the stands, the supported boat was free-standing, and the driver could pull his rig forward. When Jamie began to help with the last set of stands under the bow, Hai said quickly, "Jamie, you better get going! Mr. Jones already getting trailer ready for the next boat. He is on a mission today, and he needs to hurry. We've got this. We appreciate what you do for all us! *Cảm ơn nhiêu lắm!*"

Jamie nodded and ran to Joe's truck, and they drove straight back to the wharf. Jamie let the big rig rumble past him, stop, and turn around so it could back down the ramp again. By the time the trailer was being lowered into the water, Nigger Bob's boat was on its way in. With little effort, this boat was on the trailer, and they were lumbering back up the hill again.

So it went with all the boats of the cove. Jamie did his best to be helpful, and all the fishermen were grateful for his efforts. Even Drake said a quick thank-you when they had the *Norma Jane* on stands in his cluttered yard. Of course, Joe and Jimmy were tough on him. Jimmy beaned him with dead crabs as he approached with the ladder and Joe barked out insults and orders. But at the end of the day, Jamie had the satisfaction of having helped get all the boats of the cove successfully hauled out before the storm.

Afterwards, the captains, sternmen, and a few wharf rats gathered at the wharf. Someone had bought a case of beer, and everyone had one to celebrate the success of pulling all the gear and getting all the boats out of the water. For Jamie, the moment was bittersweet. Although it was the indisputable end of the season and he was unsure what the transition was going to lead him into next, drinking beer on the wharf with the other weary but contented men was one of the greatest feelings of camaraderie he'd ever felt in his life. And as the group looked out at the melancholic gray water of the now empty harbor, they knew that they'd all come together as a community to accomplish a truly arduous feat, and they seemed content to revel in a calming sense of success.

A movement caught Jamie's eye, and he elbowed Wiley and asked quietly, "Hey, is Bill Hand's boat still out on the mooring?"

"Yep. He leaves it out there all winter long. I hear he's got a giant piece of granite on the bottom and heavy-duty chain that's so fucking strong it could hold an ocean liner! It's been out there during some of the worst storms we've had without a problem. Plus, when you've got as much money as Bill Hand, you don't worry about losing a boat or two."

Jamie looked around at the group. "Huh. Bill didn't come down and help out today, did he?"

Wiley took a sip from his beer and mumbled, "Naw, I guess he was too busy."

A sudden gust of cold wind blew in from the water and swirled through the group of men. Drake said, "Ah, boys, did you feel that? My balls just pulled right into me with that one! It's gonna get cold as a witch's tit right quick, and then all hell's gonna break loose. We all better get home and tend to those last-minute things we need to do before Nemo smacks the shit out of us!"

The group disbanded quickly. Joe and Jimmy dropped Jamie off at his cottage with the threat that, after the storm, they'd all get together and go snowmobiling and drinking. As they drove away, he walked inside and the emptiness of the cottage wrapped around him like a shawl. A gust of wind shook the whole structure and rattled the window panes, and Jamie shivered even though he wasn't cold. He grabbed a beer from the fridge and headed to the bathroom for a shower. His night was going to consist of eating a dinner of boxed mac and cheese, drinking too many beers, and then falling asleep while reading on the couch, and although that struck him as somewhat pathetic, his body and mind were too tired to do anything but embrace the plan wholeheartedly.

The snow waited to begin in earnest until after the sun rose. Jamie watched the huge flakes being blown like icing against the cottages as he drank his coffee. The last week had been so grueling, he was determined to finally have the relaxing morning he so craved. However, when he heard the unmistakable sound of a truck coming up the driveway, he knew that his day was going to be much different than he wanted it to be. Wiley knocked but didn't wait for an answer before coming in, tracking snow onto the floor with him. He looked at Jamie with wild eyes. "Hey, man, I'm headed to town to do some Christmas shopping, and you're coming with me!"

"Uh-uh, Wiley. I'm just going to stay inside and take it easy today."

"Oh, don't be such a wimp. Besides, I bet you haven't even gotten Shelley a Christmas present yet."

Jamie rolled his eyes. "Dude, Christmas is way off and Bobbie and Clara's baby isn't due for a while. Why don't we wait for Nemo to blow over before we go into town."

Wiley looked at him with a weird expression and said, "Hey, man, do you know what today's date is?"

"No, I've lost track of the days with all the craziness of late. What is it, December twentieth or something?"

"Dude, it's December twenty-third! It's almost Christmas Eve!"

"*What?*" Jamie yelled, jumping up from his chair. "Holy shit! I don't have anything for Shelley!"

"Oh, boy; that certainly would not be received well, I'm telling you. No one wants the first Christmas together to be present-less. Plus, Vicky's sure that Clara's going to pop this baby out any minute, and she's like some kind of freakish carnie fortune-teller on these kinds a things. Get dressed and grab your cash—we're on a mission to town!"

The road was already getting coated with a slick covering of fresh snow, but Wiley seemed to be driving it at his usual high speed. To quell his fear of dying in a horrific car accident, Jamie asked, "So what are you going to get Bobbie's baby?"

"I dunno, bro. But there's a baby store there at the Corners, so we're all good. We'll find something! Do you have any idea for Shelley's present?"

"No," Jamie lied.

"Well, you can't go wrong with lingerie, dude. Or sex toys. Girls like those more than they want us to know."

Jamie laughed, but Wiley's expression told him that he wasn't supposed to.

At the Corners, they parked in the giant lot and went into the big-box baby store. After some discussion, they each finally bought a onesie, some diapers, and a couple of rattles. Once they were done there, Jamie tried not to shed Wiley too obviously, but he knew exactly what he wanted to get for Shelley and all of his friends. As it turned out, Wiley was just as eager to head out on his own, and he didn't protest when Jamie suggested that they split up for an hour.

With limited time to accomplish his shopping, Jamie nearly jogged as he made his way to the stores he wanted to visit. In that short time, however, he made it to the bookstore, the liquor store, the jewelry store, the pawn shop, and the auto parts store. When he came back to the truck with a heavy load of bags that he struggled to put in the truck bed, Wiley said, "Dude, what'd you do, buy the whole fucking store?"

Jamie grinned. "A lot of people on my list, man. Some naughty and some nice. Had to buy a big bag of coal for a certain buddy of mine!"

Wiley smiled crazily back at him. "Bull-shee-it, bro!"

Even though the windblown snow made the visibility next to zero, Wiley kept the truck at a perilously high speed on their way back toward Kestrel Cove. Jamie nervously checked his seat belt a few times, but he was more focused on trying to discern the vague shapes and objects that revealed themselves incompletely through the frosted windshield. The visibility was so bad that it was a matter of moments before either of them noticed the flashing blue lights behind them. Jamie saw them first in his side mirror and said, "Uh, Wiley? There's flashing lights behind us."

"Aw, what the fuck now?" Wiley cried as he pulled the truck over onto the shoulder—or as close to it as he could in near whiteout conditions. With the vehicle stopped and the flashing lights of the squad car lighting up the whole interior of the cab, Jamie asked in a hushed panic, "Dude, you don't have any black bags or nothing like that in this truck, do you?"

"Naw, man, we're good. Do you really think I would've stopped if we did?"

A shapeless form approached the driver's-side window and rapped on it. Wiley lowered it, and there, bundled up past all recognition was a man in a sheriff's hat. It wasn't until he spoke that it was clear that it was Sheriff Gus. "Is Jamie with you, Wiley?"

Wiley thumbed toward Jamie in the passenger's seat. "Yeah, Sheriff Gus, he's right here. What's up?"

"Clara's water broke, so they took her by ambulance to Foster's Hospital in Brementon. Shelley called me 'cause she didn't know where Jamie was. When I went over to their place, I found the cottage empty, so I figured he was with you or over at Joe's. When I saw your truck speed by right now, I figured I'd check. You gotta get that boy to the hospital, ASAP."

"Jesus! You bet I will!"

"But Wiley?"

"Yeah, Sheriff Gus?"

"Remember to drive like you're going through a snowstorm, not winning a pipeline race!"

As soon as the sheriff's car crept past them and continued down the road, Wiley gunned the engine and swung the wheel. The rear end fishtailed violently and the vehicle spun 180 degrees. The next twenty minutes of white-knuckle terror were a combination of death-defying speed and absolute disregard for traffic signs or signals. The truck was either sliding sideways through the turns, driving over what Jamie was sure were sidewalks, or barreling headlong through intersections. When it was all over and the truck slid into a space that may or may not have been a legitimate spot in the hospital parking lot, Jamie opened the door with the force of a fleeing survivor. While he grabbed the bags of his purchases out of the snowy truck bed to put them inside the cab, he saw that Wiley was sitting there motionless. "So are you coming inside, Wiley?"

"Uh, I dunno. I'm not exactly family, ya know."

Jamie looked at the dark shape of the hospital through the whiteout and then back at Wiley. "Bobbie *is* your captain, man. I think he'd be really grateful if you stopped in. Then you can get on home to Vicky."

"Yeah, I guess I can do that. Plus, blizzards always bring out the pervs, so Vick's gonna be totally busy for the next few days and nights. Let's go."

They found the Vanes family ensconced in the maternity ward's waiting room. As soon as she saw Wiley and Jamie coming down the hallway, Shelley ran over to give them each a big hug before giving them an update. Clara's water had broken, but her cervix was not enlarging. And to make the situation clearer, Shelley went on to say that it appeared that "the car was ready to come out, but the garage door just wasn't opening wide enough yet." Her hand was clammy as she took Jamie's hand in hers, and he instantly understood how anxious she was about the situation.

"Hey, it's the damn torpedoes guy!" Leon bellowed happily as they walked up.

The other members of the family laughed at his comment and smiled as Jamie made the rounds and gave each a hug or a handshake. As soon as the excitement of getting new members had abated, the group stared at the doors of the maternity ward as if they all had X-ray vision.

Shelley, Wiley, and Jamie found three chairs together and sat down. Shelley leaned in and said in a low voice, "Clara's blood pressure is rising, the baby's heartbeat is a little too fast, and the doctors are starting to get worried. They're going to give her until dinner time, but then they're going to administer drugs that will kick-start the process. Clara's healthy as a horse, so I'm not too scared. But it's not much fun being out here, just sitting around and hoping that some good news comes our way."

They waited throughout the afternoon. When Bobbie came out to give them an update, he smiled appreciatively when he saw that Wiley was there in the waiting room. He told them that the situation was the same—Clara's cervix was dilating, but it was taking its sweet time, and the doctors were still thinking that if things didn't speed up, they'd have to help it along with drugs. Bobbie looked weary, but he smiled as he waved and headed back into the ward.

The TV in the waiting room had been showing the usual afternoon drivel of daytime television—talk shows and shock shows—but suddenly it switched to network weather emergency coverage. Nemo, as originally forecast, had gathered strength and run right into the cold air mass to become a full-fledged winter hurricane. The storm was scheduled to slam into the coast of Maine by nightfall, and power outages and frightful conditions were going to make all travel in the area impossible. As if it wanted to give its own personal endorsement to the validity of this information, the wind battered the big windows at the end of the hospital hallway hard enough to make everyone in the waiting room gasp.

Then the hospital PA system clicked on. "In light of the severity of the weather and the likelihood that power will be disrupted at some point this evening, we are notifying all staff, patients, and families here in the hospital that we are now in the top level of Code White. This designation means that we are in a weather-related lockdown as we prepare for the worst winter weather conditions. In the event that we lose power, the generator is now running, and it will immediately supply all of our electrical needs. We will make further announcements as needed. Thank you."

This news did not seem to affect anyone in the waiting room. The storm's intensity had never been in question, so there was nothing new to be heard. Jamie, however, leaned over to Wiley and said, "Dude, do you want to call Vicky to let her know that you're stuck here for the night?"

He shook his head. "I'll just get a busy signal! Like I said, she's gonna be busy tonight!"

"Yeah, but shouldn't you at least try?"

"Okay, dude, I'll try."

When he got up and headed to a phone down the hallway, Shelley lifted her head off of Jamie's shoulder and said quietly, "This is all pretty exciting, huh?"

"Yeah. Are you doing all right?"

"Sure. I just want the little bugger to pop out and be healthy."

When Bobbie came out a little later, his face was ashen, but he managed a weak smile. "Well, the doctors don't want to wait anymore. They're giving her something called pitocin. It's supposed to get things going."

But it didn't. Clara's cervix still wouldn't open wide enough to push the baby out, and the doctors announced that a C-section would be for the best. This news, coupled with the fact that the TV stations had all preempted their normal schedules with reports from weathermen ranting about the malevolent maelstrom of Nemo, made the entire waiting Vanes family shift and grumble like corralled animals being circled by predators.

The sun went down, the wind continued to buffet the windows, and the stress levels of the waiting family kept rising. So, when the fatigued doctor finally came out in his operating scrubs, some in the gathering groaned because they expected the worst. The doctor, however, managed to smile before saying, "After a successful cesarean, I'm happy to announce the birth of a healthy little boy! Mother and child are resting now, and both are doing just fine. We're going to keep them both in the recovery room to make sure that blood pressures and heart rates stay good, but I would suspect that we'll be able to get them into their room before too long. Oh, and dad is doing well, too, although there were a few times I wasn't too sure he was going to make it! He'll be out to let you know when it's okay to come and visit."

The good news transformed the Vanes family anxieties into shouts of joy, and for several moments they swarmed into a hugging frenzy that got loud enough for the nurses at their station to give them a few warning looks. The celebration gradually settled down, and a new and relaxed stage of waiting began. With the dangers passed, Shelley fell asleep quickly with her head on Jamie's shoulder, and he understood just how tapped out she was from the whole experience. And after several unsuccessful attempts, Wiley was finally able to connect with Vicky, who, as predicted, was nearly worn out from all her calls. He began to slumber in his chair, too, and Jamie looked around the room and smiled before he closed his eyes and let himself relax enough to fall asleep.

The world that greeted them all the next morning was as pure in its devastation as Clara and Bobbie's baby was in its newness. Nemo had spent itself in one mighty night, leaving behind a record snowfall that had been sculpted by unthinkable wind speeds. The sun made the whiteness of the snow blindingly bright, and the silence that sat atop the white blanket reflected the shock that followed the intensity of the storm. The worst was over, but now the massive cleanup had to begin.

The baby was named Robert Nemo Schmidt. He was a large and healthy baby, and when Jamie and Shelley got their opportunity to visit, they were surprised to see how weary Bobbie and Clara were and how big Bobbie Junior was. They took turns holding him, and Jamie felt his heart flutter as he watched Shelley cradle him in her arms and kiss his forehead.

Wiley waited at the hospital until midmorning, but then became too restless to keep from trying to get home to Vicky. When they all expressed their concerns about his safety, he waved them off. As he said, if his truck could slog through the mud of the pipeline to win those races, he sure as shit wouldn't have any problems driving through a little snow. Jamie was about to point out that there was a driving ban in place, but he knew that such trivialities were not going to dissuade the boy from doing what he wanted to do. Shelley asked if Jamie wanted to go with him, but he declined because he knew that he needed to stay with her at the hospital. It wasn't until Wiley had been gone for a couple of hours that Jamie realized that his Christmas gifts were all still in the truck. But since it appeared that they'd all be stuck in the hospital for another night, he figured he'd get them from Wiley later.

As the outside world began its recovery from the storm's devastation, inside the cocoon of the hospital, the day became timeless. Jamie and the Vanes family ate their meals in the cafeteria, visited the room to cuddle the baby and chat with Bobbie and Clara, and visited with one another until there wasn't much left to say. The waiting room chairs were far from comfortable, but the roads were still too snow-covered to be driven on, and they all knew that they would be spending another night in the hospital. And although it was now Christmas Eve, they all agreed that it was better to be safe and celebrate the holiday in the hospital. After all, the family was together in one place, and Bobbie Junior's birth was the greatest present any of them could have wished for.

31

When Shelley and Jamie returned to their cottage on Christmas afternoon, they were surprised to see that their driveway had been plowed. Since they'd fully expected to have to trudge through the waist-deep snow to get to the house, the ease of driving the truck right up to it was almost a letdown. The snowdrifts and plow piles along the length of their road were above the windows of Shelley's truck, and it felt like they were driving through a white tunnel.

As they got out of the truck, they noticed two pairs of snowshoes stuck tail first in the deep snow by the doorway. A red ribbon flapped in the wind on each toe of the Algonquin-style shoes. There was a card fluttering in the breeze, and Shelley grabbed it and read, "To the young couple, from your friends in Kestrel Cove. Now college boy can walk to work in the snow, and you two can do something together that involves keeping your clothes on. HA-HA! Merry Christmas from the guys of the cove. Made with pride by Wiley."

Jamie shook his head and said, "What the hell? I can't believe it!"

Shelley gently touched the toe of one of the snowshoes. "Dammit, these are beautiful! I knew that Wiley had some skills, but I never knew he could make these! He should start his own business."

"Oh, definitely," Jamie agreed.

When they went into the cottage, there was another surprise—the bags of Jamie's Christmas presents and another giant item wrapped in plain brown paper were sitting on the kitchen floor. Jamie started to paw the paper-wrapped object, but Shelley slapped his hands and said, "We're not opening presents quite yet, college boy. I think we need a shower first."

Jamie nodded and went to start a fire in the fireplace. While he tended the fire until he had a good blaze going, he kept waiting to hear the water of the shower start, but he still didn't hear it. Suddenly, behind him, she cleared her throat. He turned to look at her, and she was standing completely naked in the doorway to their bedroom. "Do you need a hearing aid?"

Jamie was distracted by what he was seeing in front of him. "Um, I don't think so."

"I said, '*we* need a shower,' and that means you, too, bub! Get undressed and let's get clean together. Or dirty, as the case might be."

The initial excitement of an erotic shower was dulled as soon as they tried to fit into the tiny space of the shower stall. They'd never noticed that the shower walls were made of metal, but now that they were both trying to fit in, the cold metallic sides turned the moment into an awkward and wholly uncomfortable experience. Soon they were laughing so hard at the ridiculousness of the situation that they just hung onto one another and hugged as the water sprayed down on them. In the end, they decided that taking turns would probably work best, so Jamie volunteered to go out and stand by the fire. After Shelley finished up, he went in and took his shower. When he came out of the bathroom, she was lying on a blanket in front of the fire. She said breathlessly, "Oh, don't bother dressing, stud. Just get yourself down here! I've been missing you!"

Afterwards, Shelley stood up and went into the kitchen. She came back carrying the brown-paper-wrapped object and put it down near Jamie. She sat back down next to him and commanded, "Open this first!"

Jamie ripped open the paper, and there was the taxidermied head of the buck he'd shot. No photos had been taken of the momentous event that day because of the circumstances, so Jamie was startled by the overall size of the deer and the elaborateness of the rack of antlers on its head. The animal had been a regal creature, and he couldn't help but feel a twinge of guilt as he looked at Shelley's present. She seemed to read this on his face and said, "Now, don't get all weepy about killing Bambi, college boy!"

He laughed and kissed her. Then he went into the kitchen and got his present for her. As he came back with it snugged between his hands, he asked her to close her eyes. He kneeled in front of her and she opened his eyes. There in the palm of his hand was a red velveteen box. She gasped and took it from him. She opened the box and saw the diamond ring tucked into the satin fold inside. She looked wide-eyed at him, and he said, "I know that this is a surprise and all, but I just wanted you to know, Shelley Vanes, that I need you in my life. And I hope you feel the same way."

Her eyes started to well up and she wagged a finger at him. "Don't make any cracks about me being weepy, college boy, or I'll break your goddamn fingers!" She paused for a moment, then said solemnly, "Yes, I need you in *my* life, too, Jamie Kurtz!"

She kissed him hard, pushed him onto his back, and got on top of him. As they made love, Jamie wasn't entirely sure what to make of her tears falling onto his chest, but he prayed silently that they came from happiness.

The next morning after breakfast, they strapped on their new snowshoes and headed through the deep snow to make their Christmas present deliveries to Wiley, Joe, Jimmy, Drake, Jerry Shute, and Bill Hand. The air was so cold, the snow crunched and squeaked as they made their way. A murder of crows in the treetops nearby began to call raucously, so they snowshoed in silence and listened to their calls echo on the wind.

Joe was thrilled to see them. He unwrapped his gift and was speechless when he saw the replica 1851 Colt revolver that Jamie had picked up at the pawn shop. With his good hand, he pretended to shoot something at the end of the driveway. He put the pistol down and pulled out the DVD of Ken Burns's video about the Civil War. He laughed warmly as he slapped Jamie on the shoulder and hugged Shelley. He invited them to stay and have some coffee, but they declined because of the other stops they had to make. Since Jimmy was coming over to Joe's by snowmobile for a visit later that day, they left his presents there. When Joe asked what it was, Jamie sheepishly admitted that he'd given Jimmy the same video and a fancy bottle of single-malt scotch from northern Scotland. Joe rolled his eyes. "Oh, for fuck's sake, Jamie, he'll go on a bender and be quoting Civil War shit even more than you do!"

Wiley was excited to see them enjoying his snowshoes so much. He tore open the present and was ecstatic to see the entire collection of a graphic novel series about American history that Jamie had found in the bookstore. Vicky climbed down from the loft, and she was shocked when she saw the pair of Suvorna hair scissors Jamie had picked up for her at the pawn shop. When Jamie said they would be used a lot when her salon opened up, she surprised him by hugging him tightly. Wiley punched Jamie hard in the shoulder and then hugged Shelley warmly.

Jamie let Shelley hand Drake his gift. He cautiously opened the wrapping and looked at the packet in his hand for a moment before a laugh grumbled inside and came out in a hearty sound that was earnest and infectious. Jamie had found a pack of prank parking tickets that read:

> *This is not a ticket, but if it were within my power, I would love to blow up your car. Because of your moronic, asinine, and pathetic attempt at parking here, you have taken enough room for an entire fleet of UPS trucks and a city bus. The reason for giving you this is so that, in the future when you have a fit of stupidity like this, you will remember that other people just might take the law into their own hands. Besides, you clearly need to be reminded that I don't like you. May the wheels of your car fall off on your way home today, and may you get the crabs, unless you already have a case of them.*
>
> *Best wishes,*
>
> *A Pissed-Off Driver*

Drake hugged Shelley. He didn't quite smile at Jamie, but he shook the pack at him to show that he appreciated the gift. As they walked away, he nodded and laughed warmly again.

They snowshoed right up to the door of Bill Hand's house, and Jamie knocked tentatively. When the door opened, Bill Hand was clearly preoccupied with something, and a bit flustered. When he saw Shelley and Jamie, however, he grinned at them. Jamie handed the present to him, and stood back. Bill Hand looked down at it in confusion, then realized that it was a gift. He opened it and held the signed first-edition copy of Walter Whetstone's book about Gettysburg as if it were a newborn baby. Jamie chuckled, "It's for your collection in the gatehouse."

Bill Hand gave them an odd look. He opened the book and saw the inscription. He pushed the book back and said, "This is inscribed to you, Jamie. You should keep it."

Jamie shook his head. "No, Bill, I want you to have it. I couldn't think what to get you, but I want to give this to you because it's a piece of the past—both our country's and my own. It belongs with the other signed first editions down there."

"Well, thank you, Jamie and Shelley. This means a lot to me. But I didn't get you two anything!"

"Then can I ask a favor, Bill?"

"You can *ask*, Jamie…"

"Well, do you mind if Shelley and I snowshoe up to the top of Mt. Buxtor right now?"

Bill Hand seemed pained by the question for a moment, but then he smiled. "Sure, just stay on the trail that goes to the right."

"Okay, thanks, Bill. Merry Christmas."

"Merry Christmas to you two!"

The deep snow made the journey to the top difficult, but the view from there was astounding. The snowcapped world below seemed to be highlighted with the alpine light of the day, and the contrast between the white land and the black sea was breathtaking. They stood silently and took it all in. As they watched some dark clouds making their way toward shore, they knew that they should turn around and get home. They kissed before they left, but there was something in the air that made them quicken their pace as they retraced their steps to the pipeline and headed home.

The next two days felt like a true holiday. With the owner of the store giving Shelley time off, the young couple was free to snowshoe around the peninsula and enjoy being outdoors with one another. At night, they cooked elaborate meals, and when they made love, they seemed to consume each other from within. And while they read their books in front of the fireplace, Shelley kept looking down at the ring she now wore. She couldn't help but feel that the deepening of their relationship and their newfound bliss was a direct result of this piece of jewelry on her finger. They both knew this idyllic period would end when this short vacation was over, but there was a feeling that something at the very core of their relationship had changed, and their world would never be the same again.

A few days later, as Shelley was in the shower getting ready for work, the phone rang. Jamie answered it enthusiastically, but the backdraft of breath from the other end was an immediate indication of something awful. "Jamie, this is Mrs. Vanes. Is Shelley there?"

Her voice was tinny and lifeless, and he knew bad times were coming. "She's in the shower."

"Please get her now."

He put the phone down and went over to the door of the bathroom and opened it. The steam of the shower pushed him back, and he hesitated for a moment before finally saying, "Shelley, your mom's on the phone."

"What does she want?"

"Something bad has happened."

"What?"

"I don't know."

The water shut off immediately and Shelley rushed past him to grab a towel and head out to the phone. She stood dripping wet as a pool of water formed around her feet, and she looked at the receiver like it was a poisonous snake. Then she grabbed it and said, "What's going on, Mom?"

Jamie watched helplessly as her knees buckled and she fell to the floor. As the towel slipped away from her wet body, she began sobbing, "Oh no, no, no! No, the baby can't be dead! He *can't* be!"

Jamie's breath was taken away. He went to touch her, but she angrily swatted his hands away. She sobbed and listened as her mother filled her in. Finally, she stood up and said in a cold voice, "I'll be right there."

When she hung up, Jamie didn't know what to do. He tentatively reached out and touched her naked shoulder. She was shivering as she said, "When they put Bobbie Junior to sleep last night, everything was fine. But when they checked on him at midnight, he was dead."

"Omigod!"

Shelley folded into Jamie's chest and howled with anguish. He held her tight and let the spasms of despair rock her. There was nothing to say, and the two of them stood together in the morning coldness of their cottage until Shelley said softly, "I need to go over to be with Clara."

"I'll come with you."

"No," Shelley said, shaking her head firmly. "She needs her family now. I'll head over there and call you when it's okay for you to come over."

She broke away and went to dress. Jamie's clothing was wet from the embrace, and he stood numb and cold as he watched her. He knew better than to force himself to go on this trip, but he felt a gut-wrenching frustration that he couldn't do or say anything that would help. He glanced up and noticed that the windows were letting in light the color of dirty dishwater. He put out his hand as Shelley walked past him, and she grasped it tightly, squeezed, and released it. She silently got her boots and coat on and left the cottage without another word. He heard the truck start up and the fading noise as it went down the snowy driveway. Soon he heard only his heartbeat as he stood there, not knowing what to do with himself.

Later, as he sat on the couch waiting for Shelley's call and staring off into space, Joe's truck pulled in and stopped outside the front door. Joe hopped out and came right into the cottage without knocking. Jamie looked up at him and saw the man's sadness. "I guess you heard."

"Yeah."

"I just can't believe it, Joe, I just can't!"

Joe said, "Get dressed. We gotta go."

"Where?"

"I'll tell you in the truck."

"Nah, I need to wait here until Shelley calls me."

"Get dressed, Jamie. We gotta go."

Jamie stood up and said forcefully, "No, Joe, I have to wait here for Shelley to call."

"I need your help corralling Wiley. He's freaking out about all of this, and he's gonna hurt himself or someone else. You seem to be the only one able to reach the boy, so come on."

When Jamie hesitated, Joe continued, "And Bobbie needs us, too. Understandably, he's not taking this too well, neither. Once we take care of Wiley, we'll head over to Bobbie and Clara's. So get dressed so we can get going!"

Jamie did as he was told, and they shuffled out to the truck and got in. They drove silently for a while, but then Joe said, "Vicky called me all scared about Wiley. After he got the news, he grabbed a bottle of Jack and drove off on his sled. Thought about heading out on my sled to find him myself, but I don't want to waste the whole morning following the boy all over God's creation. I figure we can cover more ground in the truck."

At the first road crossing of the pipeline, Joe stopped and they rolled down the windows. He and Jamie listened for the characteristic snarl of a snowmobile engine, but they couldn't hear anything. They checked at the store parking lot, just cruising through to see if his sled was there, and then they continued on to the next road crossing and listened again. All they could hear were the wind whispers of the winter woods.

Jamie said, "You think he might be at Bobbie's house?

"No, there's no way he'd head over there yet. He needs to get drunk first."

"The wharf?"

"Nope, I doubt it. I've never known him to go there unless he's going to work."

Jamie thought for a moment. "Let's drive out to the end of the pipeline. We can start there and work our way back. I think he likes it out there."

They drove on in complete silence. Joe's facial expression was stone-like and uninviting, and Jamie watched the stark forest whiz past his window while he wondered how Shelley was doing. He felt nothing but heartbreak.

They found Wiley there. He was at the water's edge, drinking from the nearly empty bottle of bourbon. As soon as Jamie glimpsed the solitary figure across the snow-covered field, he knew exactly what he needed to do. Joe parked the truck near the gate with the no trespassing signs on it reached for the door handle. Jamie said quietly, "No, Joe, I need to go alone."

"I'm not sure that's the best idea."

"I'm not sure it is, either, Joe, but it's what I need to do."

"Be careful, college boy. I know he's your friend and all, but he's also a wounded animal right now. He's likely to strike back at you."

Jamie nodded. "Yeah, probably....Hey, Joe?"

"Yeah?"

"Whatever happens, stay here in the truck, no matter what. Understand?"

"I dunno about that, Jamie"

"Just stay here, okay?"

Joe hesitated but then agreed.

Jamie walked Wiley's snowmobile trail. In the starkly white and open world of the field, it was impossible for him to sneak up, and his entire approach was warily watched by Wiley. And, as Jamie got closer, Wiley took another big swig from the bottle and barked out, "Go back to the fucking truck, college boy! I don't need you or your talk right now."

"Oh, shut the fuck up, Wiley."

Jamie's response immediately made Wiley stiffen like a snake about to strike. "What the fuck did you just say to me?"

"I'm hurting, too, Wiley. You don't get to tell me what to do just 'cause you're in pain. I'll walk up to you and talk to you if I want."

Though he couldn't hear anything from where he sat, Joe could instantly tell that Wiley was about to snap. He started to open his door, but he remembered Jamie's request. He sat fast, but he took the sawed-off shotgun down from the rifle rack behind his head—not to intervene when the inevitable fight happened, but to protect himself when Wiley turned on him.

Down at the shoreline, Wiley said tensely, "I'm gonna give you one more warning, college boy. Turn the fuck around and go back!"

"And I'm gonna only say it one more time, Wiley: shut the fuck up! I can do whatever I want to! If I want a drink from your goddamn bottle, you can't tell me that I can't."

Wiley's eyes went wild and he nearly whinnied, "Oh, college boy, come on and try!"

Jamie didn't hesitate. He continued to move forward and even thrust his hand out as if he was going to take the bottle right out of Wiley's hands. His audacity and confidence were enough to get him the time to snatch the bottle and take a slug. He grimaced as he swallowed, and then he said, "Not as smooth as that rot-gut you make, but still smooth. Now that I'm right here, Wiley, get out of your little self-pity party and go home to sober up enough to be a *real* friend to Bobbie and Carla!"

Wiley recoiled. "Put the bottle down, college boy!"

"Stop telling me what to do! You need to man up and quit this little wah-wah session!"

Wiley's punches knocked Jamie down before he knew what was happening. When his vision went white, he wasn't sure if he was losing consciousness or if his face was just in the snow. Either way, he knew he was a dead man if he didn't get up. He stood up, but Wiley caught him with a punch to the gut that lifted him off the ground and caused his breath to be caught inside his chest. He went back down onto his knees and struggled to exhale, while Wiley stood menacingly over him.

"You fucking little asshole!" Wiley screamed, spittle flying down onto the back of Jamie's head. "No matter how close you think we are, college boy, no one tells me to shut the fuck up and then drinks my booze! Nobody!"

Jamie struck quickly. He lunged and tackled Wiley around the waist, dragging him down. The move was surprising enough that he actually got two soft punches into Wiley's face before the boy recovered enough to pound Jamie with a couple of hard punches to the side of the head. Jamie's world was spinning out of control, and he knew he needed to stand up again. Slowly, he did just that. Blood was dripping from his eyebrow and his vision was blurry, and he was so wobbly it looked like a gust of wind might knock him over. When he brought his fists up again, Wiley bellowed, "For God's sake, college boy, why the fuck are you doing this??"

Jamie rasped, "It's what friends do."

That stopped Wiley in his tracks. "What did you just say?"

"Aw, dude, after friends drink together, they fight. That's how we unwind. Get rowdy and rough—it's fucking awesome! We fuck each other up, then we're friends again. That's what friends do, ain't it?"

Wiley's own words from the bachelor party made him shake his head like he was clearing cobwebs out of it. He waggled his finger at Jamie. "Are you telling me you're lettin' me beat the shit outta you because we're *friends*?"

Jamie spit rose-colored sputum into the snow. "People like me, we use our mouths to process our emotions as we talk out our happiness or anger or sadness. But people like you, you use your fists. This baby's death has hurt you more than you'd ever say, so I knew I had to give you an opportunity to say it another way."

"Are you totally stupid? I could've killed you!"

"Yep, I was gambling that you wouldn't, but I knew it was mighty risky."

"I'd say it was more than just risky, college boy. Matter of fact, I'm still thinkin' about getting one more good shot to your head to knock you out for being so goddamn stupid!"

"Maybe I'll surprise you and land my own knockout blow!"

But he didn't. Wiley's final punch was so powerful that Jamie saw the fist just milliseconds before everything went dark. Joe would later recount how the college boy's body keeled over like a plank of wood as soon as the fist connected with his head. But then Wiley kindly, almost tenderly, scooped his unconscious friend up and carried him over his shoulder to the snowmobile, started it, and drove it back to Joe's parked truck. As he let Jamie's body slide into the snow, he said with a shrug, "I'm gonna go home and sober up. I need to get over to Bobbie's, but not like this. When this crazy sonofabitch wakes up, tell him that I owe him one. Damn, people say that *I'm* crazy, but this shithead keeps beating me on that account. Holy fuck, this boy is good people, though!"

Wiley sped away and Joe let himself breathe again. He looked down at the shotgun sitting on his lap and pointed right at the driver's door. He uncocked it and put it back on the gun rack. He got out of the truck and grabbed a handful of snow to wake Jamie up. He sure as shit wasn't going to wrestle the crazy bastard into the truck while he was still unconscious.

When they pulled up to Bobbie and Clara's house later, there were so many cars filling the driveway and the shoulders of the road, they had to park nearly in the exact same spot that they had for the bachelor party. Joe nodded at the cars. "Well, they've got people here. That's good."

Jamie grunted his approval and looked into the side mirror to check his face. His split eyebrow was covered with a butterfly Band-Aid from the truck's first aid kit, and there was dried blood crusted on it like wax. There was some slight swelling, but no darkening yet. His face was still numb from the snow bath Joe had given him, and he knew that would help keep the swelling down.

When they spotted Winston over by the woodpile, they headed right for him. He smiled feebly when he saw them and said, "Hey, Jamie. Hey, Joe."

"Hey, Winston."

Joe cleared his throat. "How's it going here?"

"Oh, 'bout as good as you'd expect, I guess. The initial shock of it all has begun to wear off, and they've started to grieve in their own ways. Clara's inside, getting lots of love from her family, and Bobbie's alone in his shop getting drunk."

Joe shook his head and spit. "It don't seem right to have this happen to people like them."

"It never does, does it? Burying your own child is, without a doubt, one thing a parent shouldn't ever have to do. Me and my Katie did it."

"Oh, that's right; I forgot about that."

The old man turned to face Jamie. "My wife and I had a child who drowned. He was nearly seven when he died, which ain't a comfort or nothing, but at least he lived long enough to see some things of this world. This poor little one didn't even live long enough to see a full moon." The old man paused and his chin quivered with emotion.

Sensing his vulnerability, Jamie quickly said, "You want me to gather another armful of wood to bring inside for you, Winston?"

"No, I got it. But thanks for the offer, though." The old man ran his hand through his hair and shook his head to gather himself. "Are you okay, Jamie? Your face doesn't seem quite right today."

"Allergies, Winston. Is Shelley inside?"

"Yep, she's a mess. She'll be glad to see you. Come on, let's go in."

As they got to the door, Winston stopped and said, "You guys go ahead inside. I think I'll just keep piling this wood up by the door. Clara's in the living room with all the rest of the family. "

"Okay, Winston."

"Joe?"

"Yuh?"

The old man spoke in a loud whisper to both Joe and Jamie. "Clara's gonna need Bobbie to help her later on. So after you go inside and see her, could you two go out to the shop and try to get him to take it a little easier on the stuff? Everybody's too scared to go and tell him that, but maybe you two fellas can, huh?"

Joe grimaced. "I ain't gonna promise any miracles, Winston. I know that, if I was Bobbie, I'd be tying one on now, too. But we'll certainly try."

"Thanks, boys."

As cold and bleak as it was outside, the kitchen's warmth and aromas had the feel of something comforting and quietly consoling. A woman was stirring a pan on the stove, and when she saw them, she wordlessly pointed down the hallway like a silent Fate. They found Clara slumped against her mother on the couch in the living room. Mrs. Vanes was so large, Clara looked tiny and shrunken next to her. Other female relatives sitting in the chairs surrounding the couch looked up sadly at Joe and Jamie as they came into the room, but they quickly returned their attention to Clara. Shelley was in one of the chairs, and when she saw Jamie, she stood up and hugged him. When she pulled back, she exclaimed, "Oh, I'm so glad you're here! I haven't been able to get to a phone to—hey, what happened to your face?"

"Nothing. Long story."

Shelley was about to say something more, but then Clara saw Joe and cried out, "Oh, Joe!"

He went over to the couch. Clara seemed too weak to get up, so he put his hand on her knee. With sorrowful eyes, she thanked Joe for coming and added, "Bobbie's in the shop. He's—"

"Yeah, Jamie and I are headed there next."

Clara was the picture of devastation. Her hair was falling out of its ponytail, and loose wisps clung to her cheeks. The way she leaned up against her mother reminded Jamie of the way an old pier sags before it falls down.

Mrs. Vanes whispered something to Clara, who nodded and closed her eyes. Mrs. Vanes then spoke directly to Joe and Jamie. "I think it would be most helpful if you two headed right out to check on Bobbie. If you could relay the message that Clara's going to need his help this afternoon, that would be good."

Clara started to cry again. Her soft, soundless sobs began to pick up a squeaky gasp like an old foot-pump organ. Other family members came over to Clara to comfort her, but Mrs. Vanes waved them off with her stubby hands. Shelley kissed Jamie and said, "Good luck out there."

Jamie and Joe went out through the kitchen door and crossed the yard toward Bobbie's shop. Joe said, "You know this is going to suck, right?"

"Yep."

"I mean, you did just let Wiley beat the snot out of you. We may have to let Bobbie do the same thing."

"Okay, but it's your turn this time."

"In your dreams, college boy!"

When they rapped on the door, Bobbie yelled, "Who the hell is it now?

"Joe and Jamie."

"Aw, shit, come on in, guys."

Bobbie was sitting in a lawn chair next to the woodstove. It was quite warm in the shop, and the room smelled of varnish, salt, and fish. He remained seated as they came in, but he shook his head and muttered something at the stove, as if he were telling it something.

"You got it nice and warm in here, Bobbie," Joe said matter-of-factly.

"Yep, no reason to sit around in the cold and freeze, right? Pull up a seat."

Joe found a lawn chair that he set up next to Bobbie's, but Jamie couldn't find another one. He saw a bucket in the corner and brought it over near the stove, turned it over, and sat down.

Bobbie asked, "Did Clara's mom send you guys out here?"

"Naw. When we saw how many people are around in the house,

we decided to come out to see how you're doing, Bobbie. Didn't want you to be alone out here," Joe said.

"Bullshit. She sent you out here to get me to stop drinkin'," Bobbie chuckled.

"Yeah, maybe."

Bobbie reached for a bottle of scotch that was on the work table next to him. He tilted the bottle back and drank heartily from it, then he passed it to Joe and Jamie. After they each took a drink, Bobbie had another big swig. Joe said quietly, "You know, Bobbie, I think Clara needs you in the house."

"Uh-uh, she's got all her family in there with her. She don't need me."

"No, she does, Bobbie. She needs you to be around to help her deal with all this."

"Well, I don't want to go in there. There's too many people in there. Too many ghosts. The goddamn crib that I spent three hours assembling is still in there! And it's fucking empty now, too! Naw, I'm staying right here. You can't make me go in there!"

Joe kept his voice even. "No, I can't, Bobbie, you're a grown man. But you know what you need to do."

Bobbie's eyes shrank to slits and his voice sharpened. "So you two assholes think you can come in here and make me feel guilty, huh? Is that what you think?"

"Naw, Bobbie, we're here as friends—"

"Well, lemme ask you this, *friends*: have either of you lost a child before? Either of ya? Naw, you haven't. The last time I checked, Joe, your kid was alive and well, right? And you, Jamie, you've never even had a child, right? So, you two come waltzing in here with your sympathy, but you really don't have a fucking clue as to what I'm going through, do you? You both think I should just buck up and go inside to console my wife and her family instead of sitting here and getting drunk! Well, fuck you two and the horses you rode in on! How the hell could either of you understand what I need to do, huh? You can't! So, I'll tell you what, why don't you just get the hell out of my shop and leave me alone?"

Joe put his hands up in mock surrender. "Okay, okay, Bobbie, we're going. Sorry to get you mad. We wanted to let you know—"

"Yeah, duly noted. Now get the hell outta here."

"Okay, Bobbie, we're going. Come on, Jamie."

"I had a brother who died."

"*Huh?*" Bobbie grunted.

Jamie hadn't expected to open up about his past, but Bobbie's melancholy and anger brought it out. "My mother got pregnant when I was about nine years old. When she first told me the news, I hated her and my father for it because I thought they were replacing me. My family was pretty fucked-up back then. My dad was all about his job, so he gave more attention to his loan applicants than to me or Mom. And my mother was too busy with her social engagements with her country club friends to spend any quality time with me and my father. So, when I first heard that I was going to have a little brother, I was really mad. But then I started to realize that having a kid brother would make it so that I wasn't alone in the world anymore. Once I understood this, I couldn't wait for the little bugger to be born. When that day came, I thought of him as a miracle—one that lasted for the thirteen days he was alive, that is."

A tear welled up in his left eye and it dropped and ran down his cheek. "I went into his room every night to check on him. I know that sounds a little creepy, but I wanted to protect him and keep him safe. On the night he died, he seemed to be sleeping peacefully when I looked in on him. I wasn't totally sure if he was breathing or not, so I touched his little wrist. When his skin was cold, I knew he was dead. I remember thinking that it was up to me to do something to save him, but I was just a little kid, and I couldn't think what to do. So I started screaming for help. My parents came running in and started their own screaming. The noise was deafening."

"Jesus, that sucks, kid," Bobbie said, sitting forward in his chair.

"To this very day, my parents blame me, especially my mom. She's sure that I shook him, but of course I didn't. And every so often, she reminds me that if I'd only checked on Simon earlier, he might still be alive. I can't argue with that, I guess. My parents have never forgiven me, and I don't think I've ever forgiven myself."

Jamie's voice trailed off and there was silence in the shop until Bobbie coughed and said, "Aw, you can't blame yourself, Jamie."

Joe spoke up in a low voice. "You know, that's true for you, too, Bobbie. Sometimes these fucking horrible things happen, and nobody knows why."

Bobbie's face shriveled with anger. "But I know *exactly* why my goddamn boy died, Joe!"

"What do you mean?"

Bobbie inhaled sharply and said in a harsh whisper, "The satellite killed him."

"What?"

"Naw, listen to me." He swiveled his neck around, looking at the ceiling of his shop. "Guess what time it was last night when I last checked on him?"

"Eight o'clock?"

"It was quarter of eight when we went up to his room, and he was alive! The next time we saw him, Bobbie Junior was dead. Do you two really think that's a coincidence? I don't fucking think so! That goddamn satellite flew over and killed my boy. We've always thought it was up there to spy on us, but maybe it's part of a more sinister plan, huh? Maybe it's designed to kill people while they sleep."

Jamie looked at Joe, who returned the look with one of concern. The fire crackled in the stove, and Bobbie squinted angrily at Joe and Jamie. "You two don't believe me, huh? You both think I'm cracking up, don't you?"

"Naw, Bobbie, nothing like that," said Joe.

Bobbie stood up. "Well, I don't give a flying fuck what you think! We've all known that that Russian satellite is up there watching us, but maybe it's supposed to do something more than that! Maybe it's sitting up there waiting to pick us off, one at a time. If it is, then it's time that something was done to stop it. I don't know what I'm going to do yet, but I'm sure as shit not going to sit back and let it kill any more children!"

There was another moment of silence when Bobbie stopped talking. The three of them listened to the crackling of the fire, and then he took another swig from the bottle. "After I realized that Bobbie Junior wasn't breathing, I called 911. Then I went back into his bedroom and Clara was there, rocking him. When I told her that the ambulance was on its way, she ran right outside to wait. When I got out there, there she was in the front yard in her white nightgown, standing in the fresh snow holding our dead baby in her arms in the pale light of the moon. It took my fucking breath away 'cause they looked like fucking ghosts out there! Next thing I know, Clara lets out this howl that's louder than the ambulance siren, and it crackled and ripped through the trees like it was alive. I never heard nothing like it before in my life! And ever since that moment, whenever I close my fucking eyes, it's all I can hear in my head."

"Jesus, Bobbie, that's fucking horrible!"

There was another moment of silence. When Bobbie spoke again, his voice was steely. "Don't you guys see? That satellite is turning us all into ghosts down here!"

When Bobbie saw Joe and Jamie exchange quick glances, he barked, "Fuck you both!"

"Naw, Bobbie, we weren't…" Joe said, waving his hands.

"No, I get it. No one wants to hear what I'm saying. That's okay. I know what I've got to do, and I'm gonna do it. Fuck all of ya!"

"We could help you, Bobbie! We could—"

"Naw. If you two really want to be useful, why don't you go inside and tell Clara that I'll be right in."

32

Dearest Jamie,

*"Never mind, General. All this has been my fault. It is I
who have lost this fight, and you must help me out the best
way you can."*

*Robert E. Lee speaking to several of his generals after
the disastrous events of Pickett's Charge, July 1863*

*I do hate beginning a letter with an apology, but there is no way
to begin this letter without one. There were obviously more
undercurrents swirling around our household the night we had
you and the lovely Shelley Vanes over for dinner, and I should
have alerted you to them with far more up-front honesty. Because
I didn't, I am sure that you two were a bit confused as to the
reasons for the underlying stress between Maggie and myself
throughout our conversations and dinner. I only hope that you
were in no way thinking that it had something to do with your
visit or that you will have one iota of trepidation whenever we
invite you in the future. Much like Lee, I know that the
unpleasantness of the evening is all my fault, and I ask for your
help in helping me out of it.*

*I have cancer and I am leaving Bridgewater College. I know
that I am prone to overly dramatic outbursts, but the truth is the
truth. I have been diagnosed with carcinoid cancer of the colon
and small intestine. This type of cancer is slow-growing compared
with other forms, so this diagnosis is far from an immediate
death sentence. However, due to the fact that our children and*

grandchildren all live in California and the best cancer hospitals and clinics in the country are in that state, Maggie and I have decided to move to Palo Alto at the end of this academic year. After all these years here at Bridgewater and in Maine, we are still grappling with the true scope of that change.

Before you think that this is a goodbye letter, however, the real tension that was playing out on the evening of your visit had less to do with the ominous news, and more to do with the invitation I'm about to extend to you. I have been asked by the president of Stanford University to start an American Civil War program in their history department. I have accepted this offer wholeheartedly. And, as I am going to be given carte blanche to set up everything to my druthers, one of my first priorities is to assemble the team that will help me with this endeavor. It goes without saying that you are my first invitee. I can think of no one I would rather co-design this program with, and no one I would rather leave in charge whenever I cannot keep going.

The specifics of all of this are still developing, but I assure you that the wheels of the process are turning and the future is forming as we speak. Whether you will be required to be a graduate student to assist me in this is still in question, but the president of the university has mentioned scholarships and grants that may equate to a completely free ride for you. I know that you may be having second thoughts to as what your future holds, but I implore you to give this offer your utmost consideration. I cannot see another such opportunity ever arising again. I also cannot see another chance for you and I to ever work together, as the cancer will have its way with me eventually. I can think of no greater legacy than creating the greatest academic program about the American Civil War with you, Jamie Kurtz, so I hope that you will accept this offer.

Again, I apologize for not talking with you more clearly about these matters on the night of our dinner. I was worried that too much, too fast would be damaging. Now, of course, I see that what I strove to avoid became reality, regardless. Please inform

Ms. Vanes of this news and tell her that this offer to you includes some amazing opportunities for her as well. As far as I can see, this situation may be a win-win-win for everyone. Please be in touch and we can talk further about it.

Sincerely,

Walter Whetstone

P.S. Enclosed is an application from Stanford University. Due to the unusual set of circumstances behind all of this, the usual deadline for it does not apply. However, I suggest filling it out promptly and returning it to them posthaste.

33

Têt Nguyen Dan literally translated from Vietnamese to English means "the first morning of the first day of the new period," but the Tet celebration at Hai's house was not the beginning of anything good for Jamie Kurtz. And like those small and barely felt seismic events that are given credit for causing unseen damage to the internal supports of buildings that could ultimately result in their collapse, the early phone call from Jerry Shute would be the epicenter of something that would ultimately cause more destruction than it at first appeared.

Jamie picked up after three rings.

"Hey, Jamie, this is Jerry. Jerry Shute."

"Oh, hi, Jerry. What's going on?"

"Uh, your car is done."

"What?"

"Your car's repaired. You can come and take it as soon as you want."

Jamie was dumbfounded. "Really?"

Jerry chuckled. "Yeah. With all the snow that Nemo dumped on us, I've only been able to work on the cars inside the garage. So I focused all my time on finishing your Volvo. Cosmetically, there's a few more things to do, but I figure you can do those yourself and save some money. I started her up this morning and drove her in the garage a little, and it's clear that she's all good to go."

Jamie yelped, "Wow, I can't believe it! That's great news, Jerry!"

Shelley, who was drinking her last sips of coffee before heading off to the store, gave him a thumbs-up. She washed out her cup, put her coat on, and gave Jamie a peck on the cheek. Just as she was about to leave, Jamie asked Jerry, "Hey, is there any way that we could leave it right where it is? I mean, if it's in the way of your work, I can figure something out. But if it isn't, I'd like to keep it there for the time being."

Shelley stopped in mid-step. She brought her foot down slowly, and then backed away from the door and closed it. She spun and came right back into the living room, surprising Jamie when he hung up the phone. When she put her hands on her hips, he knew he was in for some kind of reaming out. "Did you just ask Jerry to leave your car in the garage?"

"Uh, yeah."

"Why would you do that?"

"Oh, well, we can't have it out in front in this snow, right? There's barely enough room for your truck out there."

"You could shovel out a parking spot for it."

Jamie looked outside and imagined shoveling the three and a half feet of heavy snow. He shuddered. "I'd need dynamite and a Bobcat to dig that out."

"That can be arranged." The tightness in her voice betrayed just how upset she was with him.

"Whoa. Why are you getting so worked up, Shelley?"

"Your car is *ready!*" she said loudly.

He was surprised by the volume of her response. "Yeah, I know it is. But why should I get it and not have anywhere to put it? I mean, it's safe right now inside the garage."

Shelley shook her head quickly. "It's probably in Jerry's way."

"No, he said it's not. He's got a couple of other vehicles in there, and he said he'll just go to work on them."

"But it's *ready!*"

"I'm confused, Shelley. Why are you freaking out on me?"

She scrutinized Jamie's face for a moment. "I guess I just assumed that, as soon as your car was fixed, you'd want to head right over there and get it. Well, your car is done, Jamie! Why are you still sitting on your ass? After all, once you have your car, you can get a frickin' job!"

"Wow. I didn't know it meant this much to you."

She started back toward the door. "I guess I hoped it meant that much to *you*, Jamie. But it apparently doesn't. Well, I've got to get to work. We can talk about it after the Tet celebration at Hai's."

She walked out and slammed the door. Jamie heard her footsteps crunching in the snow and then he listened as she got into her truck, started it, and drove off. He sank into the couch and thought about what had just transpired. He didn't think that he'd been acting irresponsibly, but clearly Shelley did. He struggled to figure out where he'd gone wrong. Her pointed comments about him sitting on his ass and getting a job were well-aimed jabs, but since he was enjoying the winter the way they'd discussed, he couldn't fathom that being the issue. He put it off as just that time of the month.

Later, as he took off his snowshoes and planted them in the snow outside Hai's house, he was startled by the number of parked vehicles in the plowed driveway. He walked up to the door, but before he could knock, Hai opened it, and the aroma of anise and the dry warmth of a woodstove knocked him back a little. Once inside, he could see that all the wharf rats, fishermen, and sternmen were wearing their best clothes and were combed and shaved like they were going out on the town, and he was glad that he'd listened to Shelley's advice and worn a nice outfit. Hai ushered Jamie through the living room, where Joe and Jimmy were standing with several other people, past Drake and Alfred sitting off in the den, and finally past the dining room, where Wiley and other sternmen stood with plates of food in their hands. Everyone nodded at him as he was pushed toward the kitchen.

Once there, he was greeted by a gaggle of Vietnamese women who bowed and shook hands with him as he was introduced. Atop the stove were two huge cauldrons that Jamie saw were full of the long-awaited *Pho,* and one of the women was ladling the soup into ornate bowls and handing them out to the waiting line of men beside her. After Jamie had his bowl filled, Hai's wife took him by the arm and guided him to the huge heaped platters of arranged food that were on the counter. She helped him to add the thinly sliced raw beef, bean sprouts, limes, Thai basil, onions, and jalapeño peppers into his bowl. After watching several men of Kestrel Cove knowingly top their bowls off with a squirt of hoisin sauce and then the fiery sriracha sauce, he did the same before heading to another part of the house to eat.

Jamie wandered until he found Wiley, who was holding a beer bottle with an unfamiliar label that featured a big "33" in the middle of a red oval. Jamie said, "Hey, what's that?"

Wiley smiled at him. "Oh, man, you didn't get a *Ba M'Ba?* I'll get you one."

He came back with two cold bottles, and they toasted quickly before Jamie said, "This is absolutely amazing! I've never seen anything like this before."

"This is one of the things I look forward to all year. I think everybody around here does."

Jamie nodded. "I just can't get over the amount of food. They could feed an army with all of it."

Wiley leaned in. "Not only that, dude, but this entire house has been cleaned, top to bottom, for Tet. Just to be invited here to take part in such an important holiday makes each of us a part of their family in a way, doesn't it?"

Jamie looked at Wiley and smiled, "Well said, man, well said."

Then Wiley put his hand on Jamie's arm and gripped it like a vise. "Dude, what'd you do to piss off Shelley? She unloaded on me when I was getting coffee at the store this morning. She was as mad as a wet hen."

"Jesus, Wiley, I don't know! All that happened was that Jerry called and told me my car was done."

"What?"

"I know—surprising, huh?"

"Did he actually use the word *done*?"

"Yep, he did. Anyway, when I told him that I didn't want to pick it up today and that I thought that leaving it in the garage was the best plan, Shelley flipped right out and got mad at me! I honestly don't know why."

Wiley raised a skeptical eyebrow at him. "You really don't?"

Jamie did a double-take. He thought his friend would share his own incredulousness over Shelley's apparent irrational anger, but his question implied that Wiley thought Jamie was in the wrong. But he still didn't know why. He shook his head. "No, Wiley, I don't. Do you?"

"Hey, dude, how have you been getting around lately?"

"On those beautiful snowshoes you made, buddy!"

Wiley nodded proudly. "Yeah. And how else?"

"Well, Shelley drives me around in her truck. Why?"

Wiley looked at Jamie to see if he got it, but nothing seemed to be dawning on him. He sighed. "Hey, have you met Jimmy's old lady?"

"Linda? Sure, a few times. Why?"

"She's got June twenty-fourth circled on the calendar. Know why?"

Jamie shrugged.

"That's the very date that Jimmy's DUI sentence ends, man!"

"Oh, that'll be good for Jimmy. What does that have to do with me?"

Wiley looked at Jamie closely, then cuffed him on the side of the head. "You take some stupid pills this morning? What the fuck do you think Linda would do if Jimmy told the courts on June twenty-fourth that he wanted to wait a little longer to be able to drive?"

The truth began to hit Jamie. "Are you trying to tell me that Shelley's tired of schlepping me around?"

Wiley got in Jamie's face and whispered, "Hey, bro, if there's one thing women hate more than anything else, it's having to carry their men. But Shelley's been doing that with you for a long time, right? If I were you, I'd go over there and pick up your car right after this little shindig! As for me, I'm gonna get another beer and then some of that delicious sticky rice and mango!"

Jamie watched him walk off and he felt sore. He didn't like Wiley's implication that he'd been a burden to Shelley, and the potential truth of the accusation made his stomach uneasy.

The warm house, the Vietnamese music, and the smell of incense transported everyone to a land that was 8,000 miles away, and the afternoon felt completely magical. But as soon as Shelley, Clara, and Bobbie walked into the house, there was a noticeable change in the atmosphere. All conversations skittered and stopped as they came out the kitchen with their plates and bowls and each took a different path. Shelley sought out Jamie and gave him a loving peck on the cheek as she sat down next to him. Clara walked right to where Joe and Jimmy were standing and started talking to them in whispers. Bobbie, however, surveyed the rooms carefully before opting to settle in a far corner away from everyone else.

Jamie looked at Shelley and smiled weakly. She rolled her eyes at him and said, "I'm really sorry for getting so mad at you this morning."

"Naw, I get it. Wiley helped me see what's going on."

"Wiley?"

"Yeah, the boy is a helluva lot wiser than I give him credit for. He explained in his own way how you're tired of schlepping me around and that I should just go pick up my car."

Shelley had a spoonful of soup up to her mouth, but she lowered it. "Jamie, I'm not tired of schlepping you around at all. As a matter of fact, I like being with you in the truck. No, there's something else bothering me."

"There is?"

"Yep, but this isn't the time or place to talk about it. Let's have a heart-to-heart later tonight."

Because Shelley's comment sounded just like what Laura had said to him before breaking up, Jamie's heart jumped into his throat and his eyes took on a panicked look. She saw his reaction and reached out to touch his arm. "Oh, hey, come on, it's nothing bad! After our exchange this morning, I realized that we've got some things to hash out that we've never sat down to talk about fully. I think talking will help us work it out. Okay?"

"Okay. Tonight we talk."

"Good."

"So, how are Bobbie and Clara really doing?"

Shelley looked up. "Ah, you know. They're still healing. But it's gonna take a shitload more time."

"Yeah, it's kinda weird that Clara's chatting with Joe and Jimmy in the living room while Bobbie's standing alone over there in the den."

Shelley whispered, "She's talking to those guys because she's really worried about Bobbie. He's been doing some strange things since Bobbie Junior's funeral."

"Like what?"

"Well, she says he doesn't sleep much these days. He seems to be spending his nights reading in his shop. He keeps making trips to the library to take piles of books out, and after he reads them all, he fills up notebooks with notations. And he's started driving to random places. He's driven to Portland a couple of times, and he's even gone up to Augusta, but he won't tell Clara why. She's worried, and she's asking Joe and Jimmy if they can intervene somehow."

"I don't think reading and learning should ever be seen as weird behavior. The man is just processing his grief through some normal channels, if you ask me."

Shelley chuckled. "Only in Jamie Kurtz's world would it be normal for Bobbie Schmidt to spend his nights reading and his days driving all over the place!"

Later, when Shelley had gone off to chat with some other people, Jamie wandered toward a bookshelf in the den to look over the titles. Suddenly, he heard a hoarse whisper. "Hey, Jamie, come here."

He turned around and saw Bobbie Schmidt gesturing to him. When he got closer, the man actually pulled him into the corner with him.

"Hey, Shelley tells me you bought a bunch of your Christmas gifts at the pawn shop at the Corners. Is that true?"

"Yes, it is. I got Joe's gun there, and Vicky's scissors, too."

"Huh. You don't say. I've driven by the place a million times, but I've never been inside. Did you notice anything else for sale there?"

Jamie shrugged. "Bobbie, the entire building is full to the gills with stuff. There's everything you can imagine in there!"

"Hmm, yeah, well, that makes sense. Did you see anything else that caught your eye?"

Jamie replayed the items in his head. He remembered seeing that there was an electric guitar and amp, a drum set, a computer, and a huge telescope still in the box. When he told Bobbie about each of these items, he seemed to nod absently until he heard about the telescope. He peered intently at Jamie. "So, was the telescope nice?"

Jamie admitted that he didn't know much about telescopes, but that the photo on the side of the box made it look like it was short and stubby like a mortar. Their conversation was interrupted by Hai's announcement that he was going to hand out the lucky money in the red envelopes, which aroused a lot of excitement among the guests. When Jamie turned to resume his conversation with Bobbie, the man was gone.

Jamie noted that Bill Hand was not at the celebration. Although he was a notoriously private person and the people of Kestrel Cove had grown accustomed to not seeing him around much, the man had been even more noticeably absent lately. Jamie made a mental note to go over to his house and visit him soon.

When Hai handed him a little red envelope, he looked down at it with uncertainty. He walked over to Joe and asked quietly, "What's this, Joe?"

"It's the Vietnamese tradition of handing out money to all the guests. Inside these envelopes could be a penny, a nickel, a dime, a quarter, a dollar bill, or, if you're lucky, ten bucks."

Jamie considered the number of guests. "That's a helluva lot of envelopes!"

His captain nodded. "Yep, it is."

"I'm not gonna take this! I'm going to hand it right back."

Joe said, "You have to take the envelope, Jamie. It'd be very rude not to accept it. Most of us just put it down on the counter and forget it there. That way, we've accepted it and been polite to Hai and his family's tradition, but our own foolishness allows them to take it back. We all save face that way!"

There was one dollar in Jamie's envelope, and he carefully placed it on the counter near the phone when he went to get his coat. Shelley was ready to leave, too, so they went as a couple and thanked Hai and his family profusely for their generosity. As they walked out into the bitterly cold air, an awkwardness hit them both. Shelley had driven to the celebration in her truck, but Jamie had snowshoed there. The crux of the issue they needed to talk about was now back in the forefront and neither one knew an acceptable way to sidestep it. Finally, Jamie decided to charge ahead. "Hey, Shelley, can I get a ride home with you? I talked with Jerry in there, and told him I'm going to pick up my car tomorrow morning."

Shelley nodded and smiled at him, but there was a darkness to her face that showed she was still troubled by something. He gathered up his snowshoes, threw them into the bed of the truck, and got into the cab. As she backed down the driveway and started driving for home, she said, "This isn't about any inconvenience in giving you rides, Jamie. You know that, right? I mean, there's a little more to it than that."

Jamie could tell that the conversation was coming sooner than he'd expected, and he felt a little sad about that. He had to admit that he'd hoped to have it later—with Shelley naked and in bed. But it was clear that she needed to get it out now.

"I got upset this morning, Jamie, because I'm worried about you."

"About me?"

"Yeah. I'm not sure you're doing what you should be doing."

"Shelley, we've talked about this before. We agreed that when lobstering was over, I was going to start enjoying winter in Kestrel Cove."

"Okay, Jamie, that's true. But what are you planning to do this spring?"

Jamie shrugged. "I thought I'd wait and see."

They were just coming up to the parking lot of the store and Shelley suddenly veered off into the lot and jammed on the brakes. Her truck hit the compacted snow of the lot and slid furiously toward the towering piles that the plows had heaved up on the edges. They both braced for impact, but just before that happened, the tires gripped enough to bring the vehicle to an abrupt stop. Jamie was about to yell at her, but Shelley was already barking at him. "How can you sit there and act like nothing has changed? For God's sake, Jamie, *everything's* changed! Bobbie Junior died, Bobbie and Clara are wrecked human beings, and I've been thrust into helping them and Momma more and more. Meanwhile, Walter Whetstone is dying of cancer and wants you to go to California with him and set up a new program in one of the top universities in the country. Yet all you do is sit around the cottage and drink or go snowmobiling with your buddies every day."

"But that's what we said I'd be doing."

"Yeah, before all this other shit happened. You have this big incredible opportunity to change your life, yet you seem willing to sit on your ass and let it pass you by."

"I love you, Shelley Vanes."

"You can't be content to just become one of the guys on this fucking peninsula. You're better than that, Jamie Kurtz!"

"I love you, Shelley Vanes."

"You don't need to keep saying that, Jamie! I know you do. I love you, too! We're talking about something else here…"

As she trailed off, Jamie calmly began to talk. "I love you, Shelley Vanes. I keep saying that because that's all I know for sure. The rest of it, I don't know. I don't know when my time is going to be up like Bobbie Junior or Walter. And I don't know for sure if I want to move to California to become an academic for the rest of my life. I don't know any of that. But I *know* that I love you, Shelley Vanes. That, I know."

Shelley was out of the truck before Jamie could react. He unbuckled his seat belt and got out, too, but by the time he did, she was pacing angrily in front of the truck. When he tried to touch her, she smacked his hand away and continued to pace. Totally frustrated, Jamie yelled, "Shelley, what the hell is the matter with you?"

She stopped and screamed back, "Do you have any idea how it feels to be the noose around someone's neck? That's how I feel. Like I'm choking you to death. It's horrible! If I weren't in your life right now, you'd be getting ready to move to sunny California and start the most exciting new chapter of your life. But you're not doing that—and it's all because of me!"

Jamie grabbed her and hugged her. She struggled in his arms and kicked him painfully in the shins, but he held tight to her. She continued to thrash, but he said soothingly, "Shelley Vanes, you're the very best thing that's ever happened to me! You're not keeping me from anything, and you're certainly not a noose! Let me enjoy this time with you. Please. For the first time in my life, I feel alive. I'm not just some kind of prodigy who's wasting his potential while creating a well of disappointment for those who supposedly want the best for me. I am finally just Jamie Kurtz, friend to some, buddy to others, and lover to the one who I adore."

Shelley heard him and stopped struggling. She hugged him back, but she was crying when they pulled apart. He wiped her tears away with his finger, but she grabbed his hand and held it tightly. "Just do me two favors, okay, Jamie?"

"Okay."

"Get your car tomorrow from Jerry."

"Done."

"And fill out the Stanford application that Professor Whetstone sent to you. Please? I will feel a helluva lot better if you'd just do that, okay?"

As Shelley watched Jamie nodding his assent, she felt a sense of deep self-loathing. She knew that he was only going to do those things because she'd made a scene and he wanted to appease her, not because he'd had a real change of heart. She also knew that she should have included herself with Clara and Bobbie when she'd made that comment about the baby's death wrecking them. And her sudden awareness of her own brokenness made the Vietnamese food in her stomach threaten to go on its own Tet Offensive.

34

March came in like a lamb that spring. As the temperatures continued to rise and the sunshine poured down, the peninsula quickly thawed and got ready for an early spring. The snow on the ground disappeared, the grass became deep green in places, and the buds on the trees swelled like nipples. Spring had sprung with such fervor, more than a few worried that the month would go out like a devastating lion. The change of seasons meant that the snowmobiles were put away and the fishermen began to prepare their fishing gear and boats for lobstering. The cove was ice-free, and Drake was convinced enough to start setting up dates for the boat-hauling truck to come and put the boats back in the water.

Jamie had kept both of his post Tet-celebration promises to Shelley. He'd gone to Jerry Shute's the very next morning and picked up the Volvo. Because the front quarter panels had been salvaged from different vehicles, one side of his car was now snow-white and the other chocolate-brown. Jamie didn't care in the least because when he turned the key, the engine purred more smoothly than it ever had. The steering felt a little tight, but Jerry swore it would work itself out. Jamie was shocked when the mechanic announced that, after Drake's payment deduction, he only owed $279.67. But when he started to argue that the figure was too low, he saw that Jerry was slightly insulted so he just paid him. When he was ready to drive away, Jamie wasn't surprised when the mechanic handed him a coffee can full of nuts and bolts, just as Joe and Jimmy had prophesied all those months ago. He looked down at the greasy pieces of metal and laughed. Then he put the can down between the front seats as a monument to it all, and drove the car out of the garage and into the wintry world.

Having a car immediately had a huge impact on the rest of Jamie's life. He was now able to drive to the store to visit Shelley more often and go over to both Joe's house and Wiley's cottage for daily visits. He even drove into Brementon and filled out the Stanford application with Walter Whetstone in his office on the Bridgewater College campus. The old professor was overjoyed at this, and he kept pushing Jamie to commit to the plan. But Jamie would not do that. He just kept saying that he needed to wait and see what happened this spring before deciding.

Shelley was generally happier, but she also saw with raw clarity that the showdown the two of them were working so hard to avoid was, in fact, inevitable. No matter how much they tried to ignore it and shove it into a corner, they knew that it was patiently waiting for just the right moment to spring back out. And after spending many nights talking together, Shelley saw their situation as a Mexican standoff. The truth was hard to ignore: Jamie's future was in California and hers was tethered to Kestrel Cove. And even though they loved one another and wanted to be together, there was no way to remedy the oppositional nature of their futures. It vexed her that Jamie stubbornly held on to staying in Kestrel Cove. No matter how much she argued that they could do the long-distance relationship thing until she was free to come out to join him in California, he continued to shake his head and declare that that was not an option. His lack of flexibility on the issue made her uncomfortable beyond words.

Mrs. Vanes's pulmonary embolism decided the issue. When Shelley found her mother nearly unconscious, wracked with shooting chest pains and spitting up blood, she immediately called for an ambulance. And as they rode together to the hospital in Brementon, Shelley felt like she was inside a compactor that was crushing her and forging her new reality. She knew that since Leon was more or less useless in taking care of her mother and the children, it would inevitably fall to her. Shelley now knew that she would never be able to leave Kestrel Cove while her mother needed her.

When Jamie arrived at the hospital and tried to comfort her, she stiffened at his touch. She knew she should be eternally grateful for his presence, but she felt nothing but nausea. Jamie acknowledged this by staying in the periphery of the hospital waiting room, away from Shelley and the rest of the family. He wasn't sure about the reasons for her apparent cold shoulder, but he was comfortable enough swimming in the less visible back currents, helping out wherever and whenever he could.

Mrs. Vanes's doctors suggested an initial treatment plan of giving the anticoagulants and thrombolytics a chance to dissolve the clot. If that was successful, a more invasive procedure could be averted. The family waited with bated breath to see what would happen next, and Jamie was with them during that stressful time. He just sat several seats away from Shelley.

When the clot finally responded to the treatment and disappeared completely, the family's celebration was abbreviated by the dire warning that Mrs. Vanes needed better care at home to prevent this from happening again. Shelley knew what that meant—she would have to become the full-time caretaker of her mother. After all, the family could not afford to pay for a visiting nurse, Clara was in no shape to take on such an endeavor these days, and the brother in Portland, although concerned for his mother's health, was unable or unwilling to contribute enough time to make the situation better. So, by default, it all fell on Shelley.

Mrs. Vanes was transported back to her home, and many pieces of the puzzle still had to be fit into place. While it was understood that Shelley would be moving back into the house, she needed to figure out whether she could continue to work a few shifts at the store and whether she should move all of her stuff out of the cottage. Unfortunately for Jamie, she remained unapproachable as she wrestled with these decisions. Those around the situation, especially Joe and Wiley, wondered quietly how long Shelley and Jamie's relationship could take the warping and stretching forces it was now encountering. Being realists, they all figured that it would come apart before the summer.

Jamie, however, was completely at peace. As soon as he'd heard the diagnosis of Mrs. Vanes, he knew that he was not going to leave Kestrel Cove. His plan was to stay in the cottage for another month and then move back into his tent on the site by the store. The weather was continuing to be perfect, and he would help Joe and Jimmy get the lobstering gear ready for the season and help Shelley with her mother. He hadn't told Walter Whetstone that he would not be going to Stanford with him yet, but he figured that the professor, although disappointed, would surely understand and give him his blessing.

The mistake that Jamie made was telling all of this to Shelley during one of their short times together at the cottage. She was there to pick up some clothing, and although she had convinced herself she would not engage in a painful confrontation with him, each declaration of his new life plan felt like a punch to her gut, and she began shrieking at him that she would not, could not, be the source of such a monumentally stupid waste of talent. But it was like verbal sparring with a Buddhist monk—she'd swing with an emotional rebuttal and a cutting truth, and he'd just calmly and selflessly parry it. When it was clear that she was unable to convince him to see the situation her way, she even resorted to using the threat of just plain breaking up with him. But even as she said these awful words out loud, she knew that this threat didn't carry an ounce of truth: she didn't want to be apart from Jamie Kurtz at all; she just didn't want to be the one responsible for his missing out on an amazing opportunity such as Stanford.

After their confrontation, she kissed him and drove away with a forced smile on her face. When she stopped at the end of the driveway to look for oncoming traffic, she knew she needed to throw up. She barely got the door open before the contents of her stomach began to spew forth onto the ground. She wiped her mouth and closed the door when the heaving and retching were finally over. As the engine idled roughly, the solution came to her. As excruciatingly painful as it was going to be, she saw what needed to be done and how to do it. And, although it would break her heart and Jamie's, too, it was ultimately less destructive than allowing things to unfold the way he had laid it out. She began to drive toward her mother's house, knowing that she had to find some time to talk to Wiley and Vicky later that day. One of those two had enough love for Jamie to help her with her horrible plan, and the other one had the ethical flexibility to understand and forgive it all.

After helping her mother for a few hours, Shelley lied and said that she had to help out at the store. As she drove back toward the cottage, she cried about what she was planning to do. And even though she knew it would make matters more complicated and add exponentially to the level of the heartbreak, she knew that she needed to make love with Jamie Kurtz one last time. She found him reading in the living room, and she satisfied this yearning completely before lying to him about going to work a shift at the store—and heading right over to Vicky and Wiley's instead.

Two days later, Jamie was pleasantly surprised to find Shelley's truck parked at the cottage when he came home from another day of painting buoys with Joe and Jimmy. He noticed Wiley's dirt bike propped up against the house just as he opened the door and walked in. When his eyes adjusted to the darkness, he was caught so off guard by the trail of clothing on the floor that he stopped dead in his tracks. The trail ended in the living room, where two bodies lay twisted together in an impassioned embrace. At first, Jamie's brain refused to acknowledge what he was seeing, but then it hit him with walloping clarity—Shelley and Wiley were naked on the floor, entwined and kissing passionately. Jamie made a choking sound, and the two struggled to stand up, yelling shocked curses.

"What the hell's going on?" Jamie yelled back.

The two of them tried to cover their nakedness with their hands and arms, but they couldn't. All Shelley managed to say was, "Oh, God, Jamie! I'm so sorry!"

Jamie's eyes grew larger and then narrowed to an angry squint. "How long have you two been doing this behind my back?"

Wiley shrugged. "Hey, man, Shelley and I used to date at the end of high school. We both knew we couldn't be a couple, but we've stayed friends with benefits ever since. I'm really sorry, dude, that you had to see this."

Shelley put her hand out and her voice broke. "Jamie, I can explain. Let me tell you—"

"*No!*" he screamed, and staggered backwards a few steps. "It's all been a lie, Shelley? This whole thing was nothing but a lie?"

Her voice cracked again as she said, "No, Jamie, not a complete lie. I love you, but I guess I'm no different from Angie Williams in the end."

Jamie inhaled sharply. "Oh, my God! I can't believe you two would do this to me. I really thought you were my friends!" He put his hands to his head and croaked, "Holy shit, does the whole town know about this?"

"I doubt it, bro. Shelley and I've been real careful, but you know how news gets out and travels in this place."

Jamie shook his head. "Everyone's been laughing at me this whole time! Here I've been thinking that everybody was happy for us, but they've all known that you two are fuck buddies! Jesus H. Christ, I'm gonna be sick!"

He took a step back toward the kitchen and Shelley wailed, "Don't go, Jamie!"

He turned and waved his arms in front of him. "Oh, I'm gonna go, Shelley! I'll find a place to sleep for the night, then I'm coming back to get my stuff out of here tomorrow and get out of this goddamn town! Just don't be here when I come back, okay? Either of you! I just can't believe you'd do this to me! I just can't believe it!"

They listened to him slam the door and drive away in his Volvo. Shelley began to sob uncontrollably and Wiley hugged her. He was choked up enough that his voice was soft and fragile when he said, "It was for the best, Shelley. You did the right thing."

35

In a poll conducted by the *Bangor Daily News*, sixty percent of the participants in the survey did not know the name of the current governor of the state of Maine. Seventy-five percent said that they would not be able to identify the man from a photo. Whereas these results would be damning to most politicians, this anonymity suited Governor Turk Willis fine. What it told him was that he was doing things just right. In his eyes, only a truly independent politician was able to fight the good fights in Augusta to make necessary changes and enact the needed reforms without polarizing the situation. He'd seen enough governors who were unable to avoid the slings and arrows from the normal party warfare, and their recognition was far higher, but it came only from hatred and political scorn. When he looked at his high approval rating at the same time as the low recognition numbers, he felt as ghostly and powerful as he had while serving in Vietnam.

While he and his campaign managers were quite willing to advertise that he'd proudly served in the military, they were very careful not to bring up too many details. Being a veteran was a badge of honor that led to votes and political victories, but being a tunnel rat only meant trouble. Just trying to explain how a sane young man could crawl through the snake-infested underground tunnels of the Viet Cong to kill his enemy with pistols, knives, shovels, and his bare hands made Turk Willis sound more like someone who needed shock therapy, medication, and possibly hospitalization than a viable political candidate. And for most voters, the fact that he'd served in Vietnam was more than enough to gauge the man's abilities and beliefs. They didn't need any more details on the matter.

But one of the best things that came from Turk Willis's obscurity was a sense of security. He wasn't noticed by many people when he ventured out into the world, and the man had absolutely no enemies. Sure, he needed some protection as a public official, but it was hard to think of either Vince Evans or Jack Bell as bodyguards. These two high school buddies had gotten their jobs as clear friendship favors, and neither man was properly trained or physically fit enough to actually guard the governor. Their role was merely to walk next to him wherever he went and make it appear that he was protected. Who they were trying to fool by doing this was debatable.

So when Turk Willis left the State House early for the luncheon of young Republicans at the VFW hall in the nearby town of Gardner, it was frighteningly easy for Bobbie Schmidt to knock these two men out as they walked with the governor toward his car in the State House parking garage. As a matter of fact, when Bobbie jumped them, he could have sworn that one of the men emitted a high-pitched scream that, under other circumstances, would have been amusing. But the seriousness of his mission prevailed, and he used his homemade blackjack—a tube sock loaded with D batteries—to knock the two men out with two swipes. After that, grabbing the governor and shoving him into his waiting pickup truck had been easy because the man was in too much shock to resist.

Ironically, the truth was that the governor's obscurity hadn't created security, it had spawned apathy. Even after Vince Evans and Jack Bell came to and alerted the authorities to the fact that the governor of Maine had just been abducted, many law enforcement officials were crippled by doubt and disbelief. When the announcement finally went out, some police officials actually looked at the calendar to make sure the call wasn't some kind of April Fool's prank. This hesitation gave Bobbie Schmidt a substantial head start. By the time the police cars were peeling out of their parking lots, his truck was already on the back roads that would take him to his intended destination.

Turk Willis sat completely silent as the truck whirled along. Although initially surprised by the attack, the decorated war veteran was now clearheaded and in complete control of his emotions. Eventually, he said, "Son, do you really expect to accomplish anything with all this? All you're gonna do is get someone hurt."

"Sorry, sir, but I've got to show you something," Bobbie said without taking his eyes off the road.

The governor certainly wasn't scared or even nervous. As a former tunnel rat who'd killed forty-five enemy soldiers in hand-to-hand combat during his two tours, Turk Willis was a man who did not tend to get either scared or nervous. Ever. He'd already done his own quick assessment of the situation and found nothing in the abduction worthy of concern. There were just enough clues around the pickup truck for him to infer that the driver was a lobsterman, and nothing in the man's tone or actions spoke of anger or a real threat. Turk Willis was simply intrigued as to why a lobsterman would go through the trouble of knocking out two security men to hustle the governor into a pickup and entice the law enforcement community to chase him, especially when he could have easily walked into the governor's office on any given day and chatted right there with him.

On the other hand, the governor felt a growing sense of anger—and it wasn't toward his kidnapper. The apparent lack of response from law enforcement made Turk Willis simmer with rage. How many drills did they have to go through to practice what to do in case of a scenario just like this one? Bile churned in his stomach as he imagined the comically inept responses of the law enforcement officials, and he swallowed hard and said dryly, "You do know, son, that you're not going to get any money from this, right?"

Bobbie Schmidt scoffed, "It's not about money, sir. You just gotta see something."

"You know, you could've made an appointment. I would have gladly and willingly come with you to see whatever you're going to show me now."

"You wouldn't have come, sir. There's no way to make it all sound believable. It's something you've just gotta see with your own eyes. This was the only way, I swear."

"What am I going to see, son?"

"You'll see."

"Huh. I'm not much into guessing games. Can you at least tell me where we're headed?"

Bobbie thought on this some and said, "To the coast, sir."

The governor cleared his throat. "Where on the coast?"

"Why are you asking all these questions?" Bobbie said, a note of irritation creeping into his voice. "It's not like you're wearing a wire or anything."

The governor looked hard at the boy and smiled. There'd been a recent battle in the legislature over whether the governor should be allowed to wear a microphone and recording device for an upcoming documentary made by Maine Public Television about the workings of state government. It had been ultimately rejected for fear that important security details would be leaked outside the political arena of Augusta. What those details might be exactly, and why anyone would be worried to have them known, were two questions the governor had not understood, but the motion had been voted down nonetheless. Bobbie's comment about him not wearing a wire made the governor *like* this crazy lobsterman.

Turk Willis said, "Well, ya see, since there doesn't seem to be a single goddamn State Trooper who's gotten out of the Dunkin' Donuts fast enough to get on the road to chase us yet, and I figure that you and I are going to be spending some time in this here truck, I was thinking that we could talk a little."

"Okay."

"Well, son, to start with, I don't know exactly how I became your enemy."

Bobbie shook his head. "Naw, you're not the enemy, sir. I actually need your help. I'm hoping that, after you see what I'm going to show you, you'll become my ally and a friend to all of Kestrel Cove."

"Oh, is that where we're headed?"

Bobbie grimaced at having given it away too early. "You probably haven't heard of it, huh?"

"It's a small fishing community south of Brementon, right?"

Bobbie glanced over with a grin. He was impressed. "Well, I'll be damned."

"I've never been there, as you probably know, but I've been to the Corners. I was there once to open a new store where they fry all their ice cream. It seems ludicrous to me that people need to spend good money on a fried scoop of vanilla ice cream, but I honestly don't understand this new generation. I do, however, understand that that whole area is a symbol of rebirth and that this state could use more of that."

Bobbie scowled. "Well, I'm not taking you to see any rebirth, Governor. Just the opposite, actually. I'm gonna show you something that's been a symbol of fear and intimidation for generations. And I've learned firsthand that it's now become an agent of death, too. All of us in Kestrel Cove have been telling ourselves that we've just got to live with it 'cause no one would believe us if we tried to tell them about it. But after today, it won't be our dirty little secret anymore. That's why I need you to see it, sir."

"What is *it*? You keep saying it, it, it—but what the hell is *it*, son?"

"You'll see, sir, and then I'm sure you're gonna do something about it. That's why I'm doing all of this!"

"Okay, you said that *it* has been killing people...do you have any proof of that?"

Bobbie drew a small photo from the pocket of his flannel shirt and put it in the governor's hand. Turk Willis looked down at the picture of a newborn baby. He felt a rush of electricity go through his system because, if this photo was of this young man's dead baby, he realized there might yet be a reason to be afraid, and he had the first pang of discomfort. He knew better than most men that the anger over a dead child could sometimes make normal and gentle people do very bad things. He said quietly, "What was his name?"

Bobbie gulped, "Bobbie Nemo Schmidt."

"When did he die?"

Bobbie took a heavy breath and glanced at the speedometer. "A little over two months ago."

"And the thing you're going to show me killed him?"

Bobbie looked over at the governor with a sense of relief. "Yes, sir, I believe so."

"Well, then I want to see it. Perhaps you should have led the whole conversation with this photo to get my attention. If you think something is killing children, I want to see it. Now, you know my name, obviously, but I'm tired of calling you 'son' like some kind of old Western movie."

"It's Bobbie Schmidt."

"Okay, that's better. Hello, Bobbie Schmidt, I'm Turk Willis."

The governor beamed as if he were in a photo shoot at a press conference. Bobbie's serious expression turned into a smile, and he admitted to himself that this governor was a cool operator, given the circumstances.

"So, what's your plan now, Bobbie?"

"Get you right to Kestrel Cove, sir."

The governor chuckled. "Oh, I hope you've got something more than that planned. You've obviously done some prep for all this, but I think once the cops and sheriffs get off their asses, it's going to get a little dicey!"

"Knew it would somewhere along the way, sir."

The governor clicked his tongue and tilted his head in thought. "The way you drove slowly and smoothly away from the State House parking garage probably means that no one noticed our departure. And even when they wake up, Vince and Jack won't know which way we went. So that means probably no one knows at this very moment what's going on. But as soon as they do, the State Troopers will load up on I-95 and the Maine Turnpike, since it's protocol for the main highways to be monitored, and then they'll let the local sheriffs patrol the back roads. I'm sure they'll put a lot of eyes on Route 1, too. So, until they get something airborne, you're pretty safe going this way. But ultimately, we're talking roadblocks and searches, Bobbie. I think that getting past them to Kestrel Cove is going to be pretty tricky."

"If I keep to these back roads, sir, we'll be just fine. Like you said, no one knows who I am, the color of my truck, or where I'm taking you. Maine is a big small state, if you know what I mean, and there's a shit-ton of back roads that go in every direction. All the helicopters and planes in the world can't go everywhere at once. I think we'll be fine."

"Well, good, Bobbie, since I really don't want to end up being killed in a high-speed pursuit or in a shootout or something like that. That won't accomplish what you're after, will it?"

"Right."

"I'm just hoping that you're prepared for the whirlwind of attention that's going to come our way when they do find you, that's all. For both our sakes."

"Do you know your Maine history, Governor Willis?"

"You can call me Turk, Bobbie. And I would say that I know Maine history as well as anyone, I guess. I get half the questions correct on that high school quiz show on Channel 8 on Saturday nights."

"Huh, that's better than me," Bobbie said with a grin. "Well, do you know what was taking place from 1927 to 1933 in this country?"

"Um, just before the Depression and the Second World War and just after the First World War? Oh, that would be Prohibition."

"Very good. Now, during that time, did you know that Maine was a major player in the black-market alcohol industry? Canadian producers, New England rumrunners, Maine fishermen, local bootleggers—they all worked to get the booze in and out of Maine to keep the real drinking establishments going during the dark times. And Kestrel Cove was one of the busiest ports on the entire coast for this kind of activity."

"I'm not sure what this has to do with our current situation…"

"I won't bore you with the details, Governor. Just know that my grandfather talked to me about those times quite a bit. He never admitted whether he was directly involved or not, but I know that he worked with Oliver Muldoon back in those days, and that that man was involved with the business of bootlegging. With all that illegal booze coming in and being transported through Kestrel Cove, do you want to take a guess at how many people were arrested during those years?"

"I wouldn't have the foggiest idea."

"None. Not one person from Kestrel Cove was ever captured or arrested. Whenever the G-men would shut down one route and be ready to sweep in for an arrest, the runners would switch to another route and sneak past. The shore would be lined in one area waiting for a shipment, and the delivery would be made to another. They never caught them. Never. So if you think that I'm worried about a bunch of Keystone Kops trying to catch me on these back roads, you're wrong. You and I are going to get to Kestrel Cove without too many worries or hassles, and then you're gonna see what I'm hoping for you to see."

"Well, it's all well and good to talk about history, Bobbie, but this is the modern world. I think it's going to be a tad harder getting *me* to Kestrel Cove than it was to get *liquor* in there."

"You're missing the point, sir. I wasn't really talking about bootlegging, I was talking about escape routes. I know for a fact that there are more ways to get from here to Kestrel Cove than there are loopholes in that last bill you passed about cutting the fishing season short."

The governor laughed. "Well, I'll be goddamned! That was a great political jab! You know, this may sound crazy, but after this is all over, would you be interested in a place on my staff?"

"Naw, lobstering keeps me pretty busy, sir, when I ain't kidnapping the Governor of Maine."

Bobbie kept to the established speed limits. There was no rush, and he didn't want to attract undue attention. Pickup trucks were the most common vehicles on the Maine roads, so no one would think twice about a weathered pickup with two men in the cab driving southward. When Bobbie slowed, stopped, and then turned right onto another side road, the governor asked, "And where does this one come out?"

"We'll zigzag these back roads right into Kestrel Cove, sir."

The governor raised his eyebrows. "You got a backup plan if any these roads are road-blocked?"

"You still don't get it, do you, sir? This isn't a seat-of-my-pants kind of operation. I didn't wake up this morning and suddenly decide to kidnap your ass and bring you to Kestrel Cove! I started planning all of this the moment we put my dead baby boy in the ground. I've had nothing but time to think about and plan all these details. I know my family and friends have thought I've been acting strange these last two months, but they've all given me a lot of space to let me grieve in my own way. I started checking you out, researching your history, learning your schedule and routines. I spent day after day thinking how things were going to go down and planning escape routes. So, sir, I know for a fact that I'm ready for any kind of roadblock."

"Don't get too cocky, Bobbie. You might have gotten the jump on 'em so far, but someone is going to figure out where you're headed, and then they'll start coming for you."

"It'll be too late by then."

The two rode in silence for a while. The governor didn't like Bobbie's last statement because it had the ring of a suicide mission. He leaned forward and looked at the fisherman with concern. "No one is going to die today, right, Bobbie?"

"No one is going to die, Turk. You have my word on that one."

The governor nodded and started watching the landscape whiz past his window. Bobbie made a sharp left turn onto another road, went a short way, and then took a quick right turn. The governor pursed his lips because they were now on roads that were beyond back roads. He had to admit that they were probably flying completely under the radar now, and the ease with which they'd done this unnerved him slightly.

They drove into Brementon and past a Brementon Police squad car, but there was no one in it. Now that they were in the midst of a town, the governor wondered if he should cause a ruckus to attract attention. But he knew he shouldn't. He was now intrigued enough that he *needed* to see whatever it was this fisherman wanted him to see. This realization surprised him. He wanted to ask Bobbie if it would make more sense for him to make a couple of phone calls to call off the search. If he did this and told people not to worry, the whole situation could be de-escalated to a safer level. He'd started to like this fisherman too much to want to see him killed in a shootout.

But it was a group of protesting college students who unwittingly acted as agents in exposing them. Thirteen students from the Bridgewater College Gay, Lesbian, Transgendered, and Straight Unified Front were on the corner with hand-drawn placards supporting an amendment to the Maine State Constitution making same-sex marriage legal in Maine. In a recent interview in a trendy magazine from Portland, it was none other than Governor Turk Willis who, because of his staunch Catholic upbringing, admitted that he was morally against the bill. So when some of these protesters saw the pickup truck go by with none other than the Governor of Maine in the passenger seat, they not only took notice, they went into a frenzy of rage and taunts. Their very public reaction alerted others nearby that Turk Willis had, in fact, just driven past.

In a matter of minutes, this shocking news hit the airwaves. A large contingency of State Police cars sped on their way, lights flashing and engines revving, to the general vicinity of Brementon to apprehend the kidnapper and get the governor back safely. The seriousness of the situation called for the Air Wing Unit of the State Police to be called into action, and the unit's two Cessnas took off and headed right to the area to get an aerial view of the pursuit. Moments later, the TV stations in Portland caught wind of the chase, and their helicopters took to the air and were en route to give viewers the best aerial shots of what promised to be a tense hostage situation.

Bobbie, unaware of any of this, turned onto another back road with a sense of confidence. He said, "We're on the straightaway to Kestrel Cove, Governor, but I've gotta warn you about the frost heaves."

"Frost heaves?"

"Yep, this road gets the worst frost heaves. If we do have to pick up speed, sir, this is going to become a very bumpy ride. You might want to buckle up and hang on."

The governor was already buckled in and he had been holding on, but now he looked around for better places to grip. He noticed that the speed of the truck was still well within the speed limit, but he worried about the high-speed pursuit that seemed inevitable. He didn't need to worry for long. Blue flashing lights came out of nowhere and took up position behind Bobbie's truck.

"Dammit. I'm gonna have to speed this up, sir. Sorry, but it's gonna get a little rough."

He gunned the engine and the truck surged forward. The whine of the tires rose an octave or two, and the squad cars behind them struggled to keep up. Bobbie counted four sets of flashing lights behind them, but, in the distance, even more were coming on quickly. His cell phone rang. On the third ring, he answered it. "Oh, hey, Wiley...Yeah, you don't say...Yep, that is my truck...Yeah, he's right here. Uh-huh...Naw, I've got a plan...Yeah, maybe...Naw, you stay out of the way, buddy...No, I mean it, Wiley, I've got this one...No, I want you to just stay the fuck out of the way! Whatever you do, stay out of the way. The last thing I want to do is get you involved with any of this...Okay, talk to you later."

When the governor looked at him with upraised eyebrows, Bobbie shrugged. "My sternman. He likes to listen to a police scanner, and you and I are all over it now, as you can imagine. When he heard that a dark pickup truck was headed to Kestrel Cove with you, he put the pieces together. They haven't announced that it's me driving yet, but they'll get the license plate number soon enough."

"You're not going to be able to hold them off for very long, you know that, right? You're running out of time, Bobbie."

"We'll see, Governor."

When they came to the first frost heave, the governor saw the small orange sign with the word BUMP printed on it just before they hit the raised piece of pavement and the truck went airborne. The rough landing made the governor swear like the ex-marine he was.

He looked back as the pursuing cars hit the frost heave and lurched into the air. The flashing lights bucked up and down as each vehicle jumped the frost heave, and the governor shook his head. "Are there more of those?"

"Ah, they're just starting, sir. This road gets 'em wicked bad during the winter, but then they get pushed back down during the summer. This is the worst time of year for 'em. Usually, I slow down, but obviously I can't do that today. I'm sorry about that."

The next time they saw a little orange sign, the governor grabbed the dashboard, but it didn't help lessen the impact after the jump, and he felt a bit like a bronco buster as his body flopped around in the confines of his seat belt. The governor clucked his tongue and said, "This must be marshy land."

"Yep, it is. Does a number on the pavement, doesn't it?"

They hit a long stretch that was a washboard of frost heaves, and governor shouted, "For Pete's sake, this is fucking horrible!"

Bobbie smiled at the man's cursing, but he said reassuringly, "I'm sorry to be smashing you to bits, Governor, but we've got to keep those guys behind us."

"Why would they be hanging back there like that? I mean, I'm wanting to see whatever the hell it is you want me to see, but I can't figure out what the hell they're doing back there."

Bobbie said calmly, "They know they've got me trapped, sir. We're driving down a peninsula, which means we're going to run out of road at some point. Why endanger you or themselves by forcing my hand too early, right? Especially when they don't have to."

"But you seem fine with that, Bobbie."

"Like I keep saying, sir, I've got a plan. I was hoping to avoid detection as long as possible, but I've known that it would all come to this eventually."

"The sheriff of Kestrel Cove probably knows we're coming his way, right?"

"Of course he does. He's a good sheriff and he listens to his scanner, too."

The governor was curious about Bobbie's confident tone. "But you don't sound too worried."

"He's not part of the problem, sir; he's actually part of the solution."

"How can you be sure?"

"'Cause it's damn hard to enter a car chase when your car is broken down."

The governor laughed. "You've got this thing pretty figured out, huh? Seriously, whenever the dust settles on this, I want you to think about coming to work for me on my staff!"

"And give up all of this?"

They swung around a wide corner and hit another patch of frost heaves. The pickup bucked and bounced, and the governor looked back again at the pursuing law enforcement cars. The pounding of the frost heaves had taken its toll on them, and they were slowing down just a little. This allowed Bobbie to accelerate and put more distance between them. The road suddenly jerked hard to the left and he expertly put his truck into such a sharp turn that the tires squealed. When he came out of the steering correction, there was a big dump truck blocking the road ahead, and Bobbie calmly aimed the pickup at a clearing off to one side. "Hold on, governor, here we go again!"

The governor had little chance to brace himself before the truck jumped off the road and landed in the muddy tire tracks of the pipeline. The front tires sank a little, but the momentum of the truck ensured that it kept plowing ahead. They hit a small embankment and sailed into the air again. Muddy spray covered the windows, and

Bobbie turned on the wipers to clear the windshield enough to see. Over his shoulder, the governor saw that the first squad car had followed them off the pavement and onto the muddy ground, but it had stopped so suddenly in the mire that the following car had crashed into it. Blue flashing light spread across the clearing, but the cars were no longer moving.

"Those patrol cars got stuck," the governor said in disbelief.

"Yeah, if you hit that jump too far in the middle, it's like a La Brea Tar Pit with that mud. They're gonna need a tow out of there."

"What *is* this thing?" the governor said, pointing straight ahead at the clearing they were driving through.

"The old fuel pipeline from the fuel dock to the Naval Base. For the residents of Kestrel Cove, it's a charter road."

"Was that a roadblock back there?"

"Naw, looked like Drake's bait truck might have had a flat tire. It won't take long to fix, if there's a spare."

"I take it Drake is a friend of yours?"

Bobbie glanced quickly at the governor. "Kestrel Cove is a tight-knit community, sir."

Suddenly, he slowed down, brought the truck to a stop, and put it in neutral. The governor was confused. "What're you doing, Bobbie?"

"Shifting into four-wheel drive, sir. The rest of the trip is going to make those frost heaves look like a nice Sunday drive."

Without waiting for a reply, Bobbie hit the accelerator, and all four wheels spun and spit mud into the air. The truck sloshed and squirmed back up to speed. When they came to where the pipeline crossed the road, he didn't slow down. The truck hit the embankment, went airborne again, and landed on the road with a thump and a clash of metal. The governor was sure that the axles had snapped, but Bobbie kept his foot on the accelerator and the truck sped forward and down onto the pipeline again.

"Does this pipeline keep crisscrossing the road like that?"

"Yep."

"Isn't that going to cause a problem for you?"

Bobbie shook his head, but kept his eyes straight ahead. "Naw, that bait truck is gonna give us time to get far enough ahead, and the only cop who really knows the pipeline is the Kestrel Cove sheriff, but he's probably trying to find his distributor cap at this very moment."

The governor exhaled roughly. "You and your friends are digging your hole deeper and deeper, you know that, Bobbie?"

Bobbie chuckled. "They don't know anything, sir. They're completely in the dark about my plans. They're just reacting to help a friend in need, I guess."

◊◊◊◊

At that moment, Jamie was totally unaware of the unfolding drama. He was packing up his belongings in the cottage before taking off and heading far away from Kestrel Cove. He was still so confused and saddened by the betrayal he'd witnessed the day before, he wasn't entirely sure where he was or what he was doing. He hated to slink off like a beaten dog with its tail between its legs, but when your girlfriend cheats on you with your best friend, there's not much left to do but get the hell out of Dodge. So he shoved everything that was his into his duffle bags and put them in his car. He just needed to get far away as quickly as he could. Far away from Shelley. Far away from Wiley. Far away from everyone in this stupid little town who had been laughing at him the whole time. And the best way to do that was to do it quickly, like pulling off a Band-Aid.

He went back in for one more walk-through to look for anything that he'd missed. He stood in the ridiculous slanted kitchen and looked over the little cottage. The memories of the last six months flooded back like an incoming tide and the images of laughter and love and happiness swirled around him. He wanted none of those happy memories to be true. They hurt more if they were real, and he wished he were waking from a dream. But the fact of the matter was, he'd been very happy back then, and now he wasn't. There was nothing left for him here, so he turned and headed out to the Volvo. He wanted to stop by Bill Hand's to say a proper goodbye to him. He owed the man that much.

◊◊◊◊

The truck sloshed and bucked over the rough terrain until they were totally engulfed by a spruce forest. Here, Bobbie deliberately pulled the truck into an opening in the trees and brought it to a complete stop near a large tree. The governor could see that some of the saplings had been cut down and the area had been raked. Bobbie turned off the engine, and he and the governor sat in silence for an awkward moment. Finally, Bobbie spoke. "Well, governor, this is where you get to make a decision. You see, I don't have a weapon or nothing. I really can't force you to get out of the vehicle and walk with me to see what I want to show you. If you decide that you aren't going to go with me now, I'm not gonna try and make you. I know that you were a tunnel rat in the war, so trying to grab you and carry you to where I need to get you would end very badly for me. I *hope* you'll follow me the rest of the way on foot, but I'll understand if you take off through the woods. It's going to be a bit of a hike and climb to see what I gotta show you, so if you're going to opt out, now's the time."

The governor looked out his window into the trees and shrugged. "You planned each and every detail of this escapade, and now, when we're close enough to see your goal, you're willing to throw your fate into my hands?"

Bobbie nodded. "Yep, that's the way it has to be sometimes."

The governor smiled. "Well, let's go see this thing you went through all this trouble to make me see. I just hope it's worth it!"

"Oh, it will be, sir."

As the governor got out of the truck and shut his door, Bobbie hopped out and grabbed a bundle of material that turned out to be a camouflage sheet that he used to cover the entire truck. It was now so well concealed, only someone on the pipeline who stopped to look would find it. The governor admired the fisherman's thoroughness with a hearty clap on the shoulder. "Well, Bobbie, where are we headed to now?"

"To the top of Mt. Buxtor, sir."

"Lead the way."

The men bushwhacked through the woods in silence. They could hear the sirens in the distance and a couple of aircraft circling overhead. The woods were soggy and muddy, and the walking became harder as they gained a little elevation. Several times, Bobbie turned around to offer help to the governor, but he waved him off each time. The governor was wearing a pair of nice oxfords, which kept slipping unmercifully in the soft mud.

Bobbie's cell phone went off and he answered it. The governor quickly ascertained that it was the fisherman's hysterical wife chiding him, and although Bobbie tried to soothe her, it was obvious to the governor that the wife, whose name was Clara, was so furious that nothing the man said was going to erase the stain that his actions had · caused. Before hanging up on her, Bobbie ended the phone conversation with, "I love you, Clara."

The two men continued on for a while and then the governor finally said, "Is it really worth all of this trouble, Bobbie? You're probably going to go to jail, and it's clear that you've pissed off your wife completely. Is it really worth all this?"

Bobbie stopped and looked down into the governor's face with eyes that blazed with raw energy. "How can you ask that, sir? You saw that picture of my dead son! You know what something like that does to a person? To a couple? And now I've got a chance to stop it from happening again to someone else—isn't that worth all of this?"

The governor nodded, and they continued scaling the hillside. Their path came to a trail, which made the walking much easier. Bobbie stopped when he heard an airplane fly overhead, but it seemed to pass without seeing them and the two men pushed on.

A moment later they heard the first gunshots.

◇◇◇◇

Jamie parked the loaded Volvo next to the gatehouse. All he wanted to do was to hike up the driveway, say goodbye to Bill, and then hike back down and leave town without causing a stir. But as he walked up the hill, he noticed that the road had been chewed up by some very recent traffic. Then Jamie heard gunshots coming from above. He stopped for a second and, contrary to what every ounce of his common sense said, he began jogging up the hill toward them. He was too worried about Bill Hand's safety to stop.

◇◇◇◇

"Those were gunshots, Bobbie! That's not good!"

"No, it's not. And truthfully, I can't figure out what the hell is going on, governor. I planned that you and I might have to hide out from people pursuing us, but heading up into a gunfight was never part of it. It doesn't make any sense, actually."

"You sure you don't have any accomplices?"

"No, sir, I don't. I did all the planning and prep for this myself. No one knew what I was going to do and no one knows where I'm headed with you, so that's what doesn't make any sense to me!"

The trail came into the clearing that surrounded Bill Hand's house, and Bobbie and the governor crouched behind a fallen tree to survey the scene. They could see FBI agents taking cover from gunfire that seemed to be coming from the main house. Bobbie looked at the governor and shrugged his shoulders. He whispered, "I swear, governor, Bill Hand is not any part of this. I never spoke to him about it! As a matter of fact, I was more than slightly worried that he might get pissed at me for trespassing on his land."

"Bill Hand?"

"Yes, sir, he's a former computer exec who owns all this land—"

"Oh, son, I know Bill Hand. Every Maine governor for the last twenty years has known Bill Hand intimately. In my line of work, he's the kind of person you do everything you can for, to make sure he's your friend."

At that moment, the unmistakable figure of Bill Hand came flying out of the house and into the woods next to them. He rolled into the cover of the forest, stood up, looked around, and then started racing up the path toward the summit of Mt. Buxtor. The FBI agents saw him, but the shooters in the house continued to pepper the trees around the lawmen and draw their fire. Bobbie grabbed the governor's arm. "Let's follow Bill and get out of here!"

They went right through the secured gate and all the way to the summit. There, Bill Hand headed toward a large object that was concealed under a camouflage tarp. Whatever it was, it was easily three or four times taller than a man, and as Bill Hand began to remove the tarp, Bobbie called out, "What the hell is going on here, Bill?"

Bill Hand spun around to see who was talking to him, and as soon as he recognized Bobbie Schmidt and Governor Turk Willis, his face looked like he was beyond being surprised by anything that was happening. He shook his head and said calmly with his characteristic lisp, "I could ask you the same thing, Bobbie! Did you really just kidnap the Governor of Maine?"

Bobbie nodded and said, "I want to show him the satellite, Bill. I want him to see it through my telescope. That thing killed my boy, and I thought that if he could see it, he might help us get rid of it."

"Hello, Turk."

"Hello, Bill. Why is there a shootout at your house?"

Bill Hand looked back that way. "Damn FBI agents have been on my ass for the last few months. Then they swooped in this morning, and now they're making me speed up my schedule a bit."

Without another word, he yanked the tarp off and exposed a large white missile with a blue conical tip that was pointed straight up.

"Jesus, Bill, is that a *missile?*" Bobbie breathed.

Bill Hand ignored Bobbie's inane question while he quickly stowed the tarp. As he began to pull other tarps off what appeared to be the missile's command center, he said with a shake of his head, "You know, you've really screwed me up today, Bobbie. Next time we both do a major act of civil disobedience that could easily be construed as an act of treason on the same day, let's talk to one another and give each other a heads-up about the date and time, okay? You see, your little escapade with the governor unleashed the State Police planes. They've been flying over this whole peninsula, looking for you two, but they discovered my little project instead. I'm sure they've called it in by now and the whole force who's chasing you is on their way here, thinking that the missile and your kidnapping are somehow related. The guys I hired to occupy those FBI agents with a firefight aren't gonna be able to hold out too long, so I've got to get this gal into the air right now!"

At that instant, Jamie appeared, panting and sweaty from the climb. He seemed in a mild panic, and he shouted at them, slowly enunciating each word, "What the *fuck* is going on here?"

The three men stared at him with almost bemused faces. His question had been so dramatic, it was almost funny. Finally, Bill Hand spoke up. "It appears that Bobbie has kidnapped the Governor of Maine to show him the Russian spy satellite on the very same day that I planned to launch a satellite-killing missile to destroy it."

"Wait! Wait!" the governor roared. "Are you *all* telling me you think there's a Soviet spy satellite above us right now?"

Bill Hand nodded, "Oh, there is, Turk. I've got a connection in the Russian government who's told me all about it. It was launched decades ago to spy on that fueling depot, but it's still up there working."

"And it killed my boy!" Bobbie added.

The men listened as the gunfire down at the house intensified. Finally, Jamie asked, "Bill, if the satellite only comes past at eight o'clock at night, how will your missile hit it if you launch it now? Isn't it too early?"

"That part of the story is completely wrong. The satellite is in a geosync-ed orbit above us, which means that it orbits at nearly the same rotational speed as the Earth—for all intents and purposes, it just sits in the same place in our sky all the time."

"That's right! I've been looking at it through my big telescope—which is set up over there, by the way!" Bobbie exclaimed with pride.

Bill Hand continued, "And that makes it easier to kill. With the location of the satellite's orbit programmed into the navigational system of this missile, it's a straight shot."

The governor stepped forward and poked Bill Hand in the chest. "I know that this certainly isn't the time for a lecture, Bill, but sending up some kind of homemade satellite-killing missile is something that seems beyond the normal range of sanity, even for you!"

"Well, Turk, that might be true, but the benefits outweigh the costs this time. You see, this missile here is the latest technology from around the world. If it succeeds in knocking that satellite down today, it will not only get rid of something that has haunted this little community for too long, it could mark the beginning of the State of Maine as a site for antisatellite technology. Can you imagine the political clout that a manufacturing plant of these babies here in Maine would have? Destroying a satellite terrorizing the good people of Maine and creating future factory jobs—well, that's a win-win situation, if I've ever heard one!"

The light went on in Jamie's head. "Persian-speaking guests in the gatehouse, North Koreans at the dock! You've been meeting with people to get the technology for this missile?"

"Exactly, Jamie. I love this little screwed-up community, and it's been killing me to see what that satellite has been doing to it. Several years ago, I came to the conclusion that, since I knew that the satellite was real, I needed to make a plan and take the damn thing out. It's time for this community to be finally free at last. Now, excuse me gentlemen, but I've got to get this missile in the air before that whole clusterfuck down there gets up here. You all may want to stand back a little!"

Bill Hand began to flip switches on the control panels. As lights and gauges seemed to come alive and the missile hissed, Bobbie looked at the governor, who looked over at Jamie. The three men shrugged and backed up to find a place to safely watch the launch of the missile. Bobbie spoke softly to the governor. "Well, Bill has kinda stolen my thunder here, Turk, but I wanted you to see that the Russian satellite is real. After my boy died, I kinda became obsessed with the idea that it killed him. I bought a telescope and set off to find out if it was real or not. Finally, I saw it in the night sky, and I realized that, if you could see it with your own eyes, maybe you'd do something about it. Now it appears this whole thing today was a colossal waste of my time and effort."

"Hell, Bobbie, you successfully kidnapped the Governor of Maine, evaded a massive pursuit, and now we might just get a chance to watch a satellite-killing missile test-fired—hard to describe this afternoon as any kind of waste!"

In the silence that followed the governor's excited statement, the men were suddenly aware that the gunfight had started to move up the hill.

◇◇◇◇

Earlier that afternoon, a group of Kestrel Cove residents had armed themselves and headed over to Bobbie's house to help him fend off the anticipated wave of law enforcement that they reasoned would be headed there to intercept him. Once there, however, they found Clara holding the fort, lambasting the cops with a fiery and expletive-laden tirade. She was stating, in the most colorful language imaginable, that Bobbie was not there, and exactly which body parts she was going to cut off the S.O.B. when he finally did come home. The armed militia's arrival almost caused the whole scene to erupt, but when a police radio began blaring the news that a State Police aircraft had spotted a potential missile on the top of Mt. Buxtor, and a television helicopter had caught a glimpse of Bobbie Schmidt and Turk Willis nearby, the law enforcement officials immediately stopped arguing with the small army of citizens and raced off.

Once they were gone, Clara directed her abusive rantings at any-one within earshot, so the little armed militia, which consisted of Drake, Joe, Wiley, Alfred, Jimmy, and some of the wharf rats, decided that they needed to get to the top of Mt. Buxtor, too. And as their fleet of pickups drove the road over to Bill Hand's property, the group acquired new recruits along the way. By the time they reached the base of the driveway and could hear the gunfire coming from up above, the militia group numbered over thirty armed members. The assault on Mt. Buxtor had officially begun.

At the store, Shelley was like a chained lioness at her register. She had asked for a shift during the day to avoid being at the cottage when Jamie moved out, but the continuous developments in the abduction of the governor were hard to hear knowing that she was unable to leave the store and help out. People came in and excitedly relayed new details, and she was forced to watch the stream of law enforcement cars fly past the store with their lights and sirens going and wonder why her brother-in-law had done what he'd done. When she was informed that there was an armed insurrection headed into the fray and the situation seemed to be spiraling out of control, she decided that she was well within her rights to close down the store and head to Mt. Buxtor to see if she could help in any way.

As she hopped into her truck, she felt hollow and empty. She hated herself for what she had done to Jamie, even if she knew that it was for the best. She couldn't have lived a good life knowing that she'd played a role in trapping him here in Kestrel Cove. And while she now realized that she should have just talked to him about it rather than orchestrating such a horrendous scene, she felt a very small patch of happiness knowing that he was probably packed up and headed away from the craziness. So, as much as it had all torn at her heart, she was glad that he was safe from the shit-storm that was now hitting Kestrel Cove.

◊◊◊◊

With the sounds of the approaching gunfight, Bill Hand's movements took on a frenetic quality. He kept looking over his shoulder at where the road came up to the crest of the hill, but his hands scurried over the control panels like two rodents. The missile launcher suddenly came to life and swung mechanically to face more to the east. The missile was still nearly vertical, and steam started coming from its base. Bill Hand began to unwind what looked like a remote launching panel as he backed away and took up position behind a recently built rock wall.

Just then, Wiley and Joe came up into the clearing holding their guns in front of them and crouched for action like soldiers. Joe had a pistol in his good hand and Wiley had his pump-action shotgun up to his shoulder. They saw Bobbie, the governor, and Jamie crouched behind a downed tree, so they lowered their weapons and came right over to them. They looked the three men over and then Joe spoke. "Well, I ain't sure what the fuck *you're* doing today, Bobbie, and I sure as shit don't know why the hell *you're* in on this one, Jamie, but we're here to help."

Bobbie pointed at Bill Hand. "Bill's going to launch that missile and destroy the satellite!"

"No shit!" Joe exclaimed.

Bill Hand seemed to be ignoring everyone now and kept focused on getting the launch set. Wiley came closer to Jamie and whispered to him, "And how the hell did you get yourself mixed up in the middle of all this, man?"

Jamie shook his head and said in a resigned tone, "I came to say goodbye to Bill before taking off."

The impact of the statement sank in, and Joe, Wiley, and Bobbie looked at him forlornly. Joe was about to say something, when a horde of armed Kestrel Cove residents came barreling into the clearing. Drake was leading the throng. When Jamie saw Shelley in the midst of the group, his heart raced and bucked.

Drake said breathlessly, "Those fuckers are coming this way, guys! Better duck down!"

"What's going on, Drake?" Joe asked.

"Dammit, we had the situation nearly under control down there. We were holding our own against those FBI agents and the State Troopers, when *BLAMMO!* we were hit by someone much more fucking serious. They were soldiers, but they weren't wearing the usual army uniforms. More like black SWAT uniforms. They pushed us back up here and disappeared into the woods!"

The governor pursed his lips. "Ah, that's probably the Alpha Team. They're a secret unit of the Maine State Troopers that was created several years back to give us a crack unit of special forces in case something more serious ever came up that ordinary law enforcement couldn't handle alone. They've never been called into action before. If they're here, gentlemen, you all need to lay down your weapons immediately. They are trained to kick ass and take no prisoners. You all need to stand down before someone gets hurt or killed!"

Everyone looked around for a leader to give the order. It was Wiley who raised up his shotgun and yelled, "We're not a bunch of fucking pussies! We're not gonna be intimidated by anyone!"

From the corner of his eye, Jamie saw movement—someone creeping toward Wiley in attack mode. With no time to think, he acted instinctively. He rushed past Wiley and flung his body into the air just as the two Alpha Team members attempted to ambush the man they had ascertained was the gun-toting leader of the mob. The legend that arose afterward would say that Jamie had yelled "Damn the torpedoes!" but actually, he didn't say anything as he launched himself at the attackers. The two men skillfully met Jamie in midair and threw him to the ground, pummeling him with a series of vicious blows to the head. The impact with the ground had knocked him out instantly, so he mercifully never felt their punches.

When Wiley threw himself on the two members of the Alpha Team, many thought he looked like an angry tomcat being tossed into the middle of a dog fight. And as they watched this tempestuous scuffle, the rest of the gathering of Kestrel Cove residents was attacked simultaneously by the remaining members of the Alpha Team. Utter chaos ensued.

The superior training of the Alpha Team quickly and efficiently dispatched many of the mob, including Joe, Drake, and Bobbie, who'd been put to the ground in the first few seconds of the fray. After this, they went over to neutralize the rest of the onlookers. As Shelley was knocked to the ground, she heard Clara's distinctive voice and saw her sister jump onto the back of an Alpha Team member. She also saw Jamie's unconscious body on the ground nearby, and she started crawling toward him.

The violence of the scene stopped cold when the missile launched. Bill Hand had bellowed out a countdown from five, and then the missile launcher was engulfed by a thick cloud of white smoke. The missile hesitated momentarily, then it made a deafening thunder as it shot into the sky. All the combatants on the summit of Mt. Buxtor were so overwhelmed by the noise and spectacle of the launching that they stopped what they were doing and watched the missile streak away. The white contrail of its path was as fragile as the finest lace, and the wind began to wisp it away it before the missile was out of sight. The crowd seemed to be mesmerized until one of the wharf rats yelled out, "Wow! Did you just see that? That was fucking incredible! Hey, Bill, what the hell *was* that?"

When everyone turned toward the spot where Bill Hand had been standing, the man was no longer there. In the flash of the missile launch, he'd absolutely disappeared.

36

The launch of the missile left everyone on the summit of Mt. Buxtor in complete silence for several minutes. Most were waiting to see the explosion of the satellite, but others were merely too focused upward to look back down. And it seemed as if the missile had carried with it all the venom of the battle, too, as the combatants all found themselves looking at each other like they had no idea what they were fighting about. Even the members of the Alpha Team seemed unsure of what to do next, now that the chaos had been obliterated and order was restored. The peace of this moment was short-lived, however, because other law enforcement agents began to fill the clearing at the summit and indiscriminately started arresting all the participants.

In the midst of what had felt like a kicked-over hornet's nest, there was a sudden and new serenity among the militia members of Kestrel Cove. Even though they were being shackled with plastic zipties and led down to waiting paddy wagons for legal processing, everyone seemed pacified by what they had just seen. Even Wiley, once he could see that Jamie was all right, did not resist as he was restrained. It was as if the missile launch had been a completely cathartic event for them all, and they kept looking at each other with wide, satisfied grins—when they weren't looking up at the sky.

As Jamie was tugged onto his feet and cuffed, many people openly stared at him in disbelief. His self-sacrifice had been seen by all, and, since everyone had heard about his shocking discovery of Wiley and Shelley, the witnesses were in complete awe about what he had just done. With an almost reverent silence, they moved out of the way as the Alpha Team members walked him away from the scene. Wiley, who was being cuffed at the same time, said quietly, "Hey, thanks, bro."

Jamie, still half-dazed and woozy, quoted the infamous Stonewall Jackson: "Let us cross over the river, and rest under the shade of the trees."

Governor Turk Willis found himself looking up at the sky, too. He shook his head and grinned. As Bobbie was being shoved down the hill, the governor leaned over and whispered something in his ear that made the fisherman grin. What he said, nobody ever knew, and Bobbie never told anyone. The governor then made it immediately clear, however, that he hadn't been kidnapped at all—that he'd accepted a ride from Bobbie to see the launching of Bill Hand's missile and had not been able to tell anybody. He apologized profusely for not checking his cell phone to see if he had enough battery to call, and later he even convinced Vince Evans and Jack Bell to say that they had both collapsed due to low blood sugar and hit their heads on the parked cars. Eventually, all of the kidnapping charges on Bobbie Schmidt were dropped, and he only had to atone for his reckless driving during the chase down the peninsula.

Those residents who were charged for their participation in the gunfight and melee found themselves represented by Bill Hand's personal legal team, pro bono. Though there were far too many charges to excuse and ignore, the legal team of high-paid and high-profile lawyers made it so that most of the residents from Kestrel Cove ended up only doing community service or serving a short probation. Several wharf rats who had prior records could not be helped, and they slipped away silently after their bails were paid. Most understood that they'd be gone until the heat was turned down again, which most felt would happen fairly soon.

As for Bill Hand, he escaped scot-free. While the missile was in the air and everyone was staring straight up in the sky at its path, he had headed straight down the hill through the woods undetected. How he evaded the numerous law enforcement agents encircling his property was the topic of many a conversation afterward, but he'd made his way successfully down the hill and over to the wharf. Several days later, after the authorities were done processing his property and his house, they found that his skiff was not on the floating dock at the wharf and that his black lobster boat was gone from its mooring. It was anyone's guess which direction he had headed. Rum and cokes were raised high and toasts were made to thank the man who had finally gotten rid of the satellite, and many hoped that he'd be able to return to Kestrel Cove one day so they could properly thank him.

When the issue of what had happened to the man was debated in the fish house much later, some figured that he had steamed south in his boat to Boston and beyond. Others thought that he more likely headed Down East or across to Canada. Some went on Wikipedia to research which countries had a no-extradition treaty with the U.S., and since no one knew for certain how much fuel his boat actually carried, no one could argue against a voyage across an ocean or around the globe to get away. The fact that the boat was rumored to use the latest stealth technology to stay invisible to radar meant that it could go anywhere without being found. It had been clear to everyone that the boat was not an ordinary boat, so the sky was the limit as to where it could carry Bill Hand on the run.

The governor became the most important voice in soothing the situation. After he declared that Bobbie hadn't kidnapped him, and had gotten the charges greatly reduced against him, he began to explain the spy satellite over Kestrel Cove to the media. He vehemently declared that he'd personally seen the explosion of the missile when it hit the satellite. No one else on the hilltop had seen anything to indicate that Bill Hand's missile had hit its target, but the governor was so insistent, even those skeptics gave in and admitted that it was more than likely that the satellite was now gone. Behind closed doors, however, all of Turk Willis's attempts to get answers from the powers that be were stymied, and he was left feeling impotent and outclassed. And although it pained him greatly, he had to admit that they'd probably never know the real truth.

Some time later, Bill Hand's lawyers handed the governor a sealed file, and he finally got the answers he sought. He knew that he couldn't tell anyone the details about Kosmo2, but he nodded with the understanding that he *could* promise that a spy satellite was no longer orbiting above them. Those same lawyers then handed him the plans for the antisatellite missile factory that Bill Hand had proposed. It was to be constructed in Kestrel Cove on land that was owned by a nearly anonymous corporation. It was rumored that Bill Hand was its leading investor, but no proof of that fact was ever dug up. Governor Turk Willis proudly called a press conference to announce that construction was set to start on the factory in Kestrel Cove as soon as possible.

The kidnapping of a governor that was not a kidnapping, the presence of a Russian spy satellite over Maine, the launch of a home-made satellite-killing missile, the armed battle on top of Mt. Buxtor, and the disappearance of Bill Hand all kept Kestrel Cove in the national limelight for one solid week. But then the Red Sox had their opening day and the usual news items began to push those stories aside and out of view, and Kestrel Cove quickly and gladly resumed its status as a sleepy fishing village. Except now, most residents of the town found themselves happier, calmer, and more content knowing that the satellite was gone.

For Jamie, it took several days for the officials to figure out what to do with him. Although the governor had cleared him of any participation in the kidnapping, and nearly all the members of the armed militia mob also claimed that he'd had no involvement in the melee, his very visible assault on the Alpha Team members had been witnessed by too many to discount. Even the fact that Jamie had come out on the losing side of the encounter—several broken and bruised ribs and some harsh-looking contusions from the clash with the soldiers—could not make the decision of what to do with the boy any easier.

As he had to wait for his fate to be decided in court, Jamie lived in his tent on Bill Hand's land. He figured that Bill wouldn't care anymore, and he was careful not to alert anyone in the Kestrel Cove community as to where he was staying. Since he'd already made up his mind to leave town, those nights alone were very difficult for him. Joe, Jimmy, and Wiley had made several attempts to get his attention whenever they saw him, but he wouldn't respond to them.

When he finally went to court, he learned that his father had organized some high-powered support for him, and that he'd only be assessed a stiff fine. He paid the fine with his leftover lobstering money and was given the okay to leave Kestrel Cove. He could barely take down his tent fast enough. He threw everything in the back of the Volvo and started driving away without saying goodbye to anyone.

But as he approached the intersection with the wharf road, he pulled his car onto the shoulder and turned off the engine. He needed to say goodbye, not to the people of Kestrel Cove so much as to the places that were inseparable from the memories of the last ten months. To his first campsite, where he had been kicked out because the guys had shot up a bunch of gulls in a drunken party to celebrate his getting dumped by the town slut. To Bobbie's house, where the ferocious stripper had let people lick her twat and where Jamie had seen grief that was colder and deeper than any he'd ever seen before. To the wharf, where his car had been purposefully smashed by Drake's bait truck and where he'd finally stood up to Alex Pettingill. To Hai's house, where the Tet ceremony with the delicious *Pho* and the red money envelopes made him understand what it really means to belong to a community. To the pipeline, where he'd once ridden on the back of a motorbike with Wiley and been shot at by government men. To the quarry, where he'd skinny-dipped with Wiley and was exposed to the rich young campers. To the store, where he had fallen in love with Shelley. To the church, where Bobbie and Clara had gotten married and he had, fleetingly, understood true love. And to the top of Mt. Buxtor, where a battle was waged and a satellite-killing missile had made everything right again.

Jamie hesitated because he knew that, once he headed out of town, he'd be leaving Kestrel Cove on more than just a physical level. As soon as he crossed the town line, he'd no longer be considered a resident of the community. Once he left, it would be as if he'd never been there at all. There'd be more deaths, bachelor parties, fights, love affairs, weddings, deer hunting, and always more and more lobsters to catch. There'd be petty injustices and squabbles that could turn into full-blown feuds, and there would be sweet reconciliations. There'd be Drake screwing Wilma Simmons and old Ed Simmons shitting on Drake's pier to get retribution. Each and every thing he'd experienced would keep on happening, and he wouldn't ever be a part of it again.

And that was why he now sat at the side of the road. He knew that when he left the peninsula, nothing would ever be the same. Even if he did come back and visit, nothing would be the same between him and the other people he'd loved and called friends. Sure, Joe would be there to buy him a beer and Jimmy would be there to drink it with him and razz him, Drake would be there ready to insult him, the fishermen might smile knowingly at him, and Shelley might even be brave enough to try to hug him, but there would be no more depth to it all than that. He'd be nothing more than a visitor looking in. And he knew that it wouldn't be the residents of Kestrel Cove purposefully and maliciously excluding him, it was just the way it had to be. Either you were in or you were out. And if Jamie drove away right now, he'd be most definitely out—and there'd be no way back in for him. The purity of this realization took his breath away. After all, he felt closer to these people than he did his own family.

The truth was, even though Walter Whetstone might not have the time, Stanford could wait another year for him. He could stay another year in Kestrel Cove and try to heal all the wounds. He could even try to forgive Shelley and Wiley. He knew that Joe and Jimmy would take him back for another season as the master baiter, and during that year he could spend some time thinking about what he really wanted in life. Spending another year here would not be the worst thing ever, especially if he could recapture some of the good things he'd had. Maybe he could feel truly happy again.

While Jamie was thinking about all of this in his car, Drake opened the door of his house across the road. He was wearing his usual dirty khaki pants, and his shirt was unbuttoned down to his belt. He looked up and saw Jamie sitting in his car, and he froze in place in the doorway. He gave Jamie an almost imperceptible nod before turning around and going back inside. Just before the door shut, however, Jamie could clearly see Wilma Simmons standing there in nothing but a towel, and he suddenly felt like a person who'd discovered rotten tires and oil drums submerged in an idyllic mountain lake. Whatever warm dreams he was having about staying for another year in Kestrel Cove were now invaded by some of the unpleasant realities of what life there would actually be for him, and he knew what he had to do.

Jamie turned the key and started the car, then pulled the Volvo back onto the pavement until it straddled the middle line. Poised there, he felt like he was the missile on its launcher, ready to take off and fly into space. He was just about to punch the accelerator and speed away to fully realize that metaphor, when a gut-wrenching sound came from the rear of his car. He pulled forward a little and saw that the spare tire had fallen from its hidden perch and now sat in the middle of the road. Jamie laughed because he knew exactly what some of those extra bolts and nuts in the coffee can were for. He looked at the rearview mirror again and the tire was defiantly sitting there like a pile of Ed Simmons's shit on the wharf, and that made him laugh again out loud. He thought it would be fitting if he just drove away and left the tire sitting there, but the realization that stepping into a pile of human feces was far less harmful than running over a spare tire in the roadway made him get out, pick it up, and throw it into the back of the car.

As he drove away, he kept his eyes forward and never looked back. He wondered how long it would take Elmer to pack for their cross-country trip to California.

Epilogue

Sergei Volentchko's driver let him out and drove off with a metallic grinding of gears and acrid exhaust smoke into the frenetic Moscow traffic flow. Volentchko turned and entered the official door of his building like a proud tomcat strutting back home after a successful night out. The prostitute's saliva was still wet on his dick and he took pride in that mild discomfort because it was evidence of his sexual accomplishments. How many men in the Soviet governmental system could boast of having their dick sucked before the morning tea? Volentchko knew that his overall place in the grand scheme of the system might be low, but he had certain perks that made him feel like a goddamn prince. He walked through the building's security checkpoint with a confidence and air that showed that he, Sergei Volentchko, was hot shit.

But when he entered his Office of Celestial Information, there was that forest-green dossier on his desk, and his good mood swirled and sloshed like the morning turd he had flushed down at home. He put his bags down and walked over to his desk. He started to reach for the dossier and noticed the new black stripe down the face of it. That was unusual. None of the dossiers had ever had that feature on them before. He lifted it and looked at it like it was a piece of space rock that had hurtled to Earth and landed upon his desk. He always dreaded opening the dossiers, but now he opened this one up because he was unsure what the black stripe meant. He treated the contents with more veneration than he ever had, and he scanned the first sheet. It took him a moment to notice the all-too-obvious large-print words that were stamped across the top of the page: законченный.

Farther down the paper, it explained that the bank of computers that were in charge of monitoring the inputs and outputs to and from Kosmos2 had received an energy surge indicating that the satellite had been destroyed. The energy signature made the scientists who knew about such things quite convinced that the satellite was gone. With the amount of space trash and meteorites circling around the planet, most experts felt it was a miracle that any satellite orbited the Earth unscathed nowadays. The report went on to say, however, that an investigation into the matter was being proposed. Volentchko chortled at the level of ineptness the Russian government seemed to foment—wasting hours and money investigating the cause behind the destruction of a doomed satellite that had outlived its projected lifespan by two decades seemed like proof that someone's son-in-law or distant cousin was getting their insignificant job funded for a little longer. But if that was what the powers that be wanted, Volentchko didn't care.

The report also mentioned that there had been articles in the larger papers in Boston and New York of a supposed homemade missile being shot off from the very area that the Kosmos2 orbited above. Government officials thought the story lacked credibility, but Volentchko knew better, and this realization made his hemorrhoids pucker. He'd chosen to not alert his superiors about what looked like a missile launcher being built on the hilltop in that fishing village in Maine, and he knew that he could be held responsible for making the decision to ignore such an important and tactically rich target in hopes of not upsetting his own world too much. But now that it appeared that Kosmos2 had possibly been destroyed by a missile, someone could connect the coincidences into a line that led straight back to his office. The sudden image of himself being taken away for an inquiry made his scrotum tighten—he would never survive the embarrassment or, God forbid, any time in prison. He was not a man who was well suited for sodomy.

Then, on the last page, he saw the memo that made his scrotum relax and let him breathe again. There, written in official type, was the conclusion that since the Kosmos2 had outlived its expected lifespan and its usefulness, its sudden destruction was probably a blessing in disguise—the discovery of a secret satellite by the Americans could upset the delicate balance in negotiations with the European Union and the United States for a huge natural gas pipeline to the Black Sea.

The matter was now closed, and no further investigation was needed. Kosmos2 had served Mother Russia effectively and secretively for over two decades, and now there would be no more dossiers on the satellite.

Volentchko put the papers down flat on his desk and smiled. He stood up, organized the dossier's contents neatly, and closed it. He walked purposefully to the filing cabinet and put this last forest-green dossier into the proper section. He felt a huge weight float off his shoulders and he nearly back-skipped to his chair. He sat down lightly and opened his briefcase. He had just bought a new magazine from his dealer, and he brought it out of the case like it was a wrapped Christmas gift. He had never seen erotic photographs of naked women from Africa, and he was interested to see if the images excited him. For Sergei Volentchko, life had just gotten a whole lot better.

законченный

(The End)